DRYP: REVELATION

BOOK 2 IN THE DRYP TRILOGY

R.A. SCHEURING

ISBN: 978-1-7354417-1-9

For Arron, Jack and Carly

NOTE ON SPELLINGS

Although their spellings differ, the Yakima Valley and Yakama Nation tribes described in this novel are indeed related. The Yakima Valley, in south central Washington state, takes its name from the indigenous Yakama people, one of fourteen Native American tribes that constitute the Confederated Tribes and Bands of the Yakama Nation.

The divergence in spelling occurred in 1993, when the Yakama Nation Tribal Council voted to change the spelling of the tribe's name from "Yakima" to "Yakama" to reflect native pronunciation.

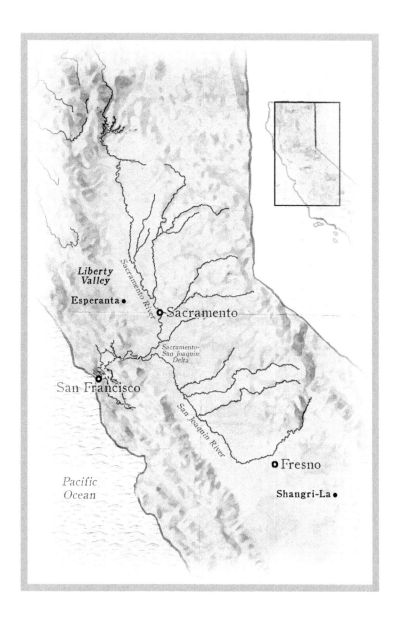

Liberty
Valley

Esperanta •

Sacramento River

◉ Sacramento

Sacramento-
San Joaquin
Delta

San Francisco

San Joaquin River

Pacific
Ocean

◉ Fresno

Shangri-La •

CQ, CQ, calling CQ. Beaming east from Northern California. Echo Sierra X-ray calling CQ, hello, CQ. Here on twenty meters. This is Whiskey Six Echo Sierra X-ray calling ...

    Is anybody out there?

ONE

JUNE, SIX WEEKS AFTER THE RELEASE OF PLAGUE

THE PLANE APPEARED ON A TUESDAY, a high speck above Liberty Valley's northern ridge, heading south in air tainted by the yellowish-brown smoke of distant fires.

Dr. Susan Barry poked her head out from under the porch overhang of her family's Victorian farmhouse and squinted against the glare.

"What is it?" the man behind her asked. He was fifty years old, and he sat shirtless in the porch's semi-cool shade, the right half of his torso wrapped in torn strips of floral cotton. His name was Alan Wheeler, and once, before the pandemic, he had been chairman of an oil company that bore his name, Wheeler Energy.

"It's a small plane, heading south." Susan pulled herself back into the shade. It was hot out, the afternoon sun burning through the haze.

"You should radio them before they get out of range," Alan said. Red spots already dotted the first layer of bandaging she'd

1

applied to his side, but she didn't notice. She was thinking that the plane was the first evidence of human life they'd seen since arriving in Liberty Valley five days earlier.

"Too late," she said. The plane was out of eyesight. Without repeaters, their radio was limited to line-of-sight communications or shortwave, neither of which would reach the aircraft.

She tied the last strip of cotton over the bullet wound beneath his armpit, trying not to flinch at the fetid stink of infected flesh.

Alan was watching her with grave eyes. "We're going to have to reach out at some point," he said. "You can't do all this by yourself."

He had a point. Since she, Alan, and Etta had arrived in the small Northern California valley, she'd been a one-woman army: watering the garden, harvesting vegetables, taking inventory of their canned and dried goods, venturing to neighboring farms to scavenge fuel for the generator, tending to Alan's wound and Etta's heart ailment. But she was also aware of what he didn't seem to recognize: as the only able-bodied person at the farm, she was hardly in the position to withstand looters or any other desperate person. It was better to lie low.

She stuck the last of her gauze, which she'd used to scrape pus and dead tissue from Alan's damaged torso, into a paper bag. She could feel his eyes on her, trying to force her to make eye contact, but she focused instead on the Laura Ashley sheets —the "good ones," her mother had called them—that she'd repurposed into Alan's wound dressings. The cheerful floral print hid a worrisome infection below.

She helped him put his good arm through his shirtsleeve. Even the simplest movements hurt him, but he never cried out. The taut lines of his face told her what he wouldn't: he was barely hanging on.

Susan had his bad arm halfway into the second sleeve when

2

she heard the distant drone of an engine again. She stiffened, turned her head like a hunting dog, and searched for the sound. Against the dull expanse of the valley's southern aspect, a pale speck rose from the horizon.

The plane was coming back.

"You should try to radio him," Alan said, more firmly now.

Quickly, she pulled his shirt into place. The plane was flying lower this time, no longer passing through, but rather skimming the valley at reconnaissance level. For a breathless moment, Susan thought it was coming for the farm itself. The yard's lawn stood out as a shock of green against its dry surroundings, and if the pilot flew low enough, he would see the portable generator positioned on the patio beside the house.

Her heart began to skitter in her chest. A memory of their harrowing escape from Los Angeles rose in her mind: a thug's hand slamming her head against a car's ceiling, the sharp, shallow slash of a knife against her neck.

She glanced back at Alan. His eyes were trained, as hers had been, on the plane's near direct course toward the house. It was so low now that it could have been a crop duster.

"Get the guns," he said.

For half a second, she didn't move, but then adrenaline exploded through her body like wildfire, and she shot through the kitchen door, startling the eighty-year-old woman cooking inside.

"What on earth is going on?" Etta cried.

"We've got visitors." Susan opened the closet next to the kitchen table and spun the dial on the gun safe inside. She pulled out a shotgun, chambered two shells, and stuck two more in her pocket. She grabbed the handgun. When she went back to the porch, she found Alan, pale as a ghost and leaning heavily against one of the porch posts. "He's circling," he said.

Half a mile away, the plane made an abrupt turn east and

picked up altitude. For a fleeting moment, Susan thought the small aircraft might ascend over the sharp ridge that lined the valley's eastern edge and disappear into the Central Valley beyond. But the plane turned back, its engine idling as it drifted lower and lower, a glide path that took it straight onto the open pasture that had once belonged to her parents' neighbors, Peter and Bernadette Morgan.

Susan stared, stunned. Tall walnut trees blocked her view, but she was sure the plane had landed, because the engine's droning lightened in pitch and then ceased entirely. The pilot had brought the plane to a halt.

Susan thrust the handgun at Alan and started down the stairs.

"Where are you going?" he called after her.

She halted for only a second. "To stop them. They're after the Morgans' fuel tank."

Alan frowned from the head of the stairs. "That doesn't make sense. Airplanes burn aviation fuel."

"You can convert a plane to burn regular gas. It's not common, but it can be done." Susan knew because her own grandfather had done it.

"Wait." Alan gripped the newel post so hard she could see his whitened knuckles from twenty feet away. "I'm coming with you."

She made a split-second decision. She didn't know who flew the plane, but she knew it was better to meet force with force, and Alan's gun, even if it was held by a man whose hands trembled under its weight, was still a threat to be reckoned with.

She crossed back to the porch, took the stairs two steps at a time, and placed her shoulder squarely below his left arm. Together, they hobbled to the driveway, where a white Tacoma pickup stood beneath the silver-green branches of an olive tree. Alan collapsed onto the seat with a grunt.

"We can't let them take the fuel," Susan said. The fuel was everything. It powered the generator, which powered the pump, which supplied the clean water from the well. It turned the lights and radio on at night. It kept them alive.

She drove a straight, rapid path through the orchard toward the property line. Beside her, Alan worked the buttons of his shirt with one hand, but his fingers slipped clumsily. He finally gave up and clutched the handgun in his lap.

"They might be friendly," he said.

"We better be ready in case they're not." She crossed through a gap in the fence she'd made three days earlier, drove through a flat pasture, and then powered through a second open gate. The pilot was already working on the fuel tank's lock when Susan reached the Morgans' property line. He looked up in shock as she drove straight at him.

He's the only one, she thought. Her eyes shot from the plane, a neat-looking Cessna with a bold blue stripe down its side, to the Morgans' empty house. There was no one there.

And she had a gun.

Susan slammed on the brakes, threw open the driver's side door, and rounded the hood, shotgun in hand. The pilot seemed to have recovered himself. He rounded on her in a crouch, the bolt cutter in his hand held back in swinging position.

Make yourself big, she thought. The old advice, given to western hikers in case of unexpected mountain lion encounters, flashed in her head. Intimidation, even if it was a miserable bluff, was her best hope of deterring a dangerous foe.

She growled at him, "That's my fuel. Get away from it." Behind her, she heard the Tacoma's passenger's side door open.

The intruder was perhaps ten feet from her, far enough away that he couldn't lunge at her gun, but close enough that she still felt threatened. He said very slowly, "Didn't realize you lived here."

He looked like a caveman. A grimy beard covered half of his face, and his hair was pushed back in long greasy waves down his neck. The skin beneath his right eye was swollen and discolored.

"It's our gas," she said, pointing the gun straight at him. "Get back in your plane, and rip someone else off."

If she shocked him, it was hard to tell. His dirt-bracketed eyes shifted over her shoulder to Alan and then back to her. He held the bolt cutter as though he'd swing it at her head.

"That might be hard since I'm out of fuel," he said.

"Drop the fucking bolt cutter," Alan ordered. He stood behind the hinge of the open passenger's door, his ill face ghoulish, but his handgun steady.

The man didn't drop the bolt cutter. "I'm willing to pay you for the fuel."

Which was a pretty funny offer, all things considered, Susan thought. She let out a harsh laugh. "With what? Venmo or straight cash?"

A furrow formed between the man's brows, and he looked at her strangely. "I meant I'll *trade* with you."

He took a step toward the plane as if he meant to prove it to her, but then stopped. A curtain of wariness fell over his features.

Something felt wrong. Her eyes shot to the Cessna. Unlike its owner, the plane looked well cared for, its panels shiny, the sheen of dust only lightly darkening the blue-striped fuselage. In the rear window, the shadow of cargo poked up like a small mountain.

Suddenly she understood. *He's worried we'll take his plane.* The realization, and its implications, rang like a bell in Susan's brain.

She lowered the gun a notch. She wasn't after his plane.

Or maybe she was.

An idea, so instantly compelling that it was nearly impossible to resist, took hold of her. She raised the gun again and pointed it at his sweat-stained chest. "What's your name?"

The wariness in his eyes turned to frank distrust. "Harr. John Harr."

She smiled at him, a wolf's smile. "Well, John Harr. Perhaps we can make a deal after all." She jerked her head at the Tacoma's bed. "Get in. Let's negotiate back at the house."

———

THEY MADE him drop the bolt cutter, and now, as John Harr sat in the back of their truck, bouncing across a pasture that hadn't seen water in weeks, he wondered why the hell he had surrendered it. He had no weapon, and though he was certain he could take either of them, one-on-one, weapon or no weapon, what if there were more of them back at the house? He was taking a leap of faith, and the recklessness of it screamed like a fire alarm in his mind.

He couldn't afford another Redding. His body still bore the bruises of his stupidity.

He watched the woman in the pickup's cab. Despite her prettiness, she had a hard edge to her. Even now, over the roar of the engine, he could hear her arguing with the man, responding tersely to everything he said.

She obviously knew the place well, but Harr was pretty damned sure she didn't own the fuel, no matter what she said. There was the small matter of fences. They'd crossed through one set and were heading toward a second. As far as Harr could tell, they were about to enter a third distinct property.

He wondered what the hell he was getting himself into. Open pasture had given way to a walnut orchard. Behind him, clouds of dust rose and lingered as they sped down the rows.

It was a big farm. Trees spread in all directions, except directly in front of them, where the orchard abruptly terminated into an open field. Harr was struck not by the odd presence of an unplanted field in the midst of an orchard, but rather by what lay smack-dab in the middle of it. In the center of the fallowed soil, an enormous yellow farmhouse rose like a castle above a shockingly green yard.

They have water, he thought in astonishment. Enough of it to irrigate a garden and a lawn surrounded by ash and pine trees.

No wonder she guarded her fuel so jealously. The water didn't come from nowhere. It had to have been pumped from a well, and Harr damn well knew that meant she had a functioning generator.

She drew the truck to a halt in a widened spot of gravel driveway, beneath the silver-green canopy of a gnarled olive tree. Before them stood a detached garage, and beyond it the big Victorian farmhouse, with its graceful covered porch and tall round tower. Somewhere, invisible to him, a generator rumbled.

The woman exited the truck and circled back to him, the shotgun still in hand but no longer pointed at him. She led him across a pebbled patio to a cement stairwell, which disappeared underground to what he assumed was the house's basement.

"Take off your shirt and boots," she ordered, holding out her hand.

He didn't expect that. "Pardon?"

A flash of irritation showed in her face. "You're not coming into my house smelling like a garbage dump." She gestured at the stairwell. "There's a shower down there. When you've bathed, I'll give you a clean shirt and socks."

He did what she demanded, although it embarrassed him the way she held his shirt and socks between her thumb and forefinger, as though the smell was beyond human toleration.

She wouldn't touch his boots.

———

AS SOON AS Harr disappeared down the basement stairwell, Susan dropped the shirt and socks onto the patio and raced up the porch stairs into the house's interior, ignoring Etta's questions as she passed through the kitchen and into the hallway. She flipped the bolt on the basement's interior access door and then doubled back to the kitchen. If their visitor wanted trouble, he'd have to come out through the basement's outside entrance. Susan wanted no surprises. She went back to the truck for Alan.

He was still sitting in the passenger's seat, although he had swung his legs out. Susan could tell he was angry. "Are you out of your mind?"

She put her shoulder beneath his and helped him to standing. "He's unarmed, Alan. I made him take off his shirt and socks. I didn't see anything to suggest a concealed weapon."

"He doesn't need a weapon to overpower us."

Alan was right, of course. It wasn't lost on Susan how big Harr was and how easily he could wrestle a gun from her. But the idea that had taken root in her mind over at the Morgan place wouldn't be shaken.

There's still a chance.

She helped Alan up the porch stairs and into the family room, where she let him collapse, gasping, on the couch. She didn't know why he gasped so, whether it was from blood loss or persistent infection, but it scared her. Shadows formed between the cords of his neck. His lips were so pale she couldn't tell where they ended and the rest of his face began.

Gently, she pried the gun from Alan's fingers and placed it on the coffee table beside him, watching anxiously as his eyelids fluttered closed and the tense lines in his face slowly softened.

Behind her, Etta asked worriedly, "Is he okay?"

"I think so. He needs rest."

The elderly woman eyed Susan unhappily. "Are you sure this is wise? You don't even know this man."

"I brought him to the house to get information. He's got a plane. He's had to have seen something."

It was at least partly true. She did want information. She wanted to know what was happening in the cities or if there was any semblance of government remaining. The diminishing reports they'd heard on Susan's father's old ham radio had chilled her: the big cities had gone, followed by the smaller towns; now even the holdouts in the country were disappearing. One by one, the ham radio operators had stopped transmitting. Only Shangri-La remained.

Alan shifted on the couch. His breath came slower now, the taut lines in his face softening. Susan knew to leave him alone. The exertion of the truck ride had exhausted him. He needed to rest.

"Do you think he spotted us from the sky?" Etta was still talking about Harr. "The generator is out in the open."

Susan shook her head. "He's after fuel, Etta. He must have seen the Morgan tank when he flew over."

"Are you going to give it to him?"

The wash of water through pipes, feeding the downstairs shower, suddenly stopped.

Susan crossed back to the kitchen and picked up the shotgun. She went into the utility closet, opened the gun safe, and stored the twenty-gauge. She spun the dial and returned to the kitchen.

"I don't know," she said.

There was no point in keeping the gun out in the open now. He'd seen Alan and Susan as they really were: a desperately ill man and a lone woman. When he saw Etta's frail form, he'd know how truly vulnerable they were.

She was taking a leap of faith.

There was a knock on the kitchen door. Through the paned window, Susan could see the visitor standing on the porch. He was shirtless, and he held a used towel in one hand and his socks and dirty shirt in the other. A screeching eagle was tattooed on his chest, just above his heart.

He was wearing the filthy pants he'd arrived in.

———

SUSAN GAVE him one of her father's plaid shirts, and though it was tight around the shoulders and loose around the waist, it still reminded her enough of her dad that a powerful wave of grief swept through her. She forced herself to focus on Harr's face, to push her parents and her brother from her mind.

The newcomer had shaved, and the result had been trans-formative. She could now see the strong outline of his jaw, the austere set of his eyes. She guessed he was in his early thirties, although it was impossible to tell for sure. A face like his had seen a lot of weather, which made perfect sense when he'd told them he'd been an eastern Oregon rancher before the pandemic.

"There's a group of survivors down in Lemon Cove," Harr was saying. "They're calling their settlement Shangri-La." He sat at the round cherrywood table in the kitchen with his hand wrapped around a cup of coffee. The muffled rumble of a washing machine sounded from the utility room behind him.

Susan felt Etta's eyes on her. They'd heard the broadcasts, too. Every evening, just after sundown, the San Joaquin Valley commune transmitted scratchy reports on the shortwave: their farming operation was up and operational; they'd set up a provisional government; they wanted other survivors to join them.

"You think they're real?" Alan asked. He sat opposite Harr, a blanket wrapped around his shoulders despite the heat of the day. His cup of coffee was untouched.

"As far as I can tell, they're the only organized group in California, but the radio on my plane is not as good as yours. Maybe I should be asking you." He glanced coolly at Susan. He was referring to the radio she'd shown him earlier.

"Don't ask me. Ask Etta. She does the listening."

They all turned to the old woman, who'd been puttering around the kitchen but now sat down with a little huff. Her expression was somber. "Most of the radio traffic has dropped off in the last couple days. Even the religious stuff."

"What religious stuff?" Harr asked.

"The wacky end-of-the-world stuff," Etta said as though reading from a tedious list. "We've reached the End Times. The Tribulations have begun. Blah, blah, blah."

"*Etta*," Susan said sharply. Etta was an avowed atheist, but that didn't mean Harr was.

Etta shrugged and poured herself a cup of coffee from the carafe on the table. "Like I said, I'm hearing less and less on the radio. Today I only heard Morse code."

The news seemed to surprise Alan. He sat forward, the blanket dropping from his shoulders. "You didn't tell us that."

Etta shrugged. "You didn't ask, and besides, I wasn't sure what I was hearing. I pulled out Susan's old encyclopedia and looked up Morse code to refresh my memory. It's definitely Morse code, but the message is a bunch of gibberish."

"Do you think it's encrypted?" Alan asked, frowning.

"Could be. It started last night and has been going on and off all day."

Susan didn't know why Alan looked so concerned about an

encrypted message. "Maybe it's an automated transmission from the government, like from a satellite or something."

Etta shook her head. "They're transmitting on amateur frequencies, which you wouldn't expect the military or government to do, since they have their own frequencies. And besides, the transmissions seemed like back-and-forth conversations, not like an automated system reporting in."

Susan realized that Harr was staring at Etta like she was some kind of savant. "Etta's father worked for Motorola back in the early days," Susan explained. "She learned a lot about radios as a kid and has a ham radio license."

"I learned *a little* about radios," Etta corrected. "And I've forgotten most of it."

"When was the last time you heard from Shangri-La?" Harr asked.

"Last night."

"Anything new?"

"Naw, just the usual welcoming message, except—" she stopped for a moment, thinking, "—they're directing people to approach the town of Lemon Cove from the south now. They don't want people coming from the north."

Susan could tell this was new intel to Harr. He was frowning. "Highway 198?"

"That's what they said."

"That's odd," Alan said. "They're trying to control incoming traffic now."

"Maybe there's troublemakers from the cities," Etta suggested. "Although it's pretty quiet out there on the radio right now. It's hard to imagine that there are bands of roving marauders out there."

Alan looked over at Harr. "You said you came down from the north. What did you see up there?"

Harr peered into the interior of his coffee cup, the frown

13

still on his face. "It's pretty grim. Redding's burnt out. Yreka's a ghost town—"

"What about Sacramento?" Susan asked.

He gave her another one of his cool gazes. "I didn't fly that far south. The smoke is too dense in the Central Valley. I had to reroute west to avoid it. That's how I came across you."

Or came across the Morgans' fuel tank, Susan thought. He'd probably been hopscotching across the state looking for fuel.

Susan rose and pulled open a cupboard. She took down four glasses. "Are you planning to go to Shangri-La, then?"

"That's my intention."

"Then you'll have to cross the Central Valley at some point."

"Sure, but the safest route through the smoke is the shortest." Harr stood up. "Let me help you with that." He took the glasses from her and carried them to the table. Susan's stomach dropped when she saw his hands. A rim of dried blood ran beneath the nail tips. Half-healed scabs covered his knuckles.

He was still talking. "I'm instrument rated, which means I can fly in poor visibility, but that's during normal times. With the pandemic—" He lifted his shoulders in a shrug. "The GPS system which underpins instrument flying is questionable. If GPS is still functioning, it's probably not fully accurate, and if it's not, my instruments are completely worthless. So, if we can come to a deal on the fuel, I'll head south and cross the valley by the shortest and safest route possible."

They'd come full circle to the fuel again. He hadn't made a single threatening move since she'd brought him into the house, but his coolness made her uneasy. What was to stop him from clobbering her if she said no? He'd clearly been in a fight already. She could see it in his swollen eye and battered hands.

She watched as he set the glasses on the table, listening and not listening as Alan grilled him about what he'd seen in

Oregon. She was thinking of the negotiation that would happen after dinner, and she was weighing if she was making a terrible mistake by even trying to negotiate. She wanted only one thing really, and if he said no, she'd have put herself in a terrible position.

She looked again at his fingernails, at the dark red-black line at the end of his stubby nails, and at the subtle swelling on his weather-hardened face.

"Let's eat," she said.

———

AFTER DINNER, Harr watched as Susan poured an inch of whiskey into a cut glass tumbler and slid it across the table to him. She then poured a tiny splash of whiskey into Wheeler's glass and a bigger splash in Etta's. She capped the bottle and set it in the center of the table.

Negotiation time, he thought grimly.

It was growing dark outside, the last dregs of daylight fading into a thick black. He could see the four of them reflected in the room's bay window, clustered in the still warm kitchen.

What a mess, he thought. An old woman, a deathly ill man, and an obstinate woman who was clearly in over her head.

"Would you like a cookie?" Susan pushed a bag of Chips Ahoy cookies across the table at him. "Nothing fancy, but as close to dessert as we have."

Harr took one. He had to admit it was the best food he'd had in weeks: chocolate chip cookies, whiskey, and a dinner of spaghetti with tomato sauce and fresh strawberries from the garden. He felt a sense of vertigo, the colliding realities of the awful last days of the pandemic and his present circumstances disorienting him. The large house glowed in the thickening night like a brightly lit castle, its electric lights reflected, he could almost believe, in the sliver of yellow moon rising above the eastern ridge. If not for the grinding of the generator and the thick, unyielding darkness beyond the house's circle of light, he could almost believe drug-resistant *Yersinia pestis,* or DRYP as the public health people liked to call it, had never reared its ugly head. He felt a powerful yearning to slip into the fantasy, to forget the pandemic, to forget about the fuel, to luxuriate in the illusion of safety.

He stopped himself. Wheeler was sick as a dog, and the old lady, in her slippers and housecoat, looked like one of the shut-ins from the senior center. As far as Harr could tell, Susan was the only able-bodied person in this holdout, and once the fuel and food ran out, her grasp on survival would disappear like fog on a sunny day.

And here he was trying to talk her out of her fuel.

A little arrow of guilt shot through him. There was nothing in his plane that could replace the brief respite from darkness their fuel granted. Neither could he offer to take the three of them with him to Shangri-La, because his Cessna was, for all intents and purposes, a three-person airplane. It occurred to him that once they realized how little he had to offer, they might not make a deal, and then what would he do?

"Where've you been staying?" Wheeler asked.

"I avoid the cities as much as I can. Mainly I land wherever I can fuel. I don't stay anywhere long."

"Have you seen anyone alive outside of the cities?" Susan asked. She was watching him intently, her dark eyes trained on his face.

"Not in the last two days. I figure different communities got hit by DRYP at different times, but I think the plague's spread pretty evenly by now." He peered down at the amber liquid in his glass. "There aren't a whole lot of survivors left."

Susan sat back and crossed her arms. "And so you want our fuel to go to Shangri-La, to join their community."

She was giving him a hard-eyed look, so he gave her one right back. "I think it's the best chance for survival. They're producing food there; they've got a rudimentary government."

It's more than you have here, he thought but didn't say.

Instead, he got down to business. "I can offer you matches and a kerosene lamp. Plus the fuel for the lamp. I'll also throw in two rolls of toilet paper." He hated to give up the toilet paper since it was one of the things that was hardest to come by, but he figured a woman would want it. It was about the best deal he could offer.

She made a swatting motion with her hand as if his proposal was laughable. "We don't need any of that. I need to go to Sacramento. If you fly me there tomorrow, I'll provide the fuel *and* let you fill your tank when we get back."

Harr blinked, taken aback, and he wasn't the only one. The frown on Wheeler's face was so abrupt and furious, it would have been funny if it weren't so surprising. The old lady merely looked bewildered, as if this development was so unexpected that her elderly mind had trouble processing it.

Wheeler exploded before Harr could even react. "No way, Susan. *Absolutely not.*"

She wheeled around on him. "You just heard him, Alan. The plague's everywhere now. He hasn't seen anyone alive in two days. We'll be safe."

"*In the country,* Susan! I guarantee you that there are people still alive in Sacramento—"

Her face was flushed, and her voice rough with emotion. "That's why I want to go! My mother might still be alive. You want me to just let her die there?"

Suddenly Harr felt invisible. He knew instinctively that this argument had started long before his arrival. It was reaching a climax before his eyes.

Wheeler leaned forward and gripped the table, his face white. "It's been a week, Susan. If your family was still alive, they'd have gotten out by now."

"It's been five days."

"You know damned well that your mother wrote you that note seven days ago. People die from plague in two to three days. Your dad was sick when she wrote it. There's no way either of them is still alive."

For one moment, despite her bossiness, despite how much he distrusted her, Harr wanted to punch Alan for saying that to her. Susan paled. He heard the ragged intake of her breath.

"Besides, haven't you listened to him?" Wheeler went on. "It's too smoky to fly there."

Maybe the whiskey had softened him, Harr thought later. Maybe it had allowed him to see her not as a hard-assed woman, but rather as a brokenhearted daughter. His rational mind knew Wheeler was right. No sane pilot would fly to Sacramento in the smoke. No rational person would go back to any city right now, much less land a plane in one. But sitting at the table, in what seemed the last bright electrical light of the post-pandemic world, he thought of what she was willing to gamble for the chance to see her family again. He didn't have family, but he understood the devotion. It was tattooed on his chest.

Leave no man behind.

"I'll take you," he said quietly.

TWO

Jɪᴍ Cᴀʀsᴏɴ ᴡᴏᴋᴇ ᴛᴏ sᴜɴʟɪɢʜᴛ sᴛʀᴇᴀᴍɪɴɢ ᴛʜʀᴏᴜɢʜ white linen sunshades. It spilled light onto the blond wood flooring of the Napa Valley resort in which he was currently honeymooning.

He kicked a leg free of the bed coverings and fought a groggy urge to laugh. The woman in bed next to him wasn't his wife, and he wasn't married, but the suite in which he and Sam now lay entangled practically screamed honeymoon in Napa. An impossibly fluffy duvet lay in tangled disarray on the king-size bed. Wood-paneled walls gently reflected morning light. Everything was painted a perfect bridal white except the pale gray scattering of furniture before the stone façade fireplace.

You'd blow the budget on this place, he thought as he stretched his full six-foot four-inch length. And then he really did laugh, because there was no blowing budgets anymore. The world had become a first-come, first-take place.

Which suited Carson just fine. How else would he, a one-time UC San Francisco infectious disease fellow with crippling student loans, be able to stay in the uber luxurious neo-Victorian lodge high above the Silverado Trail? True, the resort needed some work. The five-star restaurant lay in smoking ruins, and the lobby's entire window façade had been broken out, but the rest of the resort, the bungalows and meeting rooms, looked much as they had before the pandemic: clean, luxurious, and blessed by a gentle sun. Contented, Carson rolled over, slipped his hand beneath the covers, and ran his fingers down Sam's sweet, tattooed ass.

She groaned and pulled the covers tighter around herself.

Hangover, he thought with a smile. He rose from the bed, naked, and ambled to the bathroom, where he grabbed a towel and a bottle of olive-scented bodywash. He carried these past the three empty bottles of cabernet before the fireplace, out onto the deck, and down the stairs to the gently lapping pool.

It was very pleasant out. Not a cloud dotted the sky, and in the heavy trees beyond the open meadow and pool, he heard the lazy back-and-forth of birdcall. Every so often a breeze stirred the branches.

No, he wasn't in a hurry to leave the Carneros.

He stepped into the turquoise water and rubbed his skin with bodywash, carefully avoiding the plastic-wrap bandage on his upper arm. Beneath it, a new Mayan sundial tattoo healed, courtesy of the sleeping tattoo artist in the bridal bed.

Sam. He felt the stirrings of desire as he soaped his body. He'd found the twenty-six-year-old walking along the road three days earlier, looking disoriented and grief-stricken, her two-tone black-and-red hair knotted and falling halfway down her tattooed back.

He was lucky to have found her. Despite her ink and dye, she was sweet and stupid, which suited his needs perfectly. With a tenderness normally foreign to him, he'd decided to let her sleep.

The first throb of a familiar headache struck as he lay sunbathing on one of the poolside chaise lounges. It began as it always did, with an ache behind his left eye. Dread pooled in the pit of his stomach, because he knew what would follow: the ache would become a band, and the band would begin to squeeze the living shit out of his brain.

Goddamn, he thought bitterly. *It's only been two hours!*

He rose from the chaise lounge and returned the way he'd come, first up the flat stone steps and past the fountains that no longer flowed. He tried to hold on to solid things, but the patio furniture and railings began to waver and fade before him. He knew from experience that if he didn't get his pain medicine, he'd soon be prostrate on the floor.

The desperate violence with which he threw open the bungalow door must have startled Sam, because she looked up from the bed with mascara-smeared eyes and asked, "Are you okay, Jim? Why are you crying?"

"Shut up," he said as he walked past her to the bathroom and slammed the door. In the mirror, he caught a glimpse of his tearstained face.

He knew he didn't have much time. Maybe two minutes at most. He withdrew a syringe from his travel bag and dug around for an alcohol swab. When he couldn't find one, he pulled out drawers and dumped them on the floor.

Fuck the pandemic! he wanted to scream. *Fuck it all!*

With clumsy fingers, he broke off the ampule's top, stabbing himself as he inserted the needle into the little glass vial. A moment later, he popped the needle into the vein in the crook of his elbow.

Somewhere far, far away, the doctor in him cried, *You didn't clean the skin first!*

But the patient in him didn't care. The headache was all that mattered, the single most important thing in the deep center of his brain, in the place where need outweighs reason, and terrible mistakes are made.

———

HARR'S AIRPLANE WAS A WORKHORSE. Susan gazed at the long cracks in the worn leather seats, smelled the machinery stink of fuel and aluminum.

"Put this on," he said, handing Susan a headset.

He didn't say anything else. He ran the preflight checklist without speaking to her, and later, when they were airborne, he continued to ignore her. He seemed preoccupied by the gauges before him. He kept looking out the windows and then back at his instruments.

She could barely see the ground through the smoke. Occasionally the square patchwork of orchards and open fields materialized below them, but the view disappeared as quickly as it appeared, swallowed up in yellow-brown air.

A twenty-five-minute flight. That was what Harr calculated it would be. Short enough that the round trip could be concluded by noon, but long enough to make her nerves scream.

She forced herself to think of her family—her brother, Steven, his wife, Amanda, and their children; her mother and father. They'd all been caught in Sacramento in the pandemic's dark final hours. She kept thinking of the boulevard near Steven's house, wondering if it was long and straight enough to land.

"In and out." Harr's voice, tinny and abrupt, filled her headset. "Twenty minutes on the ground. No more."

She nodded. She knew the plan, had agreed to it the night before, but still, her heart pounded at the number. Twenty minutes. She'd have to move very fast.

There was a crackle of static and then Harr's voice again in her headset. "There's Sacramento International there," he said, pointing at the airport. "We're just north of city limits. I'm going to need you to help me find the road."

Through the haze, Susan could just make out the airport's fuzzy runways. Not far away, the parallel lines of Interstate 5 slashed southward through open farmland toward California's capital city.

There was no movement anywhere.

"Follow the interstate in," Susan said.

They were flying at a thousand feet now, low enough that she could see a long train of stalled cars stopped on Interstate 5.

"Where now?" Harr's voice crackled in her ear.

They were over the northern reaches of the city. Postage-stamp-size houses winked through the smoke, separated by short straight streets and lollipop-shaped cul-de-sacs.

"There," she said abruptly. She pointed at the wide boulevard that bisected Steven's neighborhood. It was the widest street in the northern suburbs, a straight four-lane stretch of asphalt from which the narrower streets of the neighborhood sprouted.

"Is that long enough to land?" Susan asked.

"Should be," Harr said, but she could tell he wasn't paying attention to her. He circled lower this time, his brows furrowed as he stared at the streets below. "They've erected roadblocks."

He was right. Piles of patio furniture and children's toys had been stacked at each entry point to the neighborhood. Bicycle tires poked up from heaps of what looked like torn-up fencing.

"A quarantine within a quarantine," she breathed.

"Either that or they were trying to keep looters out." Harr was frowning. The boulevard itself was not blocked, although every street branching off it was. "Where is your brother's street?"

Susan pointed to where she thought it was, although with the smoke and the cookie-cutter subdivisions, the houses and streets all looked alike.

Harr landed with a precision that would have impressed her

if her heart hadn't been pounding against her ribs. The Cessna's engine roared like a bullhorn, announcing their arrival to anyone within a mile.

"Twenty minutes," Harr repeated. He was squinting down the long boulevard to where the asphalt curved and disappeared behind the browning field of what looked like an elementary school. The furrow between his brows had deepened to a canyon. "The plane is exposed here. You've got twenty minutes max. Then I'm taking off."

She didn't waste a second. She pulled her backpack on and took off at a trot for the nearest cross street. Behind her, she heard Harr cut the Cessna's engine.

By the time she scrambled over the first barricade, she was gasping. The smoke burned in her lungs and made her eyes water. She scanned the empty street, looking for Steven's house, but she couldn't find it. In a flash, she understood why.

This wasn't Steven's street!

Frantic, she scrambled back up the barricade, looking for the street sign. She found it half-hidden by the wilting branches of a maple tree.

Catalpa Drive. Steven lived on Edgewood. The streets were alphabetical. She'd missed his street by two letters.

Twenty minutes, she wanted to scream. *No more screwing up!*

She dropped back down behind the barricade, avoiding the boulevard. She didn't want Harr to see her wasting precious time running back and forth. Instead, she ran the opposite direction, down Catalpa to the next cross street. She rounded the unbarricaded corner and sprinted for her brother's street.

There are no painted red crosses! Nearly every house in Los Angeles had borne the awful mark of plague, but there were no red crosses anywhere in Steven's neighborhood. There was only a heavy stillness, more ominous than the barricades, more ominous than anything at all.

"Steven, open up! It's Susan!" she cried when she reached her brother's front door. No call answered her pounding fists, and after a minute, she gave up and rounded to the side yard, throwing her shoulder against the gate.

It was only when she reached the back that everything disappeared in a haze. Certain details stayed with her: the line of six graves dug into the browning lawn, the first carefully mounded, and later ones so sloppy that she could see clothing and fingers poking through the dirt. She remembered a seventh hole, not yet filled. But the body she discovered minutes later in the family room seemed to have evaporated from her consciousness. Had it been Steven or her mother? It didn't matter.

Seven family members. Seven corpses. Something died in her soul.

———

HER MIND SKIMMED over the next minutes. The parts of her brain that processed memory and emotion shut down. The part deep inside, concerned with a backup plan she didn't even know existed, took over. She threw open cabinets and cupboards, stuffing the backpack with anything she could find: medicines, toothpaste, dental floss, soap, bandages, matches. She flung open the storage cabinets in the garage and found laundry detergent and a whole bottle of bleach.

She checked her watch. *Two minutes left.* In her head, she could hear Harr firing up the Cessna's engine, the propeller beginning to spin as he readied to take off.

She was halfway down the street, the laundry detergent and bleach in either hand, the pack pounding against her back, when she heard a cry.

25

THREE

THE SOUND WAS FAINT, HIGH-PITCHED, AND TO SUSAN'S ear, full of suffering. She froze, wheeled around on the sidewalk, and craned her head to listen. The crying seemed to come from one of the houses closest to her, but it was impossible to tell which.

You've got twenty minutes max. Then I'm taking off.

She dropped the bleach and ran to the nearest house. "Hey, everything okay in there?"

The crying rose in pitch. Susan's heart began to race. When she pulled on the door handle, it didn't give.

In the back of her mind, a clock ticked off the seconds remaining until Harr left her behind. Sixty, fifty-nine, fifty-eight ...

With her eyes closed, she swung the laundry detergent bottle as hard as she could at the front window. The resultant collision sent glass everywhere; something sharp like sand whipped into her face.

Thirty-five, thirty-four, thirty-three ...

The next moments disappeared in a blur of stench and darkness. She scrambled through the window and fell into the living room. She charged down a dim hallway and banged into a kitchen.

She found the little girl, clad only in a diaper, lying on the family room floor. Around her a corona of upended sippy cups and Cheerios lay scattered around on stained carpeting.

"*Oh god*," Susan breathed. The ammonia smell of concentrated urine was overpowering.

Susan looked at her watch and felt her heart slam against her chest. *Two minutes late!*

She dropped to a knee and put a hand to the child's forehead, felt the heat of the toddler's skin. The little girl was sick, desperately sick, but there were no telltale blotches on her skin, none of DRYP's strangled coughing.

No more time! Susan shot one brief glance at the body on the couch, at the remains of the parent who, in desperation, had filled sippy cups and piled Cheerios and placed them with the hope of what? That the child might live a few extra days? That someone might come and rescue her?

It didn't matter. Nothing mattered.

Susan swept the little girl into her arms and ran for her life.

———

THE MEN APPEARED at minute twenty, two dark figures small enough on the horizon that Harr at first wondered if his eyes were playing tricks on him. His binoculars told him they weren't. The two specks grew larger. With a sinking feeling, Harr realized both men carried guns.

Shit. The plane was out in the open, in the center of the boulevard, a straight shot from where the men approached, a half mile away.

He tossed the binoculars on the seat and reached for the rifle in back, and then stopped himself. The men weren't attacking. In fact, they walked toward him in an unhurried manner. They could be friendly.

But the fight at the Redding airport was too close in memory, and Harr was no longer willing to take chances. He flipped the Cessna's master switch, cracked the throttle, and then peered at the barricade over which Susan had disappeared twenty minutes earlier.

Where the hell was she?

For a second, time seemed to stop. He looked at the barricade and then the men. He watched as they seemed to move in slow motion, as their mouths opened to shout, as they raised their weapons.

The snapping noise that followed, so close to his ear, shouldn't have been a surprise, but somehow it shocked the shit out of him. Instinctively, Harr threw himself across the passenger's seat, his forehead banging against the fuselage.

Two tours in Afghanistan roared instantly, electrically alive in his brain.

The second crack sounded louder than the first. Harr scrambled upright and turned the starter key. The engine spluttered and then roared.

Somewhere, beneath the din of the Cessna and his own surging breath, he heard the first *pling* of a bullet striking metal.

Where is she? his brain screamed.

He shot a glance over his shoulder. The smaller man was openly running at him now.

He looked over the barricade, down the empty street on which she'd disappeared, as the plane rolled past the intersection. She wasn't there.

Another *pling* sounded somewhere behind him. He searched around futilely for his headset. It sat, useless, on the passenger's side floor.

Harr couldn't believe it. He was leaving Susan behind. He

rolled down one block, then the next, the plane growling as it gathered speed.

She appeared at the third cross street, climbing and then stumbling over its barricade. Her mouth was open like she was yelling, but he couldn't hear her. She was screaming one word over and over again, her face contorted with a desperation that sliced like a knife at his heart. He knew what she was saying. The word blared in his mind, a Klaxon call:

"Wait!"

———

HE HAD the strange feeling of time slowing. He remembered slamming on the plane's brakes and shoving the passenger's door open. He remembered how she ran, awkwardly, her leg buckling as she sprinted across the boulevard. It wasn't until she was fifteen feet away that he realized why. She was carrying something that threw her weight off. She shoved the object through the open passenger's door.

The stink of shit and piss was instantaneous. A mess of arms and legs and crap-soaked diaper landed on the seat. She tried to crawl in after the baby, but her backpack caught on the door frame and hung her up. Harr pushed her neck down hard, just as another *pling* sounded. He grabbed the top of the pack and hauled her in.

Her head collided, face first, against the yoke. Harr heard a sharp cry, and then she was shoving at him like a madwoman. In some part of his mind that wasn't concerned with the fact that they were being shot at it, he realized she was trying to get off the baby.

"Stop wriggling!" he shouted. The backpack and her body and the baby crowded the cockpit and made piloting the plane impossible. Harr yanked the pack from her body and shoved it over the back of the seat. She let out a yelp of pain.

"Close the door!" he shouted over the grinding engine and the crack-crack of rifle fire.

The Cessna was already rolling. Peripherally, he was aware that she had righted herself in the seat, but he wasn't looking at her anymore. He was looking down the boulevard and thinking he was going to kill them on takeoff. The roadway curved to the left ahead, the straight stretch of asphalt too short to safely get in the air.

He didn't have a choice. He gritted his teeth and pushed full throttle. The Cessna's engine rose to a roar.

———

THEY CLEARED the houses where the boulevard curved by no more than two feet. Harr's heart hammered in his ears, blotting out the sound of the engine, the weird low whine of the baby. He stared straight ahead, into the smoke, and forced himself to focus. It occurred to him that many things were wrong. The plane had an unknown number of bullet holes in it; he didn't know where the bullet holes were; the smoke was so thick he couldn't see; but most baffling of all, for some reason, the woman beside him looked like the victim in a slasher film. Blood streamed down her face in great, horrifying rivulets.

She didn't say anything. She clutched the baby in her arms, her head bowed, the baby's face turned to her breast. Harr realized she was shuddering, that she couldn't hold herself still.

Astonishment and an explosive rage warred within him, but he pushed the conflicting emotions down. He was doing the most dangerous flying of his life, and he knew if he lost his focus even for a second, they could all die.

———

WHEN THEY LANDED at the Morgan property twenty minutes later, she pushed open her door and, without a word, carried the baby into the house. Harr stared after her, the jagged edge of adrenaline still razoring through his veins, astounded that she'd leave him without saying a word. A door slammed somewhere. The still heat of the day wrapped around him and squeezed.

He felt amped up and outraged, and he knew with certainty he shouldn't fly again that day. But he didn't know what to do with himself either, and the pressure in his chest was so bad he thought his heart might explode. He checked the Cessna for damage and discovered four bullet holes in the fuselage and wings. He thought the plane would still fly, but the damage would eventually require repair, and that wouldn't be easy to accomplish when there probably wasn't a goddamn airplane mechanic left on the entire planet. He grabbed the backpack from the rear of the plane and stormed into the house.

He found Susan in the bathroom, kneeling by the tub. The room looked like a bomb had exploded in it. Susan's black doctor's bag lay upended on the floor next to a water bottle. Every drawer and cabinet in the bathroom had been flung open.

"What's wrong with her?" Harr stared down at the little girl in the tub in shock. The toddler's crotch was so red and denuded of skin that it looked like she'd been dipped in boiling water.

"Diaper rash. She's been wearing the same diaper for days." Susan poured a thin stream of water over the child's stool-covered legs. The child let out a weak wail. "She's also dehydrated. Maybe she has an infection."

She rattled off her suspicions tersely, her face a mask of fierce concentration.

"Do you know her?"

"No." Susan poured more water, blotted a washcloth along the child's legs. "I found her in a house on my brother's street. She was the only person alive. Hand me that towel."

Harr watched as she lifted and gently wrapped the toddler. It was only when Susan came to her feet that he got a good look at her face. An inch-long slit gaped open above her right cheek. The eye above was already turning black.

"How'd you hurt your face?" he asked. Besides the laceration, a constellation of smaller cuts oozed blood.

"I had to break a window to get into the house. Can you bring me my doctor's bag?" She disappeared down the hallway.

He swept up the doctor's bag and followed her. He'd seen cuts like hers before. They happened when you got punched. Or when your head got slammed into the cockpit yoke.

"Glass cuts don't give you black eyes, Susan."

She was in one of the bedrooms. She laid the toddler down on the bed and threw open the curtains. In the resulting light, her face looked even worse. She spat out orders like a drill sergeant. "I need a measuring cup and spoon. And more water. A thermometer, if you can find one."

She didn't even bother to look at him. He stared hard at the side of her face, dropped the doctor's bag on the floor, and walked out.

He knew the basics of the house's layout because he'd slept there the previous night. It was one of the few homes in the valley that didn't have a dead person in it, and Susan, knowing that, had offered it to him as a place to sleep. But even though the house was relatively clean and gave Susan a place to quarantine after her visit to Sacramento, it didn't have electricity or running water, which would make nursing a sick kid there very difficult.

He brought her the measuring cup, spoon, and what was left of the water.

"Just put them on the nightstand, would you?" She was sitting bedside in a chair, scribbling something on a pad of paper. She didn't even look up. "Thanks."

She was bossing him around again. He gave her the stink eye for a solid five seconds and then walked out.

FOUR

Rolando "The Reaper" Bravo was pretty sure he was the last person alive in Fairfield. He stood on the mat in Eddie King's MMA Gym, surveyed the stacked weights and heavy bags, and thought, *Fuck me.*

He was out of food and nearly out of water. Which meant he'd have to leave the gym.

But he didn't want to leave the gym. He hadn't seen or heard another person in more than forty-eight hours, and the silence outside scared the living bejesus out of him.

He dropped and pushed out fifty push-ups.

Discipline, Rolando! Eddie's voice rang in his head. *You got to want it to win it!*

Win what? A wave of terror swept through The Reaper. Eddie didn't prepare him for this.

Rolando's heart began to skitter in his chest, his breath catching raggedly in his throat. He felt as if some internal circuit breaker were tripping, and that the horror and the stillness outside were big yawning things, a black hole of terror from which he couldn't escape.

He had to leave the gym. The toilets no longer flushed, and

the water didn't run. The place smelled so bad he couldn't stand it. But outside seemed impossible. True, he hadn't heard any weapons fire recently, but Rolando wasn't stupid. Eddie's gym was on the outskirts of town, in a warehouse district filled with plumbing supply and tile stores. The Reaper bet people were still shooting each other at the mall and in the outer suburbs.

He rose and paced in a tight circle. No, he'd have to go out there, and though Rolando knew he could take anyone in hand-to-hand combat, he also knew that all the MMA training in the world was worthless against a gun. He'd wind up like those Chinese warriors, the Harmonious Fists or whatever they were called, who thought martial arts would protect them against the firepower the Americans, Europeans, and Japanese rained down on them during the Boxer Rebellion. Rolando was pretty sure they'd been mowed down in droves.

Which meant The Reaper needed a gun.

Which meant The Reaper had to leave the gym.

But first things first. He dropped for another fifty push-ups and then did another round of drills. Deep inside, he knew Eddie would have been proud.

———

SIXTY MILES TO THE NORTH, Alan Wheeler sat on the porch of Susan's parents' home, listening for the drone of a small plane's engine. It came, more or less on time, over Liberty Valley's eastern ridge, sometime after noon.

He should have felt relief, but he didn't. The Morgan property was no more than a half mile away, but because walking farther than twenty feet sucked the life out of him, the house where Susan meant to quarantine might as well have been on the moon.

A wave of restlessness washed through him. He rose and

dragged himself across the house's wraparound porch, gasping as if he were climbing Mount Everest.

He wanted to look at the solar panels. They stood in two rows, beyond the yard, in the open space between the barn and the thick cottonwood trees that lined Liberty River. He'd been thinking about the solar panels a lot lately.

When he'd first asked about them, Susan had explained, "They power the irrigation pump down in the river."

Which wasn't exactly right, Alan knew, but he didn't bother to correct her. The solar panels were wired to feed electricity to the grid, which would then in turn deliver electricity to the pump. It was a complicated arrangement, which in good times earned Susan's father a credit on his electricity bill, but in bad times, like the present circumstances, didn't help with anything. The solar power system was designed to automatically turn itself off any time the grid went down. As a consequence, all those beautiful panels were basically doing nothing.

Alan closed his eyes, tried to think. The sun was hot against his head, a glaring reminder of the solar energy that the panels weren't using. If he could rewire the system and override the automatic shutoff, he could use the panels to directly generate power for the house and farm. They'd effectively be freed from the generator. With luck, the solar power system would last for years.

If we live that long.

He pushed that gloomy thought from his head, opened his eyes, and squinted at the system, trying to guess how many kilowatts the panels could generate. He looked at the house and tried to estimate how much battery storage he would need to power the refrigerator and range. He made calculations in his head about which appliances they could use and which consumed too much electricity. He thought about the domestic well.

And then he let out the ghost of a laugh. The irony of his situation—that he, the chairman of a major oil company, was trying to figure out how to jerry-rig a renewable energy system—wasn't lost on him.

But he didn't care. The photovoltaic panels would have a functional life span of ten to fifteen years. If he got the system up and running, they could power the house and, at least on some level, irrigate enough to support a sustained food supply.

They could begin to rebuild some semblance of the life that DRYP had almost wiped out.

His mood somewhat buoyed by the possibility, Alan limped back into the house to take his afternoon nap.

———

WHEN HARR RETURNED AN HOUR LATER, he set a plastic water jug on the bedroom floor next to Susan's chair.

She looked up in surprise. "Where'd that come from?"

"The jug is mine," he said coolly, still smarting from her earlier dismissal. "The water came from your place."

She frowned. "You broke quarantine?"

"No. I went to the outside faucet, filled the jug up, and then yelled at the old lady from the lawn." He peered at the nightstand. She'd set up a notepad and pen, a measuring cup full of water, and a teaspoon. "What are you doing?"

Susan sat back and crossed her arms. "Rehydrating her. You didn't actually yell at Etta, did you?"

Harr ignored her unfriendly tone. He was looking at the notations of volume and time on the notepad, finally understanding what she was doing. Susan was spoon-feeding water to the little girl, drop by painful drop.

"Of course I yelled at her," he said. "She's not going to hear me whispering from twenty yards away."

Susan flicked an annoyed glance at him, and then reached for the teaspoon. Very carefully, she dripped a tiny measure of water into the kid's mouth. The toddler's neck muscles barely moved in response. "Did you see Alan?"

"Nope. But Etta told me to tell you he's the same. She said he's camped on the Barcalounger." He gestured at the teaspoon. "Is that even helping?"

For a second, an uncharacteristic doubt flickered in her eyes. She peered down at the listless child. "I don't know. She doesn't have a fever, so I'm guessing it's dehydration and not an infection that's making her sick. But without lab tests, it's impossible to know."

Harr didn't say anything. He knew she was some sort of doctor, but the uncertainty in her voice suggested she wasn't a pediatrician. If she wasn't such a hard-ass, he'd probably feel sorry for her.

But she clearly wasn't the sort who wanted sympathy, and she showed it once again by reaching into her pocket, pulling out a set of keys, and tossing it at him. "The gold one is for the fuel tank," she said.

He caught the keys with his left hand, looked at them silently for a moment, and then slipped them in his pocket. "The jug of water is for your face."

It took her a full second to understand. She blinked, reached a hand to her bloodied cheek, and then peered at the dark smudge of red on her fingers.

"I'll watch the kid while you wash up," he said and handed her the jug. Her hesitation to accept it spoke volumes, but he told himself not to fret about it. He made a little flicking motion to get her to leave.

By the time she returned from the bathroom, he had his first aid kit opened on the bed.

"Sit down," he ordered, inspecting her face but not meeting

her eyes. The smaller cuts would heal within days, but the slit on her cheek was another story. That one would scar.

For five minutes, she let him dab her wound with hydrogen peroxide and apply a butterfly bandage. He dotted on antibiotic ointment and then taped a gauze pad.

She was very still, a good patient.

When he was finished, he silently packed up his kit and went outside.

———

LATER, after he'd reloaded the last of his belongings into the plane's cargo area, Harr walked to the edge of the Morgan property and peered across the neighboring pasture at the tall conical tower of Susan's home. It poked above the distant walnut trees like a church spire; a vertical antenna stood in place of an apical cross.

A late afternoon breeze rustled the tall shrubs along the fence line. It took Harr a minute to realize that the quiet whisper of the trees, uninterrupted by road noise or airplane noise or any other sort of human-caused noise, reminded him of his Harney County home in Oregon, on the quiet evenings before the plague, when he had drunk a beer alone on his porch and listened, in the darkness, to life carrying on without him. On those nights, he'd felt a sort of wonder and humility to realize how inconsequential his presence was to the natural world around him. The wind blew and the animals scampered, and a whole ecosystem proceeded without him being at the center of it.

It had almost been possible, in the wild, sparsely populated high desert, to forget that seven billion people pushed and shoved on the Earth, that he himself had been thrust into one of those shoving matches in Afghanistan, and that on more than one lonely night, while he had lain sleepless in his hooch, he had thought that humans were the most fucked-up species in the world.

He had had no idea then how fragile it all had been.

His heart, a mostly ignored organ, began a slow thud. He couldn't have exactly explained what he was feeling, because words were not his strong suit. He only knew that the feeling was lonely and awful, and that it seemed to stretch across the valley and into the valley next door and across the country and the oceans beyond. He felt as if the whole silent world echoed his quiet devastation.

Which was why, he thought later, he went in to talk with her.

———

HE DIDN'T MEAN to be a Peeping Tom. His intention was to ask if she wanted him to heat up some of his canned goods for dinner. But he walked to her cracked door just as she was pulling off her blood-splattered shirt, and he, for a solid ten seconds, stared at her bare skin and the navy-blue bra strap that ran over the sharp, pointed angles of her shoulder blades.

She was very thin. Not concentration-camp thin, but near enough.

She turned as he was eyeing the narrow indentation of her waist. For a second, she just stared at him with her one good eye and one black one, and then a sort of revolted comprehension flashed across her battered features. She pulled her shirt to her chest.

He did not know how to explain why he was staring, so he pivoted instead and walked back down the darkening hallway and out of the house.

He stayed outside until the sun sank beyond the western

hills and the sky turned a salmon pink and then faded to dark red. He stayed until the heat of the day slipped away into a cool, quiet darkness.

And the whole time he kept cursing himself. As he lay awake in his sleeping bag, he felt too embarrassed to go back into the house, but unhappy where he was. The ground was hard beneath him, and the sky above messy with faint stars. The Cessna, not far distant, creaked as the fuselage cooled in the night air.

His eyes drifted to the house and the small flare of light in the bedroom. It was still burning when he finally fell asleep hours later.

FIVE

THE REAPER HEARD THE MOTORCYCLE A LITTLE AFTER eleven on Tuesday. He'd been lying spread-eagle on his back, gazing at the unlit fluorescent lighting above, when the thin walls of Eddie King's MMA began to vibrate. Shocked, he leaped to his feet and ran to the gym's one street-facing window just as a man and a woman on a Harley passed by.

Rolando's heart began to thunder. "Hey!" he shouted. "HEYYYY!"

The man didn't appear to hear him. He continued slow-rolling down the street, scanning the buildings on either side. The black-and-red-haired woman behind him leaned against the seat back, gazing off into space with a bored expression.

The Reaper threw himself at the door, unbolted it, and ran down the street. "WAIT!" he yelled.

He caught them half a block down. The biker turned, frowned, and then brought the motorcycle to a halt. Rolando flew by the Harley with his arms windmilling like crazy.

"Where—where are you going?" he gasped.

The man's face was perfectly composed, but The Reaper had the distinct impression that amusement lurked beneath his thin lips and aviator shades. "I think the better question is: Where are you going?"

Suddenly The Reaper saw himself as they probably saw him: a short, baby-faced man so desperate he'd run outside in tight red training shorts and nothing else.

"I've been working out," Rolando huffed. He jerked his head toward the gym. "At Eddie King's MMA."

One scraggly eyebrow rose above the biker's aviator shades. He looked back down the road at Eddie's gym and then back at Rolando. "This whole time?"

"Yeah, sure. I live there. It's clean." He rethought that. "Well, it was clean before the plumbing went out. Now it's like ... you know."

The chick behind the biker let out a little titter, which made Reaper mad, because he didn't like chicks laughing at him. He turned his back on her and focused on the aviator-shades man, who, now that he thought about it, looked pretty cool in his black leather pants and AC/ DC T-shirt.

"Where you heading?" Reaper asked, trying to sound equally cool, which wasn't easy because he was standing there half-naked with no shoes on.

The biker gave a friendly little shrug. "Here and there. You happen to know where the Cardinal Health warehouse is?"

Cardinal Health? They were lost! *Really* lost. Reaper stared. They were lost! *Really* lost.

"It's in Dixon. This is Fairfield." Rolando said. "I'll show you how to get there without going on the interstate. I know the backroads like the back of my hand."

The biker's lip curled as he eyed Rolando's shoeless feet. "That might be hard if you're walking and we're riding, though."

"I got a bike," Reaper said, more confident now. His sporty red-and-black Suzuki was right behind him, on the other side of the roll-up door at Eddie King's MMA.

The two-tone woman started giggling again. "How about a shirt? You got one of those, too?"

Rolando kept his eyes on the biker and suppressed the urge to drill a fist straight into the woman's tittering mouth. "What do you say?" he asked the biker.

"Sure. How long will it take us to get to Dixon?"

Reaper was feeling great now. "An hour max," he said. "Why don't you come back to the gym while I get my stuff?"

———

SUSAN WOKE to the sound of a sharp thump. For a second, she just sat there, staring at the bright sunshine beyond the curtains, confused about where she was and why. And then it came back to her. She was in the Morgans' house. She was nursing a sick kid. She'd fallen asleep on her chair and let the pad of paper slip from her fingers.

With a groan, she pulled herself upright. Next to her, the tablet lay open, facedown, where it had fallen on the floor. She picked it up and put it back on the nightstand. She then poured more water into the measuring cup and scribbled the time. With a weary sigh, she rubbed a palm against her good eye.

The next twelve hours were critical for the little girl. Susan couldn't fall asleep again.

But god, she was tired. Her brain ached with it.

The little girl let out a weak cry. Susan forced her eyes to focus on the naked little body, only half-wrapped in a sheet.

How could I have left her exposed like that? Susan thought in despair. She rewrapped the child, laid the back of her fingers against the toddler's forehead.

No diapers. No baby clothes. No sippy cup or bottle. Why hadn't Susan thought to take even one of those things from the Sacramento house?

She sank against the chair back and tried not to weep.

She dipped the spoon, brought it to the child's lips, watched the tiny muscles of her neck ripple as she swallowed.

Drip, drip, drip.

Susan pinched herself and paced as the hours slipped away.

———

JIM CARSON STARED at the Cardinal Health warehouse, perplexed. A crater stood where the front office door had once been, and black soot snaked up the side of the building. Even the windows were blown out.

"Holy shit." The Reaper's eyes were huge. He stood next to Carson, shifting from one leg to the other like he was about to jump into the ring. "They fucking bombed the place!"

Carson fought a growing kernel of irritation. "Who exactly do you mean by 'they'?"

Samantha answered for him, "The Army men." She stood next to a sand-colored Humvee that blocked the entrance to the employee parking lot. She poked her head in through the Humvee's open door and then pulled it back out. "No one here. They must still be inside the warehouse."

Not for the first time, Carson wondered at her intelligence. The parking lot was as silent as a tomb, and the building looked equally still. If the soldiers were inside, they were dead. Carson was pretty sure he could smell the fetid stink of rotting corpse drifting from the front office.

Reaper was looking at Samantha like she was a moron. "First of all, these are National Guard vehicles, not Army. And second, why would the National Guard attack a medical distribution warehouse? That makes no sense whatsoever."

He turned to Carson. "I think the soldiers were guarding the place."

Carson had to agree. Another Humvee blocked the driveway that led to the loading docks. These were not attack positions, but rather defensive ones.

"You still want to go in, Doc?" The Reaper was now swinging his arms in big round circles.

Carson ran a finger over the Humvee's hood, looked at the dust he'd picked up. It wasn't thick. He nodded. "Let's go to the loading dock."

The back side of the building was as quiet as the front. There were no trucks at any of the bays, but the roll-down doors were wide open. Carson scanned the length of the empty driveway, spying a spiderweb of fresh ruts in the lawn beside it.

"What the hell?" The Reaper breathed.

Carson squatted down, poked a finger into one of the tracks. "Dualies. The trucks came out this way." He looked back at the Humvee blocking the driveway. Whoever had attacked the building had been forced to circumvent the National Guard vehicle on the way out. Which meant the National Guard had failed in their defense.

Samantha grabbed his arm, tried to pull him to his feet. "We don't need medical supplies, Jim. Come on, let's go!"

He pulled himself free and peered over at the loading dock. Broken boxes clogged the dark openings. Loose pieces of plastic packing material had blown against the chain-link fencing surrounding the asphalt.

Carson rose to his feet and crossed the driveway.

"They could still be in there," Reaper said behind him. He was hustling to keep up.

"Maybe," Carson said. He pushed himself up through the first open bay, kicked a broken box aside, and quickly advanced to the first row of shelving units. Without electric lighting, the interior of the building was dimly lit and cavernous. He had the sense of rushed chaos, of some group having torn through the building's shelving units, emptying boxes and leaving unwanted junk in the aisles.

He listened and heard it again, a creak, something light toppling over.

"Dude, man. This isn't good." The Reaper had come up behind him. Carson could practically feel the younger man's breath on his back. "They've ransacked the place."

"Shut up," Carson whispered. He was looking for directional signs, anything that might indicate the organization of the building.

He was halfway down the aisle when an explosion of movement erupted from one of the shelving units. A bird, black like a raven, launched itself, its wings flapping furiously. Startled, Carson jumped backward. The Reaper let out a scream.

"You moron. *Shut up*," Carson hissed, watching as the bird disappeared out the loading bay door into the bright light beyond.

"Let's go, man," The Reaper cried. "There ain't nothing we need here."

But Carson ignored him. He was listening again and slowly picking his way along the floor, skirting upended boxes and scattered plastic bedpans. He was halfway down the first aisle when he smelled stool.

"Hey," Carson whispered with sudden urgency. He flagged Reaper and pointed.

Two bodies lay up ahead on the floor. The closest was dressed in the camouflage uniform of the National Guard. A pool of half-dried body fluids surrounded his hips.

"Oh, Jesus," Rolando breathed. "That smell."

"Shhh." Carson walked past the National Guardsman to the second body. The tactical gear on this one was different, the vest plain and black, the pants a basic olive green.

"Look at that," Carson whispered. The man wore a gas

mask—or what was left of a gas mask. A hole as big as his fist had been blasted through it, and bits of rotting gray matter lay scattered on the floor.

What the fuck?

Rolando could barely speak. "You think they used tear gas? You think that's how they got in?"

Carson didn't know.

"What kind of uniform is that?" Rolando asked. He seemed to have verbal diarrhea now. In the dim light, his eyes were as round as silver dollars.

"It's not military," Carson said. He turned and gazed at the bullet casings that littered the floor. "There are no guns," he said thoughtfully. "Whoever raided this place scavenged all the weapons after the attack."

Across the warehouse, in one of the loading bays, Samantha wailed, "I hate this place. I want to go now!"

"Go shut her up," Carson ordered.

He wanted to be alone. The two bodies lay before the pharmaceuticals section. He could already see the controlled substances safe had been blown wide open and the shelves inside were bare.

He shook his head, bemused and impressed by what he was seeing. Obviously, the attackers had known, with quarantines and sickness sucking up National Guardsmen, that the warehouse would be lightly guarded. They also knew to strike while the semitrucks still had fuel in them. Carson marveled at the planning and organization that had gone into the raid.

He wondered who was behind it. He wondered where they'd gone.

He was still thinking about the raid fifteen minutes later as he, Sam, and Reaper left the facility empty-handed. Every narcotic, syringe, and alcohol swab was already gone.

SIX

A QUIET KNOCK YANKED SUSAN OUT OF DROWSINESS. SHE jumped in her chair.

"Sorry. I didn't mean to frighten you," Harr said.

He stood in the doorway, his sleeves rolled up to his elbows, looking down at her and the child with an expression she could only describe as *wary*. "I made some dinner. You think you could leave the kid for a moment and eat, or do you want me to bring you a plate here?"

She peered down at the toddler. The little girl's eyes were drooping closed, not in the glassy-eyed way of earlier, but rather in the exhausted way of a child recovering from severe stress. Susan guessed she would sleep for hours.

"I can leave her." Susan checked her notations, calculated the volume she'd managed to get into the girl. "I've probably got half an hour until I need to give her more water."

"Then let's get going. Dinner's on the table," he said brusquely. He was already halfway down the hallway, the wooden floors creaking under his weight.

She had to hustle to keep up. "Where'd you go today?" She'd noticed the Tacoma had vanished from the yard.

"Hunting." He didn't break stride.

"Any luck?"

The smell answered her question. It hit her the minute they stepped through the kitchen doorway. "What is that?"

He finally stopped and stepped aside, his expression both defensive and mulish.

She wasn't sure she was seeing right. On the kitchen table, two plates sat atop cloth placemats, and absurdly festive napkins lay beneath forks and knives. But what really astounded her was the turkey. The golden brown bird rested, center table, on an antique china platter.

Harr was watching her with an unreadable expression. "I shot it down by the river. There are quite a few wild birds down there. You need some population control."

She wasn't really listening to him. She was looking at the other dishes, the baked beans and the dark red cherries, and thinking that she'd been so preoccupied with the sick girl that she hadn't noticed him clanking around the kitchen. Suddenly a wash of emotions, so tangled that she couldn't hope to pick out its threads, engulfed her. She couldn't really move. She just stood there like a frozen person.

Harr pulled out a chair for her. "I hope you're not vegetarian," he said.

A little croak of laughter, almost like a huff, erupted from her. "Nobody's a vegetarian anymore."

"That's good, because the tofu aisle in the supermarket is pretty picked over," he said as he sat down across from her. He proceeded to slice off a thick slab of breast for her and a thicker one for himself. He then scooped a mound of beans on each of their plates and pushed the bowl of cherries at her. "Dig in," he said.

She didn't move. She held the knife and the fork flat on the table before her. "How'd you cook the bird?"

He gave her a strange look. "Outside, over a fire."

"Ah yes, of course," she said. It made sense. There wasn't any power to the house.

She felt a bubble rising in her chest, shoving against her sternum and pushing against the tightening in her throat.

"I'm sorry about your plane," she said.

He looked at her blankly. "Pardon?"

"It's my fault it's damaged. I was late getting back."

When he looked at her with a dumbfounded expression, the bubble burst through its bottleneck, and she began to cry.

———

HE HANDED her one of the colorful napkins, and because he didn't know what else to do, he watched helplessly. Her shoulders sagged and shuddered. She dropped her head, so that he could not see her cut-up skin and blackened eye.

He was afraid to touch her, uncertain if he'd offend her. So he said the first thing he could think of, which was an awkward, "There are four bullet holes in my plane, but it's fine. It'll keep flying."

Her head came up. "It will?"

It pained him to see the exhausted worry in her eyes. "Did you think it wouldn't?"

"I didn't know. I thought you might have to get it repaired."

"Nah, the plane is fine," he said again. "The holes are small, nothing to be worried about." He poked a fork in the direction of her plate. "Eat."

She ate.

———

HE WAS WRONG, of course. But he didn't know it then. He only knew he wanted her to sleep awhile, and if he was going to stay up watching the kid, he needed caffeine. He pushed his plate away. "You had enough?"

She smiled at him for the first time. It was a teary smile, but it was real. He thought it looked kind of pathetic in the middle of all those cuts and scabs.

She sat back and put her hands on her nonexistent belly. "I ate half that turkey."

He rolled his eyes and picked up their plates. "Hardly. I'm making coffee. Want some?"

She nodded, eyeing the turkey carcass. She was different now, nicer. "Can I take the leftovers to Alan and Etta?"

"Nope, but I'll do it." He set the plates by the sink and fired up his camping stove. He put a pot of water on top, and then sank back in the chair opposite her. He felt like he could talk more easily now, that some sort of barrier had been broken.

"You know, if all the kid has is dehydration, you probably don't have to quarantine anymore," he said thoughtfully. "You're not sick and neither is she."

Her face clouded for a second. "I'm not one hundred percent sure of that."

"Seems to me that if you wait to be a hundred percent sure about anything these days, you're going to be waiting the rest of your life. You can risk it, Susan."

She eyed him seriously. "That must mean you want to leave. When?"

"Tomorrow probably." He'd been thinking about it, and now that the kid seemed like she was on the mend, it seemed the right time to go.

She nodded.

"You should come with me." He blurted out the words before he knew what he was saying.

Apparently, he'd shocked her, too, because she looked at him blankly and said, "Me?"

"Yeah. Bring the kid."

She was silent, and for half a second, he thought she might say yes, but then a furrow formed between her brows. "I can't leave Alan and Etta."

"We'll come back for them. We'd only need to leave them for a few days while we get established at Shangri-La. In fact, I'd fly back for them myself. You and the kid could stay in Shangri-La."

It was a good idea, he thought. It made sense.

But she wasn't convinced. "What if Shangri-La won't accept them?"

"We can convince them to take them. They seem pretty welcoming on the radio."

"Even for two sick people who can't work?"

What she said was true. Alan and Etta would be a drain on any settlement. In the harsh calculus of survival, they had nothing to offer.

But he didn't say that. He said, "If they don't accept them, I'll bring you back here. I'll find the fuel. Don't worry."

She shook her head. "There are a lot of other risks besides finding fuel, John. What if Alan or Etta gets sick while I'm gone? You don't even know what Shangri-La is really like. They could be worse off than we are here, for all you know."

He doubted it. "Animals run in herds for a reason, Susan. Shangri-La has at least twenty people that can work together. You're basically a one-man army here. The odds are obvious. Go with the herd."

It was like talking to a wall. She shook her head. "You go. Find out if Shangri-La is what you think. And if it is, have them radio us. We know what frequencies they broadcast on. We'll listen."

Across the room, the camp stove let out a small hiss. He stared at her battered face, at the set of her too-thin shoulders. He didn't say what he felt, which was you couldn't be a hundred percent sure all the time. Sometimes you just had to take risks.

But her expression told him she'd already decided, and nothing he could say would change her mind. She'd rather stay here, in a place with gargantuan but known challenges, instead of venturing forth in the hopes of finding something better. It was an overly cautious and potentially suicidal decision.

Yet he couldn't bring himself to condemn her. It was clear she was dedicated and selfless. He'd seen the same qualities in Afghanistan, in the medics who so willingly put themselves in harm's way to save others.

He gazed at her for a long minute, at the dark, shadowed eyes and the cut he knew he'd put on her cheek. In the fading light, her face looked tragic and somehow, despite the black eye and cuts, beautiful.

"I'll come back for you," he promised. "It may take me four or five days to get squared away in Shangri-La, but once that's taken care of, I'm coming back."

THE FEVER STARTED in the night. Jim Carson woke, freezing cold, in darkness.

It took a moment to remember where he was. In the dim moonlight, he could just make out the stacked videotapes piled on the dresser and his dark reflection in the mirror overlooking the bed.

Truck stop motel, he thought miserably. The only place left on the planet that still had VCRs.

He shivered and put a hand to his forehead. Beside him, Sam shifted and mumbled groggily, "You okay, Jim?"

"I'm fine," he said.

But it wasn't really true. Fever burned against his fingers. Every bone in his body ached.

He dragged himself to his feet, nightmarish memories of a needle injected through dirty skin spinning like a kaleidoscope image in his head. What had he been thinking?

He hadn't been thinking. He'd been so desperate for a hit that he'd injected like a goddamn junkie.

He flashed his Maglite at the crook of his elbow, half expecting to see angry red streaks, but instead seeing the pale blue rise of his veins. He felt his pulse. The slow bump-bump-bump of his heart pushed back at him.

So maybe no bloodstream infection after all. But still, something else was wrong with him, because how else to explain the pain in his bones and the exhaustion that made him want to curl into a ball and shudder?

He scrambled in his travel kit for ibuprofen, popped three, and then swallowed an OxyContin. In the flashlight's beam, he could see his reflection in the bathroom mirror: the hot-pink blotches on his cheeks, the scorching intensity of his eyes.

He tried to think of where the infection had come from. He doubted the medical distribution center, but perhaps he'd caught something in the nursing home they'd visited afterwards? God knew, there had been enough dead people in that dump to infect half the world.

Or maybe it was this awful motel room. His mind was playing tricks on him. He could have sworn a million bedbugs were marching across his skin.

It was enough to make him crazy.

One more OxyContin, he thought. He needed to quiet his mind, to get some sleep.

He dry-swallowed another pill and staggered as it took effect. Some sleepy part of his mind knew he was treading on dangerous territory, that the space between relief and overdose narrowed the more tolerant his body became to narcotics, but at the moment he didn't care. He was tired and felt like shit, and at the bottom of his heart, he knew he was too smart to OD. He was Jim Carson, after all, a doctor who had once trained at that pinnacle of academic medicine, UC San Francisco. He knew how to titrate medications, knew what lines not to cross.

Relief swooshed in and with it, drowsiness. He wandered back into bed and slipped beneath the unwashed covers. Before long, he fell into a thick, dreamless sleep.

SEVEN

Susan stood in the yard as Harr readied the plane for takeoff. It was only ten o'clock, but already her shirt stuck to her back. She could feel the hot sun burn her scalp.

Harr waved, a quick jerk of his hand, and she waved back. The Cessna began to roll, its fat wheels bouncing on the dried ground, the engine roaring. A minute later, Harr was airborne, flying southward into the haze.

She stood, listening for a minute to the fading engine, and then the valley became its still self again. One bird, brave against the rising heat, let out an irritable squawk.

She returned to the Morgan house and started the cleanup. She washed the dishes from the night before and then packed up the sheets and blankets she and the girl had slept on. She tried to focus on practical matters: how she could make diapers and clothing from the sheets; where she could find safety pins; if she could find milk.

And yet, when she finally packed up the truck to return to her childhood home, she couldn't help feeling deflated. The valley seemed too quiet, the brown hills too dry and dull.

Snap out of it, she told herself. There were vegetables to harvest, and medical care to administer. She had no time to sit around and mope.

But still, when she saw Etta descending from the Victorian's covered porch, her smile in response to Etta's "You're back!" was halfhearted.

"Quarantine's over." Susan gave a little huff as she lifted the sleeping toddler from the Tacoma's back seat.

"So, it really is true," Etta said, staring at the little girl in wonder. "Harr said you'd brought a sick child back from Sacramento. Is she okay?"

"I think so. She was pretty dehydrated when I found her, but she seems to be bouncing back." Susan carried the girl up the stairs. "Where's Alan?"

"Napping on the Barcalounger. What happened to your face?" Etta was frowning at the black eye and fresh butterfly bandage Harr had placed on Susan's cheek earlier that morning. "Did Harr do that to you?"

Susan didn't want to talk about the last forty-eight hours, not yet. "We had a rough escape from Sacramento, but I'm fine. I'll tell you about it later." She ducked through the open kitchen door. "Hi, Alan."

On the Barcalounger, Alan popped one eye open. "I thought you were coming home tomorrow."

He was still pale and the hollows beneath his cheeks too deep, but his eyes snapped to alertness. They followed Susan as she crossed the room.

"She got better faster than I thought." Susan plopped herself on the couch next to his chair, turning the little girl in her lap so that the drowsy child faced him. "Meet Emmaline. She's a little sleepy still, but she'll perk up after we feed her."

Alan pulled the lever so that the Barcalounger snapped into

an upright position. He peered at the little blonde-haired girl. "Is that her real name?"

Susan shook her head. "I have no idea what her real name is. I found her in some random house in Sacramento. So I'm calling her Emmaline after my grandma."

He made a noncommittal noise, his eyes shifting from the little girl's face to Susan's. He frowned. "What happened to you?"

She shrugged and turned Emmaline so that her head rested against her chest. "I climbed through a broken window to get to her. It's nothing."

"It doesn't look like nothing."

"It's nothing compared to a gunshot wound. How are you feeling?"

"Better." He smiled wryly. "I can walk twenty feet now."

"Gasping the whole way," Etta cracked. She had joined them in the family room.

Susan gazed at the elderly woman and the sick man, the groggy little girl in her lap. She imagined her own scabbed and wounded face. *What messes we are*, she thought.

But still, they were alive. And, all things considered, that was something. She smiled, and this time it was for real.

———

THE DEATH RATTLE began somewhere south of Fresno, about ten miles outside Lemon Cove. Harr felt the faint shudder in the Cessna's yoke and a worrisome vibration in his seat. By the time he'd shucked his headset, he knew he was in big trouble. The left wing was making a flapping noise, like a baseball card slapping against a bicycle wheel's spokes.

Oh shit. The bullet holes! The realization clanged in his head. He searched the wing for the source of the sound and saw a flutter in the narrow control surface on the wing's trailing edge. He knew immediately he needed to land.

His hands worked quickly. He closed the throttle and adjusted the plane's pitch. He checked his airspeed and saw the plane was descending too fast. All the training for this moment, the nights he'd lain awake thinking about it as an abstraction, went blazingly, electrically live.

I'm going to crash.

He couldn't see the ground. He retrimmed and searched. Through the smoke, the Earth finally popped into view.

Level off, he told himself. *Don't stall.*

But the plane seemed to have a mind of its own. The left wing let out a screech and started to shimmy. He felt the yoke begin to pull.

The long flat barn of a dairy operation came into view below him. Beyond it, dirty brown pastureland stretched at least a quarter of a mile.

He aimed for it and hit ten seconds later, the shock of the collision running up his spine in one violent wave. The Cessna bounced, rose, and then hit again.

Light tumbled. The ground pitched. He had the feeling of flying through space, of gravity upended.

There was pain, but only for a second.

———

HE CAME to with his ass up in the air. Or at least it felt that way. He was hanging by his shoulder restraints, the lap belt pulled tight against his hips.

Somewhere, far away, he heard the plaintive moo of a cow, but he wasn't sure if it was real or a hallucination. He was having trouble thinking. He couldn't understand why he was hanging like he was.

Little things struck him and then flitted away: how dry and bleached the soil looked, how the airplane creaked and moaned. He looked with a sort of detached sorrow at the mangled metal and broken glass, and thought, *Aw, shit, I've really messed up my plane this time.*

By the time he fumbled with the harness and fell in a heap against what was left of the plane's controls, the smell of gas was very strong. He dragged himself from the fuselage, managed to salvage his shotgun. He wrestled his backpack out and tried to free his camp stove.

But it was no use. The fire had already started. He reeled back and landed on his backside.

He watched in shock as his beloved plane burned.

———

JIM CARSON'S diarrhea started midday. It splattered in the toilet bowl and stank up the entire motel room.

"Oh, Jim!" Sam cried. "Was it the rice?"

She stood in the bathroom doorway, her eyes wide with anguish. He couldn't believe she was actually watching him take a shit.

Another wavelike cramp hit him. He bent forward, dropped his head, and let go again. Sam's voice faded to a drone.

"We should never have eaten that rice, Jim! Those places aren't safe. There are germs everywhere!"

In the depths of his suffering, he knew she was right. Scavenging for food and narcotics in a nursing home had been an idiotic decision. But Carson had been desperate, and his need had been so powerful that he'd shut off the part of his brain that screamed, *Don't touch anything!*

And now he was sitting on a toilet that didn't flush, shitting his guts out. "Get me Imodium or Pepto Bismol," he hissed.

Sam gaped at him from the doorway. "How?"

"How do you think?" He gripped his head, too weak to rip her head off, too weak to rip off his own. "Go to a Walgreens or Safeway. You're not helping me watching me crap."

"You think that's safe?" He could hear the uncertainty in her voice, the hesitation.

He glanced at her wearily. She hadn't bathed in days, and now, in the dim bathroom light, her black-and-red hair had lost its vibrant luster, and the ring in her nose glinted dully. But she was upright and healthy, and he knew, whether she recognized it or not, that the power balance between them had shifted.

For now.

He forced his brain to slow, to think.

"Baby," he said quietly. "I'm getting dehydrated. We've got to slow this diarrhea. And the only way we're going to do that is if you go out and find me some medication. Come on, sugar. Take The Reaper with you if you're afraid."

Carson knew she didn't like The Reaper, but he also knew she was terrified of being alone. An internal battle seemed to be raging within her. After a moment, she said, "Okay, Jim. I'll go with him."

"That's my girl."

She gazed at him a moment longer, her face unhappy. "No more scavenging, okay? Promise me this is the last time."

He didn't promise, but after she left, as his stomach knotted in on itself and his intestines seemed to turn inside out, he knew she was at least partly right. They had to be smarter about scavenging.

He rose from the pot and upended the OxyContin container into his mouth. He swallowed water and grimaced when the pills caught in his throat.

By the time Sam returned an hour later, he no longer cared

about her or the Pepto Bismol. His mind was drifting painlessly, and the worst of the diarrhea was miraculously behind him.

He was already planning where he could scavenge next.

———

HARR SAW the first plume of smoke sometime in the early afternoon. It rose against the distant horizon, a dark smudge in the murky yellow haze. When a second plume appeared, sharper and blacker than the first, Harr knew it was time to leave the road.

What the hell was burning?

For a moment, he rested in the paltry shade of a citrus tree and allowed himself to suffer. His entire body hurt. He couldn't take a deep breath. He longed to rest on a bed.

But there was no bed and certainly no rest. The fires appeared new, and there was no reason for a fire on a sunny day other than someone setting one. Which meant there was someone up ahead.

The problem was he didn't exactly know where he was. The mile markers told him he'd been on State Route 198 in Tulare County, which meant he had been heading in the general direction of Lemon Cove, where Shangri-La was, but whether he was two miles away or ten, he couldn't say.

He could only say he was beat to hell and out of water, and he hoped to god the fires weren't at Shangri-La.

With a groan, he rose and traveled on a zigzag course through the orange groves until he saw the security checkpoint on the highway fifteen minutes later. It consisted of a forlorn-looking orange-and-white-striped sandwich board with a hand-written message: *Stop Ahead. Exit Vehicle with Hands Above Head,* and a tractor trailer drawn across both lanes.

But no people. Where were the people? He searched the surrounding orchards, the gradual upslope of a treeless bluff.

Where were the people?

Dread, as still and lethal as the air around him, spread its black wings in his chest. He hung his binoculars from a strap around his neck, picked up his shotgun, and advanced.

He was listening and looking everywhere. He did not want to miss a thing.

EIGHT

Three hundred miles north, Susan Barry watched a diaper-clad Emmaline grip a set of measuring spoons. The toddler was mesmerized, grasping and releasing each spoon with her tiny hands.

"Best toy ever," Susan said, amused.

"You're going to have to find some clothes for her, or she'll grow up an exhibitionist," Alan said from the Barcalounger.

An unexpected laugh burbled up inside Susan. She gave him a pointed look. "Maybe she'll grow up without hang-ups."

He arched an eyebrow. "Maybe she'll grow up to be a nudist."

They both laughed. For a moment, Susan was catapulted back in time to the USC Cardiothoracic Surgery Department party at which she'd first met him seven weeks earlier. He'd stood by the pool, handsome and melancholic. She'd been awkward as a teenager around him.

She shrugged, pushed the thought away.

"I wish we could get her vaccinated," she said.

Emmaline tossed her spoons, came awkwardly to her feet, and toddled after them.

"Why?" Alan asked. "Measles and whooping cough are human diseases. If there isn't a human reservoir, those diseases die out."

Susan rose and handed the spoons back to the toddler. "Not all diseases are transmitted from person to person, Alan. Tetanus actually comes from bacteria in dirt. So she definitely could benefit from shots. We all could."

As she reseated herself, Susan tried to guess Emmaline's age, to remember the immunization guidelines and the shelf life of the common vaccines.

"I need to go to town," she said abruptly.

"I thought you said we only had enough gas to run the generator."

"We have enough to make one trip." It wasn't exactly true. They had enough for one trip, if they cut the generator use down to practically zero.

He looked at her for a long time. She could tell he was thinking, weighing the risks versus the benefits. "What did you have in mind?"

She let out a ghost of a laugh. "The mother of all scavenging trips. We need *everything*, Alan. Medications, food, diapers, sippy cups, children's clothing, toothbrushes, toilet paper—" She could have gone on all day.

"Do you have access to a truck with a jib crane?"

She looked at him blankly. "A what?"

"It's like a hoist," he explained. "It goes on the back of a truck. You use it to lift heavy objects."

"Toilet paper and sippy cups aren't that heavy."

"I'm not talking about toilet paper and sippy cups. How far is Davis from here?"

"Fifty miles." She gave him a puzzled look. There were closer towns than Davis. "Why?"

"It's a university town. I'm betting at least some of the solar-equipped houses there have batteries. If we can find two or three batteries, we can bring them back here."

Susan suddenly understood. "You want to rewire our solar panels to power the house and the well!"

"That's right. The batteries will store whatever energy the panels generate. With luck, we should have enough storage capacity to run both the pump *and* whatever appliances we want to use in the house."

Susan's mind raced. For days she had worried about finding fuel for the generator. Just the thought that they could use the sun to power their electrical needs made her dizzy. But theory and reality were two different things. She frowned. "Don't those batteries weigh hundreds of pounds?"

"That's why we need the jib crane."

A wave of excitement swept through her. "I'm sure we can find a jib crane somewhere. The volunteer fire department in Romulus probably has one, and if they don't, some of the bigger farms around here might."

She was probably too excited, because he cautioned her, "Don't start planning any celebratory parties yet, Susan. There are a million steps between an idea and its successful execution."

She understood. They'd have to find the jib crane and then the fuel for the truck that carried it. They'd have to find batteries, and if they managed to find the right ones, Alan would have to figure out how to disconnect them from their old home and then reconnect them back at the farm. And then there was the matter of rewiring the electrical connections between the solar panels and the Victorian. In the post-pandemic world, creating a jerry-rigged, self-contained solar power system seemed as gargantuan and challenging as building the Golden Gate Bridge had been in the 1930s.

And yet, if it could be done, it would change everything.

They'd have an inexhaustible source of clean water and could refrigerate foods. They could cook with the flick of a switch instead of building a fire. In short, they could live, at least in some ways, in the present century instead of reverting to the 1700s.

Emmaline had discarded the measuring spoons and was now trying to climb in Susan's lap. Susan glanced up at Alan. "If you'll take care of her for a bit, I'll go ride my bike over to the volunteer fire department and see what they have there."

. Alan smiled and snapped the Barcalounger upright. He looked at the little girl with a twinkle in his eyes. "Come on over here, Emmaline. I have some great stories to tell you about clothing."

"Oh, god," Susan said and went for the bike.

———

HARR SPOTTED the bodies from a hundred yards away. Nine of them hung from the second-floor railing of the Lemon Cove Women's Club, obscured intermittently by black smoke that drifted in windswept clouds in front of the broad two-story Victorian building.

Shangri-La was nothing like he had hoped. The settlement was dusty and small, more a sprinkling of buildings along the highway than any proper town. It was also on fire. The post office and ancient Richfield service station belched black plumes into the sky.

Harr hid behind one of the few buildings that weren't on fire: a small, stucco one-story house across the road from the Women's Club.

Like the unmanned security checkpoint, Shangri-La looked deserted, although Harr felt certain he was not alone. Someone was watching him from somewhere, and the feeling was so strong he pressed himself against the house's rear corner, unwilling to venture out into the open.

The bodies were male, some young, some quite old. When the smoke cleared, Harr caught quick glimpses: the bloody stab wounds, the blue, bloated faces.

Jesus, he thought. He'd never seen such a bloodbath in his life. The bodies were riddled with puncture marks, as though an entire army had bayoneted them.

A plastic grocery bag skittered down the highway before him. His eye followed the movement, just as the smoke cleared. For one brief moment, he could see the entire Women's Club building: the white balcony that wrapped around the building, the nooses hung from each post.

But his eye rested on something he hadn't seen earlier. Someone had spray-painted what looked like a P superimposed upon an X on the broad front door.

It wasn't the red slashing cross he'd seen on plague-stricken houses. It was another kind of symbol, one that lurked in a distant corner of his mind, just beyond his memory's grasp.

Harr was trying to remember when he heard the snap of a twig.

———

HE ALMOST BLEW her head off. He raised his shotgun and spun, just as a woman darted from the open back door of the house behind which he was hiding.

"Stop!" he shouted, but she didn't. She ran across the drying lawn and forced him to pursue her. Pain exploded through his injured body when he finally tackled her to the ground next to a burning shed.

She twisted wildly beneath him, trying to throw him off, but he pressed her flat and put a knee against her back.

"I'm not going to hurt you," he grunted. "Stop fighting."

He couldn't tell if she believed him. He could see enough of her face to see that her eyes were squeezed shut and that the knee in her back was hurting her. He lifted his weight, waited to see if she'd make a run for it.

She didn't. She was shaking like a leaf.

Harr didn't know what to make of her. She was young, maybe in her early twenties, and she wore tactical gear: olive-green pants, a black performance T-shirt, and what looked like a military-style torso harness. Most baffling of all, a gas mask hung from her belt.

"Who are you?" he asked.

"Don't shoot me."

"I'm not going to shoot you. Get up and empty your pockets."

There was blood on her fingers. It ran in jagged trails down across her palms and over the tattooed inner surface of her right wrist.

She turned her pockets out. Nothing but a small Bible and a few bandages. Harr scanned her body for a weapon. She didn't appear to have one.

He thought she was on the verge of fainting. She listed on her knees; her hips seemed to buckle.

He grabbed her upper arms, tried to keep her upright. "What happened here? Who did this?"

She gazed at him with pupils so large they almost eclipsed her irises. "The dragon wears a pastor's clothing," she whispered. "He atones for no sin at all."

He didn't know what she was talking about. "What dragon? What sin?" He realized he was shouting, that his voice carried through the silent streets.

But even shouting, he couldn't seem to reach her. She was falling, slipping to the earth.

She said something, but the words came out vaporous and indistinct. He dragged her limp body across the lawn, away from the fire.

"It's too late," she whispered as she faded away.

———

ETTA HELD the kerosene lamp aloft as Susan gently lowered Emmaline onto the sheets. "You should pick up a crib when you go to town. You're not going to want her sleeping in your bed forever, you know."

Susan smiled wearily. It was late, and she was tired. "She's too big for a crib. She needs a toddler bed. Can you hand me that blanket?"

Etta set the lamp on the dresser and passed Susan a small throw blanket. "Then get her a toddler bed. You should be able to find one without too much trouble."

Susan sighed. They'd just spent the previous hour devising a list of needed supplies. It would take a moving van to haul it all back to the farm. "I'll try, Etta, but it's lower priority than the other stuff."

Etta shrugged. "I guess so." She tilted her head, gazing at the sleeping toddler. "You'll have to make up a birthday for her. Kids love birthdays."

Susan draped the blanket over Emmaline's torso and legs. In the dim lamplight, the little girl's blonde hair glowed a warm coppery gold. "That's funny. I'd forgotten all about birthdays. We'll have to make up something for her. Maybe an August birthday. What do you think?"

"Isn't it hotter than Hades here in August?"

"Okay, September then." The little girl made a sleepy murmuring sound. Susan picked up the lamp from the dresser. "Come on, let's go back to the kitchen."

In the hallway, Etta asked, "What time are you leaving tomorrow?"

"Early. Did you hear from Shangri-La tonight?"

"No, just the Morse code stuff. There was a lot of dot-dot-dot, dash-dash-dash, back and forth."

"Really?" Susan frowned. She'd hoped to have heard from Harr by now. "How long were you listening?"

"About an hour and a half, while the generator was running."

That reassured Susan somewhat. "That's not very long." she said, setting the kerosene lamp on the kitchen table. "We could have missed the transmission."

Etta sank onto a chair with a weary sigh. "Shangri-La usually broadcasts between eight and nine thirty. I would have heard them if they'd broadcasted. But who knows, maybe the atmospheric conditions weren't right."

A little ripple of unease swept through Susan. She went into the pantry and emerged with two glasses and a bottle of her father's favorite whiskey. Susan poured two neat shots and handed one to Etta. "But the Morse code came through loud and clear. That argues against bad atmospheric conditions."

"It depends on where the code is coming from. If it's coming from Canada, they might have different atmospheric conditions than we do here in California."

"Can you tell where the code is coming from?"

Etta shook her head. "Not with any precision. It could be coming anywhere from a few hundred miles to a few thousand miles from here."

"Which doesn't tell us if it's related to Shangri-La's radio silence tonight." Susan spun her glass on the table, thinking. "There's an old battery-powered cassette recorder in the den. You should use it to record the next time our Morse code friends get active."

"Are you suggesting we try to crack the code?"

Susan polished off her shot and pointed the empty glass at Etta. "I'm suggesting *you* crack the code. You're the one with a mathematics background. I'm just a dumb doctor."

Etta let out a little snort. "I got my undergraduate degree in mathematics in the 1960s, Susan."

"So what? Math hasn't changed that much. I mean, Newton was doing calculus in the seventeenth century, wasn't he?"

"I'm not talking about the math." She tapped her temple meaningfully. "I'm talking about my eighty-year-old brain."

"Your eighty-year-old brain is sharp as a tack."

"Hardly, but if you want, I'll give it a shot. Of course, it would help if we could find more generator fuel. It's pretty hard to listen for code when you're only allowed an hour and a half of radio time."

"I'll work on it," Susan said, suddenly weary again. There were so many pressing issues, each as urgent as the next.

Etta rose, collected the two glasses. "You look wore out. Go to bed. I'll clean up."

Susan peered at the glasses and the bottle, and the pile of washed dishes drying on a dish towel on the counter. Her fatigue felt oceanic. Her battered face ached.

"Thanks, Etta."

She left the older woman in the kitchen and trudged through the darkness to her room, telling herself that one night of radio silence meant nothing and that she should focus instead on the Davis trip ahead of her.

But as she climbed into bed and lay in the darkness, she could not convince herself. The Morse code and Shangri-La's radio silence bothered her. That both should be occurring just as Harr was supposed to arrive in Shangri-La struck her as ominous.

But then again, it could all be coincidence. An old medical

saying flashed in her head: *True, true, and unrelated.* Simply put, it meant that two circumstances could occur and not be linked to one another. But still, the timing of it all disturbed her.

She turned on her side and gazed at the dark outline of the child sleeping next to her. It was a long time before Susan finally fell asleep.

NINE

THE YOUNG WOMAN PRAYED WHENEVER SHE COULD. OR AT least Harr assumed that was what she was doing. Every time they stopped walking, she'd drop to her knees, clasp her hands before her face, and start a tortured murmuring. It was killing them time-wise. Since they started walking that morning, they'd barely covered five miles.

Which was why, when he saw the open wrought iron gate of the Four Winds Horse Ranch, he left the highway.

"Stay here," he told the woman.

A quarter mile up a gravel road, the skeleton of a massive, half-constructed house stood next to a white barn. Closer in, three Arabian horses grazed in an enclosed pasture.

Bingo! he thought.

He eyed the Arabians, picked the two that he thought looked strongest, and then headed for the barn next to the half-finished house.

Later he would blame himself for becoming too accustomed to the idea that there was nobody left, that he and she were alone on the road. Because when he entered the barn, looking for halters, he wasn't wondering how three horses had survived the die-off in an enclosed pasture. His mind was busy calculating how far he and the woman could travel by horseback each day and how long it would take them to cross the Central Valley.

He'd just lifted two leather halters from their pegs and was heading for the barn door when the pump action of a shotgun stopped him in his tracks.

"You know," a voice behind him said lazily. "Where I come from, they shoot horse thieves."

———

TWO HUNDRED AND fifty miles to the northwest, Susan was congratulating herself on the two Tesla Powerwalls that lay in the pickup's cargo bed, when they saw the man. He sat alone in Davis's central square, on a bench beneath the wilting branches of an ash tree.

"Alan, look!" Susan wasn't sure she was seeing right. The man appeared to be reading. An open book sat on his lap.

"Wait," Alan said. Susan heard the click of the handgun's safety. He was squinting at the buildings surrounding the square.

"Too late. He's heard us." Even from her perspective, half a block down, Susan could see the man's astonishment. He stared at the truck as though he were seeing a mirage.

She steered straight across the intersection to the square.

"I don't see anybody else," Alan said. She could feel his tension, see the white of his knuckles on the gun handle.

"That's because there isn't anyone else. Come on, let's get him." She pulled the truck to the curb and hopped out. She didn't know why she didn't feel fear. Maybe it was the age of the man—he looked to be in his sixties—or maybe it was the Bible on his lap. Whatever the case, she approached him unarmed and unafraid.

"Hi," she said.

The man blinked at her through wire-rimmed glasses. She thought he might be shocked by her battered face, but what he said instead was a wondering, "You're alive."

"So are you," Susan said.

The man pressed his hands against the open pages of the Bible and said, his voice choked with emotion, "God has answered my prayers."

————

HIS NAME WAS XIANGFA YANG, and until DRYP, he had been a professor of biochemistry at the University of California, Davis. His field of interest was cellular metabolism in plants.

He was also interested in the Bible. He liked to quote Scripture.

"How does a man of science believe that stuff?" Etta huffed. She was peering out the kitchen window, across the yard, where Alan and the newcomer stood in the fading daylight, pointing and gesturing at the solar panels.

Susan stifled a smile. "The Bible is a book of mystery, Etta. A lot of scientists like mysteries."

"A lot of scientists like science," Etta harrumphed. "The Bible is the least scientific book on the planet."

Susan couldn't help laughing. Etta's atheism was set in stone. There was nothing that would change her mind about it. "I think Xiangfa is dignified. He's very polite."

"Of course he's polite," Etta scoffed. "All those Bible thumpers are. It's how they reel you in."

"Oh, come on. He's not trying to convert us. He's just expressing his belief system. Who cares if he turns to religion to help him make sense of all of this?"

Etta filled a sippy cup with water and passed it to Emmaline, who sat at the table pawing at little chunks of strawberry. "I'll tell you how to make sense of all of this." She turned to give Susan an imperious look. "You deal with facts. For example, there was a bacteria called *Yersinia pestis* that became antibiotic-resistant, and it killed nearly everyone. Consequently, there's only a few of us left alive. If we don't utilize science and technology to pull us out of this mess, we'll either die or wind up living like armpit-scratching cavemen."

Susan looked out the window to keep from laughing. Outside, Xiangfa was making a sweeping, pointing motion from the solar panels to the barn, while Alan nodded thoughtfully.

"Looks to me like Xiangfa's working on technology right now," Susan pointed out. "Scripture or no Scripture."

Etta looked unconvinced. "As long as it stays that way," she said firmly.

———

THE SUN GLOWED a deep orange red on the western horizon when John Harr finally got the quail on the campground grill.

"You're a helluva shot," Alejandro Mendoza said. The young horseman leaned back against one of the county park's picnic tables, his booted feet stretched out before him. Behind him, the slow-flowing Kings River glowed like a fiery ribbon beneath the salmon-colored sky. "Where did you learn to shoot like that?"

"Eastern Oregon, down near the Malheur refuge." It had

only been two days since Alejandro—or Hondo, as he preferred to be called—had held the gun to Harr's back at the half-finished horse farm. In the ensuing forty-eight hours, much had changed. The young man had volunteered to accompany Harr and the woman on their trek northward. Best of all, he was willing to share his horses.

The corner of Hondo's mouth twitched. "Seems like fishing might be easier, boss. We should stop at a sporting goods store, you know, and scramble up a couple of poles."

"I'm not going into town."

Harr added another positive characteristic to the list of Hondo's virtues: the former farmworker wasn't in the slightest bit fazed by Harr's taciturn nature.

"Who said anything about going into town?" Hondo uncrossed his legs and then crossed them again. Both men were sore from a long day in the saddle. "There's got to be a bait shop somewhere along the river."

Harr slid a skeptical gaze Hondo's way. The Kings River, at least along the stretch they'd been following for the past two days, had consisted of a lot of exposed gravel and not a whole lot of water. Harr doubted there was a bait shop within fifty miles. "Don't get attached to this river. We're better off following the San Joaquin."

Hondo grunted. He shot a glance over at where the woman prayed, in the shade of a gnarled oak tree, not far from where the horses grazed on a small patch of yellowing grass. He turned back to Harr with an uncharacteristically somber expression. "Listen, I'm not saying it isn't doable, but the San Joaquin isn't much of a river either. There are parts of it that are nearly dry and other parts of it that are a marshy mess of small channels. Following it is going to be like crossing a desert and then getting bogged down in a swamp."

Harr gazed out across the campground, across the rocky riverbed and the shallow thread of water meandering down its center. He knew the risks of following the San Joaquin. He'd been thinking about them all day. But the alternative—to follow the Kings—struck him as an even worse choice. He was pretty sure the lower stretches of the river flowed south, and even if some branch of it still drained into the San Joaquin River to the north, he was fairly certain that branch was dry. Harr knew enough of pre-pandemic California water management to know that practically every river that crossed California's massive Central Valley had been dammed and diverted to serve agricultural and metropolitan uses.

"We can make it," he said.

Hondo didn't seem so certain. "Or we could hold off, park ourselves by the river, and wait out the summer."

Harr opened a can of pears and stuck a fork in it. He was thinking of how long it would take them to cross the Central Valley and head north to Susan's farm. He was pretty sure they could make the trip in a less than a month.

"One day," he said, seemingly out of nowhere.

Hondo gave him a confused look. "One day what?"

Harr pulled the skewers from the fire and used his knife to pry the meat onto a plate. "We make a run for the San Joaquin tomorrow. When we get there, you get one day to scavenge. Then we ride."

"That won't give me much time to gather goods," said the younger man.

"Exactly. We'll live off the land, move fast."

Hondo glanced over at the woman, who was reduced to a black silhouette in the fading light. "What's wrong with her anyway?"

Harr shrugged. He'd given up trying to get her to talk. "She's traumatized by what happened at Shangri-La, I guess."

Hondo frowned. "I don't get it. Shangri-La wasn't a religious place. It was more of a hippie camp. Everyone smoked a lot of weed and hung out at that Women's Club building."

Harr and Hondo had discussed this before. After nearly everyone Hondo had known died, he'd left the grape fields where he'd once served as foreman and met up with a young woman who had told him about Shangri-La. They'd gone together to the settlement. She'd stayed, and he'd moved on to the half-finished horse farm. Hondo wasn't a hippie kind of guy.

"Maybe she wasn't part of Shangri-La," Harr suggested.

"You think she was part of an outside attack?"

Harr shrugged. "Dunno. It could have been an internal dispute, for all we know."

Hondo shook his head. "I don't think so. Shangri-La was peaceful when I was there, and even if there was trouble brewing, why would only men be killed?"

Harr had to agree. An internal dispute didn't make sense. A group of previously peaceful women were unlikely to turn on their men and boys, much less stab them a hundred times and string their corpses up from the balcony of the Women's Club. The murders had been too vicious, almost like a warning. But a warning for what?

"Fifty bucks says it was an outside attack, and another fifty says that woman was part of it," Hondo said. "No one at Shangri-La dressed like a soldier. They were tie-dye and flip-flop people."

"She had a gas mask when I found her."

Hondo stared at him. "What? Why?"

"I have no idea."

The shock in Hondo's face abruptly turned to anger. He cupped his hands around his mouth and shouted, "For fuck's sake, woman! Quit your praying or I'm going to eat your dinner!"

The woman lifted her head and stared their way for a long, expressionless moment. In the waning light, her eyes looked like two empty sockets. She rose and walked toward them, her military boots kicking up little clouds of dust.

TEN

The thermometer on the barn read 109 degrees. Susan stood in the shade of the metal-sided structure and stared at the still unconnected solar panels with a rising sense of dismay.

Two days wasted! The batteries sat in the barn, Alan and Xiangfa sat in the house, and the sun, white-hot and relentless, was baking them alive.

Susan speed-walked across the yard to the porch. She didn't want to be in the blazing heat any longer than necessary.

Alan greeted her at the kitchen door, his face a mask of concern. "For god's sake, what are you doing out there? You'll give yourself heatstroke."

"I wanted to pick the last of the strawberries." Susan carried a sorry-looking basket of the fruit to the kitchen table. "Maybe we'll get apricots in a week or two. It's hard to say without irrigation."

Alan peered at the pathetic-looking berries. "They look half-cooked."

Susan plopped into a chair. "That's because everything is wilting out there without water. Where are Etta and Xiangfa?"

"In the basement with Emmaline. It's cooler down there."

Susan nodded. Without air-conditioning, the internal temperature of the house had risen to the high eighties. Even the furniture felt hot to the touch.

"I hope Etta is being civil to Xiangfa."

"Oh, she is. Whenever he quotes Scripture, she turns bright red and looks like she's having a stroke, but she doesn't say anything. She's showing remarkable restraint."

"For Etta."

Despite the heat, they both laughed.

Alan turned serious. In the dim interior light, he looked skeletal, the shadows accentuating the hollows of his cheeks. "We can't keep waiting on the solar panels. Xiangfa and I are going to start working on them tomorrow morning."

She stared at him. "No way. You'll kill yourself."

"No, I won't. We're almost out of generator fuel, Susan. Once it's gone, so is water from the well."

She knew this. She'd been thinking about it all day. But still, she didn't want him keeling over in the heat. "The heatwave's going to end eventually, Alan. They don't last forever."

"There was a heatwave in England that lasted sixty-six days back in 1976. It was the hottest summer in three hundred and fifty years. It could happen again."

"How do you even know this stuff?"

"Climate change was a big deal at Wheeler Energy. My point is that we can't keep waiting. We're almost out of generator fuel, and I need to charge power tools."

The determination in his expression made her want to weep. He was so frail, too frail to work out in the blazing sun, but what other choice did they have? If they ran out of fuel, she'd have to haul water from the river, and if she had to haul water from the river, she had to filter or boil it before they drank it. Her workload would become near impossible.

Outside, the sky faded from warm orange to cool gray.

"Okay," she said. "How long will it take to charge your power tools?"

"Up to three hours."

That would burn up three precious gallons of fuel. She tried to think of all the other tasks they could accomplish during that short period of time with electrical power—bathing, storing clean water, checking the airwaves futilely for word from Shangri-La—but the thought just depressed her. They'd be living with increasing scarcity until Alan got the solar power system up and running.

She corrected herself. *If* he got the solar power system up and running. Neither Alan nor Xiangfa were electricians.

With a weary sigh, she went to turn on the generator.

———

HONDO LIKED TO SING. Every so often, as they clopped their way along the pastureland that separated the Kings River from the San Joaquin, the young man broke loose in a deep baritone. It would have been a welcome distraction if not for the scorching heat.

Harr was worried. The woman listed in her saddle, and the horses' sweat stunk of stress. Harr wasn't certain how much further he could push them in the heat but realized he didn't have a choice. They'd entered a no man's land of infrequent shade and non-existent water.

For the twentieth time, Harr consulted the Fresno County map he'd taken from a service station, trying to figure out where they were. He thought they were close to the eastern fringes of Fresno. He was pretty sure the dark smudge on the western horizon was houses.

What he didn't expect to find was a body disposal site out

on the open plain. The pits were as long as a football field. Mounds of displaced dirt rose like small mountains along the trenches' sides.

"Oh, shit," Hondo breathed next to him. "*Holy* shit."

The stench was awful. It rose above the tangled, partially covered limbs and oozed across the cleared soil to where Harr, Hondo, and the woman sat upon their horses.

Harr's stomach pitched. Like every survivor, he'd seen his share of dead bodies, but the size of the pits before him stunned him. Hundreds of bodies lay in rotting piles next to abandoned bulldozers. Thousands more lay in twisted heaps in the trenches.

"They didn't even try to wrap them," Hondo said. "They just bulldozed them in there."

"They probably ran out of people to run the site," Harr said, remembering his own work in body disposal at the Burns hospital. In the end, it had only been him and Dr. Fisk, and then Dr. Fisk had died, and Harr had finally given up wrapping bodies and trying to keep order. Just as the people who'd worked this site had finally given up order.

Beside him, the woman suddenly began to wail, a strange, feral noise unlike any human sound Harr had ever heard. She was staring at the bodies with a wide-open mouth, her face twisted in an agonized grimace.

She knows.

The thought came to him, as horrifying and certain as the thousands of bodies before him. She knew what happened in Shangri-La. Just as she knew why a once controlled and rare bacteria suddenly acquired the capacity to kill almost everyone on the planet. Her knowledge was a black thing, so powerful and self-damning that he felt it pulling at his soul.

"Who did this to us?" he asked her in a voice he didn't recognize as his own.

She didn't answer him. Her dark eyes were fixated on the pit before her, that eerie cry still issuing from her mouth.

Somewhere, faraway, Hondo cried, "John, let's get out of here!"

The horse shifted beneath him; he reached a hand for her arm. He had the sense of something giving way in her, like a dam that is overtopped and crumbles beneath an onrushing wall of water. He felt the presence of evil everywhere.

"John! Goddammit. John!"

It was Hondo's voice, near panicked.

But Harr could not move. The horses began to scream, a rim of white terror flashing around their eyes. The woman was staring down at the bodies. She picked up the reins and dug her heels into her horse's sides.

Later, it seemed to Harr that time had folded in on itself. He remembered Hondo pulling alongside the woman and seizing her reins. He also remembered how, at the same time, he hooked his own hand around her torso harness. The Arabians reared up on their hind legs. Harr watched as the woman toppled from the saddle.

He had her. He yanked hard on the torso harness, held her on the horse.

Hondo was shouting, "You batshit crazy, loco woman! You wanna go in that pit? I'll put you in that pit."

All the while, the horses screamed. Harr had never heard such an awful sound in his life. He could have sworn it was human, a thousand agonized voices crying out.

Maybe I should let her die, a voice inside said. *Maybe I should die, too.*

Anything to stop the screaming of the horses.

He did not remember the rest. His memory came back to him later. The same dreary, dry landscape came back into focus, the same barren alluvial fan. Only the trees in the distance signified that they were at long last approaching the San Joaquin River. With a start, Harr realized the pits were far behind them.

"What the hell was that about?" Hondo demanded. The younger man's face was pale, and Harr thought, completely freaked out.

Harr glanced at the woman. She rode along beside them, the torment gone from her face, her expression as dead as it had been before the pits. Harr shook his head, mystified.

"I don't know," he said.

———

THEY REACHED the San Joaquin River two hours later. The waterway wasn't what Harr expected. A torrent raced down the shallow canyon, half submerging scrub trees and scraggly pines.

"I thought you said this was a low water river," Harr said.

They were just north of Fresno, in the gently upsloping foothills of the Sierra Nevada mountain range. The rush of swiftly moving water filled the air.

Hondo peered up and downstream, a frown on his sweaty face. "They must have increased the flows out of the dam before all hell broke loose. Either that or the dam's about to go."

Harr glanced at him in alarm. "What do you say that for? It was a pandemic, not an earthquake." He pulled his binoculars out and looked for a place to cross. There wasn't one. The channel was too wide and the water too swift. Half-submerged shrubbery poked above the rushing surface. "We're going to have to find a bridge."

"There's got to be a bridge downstream in Fresno," Hondo said wearily. The heat, the long ride, and the shock of the burial pits had taken their toll. Hondo looked beat, and the woman seemed even worse. She was curled up in the dirt, in the shade of a scrub oak, already asleep. "And who says we need to cross the river anyway?"

Harr put the binoculars back in their case and slid them in his backpack. He pulled out the map and pointed out the obvious. "The city of Fresno abuts this side of the river. Farmland abuts the other. Which side would you rather be on?"

Harr knew he won the point. The pits, only a few hours distant now, lingered in his mind like a black stain. Harr had no stomach for the deathscape the city promised, and he wasn't sure the woman could take any more anyway. Since the pits, she had slipped into a catatonic silence. She didn't even pray anymore.

But mercifully, the horses seemed to have withstood the stress of the day. They grazed along the riverbank, in the shadows cast by a cluster of cottonwoods. Harr gazed at them, thoughtful. "We'll need to take it easy tomorrow. There's a bridge upstream of here, closer to the dam. We'll cross there and then rest."

In the deepening light, Hondo's face looked older, less enthusiastic. "How far?"

Harr shrugged. "Five, maybe six miles."

Hondo nodded with no enthusiasm whatsoever. "You might have a hell of a time getting her back in the saddle."

Harr peered at the woman. She lay in the dirt like a dog on its deathbed, her face, even in sleep, pulled in and suffering.

He'd seen soldiers shell-shocked by war, so messed up they wouldn't eat or work, but he'd never seen someone like her. It was as if some vital thing in her had finally been broken, and all that was left was a body.

Later, when he called her to dinner, she didn't even raise her head.

ELEVEN

ETTA CHARGED INTO THE KITCHEN, JUST AS THE LAST embers of sunlight died on the western horizon.

"I just heard from another group," she gasped, leaning hard on the granite counter, her chest heaving from hurrying.

"Where?" Alan asked. He was sitting at the table with Xiangfa, a pen and pad of paper on the tablecloth before them. Not far away, Susan spooned chopped-up apricots between Emmaline's orange-stained lips.

"In Yakima Valley—" Etta's excitement was palpable. "Up in Washington. Congressman Roger Cortese is their leader ... there's thirty-six of them."

"Thirty-six!" Susan looked up, astounded. It was a big group, bigger than Shangri-La. "How'd you find them?"

"Shortwave. They answered my CQ."

Susan's stomach dropped. CQ was ham radio shorthand for Calling Any Station. Etta had been transmitting without telling the rest of them. "Etta!" Susan cried. "How could you?"

The old woman gave Susan a defensive look. "What do you mean, how could I? Do you know how hard it is to find people on shortwave? One night atmospheric conditions will be right

90

for transmission on certain frequencies and the next night on other frequencies. We can't just wait around to come across someone's transmission by luck, especially when we're running out of generator time. We have to actively *seek out* others."

"And wind up like Shangri-La?"

"You don't know what happened to Shangri-La," Etta said hotly.

"I know we haven't heard from them in days," Susan shot back. *Not to mention, we haven't heard from John either.*

"Did they tell you where in the Yakima Valley they were?" Alan asked.

Etta shook her head. "I barely got them to admit they're in the Yakima Valley. They're not exactly like Shangri-La, blabbing their information all over the airwaves."

Susan stifled a sigh. There was no use arguing with Etta about radio transmissions. It only made the old lady more cantankerous. She turned to Alan and said in a muted voice, "Yakima's a big agricultural area, lots of apple and pear trees. Quite a few vineyards."

Alan looked over at Etta. "Did they say anything else?"

"Yeah. They've been in touch with a group in Colorado and another one in Illinois. They've set up a radio network for communication." Etta gave Susan an I-told-you-so look.

"Anything in Texas?" Alan asked.

"No. They picked up something from Georgia, but only on one night, and the transmission was so broken they could barely understand them. They're not counting them as a settlement until they hear from them again."

"What about Shangri-La?" Susan asked.

"Same as us. They last heard from them five days ago. About the same time as the code started."

For the first time, Xiangfa spoke up. "What code?"

Etta explained the strange code. "I've recorded some of it,

but I'm afraid I haven't been able to make heads or tails of what it means."

"Do you mind if I take a listen?" Xiangfa asked.

Etta eyed him with outright skepticism. "Do you know cryptography?"

"A little," Xiangfa said modestly. "I played with it when I was younger."

Susan tried to be diplomatic. "Two minds are better than one, Etta."

"Fine," said Etta testily. "But there's something else you need to know. They said they're armed and ready."

The room went silent. Alan said very carefully, "What does that mean?"

"I don't know," Etta said. "Shortwave is dependent on atmospheric conditions. Signal fluctuates. I was having a hard time hearing them at the end."

———

THE REAPER WOULDN'T STOP BITCHING. He bitched when they scavenged in the giant strip mall off the interstate. He bitched when they scoured the bare shelves of the AMPM minimarket. He bitched when they went through the empty storage unit of the Mexican restaurant just off the highway. Carson was getting tired of all the bitching.

"For god's sake, would you shut up?" Carson muttered wearily.

Reaper grunted unintelligibly and kicked one of the pots on the restaurant's shabby linoleum floor. It shot across the kitchen and banged against the walk-in fridge.

"There's nothing here, man," he cried. "She doesn't know what she's talking about."

Sam pulled a can of green chiles from a drawer and shoved it in his face. "What about this?"

He pushed the can back at her so hard it almost smashed into her nose. "You're such a dumb fucking bimbo. What are you going to serve that with? With the cheese and tortillas we don't have?"

"*Enough*," Carson said sharply. The younger man had turned almost feral in the past few days.

Carson stepped between them. The Reaper leaned his head so that he could maintain eye contact with Sam. Sam was doing her best to stare back, but Carson could feel her shaking. She was terrified.

Carson understood implicitly what he had to do. "What the hell is wrong with you?" he snarled into The Reaper's face.

"I'm fucking hungry. That's what's wrong with me." He turned and glared at Carson.

There'd be no backing down with The Reaper. In his current state, The Reaper understood only one form of order—dominance—and Carson fully intended to dominate.

But Carson also knew that domination was a form of leadership with no lasting legs. If basic needs, like food and shelter, weren't met, rebellion was certain to follow.

"Get the bikes," he ordered. When Sam didn't move, he snarled, "That means you, too."

"Where are we going?" She looked at him with pleading eyes.

"Where the food is," he barked out. "Bring the bikes around front. Don't talk to each other."

Sam and The Reaper eyed each other like two wild dogs as they disappeared out the door that separated the kitchen from the rest of the restaurant. A door opened somewhere out front and then slammed shut.

Alone, Carson let his gaze wander over the steel counters

and blackened grill. Even now, seven weeks after everything had gone to hell in a handbasket, the stink of stale grease lingered in the kitchen. A parade of ants swarmed on the sticky surfaces.

But no one had bothered to leave behind any food.

A little flame of anger ignited inside him. Where was the food? Where were the medications? Surely, in a country that once held more than three hundred million people, someone would have left behind something decent to eat and an OxyContin or two.

But no one had left anything. The stores were empty, and so were the restaurants. Even the houses had been picked bare.

His head began to ache. His left eye throbbed.

He reached into his pants and withdrew a small ziplock bag. In it were his last three MS Contin. He dry-swallowed them all.

Through the small kitchen window, Carson saw a long straight row of almond trees. It occurred to him that they were still in farm country, that the roadside restaurant in which they were scavenging sat at a dusty interchange somewhere between San Francisco and Sacramento.

He squinted. The almonds were green, too immature to eat. But there had to be other crops elsewhere, Carson realized. He remembered the organic veggie boxes that had been popular with doctors at UC San Francisco, how they claimed to be "locally sourced," farm-to-table food. Where were those farms?

Esperanta. The name came back to him. A little town at the mouth of some little valley whose name he couldn't remember. They called it the "Breadbasket of the Organic Belt."

He'd been there once, on an agri-tour the department had set up. How he'd rolled his eyes at those poor farmers, eking out subsistence on their small, organic farms!

But those farms were far better suited to the post-pandemic world than the giant, single- crop ag land outside the restaurant's windows. Who needed two hundred acres of green

94

almonds, when an organic farm might have a few acres of berries, peaches, and tomatoes?

He closed his eyes, felt the smoothing of his headache, the slow lazy onset of relief.

Esperanta wasn't far, maybe forty miles. They could get there by mid-afternoon.

A little smile formed on his thin lips. They'd find food there, he was certain of it.

And as he recalled, there was a small family medicine clinic in town as well.

———

JOHN HARR STUDIED the river as they rode. The further upstream they went, the wilder and more turbulent the water became. It roared down the center channel in an angry green torrent.

Hondo raised his voice above the sound. "You think the bridge is out?"

"I doubt it." The water was high, but it wasn't that high. Even so, Harr wasn't keen to get anywhere near it. Shrubbery and cottonwood trees choked the channel, turning the river into one giant obstacle course.

A downed branch sailed by on the main current, catching on a half-submerged scrub oak, and then spinning itself free. "I've never seen the San Joaquin like this," Hondo said uneasily. "They must have shut down the diversion canal before everything collapsed."

Harr steered his horse up the bank onto higher ground. "What canal?"

"The Friant-Kern. The feds used to divert pretty much the whole river down it to supply farms and towns in the lower valley. It's a big-ass canal. Comes off the dam."

Harr peered upstream, tried to spot the giant dam in the distance. "You think they stopped diverting because of the pandemic?"

Hondo shrugged. "Could be. Those canals cost billions. You can't exactly control flows with no one running the dam."

A great blue heron lifted from the riverbank in front of them and took flight. Harr imagined the last-minute decision making by the dam operators. Keep water flowing down the canal on the off chance someone might need it downstream, or send it where nature meant it to go? He was looking at their decision right now. "It certainly makes it easier for us. There's no way this river is drying up downstream, not with that kind of water going down it."

They rode in silence, the woman trailing a half horse length behind them. Since the pits, she'd given up managing the horse by herself. Harr and Hondo were forced to take turns leading her Arabian. It slowed them down even further.

But Harr wouldn't leave her behind. The pits lingered in his brain, his experience there as baffling and troubling as ever. He kept feeling the dark, awful pull of massive trenches, the dark, suicidal pull of her.

Sooner or later, she was bound to open up and tell him who had decimated Shangri-La, and why. She'd tell him what she knew of DRYP's origin.

He told himself finding out this information was the reason for dragging her along when it was clear she didn't care if she was dragged along or not.

But inside, he knew it was more than that. She was suffering, and Harr couldn't stand suffering. It ate away at his soul.

———

THEY REACHED the bridge sometime mid-afternoon. Harr and Hondo looked over the concrete railing at the hurtling, turbulent water below.

"They must be letting a ton of water out," Hondo shouted. The river was so loud they could barely hear each other.

Harr gazed up at the dam. The massive wall of angulated concrete, perhaps half a mile upstream, stretched from one edge of the canyon to the other.

"There's nothing coming out of the spillways," Harr shouted back.

"The water is probably coming out the bottom, where the turbines are."

It didn't make sense. There was too much water in the riverbed. Even if the dam operators had decided to release at maximum capacity through the penstocks and hydroelectric tunnels, it would never raise the river flows to such a high level.

Hondo turned to Harr with fear in his eyes. "You think the dam's going to go?" he said. "We should probably head to higher country."

Harr pulled his binoculars from his pack and scanned the concrete structure. Aside from the white mineral streaks of normal seepage, the dam's concrete structure looked uncompromised. He checked the turbidity of the water below him. The water was opaque, but not the muddy brown one would expect with an imminent collapse. He thought it possible, with full releases and no diversion into the Friant-Kern Canal, that the river could naturally have flows this high.

But it didn't feel right. The river was damn near at flood stage. A cool wind rose off the roiling water.

"I think we should cross and ride along the upper edge of the gorge—"

Harr had barely gotten the words out when a high, strangled scream rose above the river's roar.

Harr's heart stopped. The woman was clutching her chest, her face as white as a sheet.

Below the railing of the bridge, an X with a superimposed P had been spray-painted on the concrete. It was the same symbol he'd seen on the Women's Club at Shangri-La and the same that had been tattooed on her inner wrist.

"What the hell?" Hondo cried, struggling to control his horse. The woman's scream and the rush of the water had unnerved the Arabian, and now it pranced sideways, whinnying as though it wanted to bolt.

"Quiet," Harr said. There were words sprayed in long, sloppy letters on the narrow lip of concrete below the symbol. He climbed down from the saddle to look.

Et cognoscetis veritatem

Harr turned to the woman. "Do you know what this means?"

Her voice was barely audible over the roar of the river. "It means 'His is the truth. The only truth.'"

It was the first time she'd spoken directly to him since he'd found her in Lemon Cove. He kept his voice calm, just loud enough to be heard over the river. "Who wrote it?"

Her hands jerked on the reins. The Arabian clattered backward.

"The Brotherhood," she said hoarsely. "They've come this way."

"Who is the Brotherhood?"

She shook her head mutely, tears shimmering in her eyes. Harr sensed he'd pushed too close to the truth, that her hysteria was rising again.

"You don't need to tell me if you don't want to," he said gently. He reached out and took a slow step toward her. "Just come down from there. You're not safe with the horse jumping around like that."

For a moment, he thought he had her, that the agony in her eyes faded enough that she could see his outstretched hand.

"No one is safe anywhere," she said. "Carlos will hunt us down until there is no more of us left."

Harr didn't know what she was talking about. "Who is Carlos?"

He was very close. Another step and he could grab the reins.

She held her left hand out, the rein in her hands. "The devil."

Her answer was too much for Hondo. The young man exploded, "Jesus fucking Christ, John. I can't listen to this anymore. She's crazy!"

But neither Harr nor the praying woman looked at him. Harr's eyes were locked on hers, on the tears running down her filthy cheeks.

"Come down from there," Harr said again. "Take my hand."

She shook her head. "You are the only one who can stop him. You must stop him."

He sensed her slipping from him. "Where is Carlos?" he asked, trying to keep her focused, trying to stop her from spinning apart again. "Tell me where he is."

But she wasn't listening. "You are the only one who can stop him."

She drove her heels into her horse's flanks just as Harr lunged. The Arabian bolted across the asphalt.

Harr shouted something, but his words didn't register in his brain. He was only conscious that the horse had locked its legs at the bridge's railing and the woman had disappeared over its head. Harr watched in horror as her body sailed beyond the concrete barrier and into the roiling water below.

TWELVE

He didn't think about it. He jumped in after her.

Rushing, green darkness engulfed him, and the shock of cold mountain water jolted like electricity in his chest. He thrashed upward toward the murky light.

He couldn't breathe when he surfaced. Something was wrong with his diaphragm or maybe his throat. He sucked for air, but he couldn't seem to draw it in.

She was up ahead of him, her dark head bobbing above the water. A little bolt of terror shot through him as he realized she was heading straight for the concrete remnants of a previous bridge. He swam hard, trying to catch her. Her head hit the side of the pier and disappeared downstream.

"John, watch out!" A voice, far away, called from the bank.

But Harr didn't pay attention. He was trying to cross the current, his hands stabbing into the water, his legs kicking like hell. He didn't make it. The side of his shin hit the pier, and his body jerked and spun in the water. A second later, he was under water again.

When he surfaced this time, he was in the middle of a straight stretch of current. For a second, he let the water carry him along, trying to catch his breath, but then he spotted her dark head downstream again, popping up as the river abruptly dumped over a submerged rock shelf. He followed her feet first, praying she'd cleared the chaotic froth below.

She had. He caught her as the water narrowed. For a second, he just clutched her body to him, trying to catch his breath, which wasn't easy because his throat felt like it had closed on itself. The current spun them again and sent them sideways.

"John, John! Look out!" On the bank, silhouetted by sunlight, Hondo was screaming.

For a blank second, Harr just stared. A corona of sunlight surrounded Hondo and his charging horse. Harr felt as though he were looking at a painting, at some heartbreakingly beautiful scene rendered in oil.

And then he hit. The force of the collision knocked the breath from his body. Something crumbled on his head and tore at his face. He could not see what he was pressed against. He was only aware of the monstrous power of the water and the heavy weight of her body smashed against his.

He tried to turn, to push her away from him, but the current was too strong.

I'm going to drown, he thought.

The fact shocked him, ricocheted around his brain.

He pushed again, wildly, but it made no difference. The water was winning. Rays of light flickered, but the river swept them away.

———

MAYBE SHE SAVED MY LIFE, he would think later. Maybe the weight of her body had been just enough to do what the water alone could not: break the branch that held him fast.

He didn't know. He only knew that the pain in his back suddenly shifted, and he and the branch were moving. The light through the water was very bright.

He swam toward it. Noises he didn't recognize came from his mouth when he surfaced. He couldn't suck in enough air.

"John, grab the stick!" a voice shouted.

Harr's legs felt like jelly. He tried to kick, to control his position in the current, but there wasn't any power left in him. He could only float, as the river swept him along.

He fixed his eyes on Hondo's form along the bank, on the branch the younger man held out into the river.

One chance, Harr thought. That was all he had.

He kicked and thrashed. He blacked out the river and the trees, the light and the roar of the water. He focused only on the outstretched branch.

When his hand closed on bark, he held on like he was holding the hand of God.

————

HE WAS LYING ON GRAVEL. The uneven surface poked at his back. But he couldn't move because he couldn't stop gasping. It was all his exhausted body wanted to do.

"Jesus, man, are you okay?" Hondo's face was above him, his eyes wide with fright.

Harr lifted a limp hand against the sun above and let it flop against his eyes. He was trying to control his breathing, to speak words, but he couldn't seem to do anything other than lie there and suck in air. His body felt boneless, like the very life had been drained from it.

"Jesus, brother, I thought I lost you for real." Hondo was on his knees, panting. Harr realized that they'd gone far downriver, that the landscape had changed from shrub- and tree-choked

shrub- and tree-choked

canyon to a sparser escarpment. Rows of citrus trees peeked over the canyon lip.

"Where is she?" Harr was trying to sit up, trying to find her.

"She's dead, brother. She didn't make it."

Harr saw her body then, on the gravelly bank ten feet downstream from him. Hondo had had the grace to close her eyes, or maybe, Harr thought, she had had enough of seeing the world and closed them herself. He didn't know.

He only knew a grief he couldn't put words to. It opened in his heart and spilled from his eyes. He tried to find a reason for any of it, but he could find none.

She was one more lost life, as tragic and senseless as any, but to him, who had tried to keep her with him, the most devastating of all.

———

WHAT THE HELL am I doing? Susan thought.

The sun was not as hot as the previous few days, but hot enough that she questioned her sanity. Had she really volunteered to ride a bike eighteen miles to Esperanta?

Only mad dogs and Englishmen go out in the noonday sun, she mumbled as she pedaled through Liberty Valley's southern opening.

But so does Susan Barry when she needs a circuit breaker for a solar panel hookup.

Sweat poured down her back. She pedaled harder. The narrow gap that marked Liberty Valley's southern terminus was only wide enough to accommodate Liberty River, an irrigation canal, and the two-lane highway on which she rode. Most of the development lay a few miles further, where the flat planes of the Central Valley began.

Susan eyed the steep hill ranges on either side of the road.

In earlier times, when she'd returned to the farm, she'd loved the dramatic entrance to the valley. Even now, she couldn't help admiring the towering uprise of golden grass and rugged chaparral.

Fire country, her father had said. *It may look pretty, but don't ever forget how fast fire can whip through this vegetation.*

Susan let out a rueful laugh. As if fire was a problem now. She'd read somewhere that 95 percent of wildfires were caused by man, by downed electrical poles, fireworks, or a host of other careless actions. With almost no humans left, the risk of stampeding wildfire had become vanishingly small.

But that didn't mean there weren't other types of fires. She sniffed the air. A trace of smoke lingered, leftover from the Sacramento blazes. She wondered how much longer the big-city fires would last. At some point they had to peter out.

Harr.

The name crept into her mind, unbidden. She tried to push it away, to keep it locked up in the unhappy box it belonged in.

He hadn't come back.

Above her, seven turkey vultures drifted in the pale blue sky. She watched their black silhouettes circle and rise. It was an amazing achievement, really, given that they hardly ever flapped their wings.

Forget him, she thought. *Let it go.*

She gazed beyond the narrow gap between hill ranges to the unimpeded, flat farmland of the Central Valley. The empty landscape seemed to stretch forever; already she missed the protective embrace of Liberty Valley's ridges.

Two more miles, she told herself. *Keep going.*

She hoped the Ace Hardware in Esperanta hadn't been looted. The possibility that she had ridden eighteen miles for nothing was just too awful to bear.

———

THE PROBLEM of supplies was a real one, Susan thought as she scanned the shelves at Esperanta's Ace Hardware. She shoved a forty-amp, twenty-amp, and fifteen-amp circuit breaker into her backpack. She checked Alan's list and rounded up four three-amp fuses and one thirteen-amp one.

But she had less luck with her own wish list. The battery section was cleaned out. No water filters or iodine tablets remained on the shelves. Even the dish soap and laundry detergent were gone.

She'd have a hell of a time finding all the things they needed.

She heaved a sigh and was heading out the door when the hardware store's walls began to shake. For a blank moment, Susan thought an earthquake was rattling the building, but then she looked up the road to see two motorcycles approaching. Her mouth dropped open in shock.

The bikers drew to a halt in front of the store. "Hello," said one of the drivers, a tall leather-clad man in aviator sunglasses. He cut his Harley's engine and said in a soft Southern drawl, "I didn't expect to find anyone in *Esperanta,* of all places."

"Neither did I," said Susan, taken aback. Her gaze shifted to the tattooed woman clinging to the man's back and then to the small, feral-looking man on the other bike, who removed his sunglasses and stared at her with dark, unblinking eyes.

None of them were clean. Oil glistened on their faces, and circles of sweat stained their dirty shirts.

The woman leaned around the leather-clad man and exclaimed, "I can't believe we found you! We haven't seen another person for *days,* have we, Jim? It's been nothing but dead people and driving town to town looking for food—"

"Sam," Jim interrupted her. "The lady doesn't care if you're

105

happy to see her. Can't you see she's nervous?" He gave Susan a pleasant smile. "Don't worry. We're friendly."

Susan wasn't sure if it was true. It was impossible to see the leather-clad man's eyes behind his aviator shades, and there was something strange in the way he smiled. "Where'd you guys come from?" she asked.

"Bay Area," he said, tilting his head toward her bicycle, which was propped up against the hardware store's front window. "You ride that here?"

Susan felt the eyes of all of them on her: the flat, animal stare of the little man, the hungry, avid look of the tattooed woman, and the amused gaze of the leather-clad man.

"Well, you know what they say," Susan answered. "When fuel is short, pedal power is plentiful."

The leather-clad man nodded and laughed pleasantly. "Very true. You live close by?"

Susan didn't know why she felt uncomfortable—maybe it was the vaguely intrusive way the leather-clad man kept asking questions, or perhaps it was the hollowed-out, hungry look they all wore—but her heart began to bump in her chest and she didn't want to answer questions anymore. "If you're looking for food, there are farms not far from here. They're not irrigated because of the grid failure, but I'm sure there's still edible stuff out in the fields."

The leather-clad man ignored that. "What have you got there?" he asked, his eyes on the circuit breakers poking through the unzipped portion of her backpack. "You doing electrical work?"

"Trying to," Susan said. She zipped the compartment and slung it over her back.

"Rolando here knows how to do electrical work, if you need help."

Susan pulled the bike from the wall. "We don't need help. It was nice meeting you. Good luck on your travels."

She was halfway down the raised sidewalk when the leather-clad man called after her, "You don't have to leave. We'll just move on if we're making you nervous. Come on, guys. Let's go."

Susan watched as he reached for the ignition switch. The woman behind him looked disappointed but didn't fight him. The little man just stared at Susan, frowning.

A little voice inside her cried out, *They're hungry and you're refusing to help them!*

The Harley roared to life. With an unfriendly glance, the little man slipped his sunglasses back on and fired up his own bike.

"Wait," Susan blurted out. "Don't go. Join us for dinner."

The leather-clad man cut the Harley's engine again, a smile once again curving his lips. "Are you sure?"

"Of course," Susan said, but she wasn't sure. Not at all.

"How many of you are there?" the leather-clad man asked. He twirled his finger in the air. "You know, where you're doing all the electrical work?"

"Five."

The leather-clad man let out an appreciative whistle. "And you're already working on electricity. I'm impressed." He glanced at the bike and at her backpack with what Susan could have sworn was a satisfied expression.

He drawled, "Come on, Rolando, let's give this lady a ride."

———

THEY NEVER LEFT. One night became two and then three. Soon a week passed.

Throughout it all, the tall, thin one named Carson said that they would need to leave, that there were places they needed to go. But they never packed up or made any move to vacate the Morgan house. Their motorcycles remained in front, exactly where they'd parked them on the very first night.

Susan watched with unease as the newcomers quickly made themselves at home. They showed up for every dinner. They liked to linger long after nightfall.

One evening, Carson said, "All we need is one hundred and ten men and women of reproductive age, and we'll have enough genetic diversity to survive."

They were sitting on the Victorian's wraparound porch, drinking 7UP that Carson had found on one of his scavenging trips. It was one of the best things Susan had tasted in weeks.

Alan looked at him skeptically. "Where do you get that number?"

"From a French mathematician." Carson kicked out a leg, leaned back in the wrought iron patio chair. "Before DRYP, there was a real effort to determine the minimum number of people necessary for a self-sustaining space colony. Space travel may seem laughable now, but those mathematical estimates of minimum colony sizes are still quite useful. They give us a starting point on how many people we need to survive as a species."

He sounded so authoritative, as if he were used to lecturing.

Susan did a quick calculation in her head. "If DRYP's survival rate is one or two in a million, that means there are only forty to eighty survivors in California. That's not enough for your model."

Carson nodded. "That's right. Especially since not all of those forty to eighty are going to be of reproductive age."

He didn't look at Etta, but the implication was there.

"And of your forty to eighty," Carson went on, "probably some of them didn't survive the collapse for other reasons."

He didn't look at Alan, but again the implication was there.

"But before you start panicking and claiming an extinction event," Carson continued, "remember that your one-in-a-million survival rate is just an estimate—"

Susan frowned. "From one of the most brilliant medical geneticists on the planet."

Carson smiled. "Of course, but Tom Hodis calculated his survival estimates based on a limited data set during a fast-moving pandemic. Were he still alive, I'm sure he'd concede that his estimate was rough at best."

"That's right," Alan agreed. "The survival rate could be higher."

"Or it could be lower," Susan pointed out.

Carson's pale blue eyes lingered on her face. "But don't you think it's better to approach our situation optimistically, Susan? You mention that there is a settlement up in Washington. What's stopping us from joining up with them?"

"About six hundred and fifty miles," harrumphed Etta.

The smile dropped from Carson's face. He gazed at Etta coldly. "Six hundred and fifty miles is not far. The pioneers travelled thousands of miles with just Conestoga wagons and oxen."

Susan slid a glance over at Alan. She could tell he was taking Carson seriously, that the newcomer's discussion of survival rates and sustainable colonies intrigued him. "If you're really interested in getting one hundred and ten reproductive-age people together, then the Yakima settlement isn't enough," he said. "They've got thirty-six people there, and we have no idea how old they are. We'd need to bring together several settlements."

The smile returned to Carson's face. He reached a hand over to Sam, who was seated next to him, and gently stroked her cheek. "Or find people who aren't in settlements. I found you walking along the road, didn't I?"

Susan didn't consider herself a prude, but the frank sensuality in Carson's caress made her uncomfortable, as did the undeniable adoration in Sam's eyes. The black-and-red-haired woman gazed at Carson like he was a god. "Yes," Sam whispered. "And we found Reaper when we were riding around, too."

"Just as we found you, Susan," Carson added, turning his pale eyes on her.

"And you found me," added Xiangfa. "I must agree with Carson on this. The fact that we've encountered so many others simply by chance argues for a higher survival rate than one in a million."

Susan reluctantly agreed. They *had* found a remarkable number of people just by accident. But still, finding even more people in such a limited geographical area was statistically unlikely even with a higher survival rate. Especially since they were nearly out of fuel.

Alan seemed to read her mind. "Probably a more effective, less resource-intensive way to find people is to use the radio and set up some sort of signage system," he suggested. "We could draw people to the valley rather than go out and look for them."

Susan glanced at him, dismayed. By the way he spoke, she could tell he'd been thinking about this, even before Carson and his cronies appeared.

Once again, Harr's words came back to her. *There is a reason animals run in herds, Susan. Go with the herd.*

Alan wanted a herd, and so did Carson. Which meant that Alan had accepted Carson's presence in the valley as a permanent one.

She didn't know why that bothered her, but it did.

She said testily, "Shangri-La tried to draw people to their

location, and look what happened. They've been off the airwaves forever."

"That doesn't mean something terrible happened to them," Alan said.

Except Harr promised me he'd radio us when he got there, Susan thought. *He promised me he'd come back.*

"You're being too cautious, Susan," Carson said. "The only way to protect ourselves is to grow the size of *our* settlement and develop our own resources."

Our settlement. Susan shot a glance at Alan, but he met her glance with a cool nod of agreement. "He's right, Susan. The proper response to outside threat is to build resiliency into a community. We need people and resources to do that."

Susan glanced over at Etta, looking for reinforcement, but the older woman wasn't looking at her. She was watching Carson with an unreadable expression.

"Which brings up another topic," Carson said. "If we're to build a true colony, then we need some sort of government. A council of some sort. I propose we hold a vote for, say, a three-member council, with the option of expanding as our settlement grows." He looked around the group as if his suggestion were the most reasonable thing in the world.

Alan nodded. "We'll need to draw up preliminary governing documents as well."

How has it happened so quickly? Susan wondered. Carson had arrived only a week before, and suddenly he was positioning himself for a leadership role with Alan's full support.

Susan's eyes traveled the group, from Alan's thoughtful face to Etta's remote expression, from the adoring Sam to the carefully neutral Xiangfa. The one they called Reaper stared off into space with a sullen look.

She let her eyes meet Carson's. He was watching her

steadily, his small pupils like tiny black dots in the center of a pale blue planet.

Susan stood up. "Draw up all the governing documents you want. I'm going to check on Emmaline."

As she opened the patio door, she knew that everyone in the room was watching her.

———

LATER, as Carson and Samantha were undressing in the dim lamplight of the Morgan house, Sam said sulkily, "I don't know why they get all the electricity, and we only get battery-powered lanterns."

In the muted light, she looked like she'd stepped out of a Rubens painting. Her impossibly full hips gave way to a soft, fleshy belly. Warm shadows accentuated the firm contours of her breasts. Only the tattoos and the two-toned hair spoiled the impression. There was too much ink; it covered her torso like a carpet.

But Carson let the thought drift away. The evening had gone better than he'd hoped. Pleasure bloomed in his belly.

"Come here," he said. He wrapped a hand around her waist and pulled her to the bed. Once between the sheets, he slid his fingers down her back and cupped the rounded orbs of her bottom.

She was still pouting about electricity. "It seems to me they ought to share. After all, Reaper helped them get those panels working. It's not fair that we're stuck in this dark house, and they get to listen to CDs."

He fought a flicker of irritation as he pulled her closer. She was so simple, like a child really. "Baby, we've only just gotten here. We can't exactly throw them out of their house."

"What about rotating? We get the house half the days. They get it the others?"

He wanted to tell her to drop it, that Susan and Alan would never agree to that, but the Dilaudid was kicking in, and warmth was spreading in his abdomen. He felt the powerful desire just to float.

"Be patient, baby," he whispered as he shifted over her.

"She acts like a princess, all holier than thou," Sam went on. "I bet she's never had a fun moment in her life—ahhh."

Her body gave beneath his weight.

"You're right. Holy people have no fun," Carson murmured.

Her eyes looked uncertain when he put his hand between their bodies, guiding himself.

"Are we having fun, Jim?" She sounded breathless and a little pathetic.

"We are, baby," he assured her. He began to move. "You and me. Lots of fun."

He felt her muscles relax; her eyes drifted closed.

This is the way it is supposed to be, he thought as he drove himself inside her. When he was finished, he closed his eyes and let her disappear from his mind.

THIRTEEN

THE SWOLLEN SAN JOAQUIN RIVER BROKE FREE OF THE levees that restrained it as soon as Harr and Hondo reached the wide-open Central Valley floor. Newly formed marshes stretched green and lush between willow and oak. Egrets and ibises, slender and motionless in the still waters, watched warily before taking off with great heaves of their wings.

It was shocking to Harr how fast the land had returned to its native state.

But what shocked Harr more were the mosquitoes. There seemed no end to them. They rose in great buzzing swarms from the water and bit and bit and bit.

"Jesus, where did they all come from?" Hondo said wearily. Although the young man had covered his head as best he could, the mosquitoes had still gotten to his face. Raw excoriations marred his cheeks and the skin on either side of his eyes.

"Standing water and no mosquito abatement," Harr responded tersely, dragging a hand down his opposite sleeve. A dozen mosquitoes rose and then settled again. "Where's that damned road?"

"I don't know. It's got to be around here somewhere."

They couldn't find it, so they settled on high ground, or the highest ground they could find, which was a stretch of levee choked with coyote brush and elderberry.

"We should let her go," Hondo grumbled. He was talking about the black-and-white Holstein they'd liberated from one of the riverfront farms. The cow trailed along miserably from Harr's lead rope, her hooves dragging in the muck.

Harr cast a worried glance at the animal. She didn't even flick her tail to clear the mosquitoes from her flanks. "She'll make it. We need her."

Hondo gave him a pained look. "She's slowing us down, John. We can find another cow later."

Harr wasn't so sure. They'd seen countless dead livestock in fenced-in pastures. "She's the only live cow we've found so far."

Hondo slapped his neck and cursed under his breath. "Maybe, but I'm not sure I want to get malaria because you want milk and cheese for some toddler you rescued."

Despite the day's heat, a flush ran up Harr's neck. He'd said little about Susan and the kid, but clearly what he'd said had made an impression. "There's no malaria in the United States."

"How do you know?" Hondo said, gazing at the pulverized mosquito on his palm. "Seems to me that these little bastards could carry a lot of diseases. And I'm not just talking about malaria."

Harr gazed at his wretched companion, at the horses twitching their tails to clear the bloodsucking insects, at the endless soggy ground below and the thick brush and trees that made seeing the horizon nearly impossible. If not for the mosquitoes, he would have considered the desolate floodplains beautiful. But the increasing lethargy of his traveling partner was starting to alarm him.

He drew his horse to a halt and pulled out a map and

compass. Somewhere nearby, a blackbird let loose with an outraged screech.

A highway lay about eight miles due north of where he thought they were. He held the map up so Hondo could see. "We can leave the river there," he said, pointing to where the road bisected the floodplains.

Hondo let out a weary sigh. "We'll never manage that before sundown. Not with the cow."

"Yes, we will." Harr folded the map and stuck it back in his saddlebag. He looked up at the sun and made a calculation. "We can make it. Trust me."

———

THEY MADE IT, but with only an hour of daylight to spare. There wasn't enough time to find extra water or food; there was only enough time to find an empty, half-falling-down barn, in which they tied up the animals and unrolled their sleeping bags. Hondo fell asleep the moment his head touched the dirty flannel.

But Harr wasn't as lucky. He lay atop his bag, gazing up at the dark rafters above him, his mind stuck on one sorry fact.

None of the farmsteads they'd visited had working wells.

He didn't know why he'd failed to consider this, that without electricity, none of the wells would work anywhere. But somehow, he hadn't, and now he lay, dusty and stinking, thinking they'd wasted precious time away from the river. The San Joaquin, as messy and mosquito-choked as it had become, was still *alive*. The farm on which they now camped was nothing but a harbinger of what the rest of the Central Valley had become: parched, sunbaked, and dying.

He heaved a restless sigh. The darkness inside the barn was

filled with snoring: Hondo, the horses, even the cow huffed and whistled in a symphony of exhaustion.

For a few minutes, Harr just lay there, his body aching from the long days on the trail, listening to the sounds around him. And then a lone, keening howl interrupted the snoring. Harr went still, listening.

The sound was eerie and beautiful, and Harr waited for the rest of the coyote pack to sound off.

They did. Ten minutes later, the wild yipping and yapping began, a mad ruckus that made Harr wonder how many coyotes were out there, and why they'd left the fertile hunting grounds of the river for the parched alfalfa land where he and Hondo now camped.

For a second, a thought wedged itself in his brain like a wrench jamming up the gears: maybe the coyotes were after his cow. Harr rejected the idea. In his entire life, he'd never known a coyote to hunt an animal as big as a cow.

Unless the cow was vulnerable, and the coyotes were either incredibly hungry or incredibly bold.

He shook his head in the darkness. He was bone tired, so tired that his body seemed to melt into the concrete beneath him. He felt as though he could sleep for days.

But he wouldn't. A timer ticked off days in his head: fourteen since he'd drilled the Cessna's nose into the dirt; another fourteen until he and Hondo would finally clear the San Joaquin River and make their way along the coast range to Liberty Valley. Weeks were slipping away. The slowness and unendingness of it ate away at him.

Outside, one of the coyotes began to bark. They were after something; Harr was sure of it.

He pushed the animals from his mind. It was easy to get paralyzed thinking of all that could go wrong, of how changed and unfamiliar life had become in such a short amount of time. You could get caught up in the shock of it all over again.

He turned on his side, his shoulders, hips, and back aching against the hard floor. He focused on that small misery, shut his mind to everything else.

After a long while, he fell into a fitful asleep.

————

SUSAN STOOD ON THE PORCH, watching as Alan tried to raise his right arm. "You look like you're doing a Nazi salute."

"Ha ha. Very funny." He was frowning. "Is this all the range of motion I'm going to get?"

She slipped around his backside and ran her fingers along the mispositioned edge of his bare shoulder blade. "Maybe. The bullet injured your long thoracic nerve. You've got what they called a 'winged scapula.' That's why you can't lift your arm above your head."

She could feel his eyes on her face as she circled back to face him. "Is it permanent?" he asked.

She made an uncertain gesture. "I can't say. Your arm should get stronger if we start some sort of physical therapy."

She could tell she'd made him unhappy. He watched broodingly as, across the yard, Carson crossed in front of the solar panels and disappeared into the barn. "You're not exactly a physical therapist, Susan."

"No, but I can come up with a few exercises that will strengthen the muscles around your scapula. It should help with shoulder stability."

He didn't say anything to that. Instead, he stared across the yard, his foul mood so powerful that Susan felt it in her own chest. She turned away and began silently packing her medical supplies just as Carson reemerged from the barn.

Behind her, Alan said irritably, "We're going to have to give Carson the generator, you know."

She stopped packing, a frown furrowing her brows. "What?"

"Because it's not fair for him, Sam, and Reaper to live in eighteenth-century conditions while we take hot showers under electric lights."

The tone of his voice shocked her. It was abrupt, almost hostile. She gazed at him for a long moment, baffled by the change in his demeanor.

"That's fine," she said quietly. "But why our generator? There are other generators in the valley—"

He cut her off. "Because *our* generator works, and they need power now. Not tomorrow or the next day or whenever we can find another generator for them."

She couldn't believe he was serious. "But that would be sacrificing our backup power source for the solar panels. That's just dumb."

Exasperation flared in his eyes. "No, what's dumb is forcing them to stay in that dark house like second-class citizens. It's creating grievance, Susan. Believe me, I can see it in their faces."

"Then let's get them a generator. We'll do it tomorrow."

She sensed his patience was fraying. He said bluntly, "We need to give them your generator today."

"What?"

He stood up. He wasn't tall, but even so, when he looked down at her, she felt the command in his face. "No more dark nights for them. You may not wish to believe it, but we need them. They're young and strong—" he didn't say it, but she knew what he was thinking. "And we need workers if we're going to survive."

She understood this. She'd be an idiot not to, but giving Carson her generator when there were plenty of others in the valley was nothing more than a symbolic gesture, and she didn't like what this symbolic gesture suggested. "Why are you so hell-bent on bending over backward for them? As far as I can see, Carson doesn't want to do anything but scavenge and pontificate about what we need to do to save the species." She started shoving her supplies into her doctor's bag. "And the little guy, Reaper, only works about two hours a day before he begs off to go train. About the only worthwhile one of the bunch is Sam, and she's no great shakes in the brains department, let me tell you."

"We don't have a whole lot of choice in who joins us, Susan. DRYP killed indiscriminately and randomly. It didn't check LinkedIn before it struck."

She didn't say anything. She didn't want to fight with him, but she didn't agree with a single word he said.

"Don't look at me like that," he said. "Sam's a good worker, and you said yourself that Carson's smart. Why are you so wary about them?"

She weighed how much to tell him. After a moment, she said almost grudgingly, "It's not them. It's Carson."

"What's wrong with Carson?"

"There's something off about him. He's not normal."

Alan let out a laugh like she was crazy. "In what sense?"

"He has weird eyes."

For a second, Alan just stared at her. "Since when do you judge people by their eye color?"

"I'm not judging him by his eye color," Susan said. "His pupils are weird. They're always pinprick-size. That's not normal, Alan."

"What does it matter as long as he can see?"

A little flush rose above her collar. "I don't know," she admitted.

All at once the thunderous expression on his face evaporated. He came to his feet, crossed the distance between them, and took her hands in his. "History is full of imperfect alliances. Sometimes they're necessary, even when they're not ideal. You have to trust me on this."

She nodded, although she was far from convinced. There was something troubling about Carson, more than just the pinprick pupils and the way he vacillated between charm and coldness. But rather than fight over it any longer, she capitulated.

"You can give them the generator," she said. "We'll need to find some extra fuel, too."

———

HARR WAS PRETTY sure someone was following them. It was only after the second day that he figured out it was a dog. The black-and-gray animal cruised through the high grasses like a submarine on the open sea, popping his head up periodically like he was doing reconnaissance.

"You got yourself a follower," Hondo said.

They'd left the marshlands and floodplain and were now riding in the fertile farmland south of Stockton, on the lip of dirt that separated orchard and alfalfa fields from the San Joaquin's wide meandering riverbed.

"He ought to just show himself and walk with us," said Harr, watching the dog skirt the shrubby riverbank. "He'll exhaust himself picking through all that brush."

"Maybe he's afraid you'll take a shot at him."

Harr brought his horse alongside the newest animal in their menagerie: a gaunt-looking steer Harr had picked up on the fringes of the marshy floodplain the previous day. He was trying to nudge the miserable beast along. "We're not hungry enough to eat a dog."

"Especially now that we got a *herd*," Hondo agreed, his white teeth flashing in his sunburned face.

Harr rolled his eyes. "A cow and a steer don't equal a herd."

"But three horses, a cow, and a steer is damn near a ranching operation, John. That girl must be something for you to drag all this livestock to her little farm."

"Her farm's not little. Where's that dog?" Harr craned his neck, looking for the furry submarine. It surfaced ahead in the dry grasses at the top of the riverbank. Harr whistled sharply. "Come here, boy."

The dog poked its head up at the sound, and for the first time, Harr got a good look at its face. Gray-and-black spots dotted a slick furry skull; long whiskers fanned out beneath dark serious eyes.

"What a weird-looking dog," Hondo commented. "He looks like a seal."

"Probably some kind of mutt. Catahoula mix, maybe." Harr whistled a second time. "Hey, Seawolf, get your tail over here!"

But the dog didn't heed. It submerged in the grasses again. They didn't see it again all afternoon.

———

ALTHOUGH HE'D SAID he wasn't hungry enough to shoot a dog, Harr *was* hungry. So hungry that he felt hollowed out inside, as though his abdomen were shrinking against his backbone.

Hondo was also losing weight. His face had taken on a dark, sinewy appearance. His cheekbones stuck out, and the residual mosquito bites made him look like a wild thing, half animal, half human.

Harr imagined he looked no better. His pants hung low on his waist, and the veins that once popped up on his arm now resembled thick ropes. He figured he looked like a scarecrow with his dirty, oversized clothes and sunbaked skin.

But they were still alive, and that counted for something. Sometimes they got lucky and found a can of beans in an abandoned house or an apricot tree still holding a few of its fruits, but mostly they lived off what they caught on the river. If Hondo was having a good day, they ate catfish or bass. If Harr's shooting was on the mark, a duck or a goose. If both struck out, they went hungry. It was as simple and brutal as that.

But as hungry as they were, they never discussed killing the horses or cattle. A horse provided transportation and could pull a plow. A steer could provide enough meat, if preserved right, to last a winter.

That was the way you thought when there weren't any people left. The choices became starker, the expectations more tempered. You became grateful for the little things, and you tried to grab onto security wherever you could find it.

FOURTEEN

Etta was having no luck. She keyed the radio's microphone and repeated, "CQ, calling CQ. Beaming east from Northern California. Whiskey Six Echo Sierra X-ray calling CQ, hello, CQ. Here on twenty meters. This is Whiskey Six Echo Sierra X-ray calling ... Is anybody out there?"

A burst of static greeted her.

"That's someone, isn't it?" Susan asked. She sat forward anxiously, straining to make sense out of the grating noise. She couldn't.

"It could be," Etta confirmed. "But it could also be interference from the sun. Let me try another frequency."

She turned a black dial on the radio, made a note on a pad of paper, and repeated her Calling Any Station message, "CQ, CQ, calling CQ ... This is Whiskey Six Echo Sierra X-ray, here on twenty meters."

Nothing.

"You sure you have the right frequency?" Alan asked. He sat next to Susan on the den's loveseat.

"Certain. They said they talk between eight and nine

o'clock on fourteen-two-seven-five." Etta checked her watch and frowned. "It's eight fifty."

"They're not there," said Susan. Worry assailed her. Etta had said the surviving settlements radioed each other twice a week, but so far, whenever she tried to listen in, all she heard was noise.

"It could be atmospheric conditions." Etta looked down at her scribbled notes. "I could try the ten-meter band. See if we can raise anyone there."

"But that's not where they said they transmit," Susan said.

Etta pressed a small square button on the radio's front panel and started turning the black knob again. "What else am I supposed to do? They're not on twenty. I've been listening for days."

"Etta's right," Carson said. He leaned against the wall, his pale eyes trained on the radio's lighted display. "We should be widening the net, not banging the same drum over and over, expecting a different outcome."

Susan ignored him. Ever since he'd taken a seat on the "council," he'd taken to uttering dictums. Pretty soon he'd be telling them how to tie their shoes.

The background noise was very loud, and then, a male voice, scratchy and unintelligible, broke through. Etta leaned forward, her ears craned toward the radio. She adjusted the dial by micro increments.

Suddenly the transmission sharpened into an audible message. The words were unfamiliar, spoken in rising and falling tones, punctuated by glottal stops.

"What language is that?" Susan whispered.

A volley of words interrupted her. A woman's voice, clear and remarkably low-pitched, responded in clipped syllables, her response time quick. Even without understanding the language, Susan could sense the exchange was an urgent one.

"Can you tell where they're transmitting from?" Alan asked. Etta shook her head.

"It sounds like one of the Inuit languages to me," Carson said.

Susan didn't even look at him. "They sound tense."

"I'm going to try to make contact." Etta keyed her microphone. "This is Whiskey Six Echo Sierra X-ray. Can you hear me?"

The frequency went stone-cold silent for a full minute.

"Maybe you shouldn't step on their conversation, Etta," Carson chided.

"Try again," Alan urged.

Etta tried again. "This is Whiskey Six Echo Sierra X-ray, calling from Northern California north of Vacaville in Liberty—"

This time the woman's deep voice rang out in the room. She said in commanding and flawless English, "Whiskey Six Echo Sierra X-ray. Recommend that you do not identify your location. Repeat, do NOT identify location."

Etta jerked as though electrocuted, a frown creasing her brow. "Who am I speaking with?"

Silence.

Etta tried again. "This is Whiskey Six Echo Sierra X-ray, repeat, please identify yourself."

Thirty seconds passed. Then the woman's voice broadcast across the room, "Whiskey Six Echo Sierra X-ray, this is Yakama Nation. Advise do not transmit any further identifying information."

Susan's mouth dropped open. "That's the Native American tribe in the Yakima Valley!"

Etta leaned forward, the microphone only inches from her mouth. "Copy, Yakama Nation. Are you the same people as Congressman Cortese's people in—?"

This time the woman didn't wait to reply. She cut Etta off with a sharp, "Whiskey Six Echo Sierra X-ray, this frequency is not secure. Repeat, NOT secure. We will find you on another frequency. Out."

"Wait!" Etta cried. "What frequency? When?"

There was no reply.

———

HARR WOKE to a low symphony of growling. For a moment, he lay there listening, trying to determine if the sound was real. It was. It had disturbed the horses. The terrified animals were shuffling on the barn's concrete floor, whinnying in fear.

"What is it?" Hondo whispered. In the darkness, Harr could just make out his silhouette sitting up in his sleeping bag. The noise had woken him, too.

"Coyotes," Harr said tersely. "Out in the yard."

He scrambled to his feet and crossed to the barn's lone window. In the moonlight outside, he could make out five furry faces. Shadowy white teeth glinted between pulled-back lips.

Harr had never seen coyotes attack, and he watched fascinated, as the silvery figures snarled and barked and then lunged at a lone animal pinned against the barn door. The surrounded animal wheeled and counteracted, its own growl guttural and ferocious.

Sudden recognition dawned. "Holy shit, it's Seawolf!" Harr cried. He recognized the sleek seal-like shape of the dog's head, the low skulk of its body.

Seawolf was fighting for his life. He took on one coyote and then swung to defend himself against another, lunging, pulling back, and then lunging again. But his attackers were closing in on him and beginning to draw blood. Seawolf let out an agonized yelp.

"Where's that fucking gun?" Harr bellowed.

The shotgun was propped against the wall near the window. Harr grabbed it, chambered a round, and charged for the door.

The growling outside was ferocious. Seawolf was hunched low on his hind legs, his lips pulled back so that his gums showed above his snarling fangs. Harr could see the dark shadow of blood on his head.

Harr let out a roar.

Instantaneously, five sharp faces rounded on him, and Harr understood in a heartbeat that he would have to kill some of them. Low, guttural growls were directed his way now. They would lunge and tear at his skin just as they had lunged and torn at Seawolf's.

He raised his gun and fired.

The ensuing cries felt like a gut punch. Two of the coyotes jerked backward and collapsed screaming to the ground. Two others streaked across the moonlit yard and disappeared into an alfalfa field. The last coyote tried to run but couldn't. He whimpered and limped and finally in the distance lay down to die.

Harr realized he was panting. He tried to still his surging breath, to slow the spike of adrenaline racing through his body.

He turned to the injured dog and said quietly, "You okay, boy?"

In the moonlight, the spots on Seawolf's head looked blacker, the gray in his coat like silver. He gazed up at Harr with his tongue hanging out, panting heavily.

"Careful there, John," Hondo said. He stood in the barn doorway with a shovel in his hand. In a flash of insight, Harr realized that his partner had been ready to bash the coyotes and would bash Seawolf, too, if he thought the dog would attack.

"He won't bite me," Harr said, extending his hand. "Right, buddy?"

The dog stared at him, brown eyes glinting in the silver light. A dark streak of blood matted his coat beneath his left ear.

Harr knew better than to touch the dog. He kept his voice calm. "I'm just going to look at you, okay, Seawolf?" Harr scanned the dog's fur, down his legs, looking for more blood. In the darkness, he couldn't be sure.

"We can't leave him out here," Hondo said. He was standing behind Harr, maybe five feet back. "The coyotes might come back to finish what they started."

Harr's eyes drifted to the dark heaps of fur across the yard. "No, they won't. Not tonight at least. Get me some water and a bowl, would you?"

When Hondo returned, Harr poured a measure of water into the bowl and slid it about a foot from the dog's nose. Seawolf panted but didn't move. Harr realized the dog was shaking.

"He going to make it?" Hondo asked.

"I don't know." Very carefully, Harr pushed the bowl so that it practically touched the dog's nose. Seawolf lay on his side, his eyes never leaving Harr's face. He didn't touch the water.

For a minute, Harr squatted there, thinking. The dog would either make it or he wouldn't. Beyond giving him water and keeping away predators, Harr could do nothing more.

But the thought filled with him with an unshakeable sadness. He reached a gentle hand to the dog's head, half expecting Seawolf to growl and snap, but the dog didn't.

Instead, Seawolf let out a quiet whimper and rested his head against the ground.

Resigning himself to guard duty, Harr settled in against the barn's wall. He knew it would be a long night.

———

SUSAN DIDN'T LIKE how Carson fingered her medical supplies. It seemed incredible to her that an infectious disease doc could be so oblivious about leaving his germs on everything he touched.

"Nice microscope," Carson said, peering into her Nikon's binocular lenses, his middle two fingers dropping a load of microbes onto the eyepiece. "Leftover from med school?"

Susan leaned against the bed on the other side of the room and tried not to cringe. "College. We didn't do any microscope work at my med school."

Carson straightened and turned inquiring eyes at her. "But clearly you know how to do microscope work. Those are blood smears, aren't they?"

They were standing in the downstairs guest bedroom in her parents' house, a room which Susan had been painstakingly converting into Liberty Valley's first post-pandemic medical clinic.

She walked over and plucked the blood-smeared slide from his fingers. "Just playing around. Trying to refresh my skills." She slipped the slide into one of the desk's drawers.

Her actions seemed to amuse him. He leaned against the wall and smiled at her. "Very impressive, Dr. Barry. Hippocrates would be proud."

"We need a medical clinic, Jim. At least one of us should try to set one up."

He laughed. "It helps to have electricity to set up a medical clinic."

"Nothing in here requires electricity except the microscope."

"True," he agreed, pushing himself away from the wall. He walked to the dresser and lifted the lid off a glass jar of cotton balls. "But electricity is the foundation of all modern societies.

It's more important than your enviable collection of cotton balls and tongue depressors."

"You have electricity."

"We have a *generator*." He pulled open a drawer. Inside was her entire collection of medications. The white childproof caps were labeled by purpose: heart, blood pressure, pain, antibiotic. "For which we must find fuel, I might add."

"I've already told you I'm happy to help you find fuel. I know where the farm tanks are in this valley. I grew up here."

Carson pushed the drawer closed and leaned against the dresser. "You also know that most of the farm tanks are empty, Susan. We'll find a few gallons here and there, but it's not the same as harnessing the sun."

She eyed him warily. He wanted something, but she couldn't tell what. More than electricity, that was for sure.

"There are other solar panels in the valley. You know that."

"Not with batteries." He dug a finger into the plastic box containing her thermometers. "It's awfully hard to power a house with only solar panels. The sun is a fickle beast, Susan. Even here in Liberty Valley."

He was trying to provoke her. She could tell by the tone of his voice.

She cut to the chase. "Why are you here?" She was pretty damned sure it wasn't to complain about electricity.

He opened the final drawer in the chest. "I'm looking for tweezers. Reaper has a splinter from all that orchard work you have him doing."

He was lying. She could tell.

"Reaper doesn't need a doctor to fetch tweezers for him."

. He let out a little laugh. "You're right. It's an excuse. I wanted to see your clinic. It's quite impressive."

She eyed him warily. In all the time he'd been in the valley, Carson had never once indicated an interest in practicing medicine. She wasn't sure how to interpret this latest statement. "If you're looking for medical-grade tweezers, I don't have them," she said stiffly.

He came and stood over her. "What about garden-variety pluck-your-eyebrows tweezers?"

He was so tall she had to bend her neck back to look at him. "They're in the bathroom."

For a second, he just gazed at her with his pale, empty eyes. He was so close that she could feel the warmth radiating from his body.

Her breath caught in her chest. He was too close. She could smell the faint whiff of musk and something medicinal. "I'll go get the tweezers," she said abruptly.

Her shoulder hit the door frame as she left the room. She could have sworn she heard the low rumble of his laughter as she hurried down the hall.

———

IT TOOK her fifteen minutes to calm down. She walked the periphery of the orchard, on the gravel road that separated the orderly tree rows from the wild riverbed, trying to wipe the memory of Carson's pale, thin face from her head.

She was only half-successful. The curve of his lips kept intruding into her thoughts, the way he gazed at her as though he harbored an amusing secret inside. It was enough to make her crazy.

She was about to take a second lap around the orchard when Alan beckoned her from the porch.

"I thought you and Xiangfa went to the Grange," she said when she was close enough for him to hear.

"We just got back." He gestured for her to follow him into the house. "I have something for you."

All the worry and strain of dealing with Carson disappeared in an eyeblink, wiped away by Alan's obvious delight. "What is it?" she asked.

"See for yourself." He'd brought her back to her clinic. On the bed lay the biggest first aid kit she'd ever seen. He unzipped the red vinyl, flipped it open, and smiled like a proud papa. "We found it at the Grange Hall in a storage cabinet. What do you think?"

The kit was industrial-sized, separated into all sorts of practical sections: bandages, individually packaged ibuprofen and acetaminophen tablets, gloves, packets of antibiotic ointment, alcohol swabs.

Susan let out a little cry and threw herself at him. He laughed as he caught her with his good arm. "That's quite a reward for a first aid kit."

"You can't run a medical clinic without supplies."

"Especially when you have a patient needing so many of them." He released her and gazed around the room. "It looks good in here, Susan. You've done well."

She followed his gaze, allowing herself to feel a moment's pride. The clinic was infinitely primitive, but still it had a country doctor's authenticity to it. Ruffled curtains muted the harsh midday sun. The antique mirror over the dresser reflected the glass jars and rubbing alcohol bottle on top. Everything was neat and orderly. Even the bed, with its freshly laundered pillows, looked clean and well cared for.

She plopped herself onto the bedspread. "It won't last," she said resignedly. "I've got two of this and two of that, but no depth in any of our supplies. We'll run out of everything in the next couple of months."

"No, we won't. We've got critical mass now. We'll get things done."

He sounded so certain. Operationalizing the solar panel

system had changed him. He was pushing himself so hard she worried he'd suffer a setback.

"How were the solar panels at the Grange?" she asked, knowing that the Grange's photovoltaic system was the real reason for the trip.

"Too small for Carson and his friends." He sat down on the bed's edge next to her. "*But* there *is* a decent-sized house with a nice set of solar panels at the end of Road 49. If we can find another set of batteries, it'd be a good place for them to settle down."

Susan tried to remember the house. She was pretty sure it had belonged to a retired couple from the San Francisco Bay Area, who'd built their dream house up in Liberty Valley's remote hills, in a place where only outside money would build a house. The ground was too steep for farming, and the thick shrubs and trees made grazing impossible. But the view was spectacular, and the location private.

"The house with the copper eaves?" Susan asked. "It's a bit of a hoof to our house, isn't it?"

The glint of humor flashed in Alan's eyes. "I thought you might appreciate the distance."

"I'd appreciate getting my generator back."

Alan rose from the bed, smiling. "You'll get it back. We just need to scrape up enough fuel to fill the truck's tank and go battery hunting in Davis again."

She watched as he crossed to the door. "Maybe you should scrape up an electric car while you're at it."

She'd been kidding, but he paused in the doorway and nodded as though he'd already thought of it. "Hauling one back here might be a challenge, but it's a good idea."

"Why would you have to haul it?"

"Because all those electric cars have been sitting there with their batteries slowly discharging since the grid went down. They probably don't have much charge left."

"If they have any charge left." She knew enough about electric cars to know that fully draining the battery could damage it.

He smiled good-naturedly. "I'm betting we can find one with some amount of charge left."

"You sound awfully confident."

"I am," he said as he walked out the door.

———

LATER, when Susan was unpacking the first aid kit and transferring its contents into her dresser, she noticed that the wooden lip of the medication drawer protruded nearly an inch from the dresser front.

That's odd, she thought.

She was pretty sure Carson had closed it after he'd peered inside the drawer.

Without thinking, she pulled the drawer fully open. She couldn't say why she was sure something was wrong, but something nagged at her consciousness as she lifted and inspected the medications. They were all there, in the same order in which she'd placed them.

But something was different. The Norco bottle was lighter. She heard the hollow rattle of pills inside as she lifted it. With a feeling of dread, she popped the plastic top off.

Only five tablets left.

For a second, she just stared. She'd never had a huge supply of the narcotic, but she'd definitely had more than five pills.

A pit formed in her stomach. Earlier, when Alan's pain was at its worst, she'd given him OxyContin. Not much, because she didn't have much, but enough so that he could sleep at night, so he wouldn't cry out every time he rolled over.

It was more than enough to develop a dependence. Especially for a proud man who wanted to work when his wound was not fully healed.

Very slowly, she placed the pill container on the dresser. The stillness around her seemed infinite, the only sound the grandfather clock ticking out in the hallway.

She told herself that needing a few extra Norcos was no catastrophe, that Alan had ample reason to need pain medications. But the nature of the pills' disappearance ate at her. It reeked of sneaking, of a dishonesty she hadn't thought Alan possessed.

Something sad and deeply disappointed swirled inside her. Alan had saved her life and then put his own life in her hands. Those simple acts, so basic and yet so fundamentally important, had forged a bond between them, one in which trust was implicit and devotion unquestioned.

But in the quiet muted light of her country medicine clinic, she realized that she didn't really know him, at least not the man he was before that fateful day when, badly wounded, he pulled the gun on her attacker.

She gazed at the pill bottle and felt something crumble inside.

Maybe you never knew people completely. Maybe you never could.

FIFTEEN

THE MORSE CODE BEGAN A LITTLE AFTER EIGHT P.M., JUST as the moon peaked over Liberty Valley's eastern ridge.

Etta was ready. She pressed the record button on the tape recorder and stuck her head out the den's doorway.

"Xiangfa!" she hollered. "It's started!"

Somewhere down the hallway, she heard the snap of a book being closed and then the soft shuffle of feet. Xiangfa materialized just as she was sitting down.

The transmission was crystal clear, a high-pitched series of longer and shorter tones that crackled over the airways. A minute later, a shorter sequence followed, accompanied by a pause. This pattern of transmission and pauses went on for perhaps ten minutes. Through it all, Etta was bent over her desk, scribbling as fast she could.

When it was over, she looked over at the biochemist. He had his eyes closed, almost as though he were in a trance.

"How many of them are transmitting, do you think?" she asked.

Xiangfa opened his eyes. "Three," he said quietly.

"That means they are in three locations."

Xiangfa nodded. "Can you play it again for me?"

Etta rewound the tape and played it. The recording sounded scratchier than the original transmission. Again, Xiangfa listened with eyes closed.

When it was over, he opened his eyes. "Can I see your transcription?"

Etta handed him the pad of paper on which she'd scribbled a series of dots and dashes. "I didn't catch half of it. There's going to be errors."

He shook his head. "No, this is very helpful." He flipped back several pages, squinted down at her previous transcriptions. "Tonight's is longer than the earlier ones."

Etta nodded. "They must be planning something. You think we can crack it?"

"Yes."

"How soon?"

Xiangfa smiled a gentle, patient smile and bowed his head. "That, of course, is always the question."

———

XIANGFA WAS NOT a man to toot his own horn, although perhaps he should have. He was an internationally renowned biochemist who had been elected a member of the US National Academy of Sciences. He was also a respected community member who served as deacon in his church. Had anyone googled him before the Internet fell, they would have discovered these things.

But what no one would have discovered was that he had once served in signals intelligence for the Taiwanese Army. That part of his past even Google couldn't touch.

———

SUSAN FOUND Alan on the porch, leaning against the railing, staring out into the moon-burnished orchard. The faint rumble of a generator floated through the silvery darkness.

"Sounds like Carson found some fuel," she said.

Alan looked at her over his shoulder, his face somber in the moonlight. "It's only right they make themselves comfortable while we get something more permanent established for them."

It was impossible to see the Morgan house from their vantage point. The dense thicket of walnut trees obscured the house and outbuildings. Only the generator noise indicated that someone else was there, that human life was still going on.

"Etta heard the code tonight," Susan said.

"I know."

"She got a recording this time. Xiangfa thinks they'll be able to crack it."

"That's good."

Susan looked at him searchingly. His face was averted, so she could only see the patrician ridge of his nose and the sharp angle of his jaw. He looked like a Roman statue in the moonlight, his face somber and unsmiling but for all the world like that of a leader determined not to lose a battle.

She couldn't believe he'd steal narcotics. Not him. But she had to ask. "Did you take Norcos from the medicine drawer?"

He turned to look at her, a black shadow darkening his brow. "What are you talking about?"

"I'm missing a bunch of Norcos. If you needed some, why didn't you just tell me?"

He was silent for a full ten seconds. She couldn't see his expression in the darkness. "I'm not taking Norcos, Susan," he said quietly.

Something bumped in her heart. She believed him.

"How many are you missing?" Alan asked.

"I don't know. I wasn't counting them. Maybe six or seven."

"You sure you're not mistaken?"

"Positive."

He was silent for a long moment. Out in the yard, a solitary toad croaked. "You better inventory everything in your clinic," he said finally. "Does the door have a lock on it?"

She looked at him in surprise. "Just the button kind. There's no key."

"We'll change that."

She peered at him. "Do you really think that's necessary? Etta's almost always in the house."

He gave her a long look. "All sorts of people have pain for all sorts of reasons."

She couldn't believe it. "Not Etta, Alan. No way."

"I didn't say it was her. I'm only saying that we have a limited supply of medications, and you're the doctor. You decide who gets what."

"Okay," she said.

"Let's go talk with Etta and Xiangfa about the code. I have a few questions."

He pushed himself upright, the matter apparently settled for him.

She didn't follow. "I need to grab something from the garage. I'll be right in after you."

She heard the kitchen door click shut as she descended the steps. Instead of going to the garage, she crossed behind it and stood at the edge of the gravel driveway, tucked in beside the shadowy limbs of an ancient olive tree. No one from the house could see her there, but she could see something she wanted to look at.

At the far end of the property, where the orchard was at its narrowest, she could see the faint flicker of light between the thick walls of tree trunks. The Morgan house was ablaze with light. For a moment, the sound of music—a snippet of guitar, the heavy hip-hop rant of a male voice—slipped through the night air.

She frowned in the darkness, remembering Carson's visit that afternoon, how he'd smiled at her and pawed through the clinic's medical supplies.

Another riff of guitar music pierced the night. She wasn't imagining it.

They were having a party.

She wondered if that party included Norcos.

———

DAWN ARRIVED cool and pale pink, but Harr was too tired to notice. He rolled on his side and pushed himself to sitting. He wanted to check on Seawolf.

The dog didn't look good. He lay on his side, his head against the ground, one glassy eye visible, staring straight ahead.

But he was alive. Harr could see the unmistakable rise and fall of his chest, the rapid ingress and egress of his breath.

"You all right, boy?" Harr reached a gentle hand to touch the dog's shoulder. A rim of white flashed around the animal's eyes, and for a moment, Harr thought the dog might snarl at him, but the dog only whimpered, a broken, piteous sound that stabbed at Harr's heart.

There was no doubt about it: Seawolf was badly injured. His right ear was torn, and his left rear leg slashed, but none of these worried Harr as much as the wound on the dog's neck. A long smear of blood darkened Seawolf's fur and had left a puddle on the gravel below him.

"Ah, boy, they messed you up good." Harr slid the water bowl near the dog's snout and watched as Seawolf feebly lapped at it. When the dog was finished, he gazed at Harr, and to Harr's astonishment, thumped his tail once. With infinite care,

Harr poured the remnants of his water bottle over Seawolf's wounds.

"Is he okay?" Hondo said behind him. The younger man stood in the barn's doorway, his matted hair sticking up on one side of his head.

"He's stopped bleeding, but he's lost a lot of blood." Harr stroked the animal's head, careful not to touch its injured ear.

"Maybe you ought to put him out of his misery, John."

Harr kept his eyes on the dog. He knew that Hondo was not being cruel, that putting a bullet in the dog's head would end Seawolf's suffering, but he couldn't bring himself to do it. The way the dog looked at him worked on him. He felt a kinship that he couldn't quite explain.

"I reckon he kept those coyotes away from us last night. The least we can do is see him through this."

If Hondo thought this bizarre, he didn't say anything. He just stood there in the pale light, looking down at the dog and at Harr sitting on the gravel next to him, and then he let out a grunt that could have meant anything.

"I'll take the herd to the river and get water," he said. Fifteen minutes later, he had his horse saddled up and their small collection of livestock on its way.

Harr watched them disappear down the dirt trail to the river and then turned back to the dog. Long, cool shadows fell from the outbuildings across the ground, protecting Seawolf from the sun, at least for the moment. But Harr knew it wouldn't last. The heat was already beginning to build. He could feel it against his neck.

Seawolf let out a whimper. When Harr scanned the dog's body, trying to decide how to move him into the barn, he did a double take.

"Well, I'll be goddamned," he blurted out, surprise and amusement momentarily breaking through his fatigue and worry. "All this time I've been calling you 'boy.'" He scratched the dog's head. "Sorry about that, girl."

Harr could have sworn the injured dog rolled her eyes.

———

SIX HUNDRED MILES NORTH, a dark-haired man with a scarred back rose from the placid turquoise waters of a sunken tub. He was an extraordinarily handsome man, and if not for the puckered crisscross of scar tissue on his rear torso, he might have been considered beautiful. His jaw angled with the right of amount of bluntness. His lips were full enough to border on sensuous. His eyes, so dark that the pupils blended in with the irises, exerted a magnetic pull so powerful one wondered if they were God's eyes looking outward. In short, it was a face one did not easily forget or escape from. It was also a face of savagery and darkness.

Beyond the bathroom window, down in the open space at the center of the compound, a man opened the barred door of a cylindrical cage, spoke with the tattered, shackled man inside, and then closed the door again. Perhaps fifteen feet away, a third man wheeled a cart from a wooden shed. Pieces of metal, long and thin and arranged in a vertical row, glinted in the morning light.

In an hour, the people would begin their lineup. Dust would rise as they shuffled forward to accept their weapons. Some would yell renunciations when the screaming began.

The dark-haired man accepted his bathrobe without gazing at the woman who handed it to him, tied it around his waist, and walked to the window so that he might be seen by those below.

The response was as he wished it. The two workers dropped to their knees and crossed themselves when they saw him. The man in the cage slumped against his shackles. And across the yard, a woman in a second cage, a pretty, fresh-faced teenager for whom he'd once had a certain fondness, collapsed against the bars, her expression contorted with sobs.

The cold fire of his anger washed through him. It spread through the bathroom air and swept through the ventilation system. He could feel it swooping over the compound's two-story dormitories and out past the barns and laboratories. From there, it raced along the river and through the canyons and across the high plateau until it, like the river, floated out into the Columbia, and then his rage, fed and stoked by betrayal, left the river and climbed into the mountains where the survivors had scattered, warned against his arrival by the very man and young woman in the cages below.

He fingered the cross at his neck.

Death binds us, he thought.

DRYP, his brainchild and progeny, played like a silent movie in his mind, a campaign of death so monstrously successful that the thought of its incompleteness burned like fire in his soul.

The man and young woman would pay. They would all pay.

Death changed everyone. Especially when your hand held the blade.

SIXTEEN

THE CODE CONTINUED INTERMITTENTLY DURING THE DAY and night, for three days, and then stopped. Unfortunately, all other radio transmissions stopped as well, and the lengthening silence began to frighten Susan.

Xiangfa seemed less perturbed. "Probability argues against radio transmissions as an effective communication tool," he said. "There are too few survivors and too many challenges to reliably count on radio contact."

The four of them—Susan, Xiangfa, Alan, and Etta—sat on the porch, in the penumbra between the house's light and the black night beyond. Somewhere in the darkness, a breeze rustled in invisible trees. To Susan, the shivering noise sounded almost like sighing, as though the oak and cottonwood were finally, in the growing coolness of the night, exhaling the day's oppressive heat.

"Please allow me to explain," Xiangfa went on. "Radio transmissions require a radio, someone knowledgeable enough to know how to use a radio, and electricity. If we assume for argument's sake that we have a survival rate of somewhere between one in five hundred thousand and one in a million, then we would have somewhere between forty and eighty survivors in California. Let's further assume that each of these conditions—possessing a radio, knowing how to use it, and having the electricity to use it—reduces the chance of radio transmissions by fifty percent; then our forty to eighty survivors in California have a one-in-eight chance of being able to transmit by radio."

In the dimness, Etta's scowl was unmistakable. "I don't know where you get these numbers, Xiangfa."

The elderly biochemist looked at her over his eyeglasses. "I made them up. My point is not that radio transmissions have a one-in-eight probability, but rather that we should focus on what these crude numbers suggest, which is that radio transmissions are unlikely."

"If you use junk numbers, Xiangfa, you're going to get junk results."

Xiangfa remained admirably equanimous. "One must begin somewhere, Etta."

Susan hid a smile in the darkness. Ever since Etta and Xiangfa had begun the arduous task of trying to decrypt the coded messages, a bond of sorts had formed between them. He politely made suggestions and offered hypotheses, which she immediately shot down. Strangely, her cantankerous personality seemed to delight him.

"Xiangfa's right," Alan agreed. He was leaning back in his chair, a blanket thrown about his shoulders. "If you consider the other challenges—the possibility that atmospheric conditions might make communications difficult, the fact that we are in a valley with ridges that might obstruct signals—the chance of detecting a transmission is reduced even further."

"Or everyone is dead and that's why we're not hearing from them anymore," Susan said. No one else wanted to say it aloud, but the possibility remained a real one.

A sharp riff of rock and roll cut through the night.

"What the hell are they doing over there?" Etta twisted to look in the direction of the Morgan house.

"Listening to music, sounds like," Alan replied. In the muted light from the house, Susan saw his eyes fall on her face. "You're right about other survivors dying. Carson said finding clean water and food was very difficult before they joined us. It's entirely possible some survivors have starved to death."

Susan suppressed a moment's frustration. "I wasn't talking about starvation. I was talking about how every time the code starts, the radio transmissions of another settlement go off the air. Harr told me he would radio us when he arrived at Shangri-La, and he didn't. He also said he'd come back, which he hasn't done either. Pair those facts with the fact that Shangri-La has never been heard from again, and I think you can safely assume that Shangri-La no longer exists. Maybe the Yakima settlement is gone, too."

Alan shook his head dismissively. "You heard the two Yakama speakers yourself. They're alive."

"Maybe, but they said they'd find us on another frequency, and they haven't."

A figure stepped out of the darkness onto the dimly lit lawn below them. It took Susan less than a second to recognize Carson's tall, slightly stooped shoulders. She wondered how long the infectious disease doctor had been lurking there out of sight.

"Still no word from our Native American speakers?" Carson asked. He stood at the bottom of the porch stairs, his face shadowed by the dim light of the house.

"Nope. You throwing a party over there?" Etta asked.

Carson let out a little puff of a laugh. He placed a hand on the banister and said pleasantly, "No, Etta. Reaper is blasting his workout music, that's all. That's why I came over here. I was hoping for a little peace and quiet."

The statement was innocuous enough, but still, a tiny pause ensued. The infectious disease doc remained at the bottom of the stairs, gazing upward with pale, waiting eyes, while Etta, Xiangfa, Alan, and Susan looked down at him, without responding.

Alan seemed to recover his manners first. He stood and pulled out a chair. "Join us. We were just discussing the lack of radio traffic."

The infectious disease doc mounted the stairs and unwound his long body on the chair next to Alan, nodding as Alan brought him up to speed.

"I wouldn't worry yet," Carson said. "The Yakama speaker never promised to contact you at a specific time, only that she would find you on another frequency. Don't you think it's possible that she hasn't gotten around to it yet?"

"I've been transmitting both day and night," Etta said. "It's not that hard to respond. And besides, we're not talking just about the Yakama speaker. Almost all radio transmissions have ceased."

The news didn't seem to shock Carson. "You yourself have said that atmospheric conditions are fickle. What's to say that we're not having sunspot activity or whatever it is that messes up radio communications? I wouldn't overreact to this short period of reduced radio traffic."

No one said anything at first, but Susan thought someone had to. "Etta is saying that this silence could be different, and I have to agree," she said. "Twice we've heard the code, and twice settlements we've previously heard on the radio have gone off the air. What's even more worrisome is that the other settlements, the ones in Colorado and in Georgia, have also gone off the air. That's a lot of radio silence in a short period of time."

Carson leaned back in his chair as though Susan's words didn't faze him at all. "That's one way to interpret the radio silence, but consider an alternate possibility: the Yakima Valley and Shangri-La settlements don't have electricity like we do. Perhaps they're generator-dependent and have run out of fuel. Or maybe they're having equipment problems that require time to repair. What I'm saying is that you shouldn't assume the worst when there are many possible reasons for radio transmissions to pause for a few days."

A soft gust of wind stirred the trees beyond the porch. For a weighted second, no one spoke.

Finally, Xiangfa said almost apologetically, "As a scientist, I have to agree with Jim. There is a concept in science called fixation error. Basically, it means that a scientist can get fixated on one line of thought to the exclusion of others and thereby miss critical information."

Susan was well familiar with the concept. It was often used in medicine to describe practitioners who fixated on one aspect of a patient's condition while neglecting other salient signs and symptoms. The result could be disaster. But still, something nagged at her. "The code—" Susan said.

"I agree with Susan. The code is troublesome." Alan turned to Etta and Xiangfa. "Are you going to be able to crack it?"

Xiangfa nodded solemnly. "When Etta and I listened, there were pauses during the transmissions, which I am guessing are when they were deciphering the previous message and then enciphering a response. The pauses are not particularly long, which suggests to me that the code is not particularly complicated."

Etta shook her head in disagreement. "Don't let Xiangfa lull you into thinking this will be easy. We've run frequency analyses on what we've managed to record, and the code is definitely more complicated than your everyday newspaper cryptogram."

Susan wasn't exactly sure what a newspaper cryptogram was, but guessed it wasn't important. Timing was what mattered. "How long do you think it will take to crack?"

"A few days," Xiangfa said.

"Or months," Etta added. "It depends on how complicated the code is. Remember, it took two centuries to crack some of the codes from the seventeenth century."

Carson leaned forward in his chair. "I don't think we can wait a couple centuries before deciding what to do next. We need to find survivors now. The survival clock is ticking."

Again, he was pushing them to act. On the face of it, Carson was right. Individual survivors, and even people in pairs, stood a far greater risk of perishing the longer they were left on their own, but still, the code and the radio silence rang in Susan's head like a four-alarm fire bell. She glanced over at Alan, hoping he'd meet her eyes.

He wouldn't. He was looking at Carson and nodding. "I agree. The time to find people is now."

Silence fell on the group. Susan sensed the mood changing.

There is a reason animals run in herds, Susan. Go with the herd.

She gazed at her hands in her lap. *Perhaps that is the problem with being a doctor*, she thought. *You spend all your time trying to save lives*, a psychological orientation that made one reluctant to take risks for fear of harming oneself or others. Susan understood the danger of such a conservative outlook.

But she also couldn't ignore her growing certainty that the code and the radio silence were related. Xiangfa and Carson might say she was suffering from fixation error, but her brain kept coming back to two things: Harr hadn't come back, and Shangri-La was off the air.

"I disagree. I say we wait before we actively seek out people to come here. We need to find out what this code means first," she said.

There was a longer silence this time. A soft breeze rustled the trees in the yard. Somewhere in the periphery of her vision, Susan saw Alan glance at Carson. A moment later, when Alan turned to her, there was an apology in his eyes.

"This is a council decision. We have two votes for expanding our outreach measures, one against," he said. "The council has ruled in favor of finding more survivors."

———

IT TOOK Susan two days to cool down enough to accept Carson and Alan's not especially sophisticated plan for finding survivors. Mainly the scheme involved setting up a series of hand-painted signs along the interstate and lighting a tire fire in Esperanta. Susan played almost no role in the effort except to provide medical care to the first survivor who staggered into town after seeing the tall black plume of smoke there.

She was a dark-skinned, hard-faced woman named Adrienne Lewis, and she was so skeletal and cut up that Susan immediately put her in the clinic. In many ways, Susan considered it a miracle that the thirty-five-year-old former university administrator had made it as far as she had. The woman's ankles and feet were so bloody and swollen that the underlying ligaments and bones were no longer visible. To make matters worse, an angry, crisscross pattern of claw marks oozed with bloody fluid from her arms.

"The cats did this?" Susan asked, astonished.

The woman nodded grimly from her clinic bed. "DRYP must have done something to their nervous systems. I've never seen such vicious animals in my life. They jump from trees or rooftops, two or three of them at a time. You never even see them coming."

Susan whistled softly. She still couldn't get over the tale of how Adrienne had escaped Sacramento. The woman had basically fought her way out with a club. When they had found her just outside Esperanta, she still carried the bloodied weapon with which she'd clobbered cats.

"Do you think rabies could explain their behavior?" Adrienne asked.

Susan dabbed antibiotic ointment on a little horseshoe of puncture marks between Adrienne's thumb and forefinger. "I doubt it. Rabies is extremely rare, and it's mainly a wild animal disease. It's not common in domesticated cats."

"These weren't domesticated cats." The former university administrator gasped as Susan dabbed hydrogen peroxide on a particularly nasty scratch. "Or at least, if they were domesticated, they're not anymore."

"Were they drooling or staggering?"

The woman shook her head. "No, they looked like normal cats. It was their behavior that was crazed. They kept attacking me even as I clubbed them."

For a moment, Susan didn't say anything. Gently, she turned the woman's arms over, eyeing the angry spiderweb of scratches and bites. In her entire medical career, she'd never seen such a mauling. A few scratches on little kids who'd played a little too roughly with the family cat, sure. The odd bite here and there by an elderly, irritable pet. But this woman had fought off cats with a *club*.

Susan released the woman's hand and walked to the dresser. "I'm going to put you on antibiotics. You may not be at risk of rabies, but you're definitely at risk of getting an infection."

Adrienne frowned. "You have antibiotics? I thought those were all gone."

Susan pulled out an orange plastic cylinder. "I have these and that's it. You don't have an allergy to penicillin, do you?" When the woman shook her head, Susan handed over the container. "Take one twice a day until they're gone."

The woman stared. "I can't take these. This is all you have. It's not certain I'll get an infection."

Susan peered at her skeletal frame and swollen ankles. She was pretty darned sure that Adrienne, in her current condition, would get the mother of all infections. "Take them. We'll find more."

All at once the hardness in the woman's face melted. Her throat jerked as though she were trying to speak and couldn't. Finally, she said, "When I was alone in my house in Sacramento, I'd go to the second floor and watch for the cats. There were no dogs. No people. No rats or mice. Just cats, in the yards and on the sidewalks. On porches and on cars. As peaceful as can be, until you tried to go out." Her voice cracked. "You don't have cats here, do you?"

For a second, a half-suppressed memory shimmered in Susan's brain: the reflected glow of a cat's eyes in the darkness, the bloodied, half-eaten face below. A baby.

Nausea, clammy and vertiginous, washed through her.

"We don't have cats here," she said quietly. "At least, none that I have seen."

The woman's shoulders sagged, like a balloon whose air had been released.

SEVENTEEN

SEVEN DAYS PASSED BEFORE SEAWOLF WAS READY TO MOVE. For Harr, the wait was interminable. He hunted and scavenged at nearby farmsteads, and in the process procured much-needed items like fresh meat and ammunition, but restlessness dogged him; he wanted to get on the road. The feeling made him irritable.

Hondo was not so afflicted. The younger man's good spirits returned, and he was given to rhapsodizing about the benefits of their hiatus: the livestock could graze down by the river and recover from their rough travels, he and Harr were able to hunt and fish enough to regain some of the weight they'd lost, and their scavenging had yielded critical additional supplies like mosquito repellant and a length of throwing rope.

Hondo immediately put the rope to use.

"See that?" he crowed as he lassoed a tree stump for something like the tenth time. "You'll make a cowboy out of me yet."

"You have to have cows to be a cowboy," Harr said.

Hondo was undaunted. He threw the loop again, another perfect lasso. "Did you see that? It's in the blood, amigo!"

Harr left the younger man to his practice and crossed the

yard to the barn. Although the sun had begun its descent on the western horizon, enough light spilled through the barn's open door to illuminate the wooden structure's interior. The three horses stood in stalls, lazily swishing their tails against fat black flies. Two stalls over, the cow and steer lay on the cool concrete, watching with slow, lethargic eyes as Harr headed for the dog.

Seawolf met Harr halfway across the barn floor, tail wagging. Despite himself, Harr's lips curled upward. "You're looking better, girl."

It wasn't quite true. In the half-light, Seawolf looked like a bandit. Her torn right ear hung in two pieces, and the poorly healed gash on her neck looked like a cut of meat. But the pink tongue, quivering in Seawolf's open mouth, softened the impression of savagery. Harr could have sworn the brave coyote fighter was looking at him with goo-goo eyes.

"We're pushing out tomorrow morning at first light," he said, squatting down to pet her. "We can't wait any longer."

The dog held his gaze with unblinking eyes, rapid little puffs of air going in and out of her mouth.

"If you can't keep up, we're going to leave you behind. So I'm counting on you to keep up."

The dog just stayed there. For a moment, Harr gazed at her, his thumb stroking the fur just below her untorn left ear. She'd either make it or she wouldn't; it was up to her and maybe, just a little bit, to God.

Or maybe he was kidding himself. The threat of loss, so ever present that it felt as though it were woven into the very fabric of the earth, swept over him once again.

———

CARSON, Sam, and Reaper moved into their new home three days after Adrienne's arrival, which was convenient because Adrienne needed a place to stay.

"I'll move into the Morgan place," she offered. "I like being by myself, and you don't have room for me here anyway."

Susan and Adrienne sat at the Victorian's kitchen table, watching as Emmaline proceeded to make a mess of the cut-up peach Susan had prepared for her lunch. The toddler kept picking up slices and dropping them on the tablecloth.

"But there's no electricity there." Susan retrieved a stray peach slice and put it back on Emmaline's plate.

"I don't need electricity. I've been living without it for the last month and a half. I'm used to it."

Once again, Susan noted the difference between Adrienne and Carson and his friends. Adrienne had slipped seamlessly into the farm's operations, neither making demands nor trying to insinuate herself into a decision-making role. Mainly, she seemed to want to recuperate quietly and be left alone. She almost never smiled.

Susan wondered what had happened to the college administrator, whom she had lost, and how she had survived. It seemed to Susan that every single survivor shared a similar version of horror: the death of loved ones, the shock of mass death, the staggering loneliness, and the great, dark impenetrability of the future.

But neither Susan nor anyone else spoke of these feelings. They were simply too big and overwhelming, traumas that must, for survival's sake, be subsumed beneath the immediate, pressing tasks of living.

She flipped the cover of a notebook. "We're cataloguing people's skill sets. I'll read some of them off to you. Do you mind?"

"Sure."

"Can you sew or knit?"

Adrienne shook her head.

"How about any electrical or mechanical skills?"

Another shake of the head.

Susan went through the remainder of the list: medical skills, construction skills, chemical skills, farming, hunting, fishing, animal husbandry, soap and candle manufacturing, food preservation skills, and on and on. To each, Adrienne gave an unequivocal no.

Susan felt bad for the woman. "Are there any skills that I haven't mentioned that you'd like me to catalogue?"

"I don't suppose word processing and database management are on that list?" Adrienne asked bitterly. "Or attention to detail and good time management?"

Susan didn't say anything. It was clear by Adrienne's tone that she understood the skills that were once the lifeblood of her administrative job were no longer useful, but what exactly she could contribute was not obvious either. Although the former administrator was eating regularly and healing from the cat attacks, she still looked skeletal. It'd be weeks before she could do any real physical labor.

"I'm just a suck on resources, aren't I?" Adrienne said. "I know you're low on food supplies. I heard you talking to Etta."

The administrator was nothing if not blunt. Susan was beginning to realize that Adrienne was a no-bullshit kind of woman, which made it oddly easy for Susan to speak no bullshit in return. "We've got plenty of fresh produce for now, but unless we get a regular supply of meat or fish, it's going to be slow starvation over the next few months."

"Hence, the need for someone with hunting and fishing skills. What kind of fish are there in the river?"

"Bass, I guess. Maybe catfish, but no one's been able to catch either yet."

"Who's been fishing?"

"Reaper."

"Put me on it instead. I have plenty of time on my hands."

Susan stared at the woman. "Do you know how to fish?"

"No, but it seems to me Reaper doesn't either if he hasn't caught anything. Might as well let me have a shot. It's just worm and hook, right?"

Just then Emmaline let out a little squeal and slapped the table.

The administrator peered at the toddler with her frank, unsmiling gaze. "That's right, Emmaline. I'm going to catch you a bass or catfish or whatever is swimming around in that river."

"Feesh!" Emmaline cried.

Susan couldn't help but laugh.

———

THE HOUSE WAS HUGE. Maybe not as big as the Victorian, but big enough that none of them had to see each other if they didn't want to, which suited Carson, because he had things to do.

"The shop is my space, understand? You're not to go into it," he told Sam as they exited the sprawling rancher and crossed the lawn to the sparkling new, buff-colored, steel-sided outbuilding. The structure was a beaut: 220-volt electrical service, polished concrete floor, and a workbench worthy of a research laboratory. Best of all, the building had only one window.

He'd need to find some blinds for that window.

Sam clearly didn't care about the shop. She'd stopped and turned back to the house, her arms folded across her chest, her eyes sweeping the circular gravel driveway and the stately rust-colored gate that separated the ranchero from the road. "The people who owned this place must have had some money, huh?"

He slipped an arm around her. "Yeah, baby, they did."

She was looking at the yard, at the expansive patio and the dirty, but easily cleanable, waters of the pool. "I can't believe this is ours, Jim. My whole life I dreamed of having a pool. And now, look, we've got a pool." She turned to him, her eyes shiny with tears. "You did this for us, Jim. You got on that council and forced them to give us a proper home with electricity. Now we have a real home, Jim. All because of you."

It was remarkable, really, how easy it was to please her. A big house, electricity, and she was gazing up at him like he could screw her right here on the grass, right now, any way he wanted. Something stirred inside, a rush of power that tingled like champagne in his blood.

"I told you I'd take care of you, baby," he said. He let his hand slide down her back to the rounded curve of her bottom, which he pushed gently toward the house. "Now, it's your turn to take care of me."

She let out a little peal of laughter and swung her black-and-red hair off her shoulder. He watched the curved width of her bottom as she crossed the lawn, marveling at the difference between men and women, appreciating her natural and entirely appropriate willingness to submit to his will.

Desire swept through him. The natural order, so buffeted by outraged denials of difference, was now, in this little valley, finally reasserting itself. As he followed Sam into the cool interior of the house, Carson was struck by the great tragedy of the confusion over simple evolutionary realities. It had been the source of so much unnecessary discord.

He followed her down the long hallway to the master bedroom, where she, true to her sex, performed her role. He was proud of her, and pleased by her, and as the blood rushed through his head and into his groin, he knew he had at last pinpointed a truth so obvious that he felt shocked he hadn't recognized it earlier:

Forty thousand years of evolution have given rise to this very moment.

His world had fallen into place: Liberty Valley, the new house, the shop with its 220-volt electricity, and now this, a chance to live in the manner evolution had destined him to live.

He pressed himself into her, and when his release came, it arrived in a blinding wave. When it was over, he rolled off her body and fell into a contented sleep.

———

SEAWOLF MADE it three miles before giving up the ghost. Above a dusty stretch of fallow farmland, just south of Stockton, she limped down the side of the levee and collapsed in the shade of young valley oak.

Harr carefully guided his Arabian down the grassy incline to the dog's side. Although Seawolf lay with her belly on the ground, Harr was not reassured by her relatively upright position. It bothered Harr that the dog didn't try to paw away flies on her head. She just sat there panting in the dirt, as buzzing black bugs landed on her fur.

Hondo shouted down from the levee road, "She okay?"

"Not sure," Harr shouted back.

"I'm going to take the livestock down to the river while you figure it out. It's too damn hot up here."

Harr glanced up at his partner. Sunlight surrounded the younger man, turning him into a dark silhouette against the blazing sky. A second later, the silhouette was gone, disappeared over the edge of the levee. Harr could hear the Holstein moo plaintively as Hondo urged her down the riverside incline.

Harr knew where they were going. Before Seawolf's detour,

Harr had eyed the single, stubby finger of land stretching out into the river channel. It wasn't much, just a gravelly, shrub-covered patch of riverbank that offered only a few scraggly trees, but it was the best chance for shade and water now that they were approaching Stockton. Levees bracketed either side of the San Joaquin like a girdle, squeezing the river into a narrower and deeper channel with no room for any real bank.

A hot wind snapped his shirt against his back. Harr lifted his hat and rubbed a dusty sleeve against his forehead, but the breeze did nothing to cool him. He climbed down from his horse, slugged half his water bottle, and then poured the remaining contents into Seawolf's bowl. He stood in the tree's paltry shade while Seawolf lapped pathetically at the warm liquid.

Somehow, he had to get the dog to the river. He stood there for a moment, gazing down at Seawolf and then at the twenty-five-foot levee. The river, flowing softly but invisible from his position, was less than a hundred feet away.

He'd have to leave the dog.

It was during this quiet realization, as he stood in a little patch of shade at the edge of an endless expanse of parched land, that he heard the engine. Harr's head whipped up. He cocked his ears.

A solo vehicle, kicking up a long trail of dust like a contrail, was coming up the levee road. Harr could hear its rubber tires against gravel.

"Stay," he said unnecessarily to the dog.

A second later, he was bounding up the slope, shotgun in hand, equal parts wild hope and adrenaline-fueled aggression rushing through his veins.

EIGHTEEN

They called themselves Travelers, which struck Harr as a pretty accurate description, because so far as he could tell, they'd been traveling ever since the pandemic began.

"We come up from Apple Valley," the oldest one said. He was a yellow-toothed, red-faced guy who smelled like onions. "You think it's hot here? It's hot as the devil's dick there." As if to emphasize this point, he sent a stream of black tobacco water onto the dirt in front of him.

There were three of them: the onion man; a pimply, dim-looking boy who couldn't have been more than fourteen; and a red-haired, unwashed woman who Harr guessed hadn't yet touched twenty. The man sat in the open side door of a Honda Odyssey minivan, his sweaty shirtfront open so that Harr could see the dirty sag of his upper chest.

"Kayla, get me that whiskey," he barked out. To Harr, he said, "That girl will lay around, lazy as a millionaire's daughter, if you let her."

Harr wasn't so sure. The redhead looked worked to the bone. She was full-figured and dirty, and she moved as though she carried a thousand-pound weight on her young shoulders.

She dug a reddened, blistered hand into the incomprehensible pile of shit in the back of the minivan and withdrew a half-filled bottle of Kirkland Canadian Whiskey, which she handed over without looking up.

"Well, don't stand there staring at her with your tongue hanging out, boy. Help her set up the tents, you idiot," the man yelled at the boy, who'd been watching the man and the girl and the strangers from a distance.

"Where'd you guys come from?" he asked Harr.

"Shangri-La. Near Lemon Cove." It was a remarkable condensation of the past few weeks, but Harr doubted the man cared a rat's ass about the details.

"Never heard of it." He spat out the remainder of his plug and then took a swig of the whiskey, breathing out in an appreciative whoosh when the booze hit his stomach. "That's some good shit. Used to cost twenty bucks a bottle in the old days. Now we get it for free."

He held the bottle out to Harr, and when Harr shook his head, he held it out to Hondo. Hondo just stared at him.

"No takers? Fine with me. Hey, Davey, get your ass over here," he called out.

The boy lifted his gaze, saw the bottle, and dumped the unopened tent on the tarp the woman had just spread out. He took a long swig, his sharp Adam's apple bouncing up and down in his thin neck.

"Jesus Christ on the cross, boy, that's enough." Onion Man snatched the bottle from Davey and rubbed his dirty sleeve against the opening, watching with disgust as the boy wandered back to the half-erected tent site. "A sip's a sip, but that boy would drink the whole bottle if you let him. Trying to get his courage up to try to hump her again, I guess." Onion Man grinned.

When neither Harr nor Hondo smiled in response, Onion

Man shrugged. He picked at something black between his teeth, inspected it on his fingernail, and then flicked the sodden tobacco into space. "Where you guys heading?"

Harr weighed how much to tell him. True, Onion Man seemed friendly enough and had hauled Seawolf's sorry carcass five miles to the modest riverside park in which they were now making camp, but there was something disturbing about the trio. For one thing, Onion Man wouldn't shut up. For another, beneath the dirt, the redheaded woman had an unmistakable bruise on her cheek.

"There's a farm north of here, in a little valley," Harr said. "There are a few survivors there, trying to make a go of a farming operation."

"Farming?" Onion Man shook his head pityingly. "Well, hat's off to them for trying. But I got to tell you, that's dumber'n a stick. Farming ain't gonna work. Where you going to get the seed and fertilizer and pesticide? Or the water for irrigation?" He snorted out a little cloud of onion stink.

Harr felt Hondo's sidelong glance and knew instantly what his partner was thinking. Why the hell were they talking to this strange man? But Harr wanted information, so he bit back his revulsion and asked the first of many questions that were circulating through his brain.

"Where'd you find the gas?" he asked, lifting his chin at the dust-covered minivan.

Onion Man leaned back against one of the passenger seats. "If you look hard enough, you'll find it. Some of the gas stations got fuel. You just got to get into those underground tanks, which can be a real bitch, because there ain't a lot of fuel left in 'em. Sometimes we find an ag tank that someone else didn't find first. We even tried the refineries over toward Martinez—" he lifted the bottle in the vague westerly direction of the Bay Area "—but

164

I can tell you, that is one direction you don't want to go. Jesus Christ on a corn cob, it's worse than Kuwait after Saddam blew the oil wells."

"How so?"

Onion Man looked at him like he was an idiot. "'Cuz the damn refineries blew when the power went out. Their backup power and computerized controls must have gone down, and then the high heat and uncontrolled reactions started. Ka-BOOM." He spread his fingers in a puffing motion and shook his head with gleeful regret. "They're still burning, not like they were in the first days, but bad enough that there ain't nothing living around there no more." He shrugged. "Anyhow, we don't need refineries. We're finding what we need, and if we don't find nothin' for a day or two, we got ten gallons back here."

Sure enough, beneath the incomprehensible mess of black plastic garbage bags and camping equipment, Harr saw red plastic jerricans in the minivan's crammed interior.

"You going to just keep traveling?" Hondo asked. He was standing there with his hands shoved in his pockets, a skeptical look on his face.

Onion Man took a swig of whiskey and smacked his lips. "Why not? I ain't no farmer and neither is dumbass over there." He swung the bottle around, apparently referring to Davey, who was now helping the woman set up a second tent. "Kayla keeps camp well enough and can cook a decent meal. Davey, despite his idiot looks, is a solid scavenger. Seems to me that we're not doing too bad. We got food, and we got fuel. We've managed to find everything we need."

Harr said nothing. There was a certain logic to Onion Man's thoughts. In many ways, the trio was better fed than Harr and Hondo, but the endless scavenging nature of their lives held no appeal for him. It was as if they were living off the dregs of civilization with no interest in building anew. It seemed a capitulation to Harr somehow, a slippery slope into oblivion.

"You're welcome to camp with us a few days," Onion Man offered. "Looks like that mutt could use the rest."

He gestured over to Seawolf, who was curled up in the shade beneath a valley oak. The dog was sleeping peacefully, her nose tucked between her paws. Further out, closer to the river, the livestock grazed where the grass grew greener along the banks, where a little beach had been cleared. It was a nice place, nicer than the barn in which they'd passed the previous seven nights.

But Harr didn't want to stay with Onion Man, and he didn't know how to say it. So he settled on, "We need to sleep with the animals, in case there's predators."

"Suit yourself," Onion Man said and then turned toward the tent site. "Kayla," he called, irritably, "don't make a federal case out of setting up the tents, for Christ's sake. We got guests tonight. Get dinner going."

The redheaded woman looked up from the tent stake she was pushing in the ground, and Harr could have sworn he saw the flash of something hot in her face, but it was only a flash. She rose, eyes focused straight ahead, and went to the minivan's rear. Onion Man didn't look at her, as one by one, she freed three collapsible chairs from the mess inside and then set them out around the park's old-fashioned fire ring. Nor did he look at her as she hauled an old Coleman camp stove over to a picnic table. In fact, he didn't seem to be aware of her at all, as he talked and talked about zigzagging across the valley from one little riverside town to the next.

Harr couldn't help darting glances at the young woman. She was filthy and freckled, and her hair was tangled in knots. Davey, the fourteen-year-old, sat in one of the camp chairs, whittling a stick with a big, bone-handled hunting knife, watching her through half-lidded eyes.

After a while, Harr and Hondo excused themselves and went to the livestock on the river. Neither man spoke, but Harr was certain Hondo noticed the same thing he had. For a man who claimed to have scavenged everything he needed, Onion Man had only managed to scavenge two tents.

———

KAYLA DID MAKE a decent dinner of rice and beans mixed in with some sort of brown sauce Harr had never heard of, but which came in a small bottle with a green cap. The tangy, slightly sweet, slightly spicy flavor complemented the bass that Hondo managed to fish out of the river. It was the best meal he'd eaten in weeks.

But the ambience was bad. Onion Man, who went by the name of Pap, had been drinking steadily all afternoon, and now that the sun had set, his face was red, and a sort of glassiness had settled over his eyes. Harr recognized the look. It was the look that would result in one of two predictable outcomes: Pap was either going to keel over face first into his plate or turn belligerent.

The young woman was clearly hoping for the former. She kept refilling Pap's cup with whiskey.

The boy held out his cup, a chipped mug decorated with an oversized black bear and the inexplicable letters BOB, and ordered, "Gimme some, Kayla."

She didn't respond, just sat herself down next to Pap, with the bottle placed out of Davey's reach.

"Ah, for cryin' out loud, Kayla, give the boy some," Pap slurred.

For the first time, she whirled to face the older man square on. "No."

Pap rolled his eyes. "He ain't going to paw you again. He knows better'n that."

Kayla ignored him. She turned and held out the bottle, her eyes shifting from Harr's to Hondo's and then back again. In their green depths, Harr registered a challenge. "You want some?" She swung the bottle back and forth with a quick flick of her wrist.

Harr could tell she was stone-cold sober.

"We're heading out early tomorrow, at sunrise," Harr said by way of refusal. Beside him, he sensed Hondo nodding in agreement.

The news seemed to surprise her. "What are you going to do with the dog?" she asked.

Harr glanced over at Seawolf, who sat not far from the campfire, with her head up and pink tongue hanging from her mouth. The dog seemed to have made a remarkable comeback from her earlier collapse, but Harr knew the travel the next day would be just as hard, if not harder than today. "She'll follow, I reckon. If she don't, well—"

"You can't just leave her." Outrage flickered in Kayla's green eyes.

For a second, Harr saw her as she must have been before the plague and all the hardship of the road. She had probably been a pretty, fiery little thing, the kind of girl who broke young men's hearts.

"We ain' taking no dog, Kayla," Pap slurred. His face had taken on a mean cast. "Jesus Mother of Mary fuckin' Christ, you're always tryin' to pick up th' strays. Din't you learn nuthin' from the damn cats?"

Here comes the belligerence, Harr thought. He wondered if he'd have to protect Kayla, but the young redhead had obviously been here before. The little light of life, flickering for a few brief minutes in her eyes, was abruptly snuffed out. She dropped her head and said in a low tone, "It's a *dog*, not a cat, Pap. And I haven't picked up a single stray."

For a moment, silence gripped the group. Kayla looked downward, her shoulders tensed. Pap gave her a long stare through bloodshot eyes. Even Davey gazed at her, his lips curled slightly upward, an anticipatory expression on his face.

All of a sudden, the cool breeze off the water was not enough. The air felt hot with tension, as though one wrong word could ignite the night into a pyrotechnic explosion. Harr abruptly stood up from the picnic table, pointed at a nonexistent watch on his wrist. "It's getting late. Thank you for dinner, Kayla." He tipped his hat to Pap, adopting his most ingratiating country-boy voice. "And thank *you* for sharing your provisions. I can see you've managed very well during these trying times."

For a second, Pap's eyes narrowed suspiciously, but then, when he saw the bland expression on Harr's face, Pap's face relaxed into a slow, yellow-toothed grin.

Turning, Harr gave Hondo a laser stare. "Come on, Hondo. Big day tomorrow. Time for shut-eye."

For a second, Harr worried that Hondo wouldn't follow, but the younger man must have read the urgency in Harr's private look. He rose and bid his farewells.

But that didn't mean Hondo was at ease. Far from it. As the two men walked into the thicker darkness near the river, Hondo whispered fiercely, "We can't leave her with that son of a bitch."

"She knows what she's doing. Pap's drunk as a skunk, and he's carrying." It was true. Harr had seen the unmistakable handle of a 1911 Mil-Spec .45 protruding from the man's waistband. Harr took the toothpick he'd been chewing on and threw it on the ground. "It's best to let him drink until he's comatose. Shouldn't be long now."

Hondo cursed under his breath. "What if he tries to—?"

"He won't."

But Harr wasn't really sure. He'd known plenty of Paps in his life, and one thing he knew for certain was that they were a mean, unpredictable bunch. He hoped she kept refilling his cup with Canadian whiskey. He wanted Pap to have the mother of all hangovers in the morning.

Then Harr would only have to worry about the kid.

NINETEEN

The first sliver of sun crested the distant Sierras as Harr and Hondo pushed out the following morning. It was Harr's favorite time of day, the sky above still tainted with cool night, and the eastern horizon pink with new day.

But Harr was not feeling peaceful or particularly awed this morning. He felt tense. He was counting the miles he and Hondo could put between themselves and the Travelers before all hell broke loose.

"Don't go near the river, and stay off the roads," he ordered. "I'll see you in Rio Vista tomorrow."

He and Hondo had cobbled their plan together in the late hours of the night: Hondo would take the animals and cross into the fertile peat fields of the Sacramento-San Joaquin Delta, while he, Harr, would double back to the camp to liberate the young woman.

Hondo had fought the idea of separating at first. "That's crazy. There's two of them and one of you. We should take them on together. I'll take the old guy, and you take the younger one."

Harr rejected the proposition. He wanted someone to stay with the livestock. He thought he could move faster alone.

They'd argued for the better part of an hour, until finally, Harr cut Hondo off with a short, "I was in the military. I've done in-and-out operations before. I know what I'm doing."

But though he'd agreed at the time, Hondo now tried one last shot at a team attack. He turned in the saddle, his face pink from the rising sun. "An op in Afghanistan with all the firepower and technology of the US Army is not the same as an op with a horse and a shotgun, friend. I guarantee you the kid is armed, and unlike that old guy, he's not hungover. I'm going with you."

"No, you're not." Harr shot a glance at the gray, patchwork fields below the levee road. "They'll come looking for her, so stay off the roads."

"That's not going to help. All they have to do is follow the tracks to find us."

Harr's horse was antsy. He could feel the Arabian shift beneath his legs, ready to move. "They're not that smart. And even if they are, they got a minivan, not a four-wheeler. They'll be hard-pressed to chase you across a field."

It was the best plan he could come up with: Hondo would head north through the patchwork of fields that separated the labyrinthine network of sloughs and rivers that made up the Sacramento-San Joaquin Delta. Harr and the woman would head east. If all went according to plan, they'd converge on the small delta town of Rio Vista in twenty-four hours.

Hondo was looking at him, his face carefully expressionless. "You know we could just kill Pap, don't you?"

The thought had already occurred to Harr, that it would be a hell of a lot easier to put a bullet in Pap's head and take Kayla that way, but Harr couldn't bring himself to do it. There seemed just a shred of something left in him, a tie to the past in which life had meaning, even a crappy life like Pap's.

"I don't need to kill him to free Kayla." Harr hopped down

from his horse and untied his rope from the saddle's horn. He made a small loop in one end and fed the other end through it. He slipped the loop around Seawolf's head. The dog looked crushed. "You can't go with me, girl. I've got to move quick."

He walked over and handed the other end of the rope to Hondo. "Keep her on the leash for thirty minutes, then let her go. If she doesn't follow you, don't stop for her. You need to get as many miles between you and me as possible."

Hondo gazed down at him with a grave expression. "That minivan is a lot faster than a horse, John. And a rifle can cover a lot of territory that a minivan can't."

"I know that," Harr said. He put a boot into a stirrup, did a quick hop, and threw his leg over the saddle. When he was seated, he pushed his hat down on his head. "If I don't meet you in Rio Vista tomorrow, you know what to do with the animals."

Hondo gave a short nod. "Liberty Valley."

Harr didn't say anything else. He turned the horse and headed back for the campground.

————

THE FOOD ISSUE was a real one. They were drawing down on their stock. For what seemed the fiftieth time, Susan rechecked the remaining inventory in the basement.

Five pounds of sugar. Ten pounds of flour. Enough rice for maybe a month or more. Maybe two months' worth of beans, tomatoes, and soup.

The reality that these dwindling supplies suggested pressed on her soul like a lead weight: even if they managed to scavenge enough food to last through the worst of winter, they'd be in dire straits come February and March. They needed to get potatoes, carrots, and broccoli in the ground. They needed livestock.

A creak sounded, and then Alan appeared in a little circle of light at the base of the stairs. He was already dressed for work, in canvas pants and one of her father's plaid shirts. His face softened when he saw her. "I wondered where you were. What are you doing down here so early?"

"Couldn't sleep." She glanced over at the pale, gray light of dawn showing through the basement's external door. "You're up early. You heading out with Carson?"

Alan shook his head. "He likes to manage the tire fire by himself." He joined her in front of the shelving unit, peering over her shoulder at the inventory list she held in her hand. He smelled like soap and clean skin, no longer like antiseptic.

"Wow," he said with a frown. "We're really drawing down on our stock."

She placed the list back on the shelf. "That's because Carson hasn't brought us any food from his scavenging runs."

She waited for the inevitable stiffening in his posture that always accompanied her comments about Carson, but it didn't come. Instead, the furrow between Alan's brows deepened. He looked genuinely surprised. "None?"

"Oh, a can here and there." She lifted a dented can of Progresso split pea soup. "This was yesterday's contribution." She returned the soup to its place with other canned soups and picked up a jar of olives. "This one came the day before yesterday."

He held out a hand. "Can I see that inventory list?"

Susan handed over the clipboard. She watched as he flipped the pages, scanning.

"I wasn't aware he was having such a difficult time finding food," he said.

The decision to send Carson out alone scavenging had been a group decision driven mainly by the desire to conserve fuel. Carson did double duty on his daily motorcycle trip to Esperanta. He monitored the tire fire, and when he felt it was safe to do so, he also scavenged for food.

Or maybe he just said he was. "Maybe he's not actually scavenging," she said.

"How could that be? The fire is set up so that he only needs to throw a new tire on it every couple of hours or so. He has plenty of time to scavenge in between."

"Having time and actually scavenging are two different things."

She could tell she'd irritated him. She could see it in the slight flattening of his expression. "Carson said they had a hard time finding food before joining us," he said with forced patience. "What makes you think he's not having trouble now?"

"Because Esperanta had almost two thousand residents before DRYP," she said, voice rising. "You can't tell me that in all of those houses, in every cupboard and basement, there's only one can of soup and one jar of olives left. We've found way more food than that in Liberty Valley alone."

When Alan didn't immediately respond, she knew she'd finally made her point: she and Alan had scavenged twenty times more food in the rural, lightly populated Liberty Valley than Carson had gleaned in a week of daily trips to Esperanta.

But that didn't mean Alan accepted what she was suggesting. His face turned forbidding. "He's not skimming off food, Susan."

"How do you know?"

"Because I didn't see any secret caches of food when Xiangfa and I installed the batteries for their solar system. Their cupboards and shelves were bare."

"Then he's not scavenging," Susan cried, exasperated. "He's probably sitting around when he goes to Esperanta."

She realized she had pushed Alan too far. His expression soured, and he snapped, "Oh, for god's sake, Susan. Anyone with an iota of energy would go crazy sitting around all day watching a fire. He's telling us the truth. There's no food there."

Susan bit back a response, knowing to argue anymore would only result in an explosion she didn't want, but inside she felt sick. She turned and marched outside. A second later, she heard the basement door slam and Alan's footsteps on the stairwell behind her.

For the first time since she'd met him, Alan seemed to be struggling for control. He came very close to her and said in a low voice, "This is not the time to stir up suspicion, Susan. Do you understand that? You. Me. Etta. Xiangfa. All of us. We don't have room for stupid squabbles and suspicions. We have to survive with who we have, and who we have is Carson, for better or worse. He's not a murderer. He's a smart, able-bodied man who's a doctor. He's *valuable*."

She stared at him incredulously. "So we just let him do whatever he wants? Is that your solution for survival? Let him make decisions for us. Let him drive all our actions?"

Alan made a sound of pure exasperation. "You act as if he's done something criminal! He wanted electricity and a new home, and we gave it to him. That's fairness, Susan. That's how you build coalitions."

"We have to have better rules. We have to have an agreement about what is acceptable and what is not."

"Like some moral code? For what? He hasn't done anything, Susan. You're casting suspicion on him that's poisoning everything. You're fucking this up."

The profanity struck her like a gut punch. For a vertiginous moment, she couldn't speak. "Is that how you view me?" she whispered. "Like I'm *fucking everything up*?"

"No," he said. Now, there was alarm in his eyes. "That's not what I meant at all. I meant—"

She cut him off. "I heard what you said, Alan. I'll just go

fuck something up elsewhere."

She stormed blindly for the barn, almost colliding with a figure at the edge of the patio. It took a second for Susan to recognize who it was. It was Adrienne. The scratched-up, emaciated woman had heard everything.

———

HARR GUESSED it was close to eight o'clock when he tied up the Arabian. Long morning shadows stretched from a cluster of cottonwoods along the river's bank. The air smelled fresh, not yet hot.

He was about a mile from the campsite, at a long, gentle bend in the river. To the north stretched the dried remnants of a tomato field. To the west, the tortuous path of the San Joaquin.

He put his hand to the horse's head and whispered, "Be ready, girl," and then, with shotgun in hand, walked quickly along the farm side of the levee. When he reached the campsite, he climbed the levee bank, stretched himself out on the road on top, and pulled out his binoculars.

Kayla was already up. He could see her awkwardly hauling a five-gallon orange Igloo from the river's edge.

The boy, Davey, was up, too. He sat with his back against the picnic table, whittling with his bone-handled knife, his left heel resting on the previous night's emptied whiskey bottle. Behind him, the beginnings of a rudimentary breakfast had been laid out: a can of Folgers and a steel percolator, a camp stove and a carton of Quaker Oats.

No sign of Pap. Harr glassed the dusty red hoop tent closest to the water. Behind it, another tent, smaller than the first, stood with its zip flap hanging open. Inside, he could just make out the mussed-up outline of a single sleeping bag.

She must have slept in the two-person tent, Harr thought and then immediately suppressed the flare of disgust and rage that followed. He needed to keep cool, to focus on that which he'd come back to do.

The minivan's back hatch was open, but the rest of the doors were closed. Harr tried to look through the windows but couldn't see into the interior. The dappled reflection of twisted oaks and morning sunlight obscured his view.

Plan A or plan B? he wondered. He glassed the picnic table again. Nothing but cooking supplies and a kid with a sharp stick and a hunting knife.

A second later, he was in motion, soft-footing it down the levee, his right hand wrapped around his shotgun's grip, his breath coming in quiet surges.

———

SOMETIMES SUSAN LOOKED at the scar on her face and remembered. The injury was healed now, or mostly so, but a permanent pucker had formed where the slit ended near the eye. The result was that a portion of her cheek had turned inward. It wasn't horrible, but it wasn't pretty either.

She told herself not to mourn useless things like beauty, but sometimes, she couldn't help herself. Small actions, like catching a glimpse of herself in the truck's windows, triggered memories of pretty dresses and cocktail parties, of pedicures and fancy nights out. It seemed like another life entirely, lived with an obscene obliviousness to the fragility of it all.

It was better not to think of it. It was better to keep the silent pact they'd all unwittingly made: no one would speak of their loss or lament the past. To do otherwise threatened to open the black door of grief.

And yet it was almost impossible not to indulge in anticipatory mourning for all the things that they'd soon run out of—the toilet paper and tampons, the toothbrushes and laundry detergent. She'd never considered any of them precious before, but their loss would be deeply felt. There were no factories to crank out new lightbulbs or electrical wire or replacement parts for appliances and cars. They had what they would have. When it was gone, there'd be no more.

Unless we can build again, she thought. At least the pioneers knew how to spin wool and make flour. They were competent hunters. They could swing an ax and construct houses.

The list of things the survivors didn't know how to do seemed to Susan as infinite as the universe and twice as daunting. Their small achievements like setting up the solar panels and nurturing the farming operation were dwarfed by the looming shortages of everything from salt to replacement parts for their appliances.

Of course, she didn't know that the myopia she so carefully cultivated was blinding her. The airwaves were silent, and the valley was silent, and for a time at least, she convinced herself that her biggest challenge was keeping their small band of survivors alive. But later, when she looked back at those weeks, she thought, *How could I have been so blind?*

TWENTY

H<small>ARR</small> <small>HID BEHIND THE MINIVAN, NEXT TO THE TRUNK OF A</small> massive valley oak, on a patch of shadowed dirt. A warm breeze was already blowing. It came off the water, carrying the sounds of songbirds and the slow-flowing river.

It also carried Kayla's and Davey's voices. They were at the picnic table, thirty feet from his hiding spot. Through the minivan's windows, Harr could see Kayla bending over the Coleman stove, her face twisted into a scowl. "Every time the wind blows, this damn thing goes out," she said irritably, picking up the Aim 'N Flame and reigniting the burner. "What a piece of shit."

Davey didn't even look at her. He was whittling again, flicking white shavings onto the dirt beneath his legs. "Must be a real step down from the trailer you were living in before we found you."

"It wasn't a trailer, you dipshit. It was a double-wide." Kayla slapped the coffeepot onto the burner. "And for your information, my mother *owned* that house, which is a sight more than I can say about that motel your mother lived in."

Davey held up the stick and eyed its sharp point. "Oh, give me a fucking break. Do you really think it matters who owned what? Your mother lived in a house, and she's dead. My mother lived in a residential motel, and she's dead. So as far as I can tell, ownership didn't make a goddamn bit of difference how they wound up."

She filled a pot of water from the Igloo and slipped it on the stove's other burner. "I'm not talking about ownership. I'm talking about what kind of person my mother was. My mother worked hard and bought a home. Your mother, on the other hand—"

Something low and warning sounded in the boy's voice. "You didn't know my mother."

"Looking at you, I can get an idea."

"Oh, that's right, Miss I-try-to-get-Pap-drunk-every-night-so-he-doesn't-hump-me. How's that working out?"

"Fuck off," Kayla said.

From behind the minivan, Harr could see her furious expression as she marched toward the Odyssey's open rear hatch. He waited until she was digging around in the back of the van before he stepped from the shadows and wrapped a hand around her mouth, pulling her back against his body. "Don't say a word," he hissed in her ear.

Harr had to give her credit. She went still as a statue. But she stank to high heaven, and he had to fight the natural impulse to push her away.

"You going to scream?" he whispered.

She shook her head mutely, and when Harr released his hand, she turned on him, her lips puffy from his grip and her green eyes so intense Harr felt as if they'd scorch his face. "You came back," she said in a low voice. "I knew you would, John Harr. I knew you would."

"Shhh." Harr put his face very close to hers, so that his voice was barely audible. "Listen to me. Where are the keys to the minivan?"

181

Her breath smelled like old beans and rotten meat. "Pap has them," she whispered. "He sleeps with them so we don't take the car and run away."

It wasn't the news Harr wanted, but he wasn't surprised. The minivan and its fuel supply were the most valuable items in the camp. Of course, Pap would guard them day and night.

"Can you get the keys without waking him?"

Doubt flickered in her eyes. "I don't know. I could try."

Harr looked over her shoulder at Davey. The teenager stared sullenly off into space, his adolescent body slumped against the picnic table, the sharp pointed stick and buck knife, for the moment, cast on the bench beside him. There was no movement in the orange tent.

Harr made a snap decision. Very quietly, he closed the minivan's rear hatch. "I need you to get the keys from Pap, Kayla. If he wakes, tell him you need something from the minivan, and it's locked."

She looked as if she would argue, but his expression silenced her. "I'll get them," she said.

He watched as she walked back to the campsite. She went straight by the boy, who called after her when he saw where she was going, "Going back for seconds, Kayla?"

She should have told him to fuck off, Harr thought later. That would have been her normal reaction to such a taunt, but Kayla didn't say anything. She just walked, rigid-backed, to the tent and unzipped its door flap with what Harr could have sworn were shaking fingers. A minute later, she emerged, shoving the keys into her jeans pocket as she stood up.

The action was enough to attract Davey's attention. The teenager sat forward with his hands on his knees, watching as she passed. "That was quick. Pap couldn't get it up?"

That caught her up. She stopped and stuck her face in his. "You talk such a big game, you midget-peckered shit, but I know what you really are. You're a bigmouthed, zit-faced coward that no girl would ever want to fuck. But maybe you can get Pap to help you out. Boys like you like that, don't they?"

Harr groaned inwardly. Even from where he stood, behind the minivan, he could see the ugly flush rise above the boy's collar. But Kayla didn't. She was marching to the Odyssey, a hot tinge of red blazing through the dirt on her face.

The boy caught her before she'd covered ten feet, grabbing her hair with both hands and yanking so hard that Kayla collapsed to the ground with an agonized shriek. A second later, Davey's blade flashed in the morning light.

Harr's stomach did a ten-story free fall. He had just blown through plans A and B and was now hurtling toward a nonexistent plan C. He rounded the minivan's hood, drew the shotgun to his shoulder, and shouted, "Let her go!"

For a wild second, Harr wasn't sure what would happen. The boy threw a leg over Kayla and sat down hard on her chest. Kayla screamed obscenities that made even Harr blush. And somewhere in the periphery, a zipper whizzed.

"Let her go!" Harr ordered again.

"This ain't your business, Harr," the kid said, his face twisted with defiance.

They were facing each other—Harr behind his shotgun, the kid with his knife poised above Kayla's neck—in a twisted Mexican standoff.

"It's my business if you're going to hurt her," Harr said.

"Get off me, you stupid dipshit," Kayla snarled beneath him.

Harr wished she'd stop cursing at the kid. Davey's face was red as a lobster, and Harr knew one thing about adolescents: they were unpredictable as hell when provoked.

As it turned out, it wasn't Davey's unpredictability that blew up plan C and sent Harr scrambling for a plan D. It was the weird snap that buzzed beside Harr's ear and the almost instantaneous roar of a gun blast that followed. Across the campsite, a shredded black hole suddenly appeared in the orange tent's side, with Pap's 1911 Mil-Spec barrel protruding from its yawning center.

Harr didn't think twice. He threw himself on the ground as the second blast roared over his head. Somewhere behind him, he heard glass shattering, and then Davey shouting, "Get her, Pap! Get her!"

Pap sure as hell was trying. The bastard blasted a third round as Kayla ran for the minivan and then a fourth as she threw herself through the driver's side door.

For one hopeful second, Harr thought she might get away unharmed, but his hopes abruptly fizzled when a fifth round struck the Odyssey's front end. Kayla let out an agonized scream.

Harr's reaction was instinctive. He fired once, twice, and then a third time, watching as the tent puffed out and then disintegrated in a cloud of shredded polyester and pulverized fiberglass. Only Pap's blood-soaked and dirty socks poked out from the wreckage.

Harr's heart pounded, every nerve in his body wired for more combat, but when he twisted around to check on Kayla, he discovered she'd already left him. He watched in astonishment as the Odyssey tore down the levee road.

His shock only lasted a moment because someone was screaming. With a jolt, Harr realized Davey was coming at him like a missile, the knife held high above his head. Harr rolled just as Davey struck and missed. With a spastic scramble, Harr came to his feet.

"Don't do it, Davey," Harr said. "Put the knife down."

The boy's chin shook with rage. "Look what you've done," he cried. "Why couldn't you just leave things alone?"

Some part of Harr understood how the boy must have felt.

Pap was dead, and Kayla gone. In the space of five minutes, his whole world had changed. "Put it down, Davey," Harr said again. "A knife isn't going to settle this."

"A knife is the only way to settle this," the boy cried and lunged.

Harr barely evaded the blade this time. It sliced through the air, its tip so close to Harr's chest that he felt its tug against his shirt. Harr jumped back and caught his foot. A second later he was on his ass, a lightning bolt of pain shooting from his tailbone up his spine.

He'd tripped on the damned Canadian whiskey bottle.

But this observation was a fleeting one, because Davey was in motion again, and this time Harr knew he was in big trouble. The picnic table blocked his left side. The crazed teenager was coming in fast from his right. Harr scrabbled backward and jumped to a crouch, but the wooden table was too close. He sprawled back against the bench, his arm coming up to protect his face.

But the pain didn't come. All hell broke loose instead. Harr had the vague sense of something gray and black streaking down the levee and launching itself at Davey. The boy grunted and staggered as Seawolf tackled him. Harr watched the bone-handled knife fly through the air.

———

LATER, after Harr had secured Davey's knife and collected Pap's handgun, Harr gave Davey the chance to come with him, but the boy only spat out, "Go fuck yourself."

Harr shrugged and left the pimply-faced teenager at the campsite, the blasted remains of the orange tent and his former protector only twenty feet away from where he sat.

It's his choice, Harr thought as he climbed the dirt trail to the levee road. Harr understood why the kid wouldn't want to pair up with a man who had blown his protector's head off and let Kayla escape with a minivan full of supplies.

But another part of Harr thought it was wrong to leave a fourteen-year-old on his own. The kid had a tent and sleeping bag, a Coleman stove, and the cooking equipment Kayla had left behind when she'd fled, but camping equipment wasn't enough to keep the teenager alive, and Harr knew it. Despite his belief in an individual's right to choose, he couldn't help thinking maybe those rules didn't apply when you were dealing with an adolescent. He kept thinking that maybe he should turn back.

"He's just a dumb kid," he said to Seawolf.

The dog turned somber brown eyes on Harr, and Harr could have sworn the dog was thinking what he himself had to admit was true: even if he forced Davey to come with him, Harr couldn't trust the kid. Too much rage and hatred coursed through the boy's blood. Harr would always be worrying the kid would stick a knife in his back.

But still ... Harr stopped, reached down, and scratched the side of Seawolf's neck. "You take a licking and keep on ticking, don't you, girl? That's twice you've saved me."

The dog panted, her pink tongue poking out between sharp white canines. Harr resumed walking, his boots crunching against the gravel, the sun making his shirt and jeans stick to his skin.

He wondered what happened to Kayla. It was a miracle that Pap's gunfire hadn't hit the jerricans in back of the minivan. Maybe her luck would hold otherwise as well. Maybe she might survive on her own. But he didn't think so as he walked the final twenty minutes to where the Arabian was tied to a tree. The sound of her pained scream still echoed in his head.

TWENTY-ONE

It took Susan nearly two hours to pedal the distance from the farm to Esperanta, and by the time she rolled into the dead town's city limits, the sun was already straight overhead. It burned down, leaching the color from the two-story houses on the town's edge. Further in, a billowing black plume arose. Susan made a beeline for it.

She was furious. There was no use denying it. Emotion raged through her, powering her along the hot pavement, past the empty retention ponds and the broken-windowed minimart.

She found the tire fire easily enough. It burned on Esperanta's main drag, on a concrete pad that had once served as the floor of a massive lumberyard.

Carson was nowhere to be seen. A hot breeze blew, kicking up little puffs of dust on the road's shoulder and sending the tire fire's plume momentarily at a diagonal, so that the sulfuric stench of burning rubber wafted Susan's way. She flinched and pedaled out of its path.

He'd been here. She could tell. A new tire burned on the pile of rubber. Not far away, a hand-painted sign leaned against the concrete remains of a loading bay. It read: *Head North on Highway 24 to Survivor Colony. 18 miles.*

But Carson wasn't here now, nor was his motorcycle.

When he didn't appear after fifteen minutes, she began to look for him, methodically riding up and down Esperanta's grid-like streets, stopping to peer into several small, older houses and a few of the newer two-story mini mansions.

No sign of Carson anywhere.

She pedaled back to the main drag and headed south, past the fire station and the pizza parlor, out to the stucco-sided high school, and the newer, wood-shingled public library. When she reached the dollar store on the town's periphery, she knew Carson wasn't in Esperanta.

For a moment, she stood, straddling her bike, in the small strip of shade beside the dollar store's side wall, looking out away from the town. The great flat plain of orchard and row cropland that had once been America's richest agricultural area stretched before her.

How big it is, she thought with a sharp little pang. She'd never appreciated the vastness of the valley nor the monumental work that had gone into turning the once arid landscape into some of the most productive ag land in the world. At least thirty dams stored water for the valley, including one just above the gap that marked Liberty Valley's southern terminus. More than a thousand miles of canal carried that water to the growers.

And it was all falling apart before her eyes. Already, star thistle grew in a thick tangle between orchard rows. By the end of summer, the parched trees would lose their leaves and die. In a year or two, there'd be nothing but bunch grasses and coyote brush, as nature erased everything that humans had worked so hard to create.

A puff of wind lifted and tumbled an empty plastic bottle halfway across the asphalt before her. Without thinking, Susan leaned her bike against the building and went to pick it up. The label was bleached by the sun but still legible: Diet Coke. No Sugar. No Calories.

How ironic. As if sugar and calories were a bad thing.

She tossed the bottle into the store's overfilled dumpster and went back to her bike.

Carson had lied to Alan. He wasn't scavenging in Esperanta. He probably had never scavenged in Esperanta.

She stared out into the hazy distance for a minute more, then mounted her bike, and rode back to town.

––––––

HARR FOUND Kayla on the levee road, not far from Red's Custom Boatworks and Marina. She was sitting with her back against the driver's side front tire, a tire iron and a jack thrown onto the gravel beside her. Blood dripped from her arm onto her hand.

"No fucking spare," she said disgustedly as Harr climbed down from the saddle. "That bastard thought he was such a goddamn genius, but he didn't carry a goddamn spare."

The Odyssey's back tire was flat. Tattered rubber clung to bare rims. The unmistakable stench of burnt oil filled the air.

"How long did you drive on it?" Harr asked.

"Since he fucking put a bullet in it," she said, jerking her chin toward the mangled minivan's front end. "He got the radiator, too."

She was bleeding pretty bad. Harr squatted before her and eyed the hole in her sleeve. "You're lucky he didn't hit the jerricans."

She let out a bitter laugh. "He's not that good of a shot. Did you kill him? I hope you put a bullet in his head."

Harr didn't respond to that. Instead, he stood up, went to his horse, and returned with a folding knife. "Hold still."

He could feel the heat of her gaze as he took hold of her sleeve and began to gently saw away the shredded material. The wound itself wasn't terrible—he reckoned it was a ricochet and not a direct hit—but she'd lost blood and stank heinously.

"You got a first aid kit?" he asked.

"Not much of one." She was still staring at him with that unblinking, hard-eyed gaze. "Pap wasn't big on the particulars."

He fetched the kit and a cooking pot. From his saddlebag, he took a slim slice of soap and a water filter. He took all of it to the slow, green waters below the levee. Upstream, pontoon boats clinked and creaked in their marina slots. A mid-afternoon breeze ruffled the river's smooth surface. Not far away, the bridge that both he and Kayla, unbeknownst to each other, had been heading for, crossed the waterway like a thin concrete ribbon.

"Did you kill him?" she asked when he returned.

He poured filtered water over her wound, stopping when she let out a gasp. "Pap won't bother you anymore."

"I meant Davey." She gazed at him with flinty eyes.

He didn't answer, and she was shrewd enough to know what that meant. She laughed bitterly. "That was a mistake." She made as if to stand up. "Give me your gun. I'll go finish the piece of shit off."

The hatred in her eyes shook Harr. It was the kind of look that led to nothing good.

Suddenly he understood. Her dirtiness and body odor were a defense. Just as feeding Pap Canadian whiskey had been a defense. He could tell by the bruising on her cheek and the hard, bitter glint in her eyes that her efforts hadn't always succeeded, but she'd tried. He had to give her credit for how hard she'd tried.

He held out his hand. "Come on," he said.

"What do you want?" she asked warily.

"To take you to the river. You need to wash the dirt off your body."

She gazed at him suspiciously. "I ain't taking off my clothes."

"No one said you had to take off your clothes." He pulled her to her feet, led her gently down the levee to the water's edge.

She stepped into the river with wary, uncertain steps, watching him the whole time. Later, when the worst of the dirt and stink were washed from her, she let him dress her wound.

———

SUSAN WASN'T TALKING to him. That became pretty obvious by dinner that night. She stayed in the kitchen with Etta during meal prep, and then when it was time to eat, she placed herself at the far end of the circular table, where she spooned small chunks of catfish onto Emmaline's plate.

It troubled Alan. She'd always sat by him at the kitchen table and in the family room, an unspoken order to which he'd become accustomed. Now, her silent removal struck him as an angry defection.

He didn't speak much during the meal either. Etta and Xiangfa were having a hard time breaking the code and spoke of their frustrations: frequency analysis had yielded nothing, the missives were too short, they thought the code might include homophones.

Alan didn't really understand what they were talking about but nodded his assent when Xiangfa suggested using one of the computers. "I have rudimentary coding skills. I could throw together a program," the old researcher said. He didn't need the Internet.

Of course, all of this coding and code breaking would take up time, and Alan didn't like that. There were beans to be planted and tomatoes to be canned. They were still hoping to attract more survivors.

He gazed at Susan. She was watching Etta and Xiangfa with somber eyes. Even with the scar on her face, she was pretty. Even prettier than when he'd met her in Los Angeles months earlier at a University of Southern California faculty party, because then she'd only been an attractive woman in a city full of attractive women. He hadn't known her personally.

Which was perhaps the crux of the matter, he decided. Because beauty, at least for him, was more than high cheekbones and smooth skin. It was underpinned by character, the heart and soul upon which the physical trappings of attractiveness lay.

He heard her say to Xiangfa, "If you haven't heard any more transmissions, then perhaps we should limit code breaking to evenings. I could use more help in the fields while the tomatoes are ripe."

She was respectful and direct when she made suggestions. She listened to input.

But she had blind spots, and in Alan's eyes, these were significant. She didn't understand the imperative of maintaining unity at all costs. She'd never lived by the law of the jungle.

He had. He'd been forged in the crucible of business, the son of a brutal, ruthless father, the scion to a vast petroleum empire.

Her voice pierced his thoughts. She was talking about drying tomatoes in the sun. She was telling Adrienne and Xiangfa that they needed to salt the red vegetables and to keep the dust and flies off.

He wished she'd look at him. He wanted her eyes on his, to

reestablish the quiet bond that had been the hallmark of their relationship since he'd saved her from the man who'd tried to steal her car in Saugus.

But she didn't meet his eyes. She finished dinner, helped clean up, and did her usual nighttime ritual of bathing Emmaline and getting her to bed. He waited for her to finish and return to sit by him in the family room, but she didn't. She popped her head through the kitchen door and said she wanted to go to bed early.

She doesn't understand that Carson controls Sam and Reaper, he thought. *She doesn't understand that Carson has a powerful faction of his own.*

He sat in his recliner and tried to read, but his mind wouldn't focus. He kept thinking of the fragile bridge that linked them all, that none had known each other before the pandemic, that they wouldn't have selected each other as friends or colleagues even if they had. But now they were forced together, and the tenuous stake the nine of them had placed in the ground needed to be guarded, even if it meant compromise, even if it meant occasionally overlooking certain transgressions.

But she didn't seem to see the necessity. She fixated on small matters of character instead, which, in the grand scheme of things, were utterly laughable if it meant they'd die.

A wave of frustration washed through him. He wanted to shake her, to break the quiet wall she'd put up between them.

After a few minutes, he finally gave up the pretense of reading. He put his book down, rose from his chair, and, against his better judgment, went to talk with her.

———

SHE WASN'T EXPECTING HIM. That was for sure. When he knocked on her bedroom door, she opened it only a few inches. "What are you doing here?" she asked, frowning.

Behind her bare shoulders, he could see the softly illuminated sheets and the open-faced, upside-down book on her nightstand. The quiet snoring of a sleeping toddler floated out into the hallway.

"I want to talk to you," he said quietly.

For a second, she didn't respond, and then she said wearily, "Wait a minute," and closed the door in his face. A moment later, she emerged, wrapped in a dark blue Japanese print robe.

He blinked. In the dim hallway light, the red flowers along the robe's hem glowed almost like flames. "Where did you get that?" he asked.

It took her a second to understand. She held her arms out and looked down at the indigo silk. "It was my mother's. A gift from a Japanese farming family who'd come to visit. She never wore it because I think she thought it was either too geisha or too fancy."

"It's nice," Alan said. "Unexpected."

She let out a little laugh. "To be honest, I feel ridiculous wearing such a luxurious robe in our present circumstances."

"Don't. It looks good on you."

It was true. The radiant silk hung in elegant folds from her slender body, but he wasn't there to talk about her clothing. He was there to talk sense into her.

"Come on," he said abruptly, taking her hand and dragging her down the hallway and out the front door. He pulled her to the furthest corner of the wraparound porch from the family room, to a patch of darkness invisible from any of the rooms.

It wasn't completely pitch-black where they stood. The full moon hung in the sky above, spilling silver light across her hair and casting half her face in shadow. Even with her features obscured, he could read the bafflement in her expression.

"We're making progress," he blurted out.

She frowned. "You dragged me out here to tell me that?"

He positioned himself before her. "Yes. It's important. We've reestablished electricity for two houses. We've got clean water, food, and a functioning leadership structure. We've also got a program to bring new people in, and we've already brought in a new person. We have an inventory system for food, medicines, and fuel."

She folded her arms across her chest, perplexity creasing her brow. "Okay, that's great, but why is it so important to pull me out of bed to tell me this?"

"I'm not through yet. We're actively irrigating and growing crops. We're making plans for further crops. We've got a division of labor that's working."

"Right, but why are we having this conversation outside in the darkness again?"

"Because I'm trying to tell you something important." He resisted the urge to grab her by the arms, to shake her into understanding. "None of this progress would have happened if we hadn't worked together as a group."

Understanding dawned in her eyes. "That's why you brought me out here?" she asked quietly. "To bash me over the head about Carson again?"

"I'm not bashing you. I'm telling you that, for better or worse, we need Carson right now. I'm not going to lecture you on tribal dynamics, but you need to recognize that we *are* a tribe right now and we need to get along." He paused. "*We* need to get along."

There, he thought. *I've said it.* He'd lost everything—his wife and son, the company which bore his name. He couldn't bear the thought of losing Susan as well. Her opinion mattered to him. Her goodness and loyalty mattered even more.

He stood there for a silent moment, waiting for her to annihilate him, to turn her shoulder on him and walk away. But she didn't. She took a step toward him and slipped into his arms.

He held her to him quietly, aware of the fragility of his body and hers, of the tenuousness of everything.

He did not want to fight with her again.

TWENTY-TWO

THE ARABIAN WAS NERVOUS, AND A FEW TIMES WHILE they floated on the river, Harr worried that the horse would rear up and trample them all. "Shhh, Luna, shhhh," he said, stroking her frightened face.

The horse barely fit in the aisle of the leisure craft, but in some ways, Harr thought the confined quarters were helpful. He was close to her and could reassure her with his words and hands. The canopy discouraged her from rearing.

"I've seen a lot of crazy things in my life, but this takes the cake," Kayla said from the front of the boat. She sat in the curved corner of the backward-facing upholstered seating. Seawolf sat at attention on the deck next to her.

Harr gave her a half smile, because, in truth, he agreed. He was a horse man, and he knew he was crazy to do what he was doing: floating down one of the delta's nameless river channels on someone's former cocktail cruiser, with a horse crammed in the middle, and the motor burring and straining against the load.

Fortunately, the water was flat. Harr was pretty sure that was the only reason they hadn't capsized. The boat was poorly

197

balanced and probably over the limit weight-wise. One good gust of wind would tip her over.

But Harr wasn't sure how he'd make his rendezvous with Hondo in any other fashion. He'd tried to find a vehicle to drive the distance between the destroyed minivan and Rio Vista, but all he'd found in the remote stretch of river was an old Honda motorbike and the rusted-out shell of a pickup truck. So he'd opted to plunder Red's Custom Boatworks and Marina instead, which was pretty damned funny because he didn't know how to pilot a pontoon boat or how long Pap's ten gallons of gas would last, much less how to keep the whole thing from sinking if weather conditions suddenly changed.

"Where are we?" Kayla asked. She was looking at the barren, gravel rise of the levee on one side and the chain of reed-enshrouded islands on the other.

"On one of the feeder sloughs to the San Joaquin River," Harr said, but he wasn't certain. His map was designed for roads, and he'd learned in the previous two days that the delta had few roads significant enough to be on a map that covered all of Northern California. Hence, his sense of his location within the twisted network of sloughs and rivers was vague at best.

She seemed to intuit his lack of knowledge. "You're certain you know where you're going?"

"I'm certain that's Mount Diablo," he said, pointing at the distant peak that marked the convergence of the Sacramento and San Joaquin rivers and the beginning of the Bay Area. "Beyond that is where the delta dumps into the bay."

She gazed at the thick pall of black smoke that partially obscured the broad, spreading slopes of the mountain. A shadow crossed her face. "That's where the refineries are burning. Pap took us there."

He steered the boat in a gentle, mid-channel turn, between the levee and an island. "Well, I'm not taking you there. We're backtracking up the Sacramento River to a town called Rio Vista. I told Hondo we'd be there by noon."

She didn't say anything, but rather looked off the front of the boat at something in the distance. She'd been quiet since he'd dressed her arm. It was as if all the anger and the profanities had been washed from her along with the dirt. Sometimes he caught her gazing at him.

But he didn't spend much time gazing back at her. He was peering at the levees and patchwork islands, marveling at the engineering that had turned this once boggy swath of wild river and wetlands into some of California's most fertile farmland.

"What's in Rio Vista?" Kayla asked. She had her injured arm pulled to her side and her feet curled up beneath her on the seat.

"Hondo, if we're lucky."

"Then what?"

"We go to Liberty Valley. There's a farm there with a few people." He glanced from the river to her face. "There's a doctor there who can look after your arm."

She digested that without outward emotion. "What kind of farm?"

"A tree farm. There are a couple of older people there, and a lady doc and a little kid."

He was aware that the farm and the people there didn't sound particularly promising, but Kayla surprised him. She asked, "How old is the lady doc?"

Harr frowned. "I don't know. Thirty, maybe."

"Thirty?" She looked straight at him. "How old are you?"

"Thirty-three."

The shuttered expression returned to her face. "Is she your girlfriend?"

"No, I hardly know her."

"But you're going back to her."

Harr gave her a look. "I'm going back to all of them. They're the only people I know that are still alive."

That shut her up, as he had meant it to. She turned her face so that he could only see her red, clumped hair. She didn't say another word for the next hour.

Which was just as well, because a strange late morning wind had blown up, bad enough to cause small whitecaps on the water. He lifted his binoculars and searched the broad expanse of river ahead for the bypass channel that connected the San Joaquin with the Sacramento River. If he missed it, they'd have to float outward to Suisun Bay where the two massive rivers converged, and then there'd be no chance the weighed-down pontoon boat could fight the current to get back upstream to Rio Vista. In short, they'd be screwed.

Fortunately, he found the bypass channel, or at least, he thought he did. The river was so broad at this point that it reminded him of the Mississippi. He throttled up and gritted his teeth as a gust of wind sent the boat teetering sideways.

"Sit over there, Kayla," he called urgently. He needed more weight on the boat's windward side. He reached out a calming hand to the horse's neck. "Luna, girl, it's all right."

But it wasn't all right, and Harr knew it. The horse blocked the aisle, forcing Kayla to climb over the seats to get into position. Fresh red blood soaked through the gauze on her arm.

But there was no time for Harr to dwell on her wound. The boat was listing precariously, each gust snapping at the canopy and sending the leisure craft shuddering toward catastrophe. Luna, so far as Harr could tell, was half out of her mind with fear.

In desperation, Harr turned the wheel and pushed to full throttle. The boat groaned, and water whipped into Harr's face.

He was facing straight upstream, so that the pontoon's tail faced the gusts, but the gains against the wind did nothing to get them closer to the bypass channel. Even at full throttle, the pontoon boat couldn't fight the current straight on.

Which meant they had to go downstream again. Harr cut a steeper ferry angle this time, trying to protect the boat's vulnerable flanks from the wind, but the pontoon boat's engine power wasn't enough. The river boat sailed pass the bypass channel and came to a precarious rest against the levee a quarter mile downstream. Luna let out a terrified whinny.

Kayla stared at Harr with wide eyes. "What now?"

"We get out and walk," Harr said. He gripped the throttle, keeping the pontoon's nose to the bank, but the current was stronger than he anticipated, and the boat pulled badly. "Can you get back up to the gate?"

She let out a pained *mmph* as she climbed back over the seats and unhooked the gate at the boat's bow. Seawolf immediately shot through the opening and leaped for solid ground.

"Throw that pack onto the levee and then follow it, Kayla," Harr urged. "Take the mooring line with you and tie it to that tree."

He could see the doubt in her eyes. The tree was little more than a shrub and was the only live vegetation on the otherwise barren incline. But she did as she was told, heaving the pack of supplies they'd salvaged from the minivan onto the rocky slope and then stepping painfully from the boat, dragging the mooring line with her.

"Wrap it around the trunk," Harr shouted to her. "Now tie it!"

Her head disappeared into greenery. A minute later, it reappeared, and she gave him a thumbs-up. Harr cut the engine.

"Now it's your turn," Harr whispered beside Luna's ear. He tugged at the Arabian's lead line, trying to get her to advance, but the horse wouldn't budge. Cursing, Harr climbed over the steering panel to the seating area at the front of the boat and tried to coax the frightened animal by her halter.

When he saw the bow, Harr suddenly understood why the horse wouldn't move. The current had dragged the drifting boat downstream, and now a foot-wide strip of flowing water separated the bow from the levee. If he were a horse, he wouldn't jump either.

So he grabbed the mooring line and hauled the boat so that its bow rested again against the levee, but the river was strong, and the hydraulic force tore at his shoulders and arms. "Kayla, take Luna's lead line!" he grunted. "Be ready to get out of her way when she jumps."

Kayla's face was as pale as a ghost's. A clotted strand of red hair whipped against her cheek.

"Come on, Kayla," Harr urged. "Pull on the lead line. You can do it."

Kayla grasped the thick rope, staring up into the horse's face as though she were looking at the devil.

Just then, the mooring line jerked. For a vertiginous second, Harr felt the boat drift and then catch.

"*Now, Kayla!*" he shouted.

Kayla pulled, and all hell broke loose. The horse bounded forward, and Kayla's head disappeared beneath panicked gray horseflesh. Seawolf, low against the ground like a cattle dog, dodged out of the way and then charged up the levee, chasing Luna as she bolted away.

For a horrible moment, Harr thought the horse had killed Kayla. She lay on the gravel incline in a heap, but after a moment, the young women stirred and pushed herself to sitting. She gazed down at Harr dazedly.

And then the mooring line gave.

Or more precisely, the tree to which it was tied gave. A loud cracking sounded, followed by a blur of branches and roots as the pontoon boat dragged the tree like a Scottish outlaw, first down the levee and then into the river.

"*John!*" Kayla cried. For a second, he just stared at her as she went to all fours and then scrambled unsteadily to her feet.

He had the sense of wind and water and the widening gap between the pontoon boat and the levee. Without power and rudderless, the boat floated as the current wanted it to, backward and toward the central channel, ineluctably downstream to the vast Suisun Bay.

Harr took one look downstream, toward the black smoke of the refinery fires, and then upstream at Kayla, who was frantically waving at him from the shore. Without another moment's hesitation, he tossed his hat onto the boat's floor and dove into the white-capped water.

———

LIBERTY VALLEY'S newest arrival showed up mid-afternoon, when the heat was at its most oppressive and even the most stalwart of birds had given up their song. She came via a dusty blue golf cart, which she piloted to a stop in front of the Victorian.

"Who is that?" Adrienne asked, looking up from the drying screen on which she was carefully lining tomato halves.

"No idea," Susan replied. She closed the screen over her own drying rack, wiped her hands on her jeans, and walked from the patio to greet the newcomer.

The woman, a cheerful-looking blonde in her mid-thirties, slipped from the white leather seat and landed on a pair of sandal-clad feet. "Well, hello there!" she called. "I was wondering where you were. Jim said, 'Up the valley,' but he didn't say you were off the highway. I had to drive around quite a bit looking for you. I was about to give up."

Susan felt as if she were looking at an illusion. The woman's blonde hair fell in a smooth cascade to her shoulders, and a thick coat of coral lipstick covered smiling lips. To Susan's amazement, the cosmetics didn't end there. Once the newcomer doffed her sunglasses, eyes with vivid blue shadow stared back at them.

"I'm Deborah." The woman stuck out her hand. "But everyone calls me Deb. Or at least they used to before this whole shit show started. That's quite a house!"

She gazed for a moment at the Victorian, before turning her smiling glance back to the women in front of her. "And you must be Susan and Adrienne. Oh, don't look so surprised. Jim told me about you."

Susan couldn't help herself. She shot a stupefied glance at Adrienne. The other woman stared at the newcomer, stone-faced.

"You met Jim?" Susan asked.

"Oh, sure, he came cruising by on that Harley yesterday. I could feel the vibrations all the way down in the bunker."

Susan didn't even know where to start. The woman seemed to be absurdly high-spirited and chatty. "You live in a bunker?" she asked.

Deb nodded. "It's my little underground chateau. Henry had it built in case of nuclear war or a zombie apocalypse. Little did he know what we were really in for!"

"Who's Henry?"

Her eyes took on a warm glow. "My dear departed husband. We met at the hair salon where I worked. He used to come in every month for a sixty-buck haircut. That's how I knew it was true love." She laughed affectionately. "You going to invite me in?"

Susan shot another glance at Adrienne. She could tell the other woman thought the same thing she did: in the post-pandemic world, how could this woman be so relentlessly upbeat?

We don't have a whole lot of choice in who joins us...

With a sigh, Susan said, "Yeah, come in. Let's get something cold to drink."

TWENTY-THREE

Harr and Kayla didn't make it to the Rio Vista Bridge until the last sliver of sun sank below the western horizon and the sky turned a deep purple-peach. Neither spoke because they were too tired. They'd hiked nearly eight miles.

Harr was cursing himself. He'd lost his horse, dog, and two guns which had been secured in scabbards on the horse's saddle. For a cowboy, that was the ultimate trifecta of humiliation.

He'd also lost his hat. It was now floating somewhere down Suisun Bay in an unmanned pontoon boat.

Of all the stupid goddamned ideas, he thought disgustedly. *To put a horse on a pontoon boat.* He couldn't believe he'd done it. He was lucky he hadn't gotten Kayla killed.

She was clearly sagging. The walking and the heat and the blood loss had taken their toll. She trudged silently, her freckled face devoid of expression, her feet scuffing along the asphalt road.

"We're here," Harr said gently.

She looked dully at the wide, dark waters of the Sacramento River. They stood on the river's edge, on the concrete approach to the half-mile-long steel drawbridge that connected delta farmland to the small town of Rio Vista on the river's other bank.

"He's not here, is he?" she asked. Harr could see her disappointment, feel her crushing exhaustion.

Harr scanned the other bank, looking for light or some other sign of life. The riverside town was dark and silent.

"Maybe we'll bed down on this side," Harr said by way of answer. He was looking at the fields around him, at the vineyards that were closest to the river and the darkening alfalfa land further out. They had one sleeping bag between them, stuffed in the pack of supplies they'd scavenged from the minivan. It'd be better to cross the river and try to find an empty house in which they could sleep, but he didn't think she had it in her to walk another half mile.

"Come on," he said finally. He led her from the road to the only nearby structure, a red barnlike produce stand set back from the road by a large gravel parking lot. White painted letters on the building's side glowed faintly in the fading light.

Delta Farmer's Market. Serving You Since 1997.

The building was already beginning to decay. The windows were broken and the interior dark and forlorn. Not a single car stood in the parking lot.

Using his flashlight, Harr guided Kayla inside to a section of flooring not covered by broken glass or trash. She sank down, her back propped against the wall, watching as Harr fished inside the pack for the sleeping bag.

"We aren't that late," she asked. "Why did Hondo leave without us?"

Harr didn't know. He'd told Hondo they'd rendezvous at noon, and it was past eight now, which meant they were only eight hours late. Worry, deep-seated and unspoken, ate at him.

He handed her the bag. "It'll get cold tonight. The delta breezes bring in ocean air. You'd best curl up."

She didn't argue. She pulled the bag around her torso and sat against the wall, watching dully as he ran the flashlight over the store's empty display tables. There was nothing left, just rolls of plastic produce bags and empty boxes. He broke two of the latter down and brought them back to her.

"Slide this under you," he said, handing her a flattened box. "It'll give you some padding against the concrete."

She did as she was told, and he put his own flattened box next to hers and sat atop it. It didn't take long before her breath came soft and regular in the dim light.

He snapped off the flashlight. He wasn't sure how long the batteries would last, and he wasn't afraid of the dark anyway.

But as he sat there, listening to the rattle and groan of the building as the evening delta breezes cooled the rafters, a chill began to sink into his bones. He crossed his arms, closed his eyes, and tried to make his brain stop thinking.

But his brain wouldn't settle. He kept thinking of the hanging corpses in Shangri-La, and the twisted piles of limbs and torsos outside of Fresno. And then his mind would skitter to the blue-lipped, ice-cold face of the praying woman as she lay dead on the bank.

Carlos will hunt us down until there is no more of us left.

He shivered. When Kayla, asleep and murmuring, snuggled up next to him, he didn't push her away.

———

A LITTLE AFTER NINE P.M., the code started up again. When Etta heard it, she yelled for Xiangfa to come. Together, the old woman and the researcher listened to the back-and-forth tones while the tape recorder whirred.

Thirty minutes later, Xiangfa said, "Etta double-checked me. We believe this is an accurate transcription."

He sat at the cherrywood kitchen table with Etta, Alan, and Susan. He'd just slid the evening's enciphered messages to Alan.

To Alan, the handwritten letter blocks looked like a lengthy word search. They were arranged in three separate strings with no spaces to indicate where a word began or ended. Alan could see no pattern in any of it.

"You think these are three separate parties speaking?" he asked.

"Yes," Etta said. "It's a shorter transmission tonight. Like they're checking in or reporting something."

Foreboding struck him. The code was the first radio traffic they'd heard in more than a week, and though he'd argued earlier that the silence on the airwaves had been a temporary pause due to atmospheric conditions or some other benign cause, he'd recently begun to share Susan's unease.

"I think we're dealing with a Vigenère cipher," Etta was saying. She held a pencil in her hand, which she tapped rhythmically against a stack of papers. "The Vigenère cipher is a sixteenth-century polyalphabetic cipher that uses a word key. It's difficult to crack if you don't have much text to analyze."

Alan glanced over at Susan, who was sitting back with her arms crossed over her chest, a look of confusion on her face. "I don't understand," she said.

"Up until tonight, we haven't transcribed enough of the transmission to find patterns." Etta pointed her pencil at the transcription in front of Alan. "But tonight's transmission helps tremendously."

Alan looked down at the sheet. "I don't see any patterns."

"They're there." She spread out the stack of papers in front of her and Xiangfa. Alan realized they were transcriptions from previous transmissions. She swung the latest transcription so that it was aligned with the others. "This is a pattern." She underlined the letters ZJK in three different blocks of letter strings.

"That's a pattern?" Alan asked. In four dense pages of letters, there were only three ZJKs.

"It could be," Xiangfa agreed. "While it's definitely possible that the repeated appearance of ZJK is purely coincidence, the odds are against it." He looked at Etta. "It's far more likely that ZJK represents a word or letter cluster."

"Like THE or AND," Etta suggested. "Those are the two most common three-letter combinations in the English language."

"So you're saying that ZJK is either THE or AND?"

"Possibly," Xiangfa said.

Something didn't add up for Alan. "But if ZJK stands for THE or AND, why don't we see ZJK more commonly in the messages? THE and AND should appear more than three times in that many transmissions."

"You're right," Xiangfa agreed. "Which is what leads us to think this cipher is a polyalphabetic cipher. A polyalphabetic cipher uses more than one alphabet to encrypt a message. In other words, in some places THE will be represented by ZJK, but in other places, where a different cipher alphabet is used, different letters will represent THE. That's what makes the Vigenère cipher so difficult to crack."

Susan leaned forward, frowning. "Will you be able to crack it?"

Xiangfa gave a little shrug. "Cracking a good cipher is like scaling a rock wall. The granite may be smooth and seem impossible to climb, but there are handholds there. You just need to find them." He tapped his finger against one of the underlined ZJKs. "That may be our first handhold."

Etta nodded in agreement.

TWENTY-FOUR

DEB'S BUNKER WAS AT THE END OF COUNTY ROAD 96, NOT far from the gravel mine that had funded the subterranean concrete structure.

"Gravel was Henry's business," Deb said with a little shrug as she drew the golf cart to a halt on the long driveway. "Liberty River has some of the best gravel around. Henry made a good living selling it to all those construction guys."

Susan gazed from the end of the road to the wide, dusty riverbed beyond. Along this part of the river, no water flowed in its gravelly channel, as a consequence of the upstream dam near Liberty Valley's southern entrance. Rather, the river water was collected at the dam and diverted into an irrigation canal, which meandered south through the gap and out to serve vineyards and olive orchards on the Central Valley's eastern flanks. The original river channel, dry for decades, now served mainly as a source of gravel for highway and city road construction.

Or it had. Now, a lone dump truck stood in the gravel yard, and the conveyors lay idle. Only a quiet wind blew, hot and dry, kicking up little puffs of dust from tall gravel mountains.

"Come on," Deb said with a smile. "Come see my little chateau."

From the outside, the bunker wasn't impressive. Only a horizontal steel door, a foot above the ground, marked the bunker's entrance, but once Susan descended the cool, underground staircase, she quickly realized Henry had invested big money in his subterranean structure. Manufactured wood flooring and stainless-steel appliances gave the bunker a sophisticated, modern look. There was even a leather couch, placed opposite a flat-screen TV. In all, it seemed rather like an apartment, only without windows or a front door.

"This place is nice," Susan said.

"If you don't like the sun and want to live like a mole for the rest of your life. I've been down here for two and a half months. I've had enough."

Susan picked up a DVD from the entertainment console. It was *The Proposal*, featuring Sandra Bullock in a black pencil skirt and stilettos, thrusting an engagement ring into Ryan Reynolds's terrified face.

Deb came up next to her. "I've watched that one fifty times. I don't know why I do it, because all it does is remind me of what used to be. Unfortunately, Henry wasn't much of a reader, so he didn't leave me any books to speak of."

"We've got books," Susan said. It was true. The Victorian was filled with books. Her parents had been voracious readers.

Susan picked up the framed photo next to the DVDs. It was of a boy in a baseball uniform, holding his bat as though he were about to swing at the photographer. Deb ran a gentle finger over his face. "That's Hugo, my son. He was ten."

For the first time, Susan saw a crack in the woman's deliberate cheeriness. Deb gently took the frame from Susan's hands and placed it back on the console. "Henry insisted we take to the shelter as soon as the plague showed up in Sacramento, but of course, it was too late by then. Hugo was already infected, and he brought the disease down into the shelter with him. It wasn't long before Henry was infected. And then I was nursing them both." She shrugged, gazing off into an invisible nowhere. "They died within twelve hours of each other."

"I'm sorry," Susan said. She wished she could say something better than that, something more adequate, but she knew there were no words that touched the grief all of them shared.

Deb put a manicured finger to the corner of her eye, dabbed a tear away. "It's our shared legacy, isn't it? It's our burden to bear. Come on." She gestured Susan to a doorway. "You said you wanted to see my supplies. Well, have a look."

Susan nearly gasped. The supply room was as big as the living area. On one wall, a variety of lethal-looking guns hung from hooks. Along the other, cabinetry was marked with labels: Freeze-Dried, Cans, Medical, Cleaning and PPE, Fire Extinguisher, Ammo.

Deb let out a sad little laugh. "Henry was ready for the zombie apocalypse, but none of this stuff saved him."

"But it saved you." Susan pulled open the cabinet marked Freeze-Dried. Inside, hundreds of Mylar packages were organized in color-coded plastic bins.

"The mac and cheese isn't bad, but the stroganoff is—" Deb stuck a finger down her throat.

Susan pulled a package labeled Heartland's Finest Powdered Milk from a blue bin. "You have milk," Susan said in wonder.

"If you can call it that. I never liked powdered milk, but it might be good for the little one."

Any doubts Susan might have had about Deb instantly evaporated. "Really?"

"Honey, I've been living underground alone for two and half months. Believe me, I may have food and supplies, but what good are food and supplies if you're all by yourself?" She swung a dismissive hand at the storage room. "Take it all. Just take me with it. That's all I ask."

Susan eyed the recessed lighting in the bunker and the sleek wooden dining table. Silk hydrangeas in a square vase added a pop of vivid blue to the otherwise neutral-colored room.

"We're not as fancy as all this or as well-equipped." Susan figured she should be direct with Deb. "We have power for two houses, and ours is full. So that means you either move in with Carson or Adrienne, and currently Adrienne doesn't have power, so you'll probably want to move in with Carson."

Deb smiled. "I don't know. I did fine at Adrienne's last night. And besides, I'm assuming your husband will come here and transfer the solar panels and generator to Adrienne's house. There's no sense in leaving all this equipment behind."

For a second, Susan just blinked, not following. And then she understood Deb's mistake. She laughed. "Alan isn't my husband. We met on the road."

Deb's mouth rounded. "Oh! Sorry, of course. I just assumed because ..." She stopped and then waved a hand. "Anyway, it doesn't matter. You can have anything you want here. The generator is diesel, and the batteries for the solar panels are lithium."

Susan followed Deb to the generator room, the section of the underground structure where the bunker's energy equipment was stored. The only sound was the whoosh of the air circulator. "I don't know how we'll get this stuff out of here."

It was true. The equipment was meticulously installed in the small room but looked too big to carry out the bunker's narrow stairway or through the shoulder-width-wide, vertically oriented, galvanized corrugated pipe that served as the structure's secondary escape route.

Deb gazed down at the battery with a frown. "You can

214

probably disassemble the generator, at least a little, but the battery—I don't know the first thing about those things. Why would they build the generator room like this? It makes it near impossible to replace equipment if it breaks down or needs an upgrade."

Susan had no idea. That was the thing about the pandemic. You couldn't pick up a phone and ask why something was the way it was. Nor could you search for answers on the Internet. You only had your brain, and an owner's manual if you could find one. Susan felt a vast world of knowledge was disappearing before her eyes.

"How long does it take to charge the golf cart?" Susan asked.

Deb gazed at her glitzy, rhinestone-encrusted watch. "Oh, I don't know. Another two hours if we hope to get enough charge to get back to your farm. Why?"

Susan felt almost shy. "I was wondering if you would cut my hair."

Deb's eyes widened with delight. "Honey, I'd love to cut your hair. I thought you'd never ask!"

———

TWO HOURS LATER, Susan emerged with trimmed and blow-dried curls.

"Honey, you look great!" Deb gushed from the golf cart's driver's seat, running approving eyes over Susan's hair and face. "I wish you would have let me put on some makeup, though. You're such a pretty girl. You might as well play it up."

A flush crept up Susan's neck. It was one thing to indulge in the luxury of a haircut and blow-dry while they waited for the golf cart to charge, but it was another thing to show up at the Victorian looking like she was heading to a wedding. It felt wrong to focus on superficial matters when there were far more pressing tasks, like transporting the bunker's freeze-dried meals and medical supplies back to Liberty Valley.

Such guilty feelings hadn't stopped Deb, though. Her face bore enough paint to walk the runway. "Keeping yourself up is good for the spirit," she insisted as she turned the cart on. She sent the cart in a wide circle past the gravel pit's storage building and conveyors. "And we're going to need all the good spirits we can get if we're going to make it through all this."

They passed the solar array that powered the underground bunker, and the trailer that once housed the gravel pit's work office. In front of them, a field of stunted, brown sunflowers separated the riverbed from the highway.

Susan suddenly blinked and did a double take. There was no house or barn on the property, and the bunker itself was underground, its access hatch hidden behind the gravel pit's office trailer. "Did you say you met Carson out here?"

"Sure. He drove by on that Harley. I told you. I felt the vibrations underground."

Susan thought it strange that a concrete bunker would transmit the vibrations of a motorcycle, but gazing at Deb's guileless face, she had no reason to disbelieve her. No, what really bothered Susan was the fact that Carson was driving down a dead-end road like Road 96 in the first place.

"Did he find you or did you find him?" Susan asked.

"I found him. Like I said, it's been pretty lonely down there in Chateau Survival, and when I felt the vibrations, it didn't matter if it was Sasquatch or Godzilla making that ruckus. Either way I was coming up to say hi."

Deb turned the golf cart onto the highway and accelerated to a whopping twenty-five miles per hour.

"What was he doing when you found him?" Susan asked.

"Looking in the shop. It took me a few minutes to get up the stairs and push the darned hatch open. It's a nuclear blast hatch. It doesn't swing open like a regular door."

Susan didn't want to get derailed by bunker building materials. "What was he doing in the shop?"

"Just looking around. He was very nice when I walked in on him. I think I scared him half to death."

Susan frowned. Carson was supposed to be looking for food. "What's in the shop?"

Deb lifted her shoulders in a disinterested shrug. "Tools and equipment. Henry didn't have the biggest gravel operation, but there's still a lot of machinery involved in gravel mining."

"There's no food in there?"

Deb laughed. "God, no. Unless you want to eat a welder or a drill press."

"What was he looking for then?"

Deb smoothly avoided an abandoned truck on the roadside. "Maybe he was just looking around. I mean, I told him he could have anything he wanted, but he didn't take anything. He just told me to take the golf cart up the highway and I'd find you easily enough."

Susan had a hard time fathoming Carson's actions. Not only was finding another survivor a big deal, but Deb had both food and medications, supplies that Carson was specifically charged with finding. She couldn't understand why he'd just leave her and her supplies behind. "Did he say where he was going?"

"Yeah. He said he needed to go to Woodland, and that he'd see me later when he came back to the valley."

Woodland. For a second, Susan didn't say anything. She had no idea why Carson would go to a city when there were closer farms and country subdivisions where he could scavenge. "Did he say what he was doing there?"

"I didn't ask. I figured he was looking for someone or something, and it wasn't my business." She brought the golf cart through the narrow gap that marked the entrance to Liberty Valley. A hand-painted sign stood at the roadside: *Survival Colony 15 Miles Ahead.*

Susan gazed at the orchards in varying throes of death on either side of the country highway, thinking. It was possible that Carson was indeed scavenging for food in Woodland. After all, a city with sixty thousand people was bound to have several supermarkets and plenty of houses to search. But the distance from Liberty Valley to the city was close to thirty miles. She couldn't believe he'd already scavenged at all the farms and country subdivisions closer in.

Deb was talking about cutting hair, how she could help Liberty Valley's residents improve their spirits with good grooming. She thought Alan would especially benefit.

Susan was only half listening. Her mind was ticking off all the other businesses that existed in Woodland: a hospital, multiple pharmacies, gas stations, fertilizer storage facilities, and the massive distribution centers that lined the important north-south interstate on the city's eastern flank. What was in those distribution centers?

It had been so long since she'd been to Woodland she couldn't remember.

TWENTY-FIVE

Harr and Kayla crossed the Rio Vista drawbridge just as the last pink in the sky faded to a brilliant baby blue. Despite the rough sleeping situation, Kayla looked marginally better. Harr wondered how much time she had before infection set in.

Only seventy more miles, he told himself. If he could find a car and gas, he could get to Liberty Valley in a single day.

And then Susan could tend to Kayla's wound and stop the infection before it killed her.

If Susan is still alive. He pushed the thought and its attendant worry away.

"What's the plan now?" Kayla asked. She was gazing at him with those intense green eyes again, not smiling, her freckled face still puffy from sleeping on the ground.

"Scavenging. You need food," he said, eyeing the distant riverbank and the vast field of wind turbines beyond. They were still mid-bridge, atop the two-lane span, which, in previous times, rose and lowered to allow marine traffic to pass on the Sacramento River underneath. Now the segment was choked with abandoned cars, and he and Kayla were forced to walk along the steel pedestrian pathway on the bridge's outer edge. The Sacramento River, blue green and opaque, swirled beneath them.

"I meant, are we still going to that farm?"

He didn't look at her. "You need a doctor, Kayla."

"I don't need a doctor. The bullet barely grazed me. You said yourself it was a ricochet."

"You still need a doctor."

She took a quick step ahead and turned back to face him. "Forget the doctor. Let's find another van and keep traveling. I'll take good care of you, John. I promise."

He understood the plea in her eyes. She'd been abused, and he wasn't an abuser. She trusted him with her life. He said gently, "There's nothing to be afraid of at the farm. They're nice people. They'll take good care of you."

Harr hated to see the sheen of tears in her eyes. Her voice wobbled as she said, "I don't need anyone to take care of me but you."

She turned and walked ahead of him, the shadows of the steel girders rippling across her body as she walked beneath the drawbridge towers. He watched her for a moment, not sure if he should give chase or let her stew. In the distance, the sparse foliage and motels of Rio Vista came into view.

They'd have a hard time finding a car with gas in such a small town.

"Hold up, Kayla," he called out, but she didn't listen. She marched onward, stiffly clutching her injured arm by the elbow.

Harr let out a weary sigh and dropped the pack. He'd only just now spotted a lone figure standing on the far bank, just north of the bridge, beneath the tall green canopy of a cottonwood tree. Or at least he thought he saw a figure.

Harr pulled out his binoculars and focused.

Beside the figure, a group of animals grazed in an open lot.

Suddenly something dark and low to the ground separated from the bunch and streaked toward the bridge's western approach. For a moment, Harr just watched as the black blur charged across the bridge toward him.

And then Harr dropped his binoculars.

"Seawolf!" he cried.

He couldn't believe how happy he was to see that mangy mutt again.

————

"IF THAT COW were worth a shit, you'd have milk for that cereal," Hondo said, pointing at the box of Cheerios Harr was currently digging his hands into.

"She doesn't have a calf," Harr said by way of defense, popping a handful of the small circular nuggets into his mouth. The cow in question grazed in the open lot next door, beside the three Arabians and the steer. Seawolf lay stretched out at his feet. "How'd you find Luna and Seawolf?"

Hondo had secured a pair of faded white plastic lawn chairs from Tex's Boat Storage, and now they sat looking over a yard full of beat-to-shit boats and trailers. Every so often a gust of wind rattled the chain-link fence.

"That dog's a helluva herder," Hondo said cheerfully. "I found her nudging Luna down the levee road yesterday afternoon. When I asked her how the hell you lost your horse and guns, she wouldn't say."

Harr chuckled. Although Hondo joked, Harr knew his partner had been worried shitless when Luna had showed up. Harr could tell by the hard hug the other man gave him when they first reunited.

"Is she still cursing like a sailor?" Hondo asked, eyeing Kayla's back. The young woman squatted twenty yards away, down by the river's edge, where she carefully washed her face.

"Worse," Harr said, around a mouthful of cereal, an unaccustomed uneasiness gnawing at him. He was worried about the time it would take to drive the livestock to Liberty Valley. After seeing what had happened to Alan Wheeler, he knew that delaying Kayla's access to medical care could endanger her life.

But there was no way in hell he was leaving three good horses and three thousand pounds of beef behind. He figured it'd take three days to reach Esperanta and a fourth to get to the actual farm. Gazing at Kayla's bent form, he reminded himself that soldiers survived gunshot wounds before the advent of antibiotics. Not every one of them died or got a limb cut off.

But still ...

Hondo was talking about food. He kept pulling out little packets of this and that from his pack. "What are you hungry for next? I got applesauce and olives. And *this*." With a little flourish, he presented Harr with a jar of Tostito's Salsa Con Queso. "*Te gusta?*"

Despite his worry, Harr couldn't help laughing. "Pass it over, pal."

Hondo handed the jar over. "What happened in the camp?"

Harr told him, sparing no detail, including his ill-fated decision to put Luna on a pontoon boat. Hondo whistled appreciatively.

"You know we're on the edge here, don't you? We're only one dumb pontoon boat ride from oblivion."

Harr dug a spoon into the processed queso and pulled out a gooey, orange blob. "At least it's turned out okay. Thanks to you and Seawolf, I've got my horse and guns back." He nudged a toe into the sleeping mutt, who grunted but didn't open her eyes.

"Yeah, and how about your hat?"

Harr laughed softly. All things considered, losing his hat wasn't that big of a deal at all.

———

ALAN FOUND Susan sitting on a stretch of dry, flat riverbed. She was watching a great blue heron standing in the shallow waters on Liberty River's opposite bank. When Alan approached, the huge slate-gray bird squawked angrily and took flight with slow, laborious strokes of its wings.

"Sorry," he said, sitting down beside her. "I didn't mean to disturb him."

It was still cool out. Shadows from the tall pines stretched across the water.

Susan watched the long, flat trajectory of the heron's departure. "It's fine. I like watching them take off. They're like a jumbo jet, don't you think? They need a huge runway to get off the ground."

The giant bird crested the bankside cottonwoods and disappeared downriver.

Neither of them spoke for a minute. Somewhere a woodpecker hammered away, the sound echoing off the surrounding hillsides.

He thought he owed her an apology for being such a hard-ass about Carson, but because the impulse elicited the simultaneous certainty that doing so would be a mistake, he resisted. Instead, he said what he'd been thinking as he'd followed her through the orchard to this flat, rocky bit of dried creek bottom, "You seem to come to this spot a lot."

She smiled. "There used to be a bench up there on the hill." She pointed to the river's bluff, where the roots of an oak tree protruded from the eroded hillside. "It was my mother's bench. My dad built it for her so she could sit and watch the herons.

But two years ago, the river flooded and eroded the bank, and the bench washed away. I thought she'd be upset, but she just said that rivers change and we should be like the herons and find a new place to perch. So here I am, finding a new place to perch."

She was gazing at him with a look of such sadness that he felt an unaccustomed tightness in his chest and throat.

"I'm sorry," he said, and this time he didn't mean the heron.

Her throat jerked. He could see the pained upward and downward motion as she said, "You can't hang on to what was. I know that, Alan. But no matter how much I tell myself that, I can't seem to let go."

He didn't say anything. He knew she was talking about her family and the life she'd led before the pandemic, but also probably about her caution and sense of morality, which even she seemed to recognize verged on dangerously inflexible.

She was trying. He could see that.

He put his arm around her and felt her head settle against his shoulder. Together, they watched the river's other bank in silence, waiting for the heron to find another perch, but the bird didn't come.

———

THE SUN WAS STRAIGHT OVERHEAD when Hondo spotted the herd. The cows were clustered in the shade of a massive valley oak, near the half-drained remnants of what had once been a fair-sized stock pond.

"There's your herd!" Hondo cried, reining his horse to a stop.

Harr pulled next to him, wondering how the six heifers in front of him had escaped starvation and predators, when virtually all others had not. Maybe it was the water and the open field, Harr thought. Or maybe they were just damn lucky.

It didn't matter, really. What mattered was that at least one of the heifers was likely pregnant, and the rancher in him knew that was good.

They were somewhere between Rio Vista and the suburban town of Vacaville, in the mostly treeless pastureland north of the delta. The stock pond lay in a little swale between two gently sloping hills.

"Kayla, you're going to have to control your horse on your own," Harr said.

For the entire morning, he'd led her Arabian with a rope, which had slowed them down considerably. It had also created a lot of work for Hondo, since the younger man had to manage the livestock by himself.

But Harr didn't see how he could keep leading her, not if he wanted the heifers, which he certainly did. A pregnant heifer meant milk. A pregnant heifer might give birth to a bull calf.

He asked Hondo, jerking his head at the Holstein and steer, "Can you take care of these two?"

"Sure. You going to show us some of your rodeo moves?"

"I'm going to show you how to manage a herd." Harr tugged on the reins, urging Luna toward the heifers.

As he drove the animals from the shade into the sun, something pure and exhilarating rose inside him. He felt as though a bridge had at last been built between the past and this moment, and that what once had been would be once more.

———

IT TURNED out that Seawolf was not only good with Luna, but she was good with heifers, too. When the animals tried to separate from one another, she turned them back. If they went too fast, she sprinted ahead to slow the pack. Harr figured she'd must have had training somewhere, because she did it all without a word from him.

But the work exhausted the still-recovering dog, and that night, as they camped near the artificial lake of what was once Vacaville's only golf course, Seawolf lay down so close to Harr that her back rested on his boot. Not far away, Kayla slept curled up on her open sleeping bag, her slumbering face turned toward Harr.

"You sure got a way with the females," Hondo said next to him. He took a swig from a bottle of Patron Extra Anejo and pointed at the sleeping woman and dog. "Look at 'em. They won't leave your side."

"They're just tired." Harr took the tequila from Hondo and swallowed a good-sized slug. It ran straight down his throat and lit a much-needed fire in his gut. "Where'd you find this stuff?"

"Rio Vista. In the trailer office." Hondo took the bottle back and took another sip. "I've never really understood why people try to save the good stuff. I mean, my dad always told me not to drink the good tequila unless I had something to celebrate, like getting a new job or getting married. And then shit like DRYP happens, and you ask yourself what the hell you were waiting for. Every night out with your buddies was a reason to celebrate. Every paycheck that went in your pocket was worthy of a toast. We just didn't know it."

Harr let out the ghost of a laugh. Clearly the alcohol was getting to Hondo. His handsome face was rosy in the firelight and his body loose. Pretty soon he'd start talking about the meaning of life.

Harr rose and poked the burning embers. Now that they'd left the delta, it had become too hot for a fire, but the light helped beat back the darkness, so they'd lit one anyway.

"Tomorrow's going to be a big day," Harr said. "There's not a whole lot of water between here and Coyote Creek."

"There's not much water here either," Hondo said, tilting his head at the golf course's reed-choked water trap. "You forget when you're on a river that California is pretty much one giant desert elsewhere."

"Not everywhere. It's wet up in the north state, up by the border." Harr knew because he'd fished the Klamath and Eel rivers and had spent more than one chilly night camping in the rain. "But you're right. In the old days, the natives lived by the rivers and lakes, which is pretty much what we're going to do going forward." He looked over at the bottle and noticed that more than half of it was gone. "Speaking of which, you might want to save some of that for later. Being dehydrated and hungover won't help you tomorrow."

Hondo laughed. "Yes, Mother." But he obediently corked the tequila, set it down in the dried grass, and fell backward onto his sleeping bag. The firelight played over his features as he said wonderingly, "If you'd told me that I'd be riding a horse across the state of California in the middle of summer with no damn water anywhere except for that mosquito-infested San Joaquin River and delta, I'd have said you were fucking nutso."

Harr smiled. He gazed out across the fading fire at the shadowed livestock by the water's edge. They were bedded down, most with their heads still up but a few sleeping on their sides. Somewhere in the thick black beyond, crickets sawed away.

The full moon is waning, Harr thought. He stared up at the fuzzy white Milky Way. It was the brightest he'd seen it since leaving Harney County, which meant the inland fires, which had burned so fiercely weeks before, were now finally going out.

Harr looked for the Big Dipper, found it, then traced a path from its two outermost stars toward the North Star.

Beside him, Hondo snored and then rolled over.

Harr wondered why he wasn't happier that the fires in Sacramento and all the other Central Valley cities had finally burned to embers. After all, the smoke had burned in his lungs and effectively cut visibility down to virtually nothing. But he couldn't find it in himself to celebrate. It seemed as if the violence of the fires had signified something important, maybe a last, brilliant refusal of the extinction that was unfolding around him.

In the dimming firelight, Harr reached for Hondo's Patron bottle and took another swig.

———

FIFTY MILES NORTH, the Victorian's kitchen smelled like peach pie. It was late for dessert, but Deb had refused to bake while it was still hot outside. As a consequence, it was nearing ten o'clock by the time the pie was cool enough to serve.

Deb passed the first slice to Susan. "No guarantees. It's a post-pandemic pie. No eggs. No butter."

"It looks incredible," Susan said honestly.

Deb crossed the room and handed Alan a slice. "We'll see how it tastes. Can I get you a slice, Xiangfa?"

The older researcher nodded absently. He was seated at the kitchen table, looking at his laptop computer. Scattered graphs lay on the wood surface next to him.

"The keyword length is a multiple of four," he said to Etta. "I'm betting for simplicity's sake that it's four letters long and not eight or twelve. Otherwise, encrypting and decrypting would be too cumbersome to be practical."

Susan had long given up trying to understand what they were talking about. She understood the basics: that the transmissions were likely enciphered using more than one alphabet, and the transmitters had used a keyword to select which cipher alphabet to use. But she didn't understand the exact mechanism by which the keyword dictated which cipher alphabet to employ, and why it mattered how many letters long the keyword was.

"Any luck deciphering ZJK?" she asked around a mouthful of pie.

"Alan was right. It's not THE or AND," Etta said, accepting a slice from Deb with a smile. "You going to sit down and enjoy this pie with us?"

"Nah, I'm going to share a slice with my roommate back at the house. Do you mind if I borrow one of your Tupperwares?"

It seemed so remarkably normal to Susan. A fresh pie, talk of Tupperware, the warm, glowing light of the kitchen. One could almost forget, if one tried hard enough, that Adrienne and Deb were still living without electricity over at the Morgan house, and that none of them had had butter or eggs in more than two months. Susan beat down the flare of guilt that welled up inside. With any luck, the Morgan place would have electricity soon. The bunker's solar panels sat on the truck's flatbed, waiting to be installed.

Susan handed Deb a plastic container big enough for two slices. "You sure you don't want another lantern? I've charged the Coleman."

Deb waved a hand. "We'll be fine. Both Adrienne and I are early-to-bed types. We're very compatible that way."

Susan had decided that Deb would be compatible with anyone. She had a hairstylist's knack for reading people. With some, she was bubbly and talkative. With others, she was quiet and sympathetic.

Susan walked the hairstylist to the door, thanked her for the pie, and watched as Deb climbed in her golf cart and bumped across the orchard, the electric cart's headlights cutting through the darkness like mini searchlights.

229

When Susan returned to the kitchen, Alan was putting his empty pie plate in the dishwasher, and Etta and Xiangfa had their heads bent over a sheet of bar graphs. Neither had touched their pie.

"We've been assuming all this time that the transmissions have been in English," Etta was saying. "What if they're not?"

"It's in English. Look at this." Xiangfa pointed at one of the bar graphs. "If the keyword is four letters long, as the frequency analysis suggests, then ZJK spells a word."

"It's better than a crossword," Alan whispered in Susan's ear. "It keeps them entertained for hours."

Susan bit back a laugh. "It's always the three-letter words that are hardest," she whispered back.

His laughter was so soft she almost didn't hear it.

At the table, Etta said querulously, "I don't know how you can figure out what ZJK spells if you don't know the keyword."

"Like this," Xiangfa said, turning the screen so Etta could see it.

A furrow formed between the older woman's brows. "That's strange," she said.

"What's wrong?" Susan asked.

Etta looked up from the screen, her face perplexed.

"Xiangfa thinks ZJK spells GAS," she said.

TWENTY-SIX

DEB'S ELECTRIC GOLF CART WOUND UP BEING A GODSEND. It could be charged using the solar power system at the farm, and even though its range was only forty-five miles, it proved invaluable for scavenging in Esperanta. Susan and Deb were making two trips a day.

"This is my least favorite part of the year," Deb commented one day as they zipped down the valley's two-lane highway. "It's hotter'n blazes, and the hills look like they could go up in flames at any moment."

Susan gazed at the brown slopes of the Coastal Range on the valley's west side. Years earlier, a fire had burned that side of Liberty Valley, denuding the hillside of trees and leaving only scrub oak and chaparral in its place. Susan remembered the fire well. The entire valley had been turned into a staging zone to fight the blaze, which had burned one hundred thousand acres and gone on for weeks.

She shuddered to think how far such a fire would burn now without fire crews and bulldozers and retardant drops.

Deb seemed to read her thoughts. "I read once that fires can burn uphill close to forty miles per hour. That's as fast as a car.

No wonder all those poor souls burned up in all those fires before the pandemic."

They were approaching the gap at the valley's southern entrance. Deb stuck her head from beneath the cart's canopy and peered upward at the steep rise on either side, marveling, "To think little ole Liberty River cut this notch in the hills. It must have taken thousands of years to erode through all that rock and soil."

"Good thing it did," Susan added. "Otherwise Liberty Valley would be one giant lake."

Deb laughed. "And Henry would never have had his gravel mine." Suddenly she frowned. "Hey, what happened to the tire fire?"

They had left the valley now and were in the open flat farmland outside Esperanta. Susan expected to see a black plume rising above the town, but only a thin wisp of faint gray smoke scratched the sky. "That's weird. It looks like it's almost out."

A little furrow of consternation formed between Deb's brows. "We better throw another tire on. I'm still holding out hope we'll find more survivors."

Susan wasn't so sure they would. After the brief GAS transmission, they'd heard no other radio traffic, and now, after more than a week, no one else had responded to the signal fire. It seemed very possible to her that they'd found who they would find, and sending a plume of black smoke up into the atmosphere was just a wasted effort. After all, what was the visibility of the plume? Thirty or forty miles on a clear day? The odds of finding another survivor within that radius struck Susan as increasingly remote.

And then there was the danger of the fire itself. Although Alan and Carson had been careful to isolate the tire fire on a wide concrete pad, it was still an unattended fire for hours during the day. Now that they were entering the hottest time of year, Susan worried about touching off an unintended wildfire.

But she didn't say any of this as they took the wide highway turn into the middle of town. She was staring blindly past Esperanta's small shops and office buildings at three figures on horses. The horses were standing next to the dying tire fire, while their riders regarded Carson's hand-painted sign. *Head North on Highway 24 to Survivor Colony. 18 miles.*

It was like seeing a mirage. Behind the three riders, in the small park across the street, a black-and-gray dog guarded eight cows in the shade of an elm tree. It was the first organized group of people and animals she'd seen outside the valley.

"More survivors," she gasped.

———

OF ALL THE things Harr expected to see in Esperanta, a golf cart was the least likely. He couldn't believe his eyes.

He didn't grab his rifle, although he was aware that Hondo beside him had instinctively reached for his. Instead, he waited as the cart drew close enough so that he could see its occupants. His heart slammed once, hard against his breastbone, when he saw Susan's face.

She didn't recognize him. He could tell this by the stiffness of her posture and more importantly by the handgun she held at waist level. It was pointed at them in a half-assed way, as though she didn't know whether to shoot or wave.

Then her face abruptly changed. She took in a sudden breath and mouthed something at the woman driving. A second later, the cart drew to a halt and Susan leaped out.

"John?"

She seemed to be having a hard time processing his presence. Her eyes flicked from him to Hondo and Kayla and then back again. She glanced at the cows across the street.

"Sorry I'm late," he said. It was a stupid thing to say, but it was the only thing he could think of. He was conscious that everyone was watching him. Somewhere in the back of his mind, he realized he should get down from his horse.

A blonde woman emerged from the golf cart and stuck her hand out. "Looks like the cattle drive has reached town," she said, smiling. "I'm Deb. Who are you?"

The whole thing felt like a dream. In all the weeks of his journey, he hadn't quite envisioned this moment unfolding like this, with neither him nor Susan talking to one another, and all his fears about her death proven to be utterly unfounded. If anything, she looked better than he'd expected. She'd put on a pound or two, and her hair, pulled back in a wavy cascade, was clean and thick. Only the scar on her cheek reminded him of the last time they'd been together.

He found himself with two crazy impulses, one to pull her away alone, and the other to avoid her entirely, and he wobbled between the two so long and ineffectively that it was Deb who finally made the decision for him. After the rush of introductions had subsided, she insisted on taking Kayla and Susan back to the Victorian. She said Susan could better take care of Kayla's arm there.

And so he found himself with Hondo and the livestock, watching as the golf cart disappeared down Esperanta's main street, aware that Kayla's fevered eyes were fastened on his and that, deep in her wounded, angry heart, this wasn't what she wanted at all.

IT WAS TOO late to close the wound. Susan saw that immediately when the young woman shucked her long-sleeved shirt and stripped down to a dirty yellow bra. Angry red flesh surrounded both the entry and exit holes, and a yellowish fluid dripped down her arm.

"You sure the bullet went all the way through?" Susan asked.

The young woman nodded sullenly. She hadn't said much in the cart ride back to the Victorian, and now, she was even more taciturn, answering Susan's questions with only head gestures or monosyllables.

Susan weighed whether to trust her about the bullet and decided she couldn't. She'd need to probe the wound, which meant unpleasantness that Susan dreaded.

But first things first. She went into the closet and pulled out a patient gown that she'd scavenged from Esperanta's sole dental office. "Follow me," she said, leading Kayla down the short hallway from her clinic to the Victorian's downstairs bathroom. She set the gown on a little stool by the shower and slid open the glass door. "I want you to wash your body, including your hair, as best you can. When you're finished, put this gown on with the back open. Leave all your dirty clothes, including your underwear, on the bathroom floor."

Fifteen minutes later, Kayla returned to the clinic with her hair hanging in wet straggles down her back. Susan was struck by how young she was. Maybe eighteen or nineteen at most, barely an adult.

And likely traumatized, thought Susan. Harr hadn't said much to Susan, but he had whispered that Kayla had been through rough times, whatever that meant.

"Go ahead and lie down on the bed," Susan said.

She walked to the dresser and withdrew a vial of lidocaine and one of the syringes Carson had scavenged for her. Then she pulled out a sterile swab and a jug of water she'd boiled and let cool. Lastly, she set two plastic containers of medications she'd scavenged from Deb's bunker on the dresser top.

"Are you a real doctor?" Kayla asked with frank distrust in her eyes.

"I've got my MD, if that's what you're asking," Susan replied. There was no use telling her that she hadn't finished residency. Kayla wouldn't understand what that meant, and truthfully, it didn't matter, because although Carson also possessed a medical degree, so far as Susan could tell, she was the only one interested in practicing medicine.

"I told John I didn't need a doctor," Kayla muttered.

"Well, you do." Using a syringe, Susan gently squirted purified water into the wound, trying to flush contaminants from the damaged flesh. "You want to tell me how you got shot?"

Kayla gritted her teeth. "Nope."

So hostile, thought Susan. With a clean towel, she dabbed around the periphery of the bullet's entrance wound. "How about you tell me if you have any medical conditions?"

Kayla stared straight at the ceiling. "I don't have any medical conditions."

"How about allergies? I'm going to give you an injection for this exam and then some antibiotics. Any history of reactions to medications?"

Kayla shook her head. It was like pulling teeth trying to get her to talk.

"Any chance you could be pregnant?" Susan hadn't meant the question as anything more than what it was: the obligatory question doctors asked any woman of reproductive age before treating them. But it seemed to sap the last of Kayla's reserve.

"Why do you ask so many questions?" she snapped. "Just wrap the stupid thing up."

Susan let out a sigh, remembering the words one of her med

school attendings had said to her: *If you don't know the patient's pregnancy status and you need to treat, treat your patient as though she's pregnant.*

In this, Susan was lucky. The medications she had at her disposal—lidocaine, Norcos, and Keflex that Carson had scavenged—all had reliable safety profiles for pregnant patients. Susan could proceed.

Thankfully, the procedure went smoothly. After injecting the wound with local anesthetic, Susan probed the bullet path with the sterile swab and found Kayla had been right. The bullet had gone straight through the fleshy part of the young woman's arm. If Susan could control the infection, Kayla would likely retain full use of her upper extremity. When she told Kayla this, the young woman replied with a surly, "I told you I didn't need a doctor."

God, give me patience, Susan thought. She pointed at the redness around the bullet wound. "See that? That's an infection that could *kill* you. The only way we'll stop it is if you keep your wound clean and take antibiotics." Susan put her face directly in Kayla's, forcing the young woman to look at her. "This is a no-joking matter, Kayla. You need to take care of that arm."

The teenager rolled her eyes. "Fine."

For the next five minutes, neither of them spoke as Susan dressed the wound. The young woman stared ahead stonily, and Susan, who'd had little experience working with teenagers, marveled at how completely irrational Kayla was being.

"I'm going to throw your clothes in the washing machine. You stay here and rest. I want to make sure that wound doesn't start bleeding again," Susan ordered. On impulse, she opened a drawer and pulled out a white-and-blue carton, which she set on the nightstand. "If you have any concerns about pregnancy, you can use this test kit. You know the drill. You pee on the wand

and look to see if there is one stripe or two. Instructions are in the box if you want to read them."

Kayla didn't look at the box or reply, but when Susan returned ninety minutes later with Kayla's freshly washed and dried clothes, she noticed the box was nowhere to be seen.

————

LATER THAT AFTERNOON, Alan found Susan out in the barn, sorting through a box of shoes. She held a pair of tennis shoes, sole to sole, against a ratty pair of women's Nikes. With a grunt of frustration, she tossed the tennis shoes aside.

"How's our visitor?" Alan asked.

"Surly and shoeless," Susan said, tossing another pair into the discard pile. She held up the Nikes. "Look at these things. How am I ever going to find her another pair that fits?"

Alan peered at the ragged shoes, noting the holes where the big toes had poked through the fabric. Without asking, he knew they were Kayla's shoes, just as he knew the source of Susan's frustration. Kayla's shoes looked like they belonged to a child. The young woman's feet were tiny.

"What about going to the elementary school in Esperanta? Maybe some kid left their shoes behind."

"I guess." Susan stood up, rubbing the back of her arm against her forehead. "I never thought to scavenge children's shoes. I thought we just needed adult shoes and toddlers' shoes."

It was true. When they'd discussed important clothing items to scavenge, shoes had been at the forefront. But no one had discussed the possibility of a woman with size 4 feet.

Alan searched Susan's face. She looked flustered and red, far more than one would expect even in the heat. "What's wrong?"

She let out a long pent-up sigh. "She acts like she hates me. I can barely get her to talk, and when she does, she speaks in monosyllables. It's going to be hell taking care of her."

"Didn't John say she'd been through rough times?"

"Yeah, but I don't know what that means exactly. She flat-out refused to tell me how she was shot or if she was pregnant."

That startled him. "Pregnant?"

Susan began throwing the discard shoes back in the box. "Of course. We ask every woman of reproductive age that, especially if we're going to give them medications. She doesn't look pregnant, but I don't know exactly what a 'rough go' constitutes. She could have been raped for all I know."

"Or she and John could have ..."

Susan gave him a look. "Oh, come on, Alan. She's only a kid."

"She's eighteen, isn't she? That's the age of consent." Alan had only seen Kayla for a moment, but it was enough to notice she stared at Harr as though she owned him.

Susan tossed the last pair of discard shoes in the box and snapped the lid closed. "John wouldn't do that. He's not a predator."

"Who said anything about a predator? If they're having a relationship and it's consensual, there's nothing predatory about that."

It was the wrong thing to say. Susan whipped around, her expression thunderous. "Kayla is a teenager who has just gone through the end of the world as she knows it. She doesn't know what she's doing, let alone feeling."

"You think that makes her off-limits to John?"

Susan rose from her crouch. "I think that makes her off-limits to *anyone*. She needs to process whatever these rough times were. I mean, we could all use some therapy after the hell we've been through, but we're *adults*, Alan. Kayla is a *kid*. Someone has to look out for her."

He understood what Susan was saying. In fact, he totally agreed with her. But the truth was that Kayla was of the age to consent and not everyone, least of all a woman of eighteen, shared the same idea of what being taken advantage of was and what was simply consensual. It was entirely possible that Kayla and Harr had had a relationship during their time on the road, and that the young woman felt possessive and jealous, and that was the reason she'd treated Susan so frostily.

But Alan didn't say this. Susan seemed especially agitated, and after their recent disagreements about Carson, he was loath to upset her any more than he already had.

TWENTY-SEVEN

THE PROBLEM WITH HARR, HONDO, AND KAYLA WAS THE same as with the other newcomers: where to put them? Harr and Hondo elected to settle at a ranch on the small plateau across the river from the Victorian. The farmstead had both barn and corral for the livestock, as well as a fair-sized pasture that stretched from the riverbank to the sharp uprise of Liberty Valley's eastern ridge.

Unfortunately, the ranch had also been occupied when the pandemic struck, so Harr and Hondo spent their first afternoon in Liberty Valley clearing out dead bodies from the ranch's modest cabin. It was disgusting work. The corpses were so decomposed that it was impossible to tell whether they were male or female, young or old, and the house itself stank so badly that by the time they were finished scrubbing the interior with bleach and water, the chemical-corpse odor was so strong neither man wanted to stay inside the building. Not surprisingly, both men elected to sleep under the stars while the house aired itself out.

"Maybe I'll just stay out here forever," Hondo offered. He

was lying atop his sleeping bag, arms tucked beneath his head, gazing up at the great smudge of starlight above. "I'm getting used to sleeping rough."

"Don't know if you'll feel the same if a rattler sneaks into your bag." Harr was sitting on his own bag with his elbows resting on his knees. He kept thinking about the two snakes he'd seen earlier. He wasn't keen on letting them get too close.

"I'm not afraid of rattlers. If you watch your step and don't hassle them, they'll leave you alone." Hondo tilted his head and looked at Harr. "Why do you keep staring at the house?"

Across the river, the Victorian glowed like a crystal palace, a radiant white blaze of light in the otherwise dark night.

Maybe he was feeling expansive, Harr thought. Maybe that was why he answered honestly. "I thought they were all going to die," Harr said. "I thought they were helpless, that they wouldn't make it without my help. But they aren't helpless. They've got electricity and clean water and irrigation—"

"—and a golf cart—" Hondo seemed particularly enamored with the golf cart.

"—and medical care, a radio operator, and a farming operation." He broke off for a second as one of the upstairs lights in the Victorian snapped off. "That electric light is amazing. I never thought I'd see it again."

"But they only have electricity in one house."

"Actually, they have it in two, and soon there'll be three. They're building." Harr felt restlessness overwhelm him, unable to find the words that explained his feelings. "I guess what I'm trying to say is that you think the cards are stacked against one group of people and yet they survive, while the ones you think are guaranteed to survive get wiped out. I'm not saying these guys will make it through the winter, but they've made a damn good start, and with our help, I bet they will."

"Unless something like Shangri-La happens."

Something uneasy crawled through Harr's veins. "We don't know what happened in Shangri-La."

Hondo pushed himself up on his elbows. "You said that nine dudes were stabbed to death and then strung up from a second-floor balcony. You also said that the only survivor was carrying a gas mask. That seems like enough to make an educated guess about what happened to them. Someone attacked that settlement, John. They fucking *decimated* it."

Harr slid a glance Hondo's way. He said quietly, "I agree. The part I don't get is why. Shangri-La did nothing but welcome people. They weren't warlike." He shook his head, remembering the strange mutterings of the praying woman, how she'd said Carlos, whoever he was, would kill everyone. "I wish we could have gotten through to her. She didn't need to kill herself."

Hondo sank back on his sleeping bag, his face pointed up toward the stars above. "But she did, and there's nothing we can do about it now."

Harr wasn't so sure.

Carlos will hunt us down until there is no more of us left.

Across the river, the last of the Victorian's downstairs lights blinked off. Only a dim lamp burned in one of the upstairs bedrooms. Harr gazed at the flickering glow and then up at the tall black shadows of the mountains on either side of the valley.

He'd been thinking about the valley. It had two entrances: to the north, through a long, steep-walled gorge; and to the south, the narrow gap through which he'd arrived with Hondo. From what he'd seen from the air, the northern gorge could be defended easily with some dynamite and a few well-positioned men. But the southern gap was another story.

He tried to remember the slope of the mountains on either side of the river, the width of the road, and where there were trees. He thought of the weapons he'd like to have and how he'd deploy them. He spent twenty minutes mulling over these things, until the last upstairs light snapped off in the Victorian, and there was nothing but the dark valley and the silvery moonlight and the quiet rush of the river down below him.

Troubled and exhausted, he fell into an uneasy sleep.

———

"ANY USE FOR FLARES?" Deb asked. She hefted a box of the red cylindrical tubes from the hardware store's shelf and carried it over to Susan, who was squatting down in the same row, going through a box of green plastic tape.

Susan peered at the flares doubtfully. "Probably not, but bring them just in case. Maybe Alan can think of a use."

After three days of back-and-forth trips, there wasn't much left in the hardware store, and now the women were scavenging items on the off chance they might be useful later. Susan grabbed a few rolls of the green tape, shoved them into a box brimming with drip irrigation supplies, and headed outside.

The golf cart's back seat was close to full. Deb slid her box of flares into a small open space, which knocked a metal canister onto the cart's floor. She picked the canister back up, frowning at the narrow eight-inch-long spout. "What the heck is this thing?"

"Drip torch." Susan stacked her box of irrigation supplies on top of Deb's box. "You use it for controlled burns and backfires. Alan wanted one in case we ever get a wildfire."

"We're not going to get a wildfire. Didn't you say that ninety-five percent of wildfires are human-caused?"

Susan walked back into the store. "Something like that. But still, what if we had lightning?"

Deb snorted dismissively. "Oh, come on. When was the last time you saw lightning in this area in the middle of summer?"

"Never, I think."

"Exactly. So we're just wasting space hauling drip torches and the like." She peered down an aisle, trying to decide if there was anything worth scavenging. "By the way, you never told me how Kayla is doing. Is she ready for discharge?"

It was easy talk, the comfortable back-and-forth between her and Deb that normally helped pass time, but Susan wasn't into it. The injured teenager weighed heavily on her mind. In fact, she couldn't stop worrying about her. "As far as I'm concerned, yes. But she wants to move up with Hondo and John, and I don't think that's a good idea. They don't have running water, and she needs to keep herself clean so that wound heals properly."

Especially since she's pregnant, Susan added silently. The young woman hadn't even bothered to hide the test wand. Susan found it in the bathroom trash can, the two bright red stripes clear to anyone who cared to look.

Deb was digging through a box of doorknobs. "You know, Adrienne and I have four bedrooms, and if Kayla wants to be with the men, we could have all three of them move in with us. It doesn't make sense for the guys to bed down in that dark cabin across the river, when we have plenty of electricity and clean water at our place."

It wasn't exactly plenty of electricity. Susan knew the newly installed solar power batteries were undersized for the Morgan house, and the two women were still learning how to balance the load. The previous day, they'd drained the battery before sundown and were forced back into using Coleman lanterns.

But still, Deb had a point. There was enough room, if someone slept on the couch, for all five of them to live in the Morgan house. With a little bit of planning, they could all take warm showers and live by electric light.

And yet, she knew Harr wouldn't agree to it. When Susan had broached the possibility of the men leaving their ranch, Harr had said flatly, "Hondo and I worked our butts off to get these heifers here. We're not going to let a mountain lion or bear take them now."

So the two men had stayed at the place they'd dubbed the River Ranch, as hairy and dirty as they'd been when they'd arrived.

"Would you ask Kayla if she'd be willing to live with you, even if the men don't?" Susan said, following Deb down the store's center aisle. "Maybe hearing the offer from you, instead of me, would change her mind."

"Sure, honey, but did it ever occur to you that Kayla might want to be with the men for a reason? She's been traveling with them for who knows how long. People get attached."

Do they ever, Susan thought with dismay. She'd noticed how Kayla changed her demeanor the moment Harr came to check on her. The sullen look disappeared, and an intense fire burned in her green eyes. She held his hand as though she would never let it go.

For a brief, almost irresistible moment, Susan wanted to spill everything to the other woman, that Kayla was pregnant and that she, Susan, didn't have any experience delivering babies beyond a three-week OB-GYN rotation as a medical student; that Kayla wouldn't talk with her, so she wasn't even supposed to know that Kayla was pregnant in the first place.

But she wouldn't violate Kayla's privacy. It was one of the most important rules in medicine. A health care provider could *not*, without a patient's permission, disclose any private medical information.

"Have you thought about her living with Jim and the rest of them?" Deb went on. "They have extra room and plenty of electricity. Maybe she'd prefer to live with them."

Susan didn't like that idea either. The whole rock-and-roll atmosphere of Carson's house wouldn't be a healthy environment for a traumatized, pregnant teen. Susan sighed.

Deb must have sensed her distress. She came up and put a hand on Susan's shoulder. "I'll ask her, honey. It's pretty obvious she's crazy about John, but I'll try."

Susan didn't know why a teenager being in love with John bothered her, but it did.

———

THAT EVENING, Liberty Valley held its first party since the Before Times. It wasn't a blowout because there were only thirteen partygoers, but that didn't stop Jim Carson from admiring the festivities. The women were washed, and the men shaved, and someone had found a case of Corona, which everyone was sucking down except the redheaded newcomer, who sat off by herself sulking.

Sulking or no, Carson was pleased to have the eighteen-year-old join the settlement. The teenager helped skew the women's ages toward younger. Susan, Adrienne, and Deb were all in their thirties.

It was a decent start. They now had five women of reproductive age and six men who could impregnate them. It wasn't the 110 reproductive-age adults they needed, but if they could pair up with another settlement, the chances for survival were good.

He stretched himself out in his patio chair, savoring the scent of roasted venison and the sight of women carrying dishes from the Victorian's kitchen. A gentle sunset breeze rustled the ash trees and whispered across the grass.

This is how it should be, he thought lazily. The hunters, Hondo and Harr, standing beside the firepit, drinking beer and

247

occasionally poking the dying embers beneath the empty rotisserie spit, while Xiangfa, Alan, and Reaper sat at the wrought iron table on the Victorian's deck, discussing important infrastructure matters like how to electrify River Ranch. Words floated to Carson in snippets: *calves coming in the winter, electricity for all houses, irrigation for new farmland.*

They were good words, solid words, and to them, he was adding his own important one:

Chemistry.

Hydrogen, carbon, nitrogen, oxygen, sulfur, chloride. How powerful those six atoms could be when combined in different ways!

Of course, he wasn't so delusional as to think performing chemical reactions in his makeshift lab would be easy, but hell, if a bunch of criminals could make methamphetamine in a garage, he was pretty sure he could make fertilizer and old-school antibiotics with his scavenged equipment and chemical precursors. After all, he'd already proven his ability with one substance. Newly manufactured fentanyl, swooping and infinitely satisfying, floated through his veins.

Carson took another sip of beer, felt the pleasant wash of alcohol mix with synthetic opioid in his brain.

Now that he had a near limitless source of fentanyl, he'd no longer need to scavenge so desperately. He could keep the headaches, which had once been the bane of his existence, permanently at bay.

He watched the women set venison, sweet corn, and tomato salad on the banquet table. It was a feast after months of what felt like famine.

As it should be, he thought again. The men would hunt and build things. The women would tend the hearth and, with any luck, bear children.

Feeling pleased and ravenously hungry, Carson rose from his chair to claim his meal.

———

ALAN GAZED from the Victorian's deck down at the banquet table on the center of the lawn. Deb, with Emmaline propped on one hip, was calling the men to the table.

For a moment, he hesitated. He wanted to burn this moment, with its tenuous sense of plenty, into his memory.

They wouldn't starve this winter. It seemed crazy to worry about winter in the heat of summer, when the tomatoes and fruit trees were plentiful, but he was a planner by nature, and he'd done enough calculating to realize they'd run out of food by November unless they secured a steady supply of protein.

Now they had, by virtue of a small herd of cattle and two men adept with guns and fishing poles. Aside from Susan, Harr and Hondo were the two most valuable people in the valley.

Which was not to say that he undervalued his own capabilities. Like Deb, he acted as *glue* that brought people together. It was a soft skill, but a critical one. It underpinned his leadership.

But he was also relatively old and half-lame. He was pretty damned sure he wasn't valuable in another crucial way as well, although he didn't know for certain.

Yet, even with those shortcomings, he remained the valley's ostensible leader, deferred to, for now, by both Susan and Carson.

Would Hondo and Harr defer as well?

It'd been impossible to miss how the Oregon rancher had sized up the Victorian and its farming operation, how his eyes had drifted, for brief, surreptitious moments, to watch Susan's movements.

As the former chairman of a major energy company, Alan

had seen corporate board members come and go, seen how sometimes a new member came and worked himself into the operation seamlessly, and other times, how a new person disturbed the carefully cultivated sense of teamwork. Either way, Alan, as guardian of Wheeler Energy, had long been vigilant about newcomers. He was vigilant now.

He crossed the lawn and placed himself at the head of the banquet table.

When Susan sat beside him and laid a hand atop the table, he gently placed his hand, only for a second, but long enough to be noticed, on top of hers.

———

AN HOUR LATER, after the dinner had been cleared and darkness had set in, Harr excused himself from the table, ostensibly to check on the fire pit's remaining embers, but really because he was feeling out of sorts and wanted to be alone. He'd had enough of Kayla's fevered attention and Carson's strange lectures on minimum viable population size. What he really wanted to do was talk with Susan.

But the opportunity had never presented itself. Earlier he'd been busy at the spit, and she'd been busy taking care of Emmaline and preparing food in the kitchen. Later, when they'd finally gotten the food served, they'd been seated at opposite ends of the table. And then Wheeler had gone ahead and put his hand on top of hers, and the gesture had struck Harr as so proprietary that Harr found himself feeling strangely put out.

Just what was that gesture about? Feeling irritated at himself for wondering, Harr jabbed hard at the ashy remnants inside the firepit. A little cloud of dust rose in the air.

Someone chuckled behind him. "You know, if you really want to kill those ashes, you ought to use a knife." Hondo was standing in the reflected light from the house, holding two open bottles of Corona. He was looking at the stick in Harr's hand. "Something bothering you, friend?"

"Nope. You going to give me one of those beers or drink them both yourself?"

The younger man passed a bottle over. "I had to the wrestle the old lady for them. Man, she's like a hawk over the provisions."

Harr couldn't help but laugh. "Maybe she just doesn't want us drinking all her beer."

"Maybe she's just old and cranky," Hondo said, good-naturedly. "Jesus, I never thought I'd drink another cold beer in my life. And look at us!" he clinked his bottle against Harr's. "Your lady friend has a pretty good setup here."

Harr's smile abruptly faded. "She's not my lady friend."

In the half-light, he could feel rather than see the amused look on Hondo's face. "Maybe not yet, but show her some of your rodeo moves and she'll be eating out of your hand before know it."

"*Jesus.*" Harr breathed, rolling his eyes.

"What does Jesus have to do with it?" a female voice asked.

Harr's stomach dropped to his toes. Susan stood in the darkness, holding a bucket in her right hand.

Had she heard? It was impossible tell in the dim light.

"We were just talking about John's rodeo skills," Hondo said helpfully.

Harr frowned down at her. "What's the water for?"

She set the bucket on the ground. "It's for the embers. You rodeo?"

Harr could tell Hondo was grinning. "I better go," Hondo said, slipping away into the darkness, but not before Harr saw the younger man surreptitiously circle his hand in the air like he was throwing a lasso. "I promised to help take the table down."

251

She didn't even look at Hondo. She was peering up at Harr. "What kind of rodeo?"

"Don't listen to him. I'm not a rodeo rider. I'm a rancher."

"But you brought all those cattle here."

"You don't need a shiny belt buckle to round up cattle." He peered down at her, surprised that a farmer's daughter would be so uninformed. "Didn't your father have animals?"

She shook her head. "He said there was no money in it." And then she seemed to realize that might sound offensive because she amended, "I mean, I'm sure you can make money off cattle, but he didn't know how to do it."

Harr's eyes flicked from the expansive lawn to the glowing Victorian. "I'd say he did just fine with trees, but he's right about cattle. You choose to raise them more as a way of life than something that's going to make you rich." He shrugged. "I liked the lifestyle."

She smiled. "Not that money means anything anymore. I'll take one of your cows any day."

"Heifers."

"Huh?" She looked at him blankly.

"They're heifers, not cows," he said, smiling. She clearly had no clue about livestock. "Emmaline looks good. You've done well with her."

Momentarily diverted, she threw a quick glance back at the house, as though reminded of how she and Harr had first come to know each other. "Oh, thank you, but it's not really me. It's her. She's a tough little one."

"You made the right call to stay here."

She frowned. "How could you have known what happened at Shangri-La?"

"I still don't know what happened at Shangri-La."

All of a sudden, he had the strong desire to tell her everything—about the plane crash and the stabbed, hanging bodies, about the burial pits and the death of the praying woman. He wanted to tell her about Kayla's abuse and killing Pap. But the night was too quiet and peaceful, and he didn't want to scare her. He decided to stick with the broad outlines of what he'd seen at Shangri-La, which she already knew.

"You think someone attacked the settlement?" she asked.

"Yes," he said, because it was true.

No one is safe anywhere. Carlos will hunt us down until there is no more of us left.

The half-light from the house danced over the smooth curve of her cheek and the slight pucker from the scar he'd put on her face a million years ago, when his greatest fear had been whether the plane would crash on takeoff from Sacramento. He had the feeling of change, of something seismic occurring that he did not yet fully understand.

"Susan—" he said, not sure what he wanted to say, but certain he wanted to say it.

He took a step towards her, his toe connecting inadvertently with the bucket and sending a small wave of water back onto his boot. He let out a little curse.

Her lips curled. "I'm not hauling another bucket out here."

"You didn't need to haul this one out here. The fire's out."

"Alan says we shouldn't take any chances with fire."

"Alan should carry his own bucket then."

She gave him a look. "I can carry a bucket just fine."

A voice in the darkness interrupted them. "Ah, there you are," Harr cursed inside when he saw Wheeler step out of the shadows. "Is the fire out?" the older man asked.

"Yes," said Harr.

"Almost," said Susan.

Harr picked up the bucket and poured the remaining water on the fire's ashes. "It's out."

In the dim light, Harr saw a smile tug at Wheeler's lips. "I appreciate that, John." He looked down at Susan. "Emmaline's fussing. Etta's trying to get her down, but she wants you."

It was an effective way to rope Susan back in, because a moment later she was walking back toward the big house with Alan and an empty bucket in her hand.

Harr was left in the darkness, wondering if he'd just been outmaneuvered.

TWENTY-EIGHT

THE FOLLOWING MORNING, SUSAN DROVE THE ATV OVER to River Ranch. Normally Susan wouldn't waste fuel on such a short trip, but the five-mile distance from the Victorian to Harr and Hondo's house was too far to carry anything heavy, and the drip torch and flares weighed an awkward twenty pounds.

Both items were strapped to the ATV, the box of flares in the wide front basket, the drip torch on the rack behind the driver's seat.

She was pensive. She wasn't sure why Harr was avoiding the big house, but something clearly bothered him, because aside from the party, he'd only come to the Victorian once. As a consequence, Kayla had become surly to the point of nastiness.

Susan downshifted as she approached the bridge. It struck her as an irony that the River Ranch cabin and the Victorian were only half a mile apart as the crow flew, but five miles apart by road. Crossing the river was the issue. The closest bridge was in the tiny town of Romulus, two and a half miles up valley.

In truth, Romulus wasn't really a town. It was more of a cluster of modest country houses, a post office, and a grange hall.

But in rural Liberty Valley, such a concentration of buildings seemed positively city-like.

She ran into Hondo as she started southward on River Ranch's side of the river. He was riding by the turnoff for the Arlington Grade, and brought his horse to a halt and smiled when he saw her. "You looking for John? He's back at the barn."

As with the first time she had met him, Susan was struck by the easy handsomeness of the young man. His skin was tanned by the sun, which made his teeth all the more brilliant when he smiled.

She passed him slowly on the narrow country road, not wanting to startle his horse, and then crossed the oak-strewn plateau, to the wrought iron gate that signified River Ranch's boundary. It was beautiful here, the rich green of the trees serving as counterpoint to the golden hills beyond. Not far distant, the terrain steepened abruptly, wrinkling into sharp, brush-filled draws and the precipitous climb of the valley's eastern ridge. She could just make out the laborious zigzag of the Arlington Grade as it cut through cliffs and rocky crags.

As Hondo had indicated, Harr was in the barn. He stood in a stall with the same gray horse she'd seen him riding in Esperanta, a currycomb in his hand. Not far away, the slit-eared dog that seemed to follow him everywhere lay on her belly, panting.

"I was wondering who was making all the ruckus out there," Harr said, when he saw her walk through the barn's open door.

She let out a little laugh. Without the low growl of the ATV's engine to blot out the sound, the air was thick with bird-call and the restless movement of cows. She noted with a little surprise that Harr wore a handgun at his hip.

"Alan wanted me to bring you a box of flares and a drip torch," she said, setting the box of flares on a bench beside the stall. "He says if there's going to be a fire, it's going to be on this side of the river."

Harr seemed easy enough. He flicked a smiling glance her way and resumed combing. "Let's hope there's no fire."

His tone bespoke the reality of living in the American West. He wasn't panicked about fire, but it was obvious he respected it. He accepted the flares and drip torch without resistance.

"You guys getting settled in here?" she asked. It bothered her that they didn't have electricity, that they bathed in the river and lived by the light of rechargeable Coleman lanterns.

"Sure." He dropped the currycomb into a pail and picked up a long bristle brush, which he proceeded to run over the horse's coat. Little puffs of dust rose and dissipated in the air. "The flat-screen doesn't work, but other than that, I can't complain."

Despite herself, she laughed, both at ease and not at ease. Up close, Harr's horse looked even more powerful and intimidating than from a distance, but Harr seemed completely relaxed. He slid around the horse's back end, his hand riding along the top of the animal's thickly muscled hindquarters. Susan watched him maneuver with a confusing mixture of genuine interest and shyness.

"Kayla's getting better. I think we've got the infection under control."

Another easygoing flick of the eye. "That's good."

She couldn't tell if he knew about the pregnancy. His even expression gave away nothing. "She says she wants to move up here with you."

This time he didn't glance at her. He bent down instead and rubbed the brush along the horse's front leg. "That's not a good idea."

For a moment, Susan didn't know what to say. If he didn't know about the pregnancy, she felt that he should, because the young woman was obviously attached to him, and he could reach her in ways that Susan could not. But Susan did not know how to relay the information to him without violating Kayla's privacy, so she settled on trying to give the young woman the chance to tell him herself. "You know, you could visit her more," she suggested. "I think she'd like to see you."

It was the wrong thing to say. Harr's head popped up above the horse's back, and he gazed at her with an expression as flat and unfriendly as stone. Even the Arabian seemed startled. It turned its nose against Harr's arm and nudged.

"I didn't get the idea I was wanted at the house," Harr said.

Suddenly Susan didn't understand the interaction. She felt as if two parallel conversations were occurring—she dancing around Kayla's pregnancy, and he alluding to something entirely different.

She tried to reassure him. "Of course you're wanted at the house. You're welcome to come down for any reason—a shower, a meal, to wash clothes, whatever. I know you and Hondo are up here without electricity—"

"We're fine."

"No, you're not." Her eyes trailed down his dusty, sweat-stained clothes, which only seemed to make the moment worse. Pride, or something harder to read, flared in his eyes.

Without saying a word, he dropped the brush in the pail and slipped around the horse's rear end. He passed her in the stall doorway and walked outside.

When she caught up to him, he was untying the drip torch from the ATV's rear rack, his rough, work-hardened fingers working the bungee cords. "I'm assuming this is a standard order drip torch, just light the wick and drip fire," he said, his voice polite but remote.

"That's right. Alan says he filled it with a mixture of diesel and gas, so it's ready to go."

Dismay filled her. She had the sense that he didn't want her there any longer, that she was being dismissed. But she wasn't quite sure how their conversation had gone off the rails, and she still hadn't yet addressed the Kayla situation. She tried once more.

"Kayla would really like to see you. Maybe you could come over one of these evenings?"

He looked down at her for a long moment, a crack showing at last in his stony façade. Exhaustion, and she thought disappointment, hovered in his eyes.

"Okay," he finally said.

She watched, bewildered, as he left her and walked back into the barn.

———

THAT AFTERNOON, Susan brooded over Kayla's pregnancy as she drove the golf cart to Esperanta. She hardly noticed the road or the trees or the awful midday heat. Her mind kept flitting from one potential obstetric catastrophe to another—infection, hemorrhage, embolism—any of which could lead to a dead baby or mother, or god forbid, both.

There was no telling how pregnant the teenager was, although by the looks of her flat abdomen, she wasn't far along. Susan pushed the implications of that observation from her mind and instead focused on what she needed: a fetal stethoscope, obstetric forceps, a good maternal-fetal reference text. She thought she might be able to find the stethoscope in Esperanta's family medicine clinic, but she very much doubted the public library would have a useful reference book. She needed to go to a proper hospital, a prospect that filled her with dread.

Which made her think of Carson and his mystery scavenging. Clearly the infectious disease doctor had no problem going into places filled with rotted corpses, but she certainly did. The risk of disease might be vastly reduced due to the drying of the bodies, but the abiding horror of the gaping, skeletal mouths remained.

Almost as though she conjured him, Carson materialized on the two-lane highway before her. He was riding his Harley with what looked like a stuffed duffle bag strapped to the backrest. When he saw her, he drew the motorcycle to a halt.

"Traveling alone?" he asked, his eyes invisible behind his aviator shades, but his lips curved into a smile.

As always with Carson, she wasn't sure if his thin-lipped smile was one of mockery or just a consequence of unfortunate facial structure. Somehow she suspected the former. "There's nothing dangerous out there except rattlesnakes and heatstroke," she said, reluctantly turning off the golf cart.

His face lightened, one eyebrow arching above his shades. "You no longer fear your fellow man?"

She immediately regretted turning off the cart. She didn't want to have an argument with him about how many survivors there were left and whether they should still be looking for them, not out here, not when she was feeling so inexplicably out of sorts.

But she couldn't help herself. She snapped, "The only scary person out here is you." She eyed the duffle bag with a frown. "Where've you been?"

He made a vague gesture. "Oh, here and there."

Once again, his vagueness irritated her. "What's in the duffle bag?"

"Ammonium nitrate."

Of all possible substances, that was the least expected. Her mouth dropped open. "Are you nuts? That stuff is dangerous."

Admittedly she was no expert about ammonium nitrate, but she did know it had been used to construct the Oklahoma City terrorist bomb and had consequently been outlawed in California.

Carson looked unperturbed by her shock. "It's only dangerous if you don't know what you're doing. Farmers used ammonium nitrate to fertilize their farms for decades before McVeigh did a number on the Murrah building. None of them blew up."

"But why do you need it?" Susan eyed the duffle bag warily. "We've got fertilizer."

"But we don't have nitrous oxide. Did you know that I can make laughing gas with ammonium nitrate? You may think we're all healthy now, but one day, one of us is going to need a tooth pulled or some type of operation, and I don't know about you, but I'd rather laugh goofily than bite a stick like some frontier yokel."

She didn't say anything, hung up for a second on how Carson could possibly get the anesthetic gas into the tanks in which it was normally stored, but she didn't perseverate. She wanted to know what else Carson was up to. He'd now openly gone rogue.

"I want to see your lab," she said abruptly.

He tilted his head and gazed at her, eyebrows raised in surprise. "I had no idea nitrous oxide excited you so. Maybe I could manufacture one of the fluorinated anesthetic gases. Would that—?"

She cut him off. "It's not the nitrous oxide I'm concerned about. It's what else you're doing in there."

He laughed. "My, my. When did you become so suspicious?"

"I'll be by your lab tomorrow afternoon."

"Alone, or shall I expect the rest of the UN inspection team?"

Don't react, she told herself. *Don't let him provoke you.*

"Just me," she said.

His smile broadened. "If that's the case," he said, "I look forward to it with pleasure."

———

OF COURSE, it didn't work out the way Susan anticipated. She wouldn't tour Carson's lab the next day, but she didn't know it as she drove, perturbed, into Esperanta that afternoon.

She only knew that Carson was not reporting what he was doing or scavenging, and that in doing so he was violating the compact that the valley's members had committed themselves to: they would operate, in the open, as a coordinated unit.

These thoughts dogged her as she lobbed a rock through the family medicine clinic's front window. The plate glass window shattered and cracked, leaving an arm-sized hole that opened into the small clinic's waiting room.

For a moment, Susan let regret wash Carson's mocking face away. She hated breaking windows, knowing that there would be no way to replace them, and that she, whether she wanted to or not, would be contributing to the building's accelerated decay.

But whoever had been the last to leave the building had elected to lock up, thus forcing Susan into destruction she loathed. With a regretful grunt, she finished the job, knocking out the rest of the glass with a hammer she'd brought along from the farm.

The waiting room was empty, the chairs spaced in a futile effort at social distancing. With a pang of sorrow, Susan spied the signs that exhorted patients to wear masks and to alert the front desk if they felt fever or any other symptom of DRYP. As if wearing a mask or sitting six feet apart had made a difference. As if alerting the nurse you felt sick had changed any outcome.

But she didn't dwell on these thoughts. She moved quickly

into the exam rooms instead. Like other medical facilities, this one had been stripped clean of PPE and IVs. But there were other supplies she wanted and needed: speculums, urinalysis test strips, a rolling blood pressure cuff and pulse oximeter, an EKG machine. She loaded what she could on the blood pressure machine's stand and dragged the heavier EKG cart behind her. She was halfway out the door before she realized she wasn't alone.

Two men and a woman stood on the short walkway that separated the clinic from the parking lot. Each was carrying a shotgun.

"Are you from Liberty Valley?" the woman asked, stepping forward and lowering her gun. She was young, maybe in her late twenties, and she spoke in a deep contralto that was simultaneously authoritative and strangely familiar. Behind her, two men in hunting camouflage and ragged facial hair kept their guns held high.

With her hands up, Susan stared at the woman, racking her brain trying to figure out if they'd met before.

"I am. Who are you?"

"Paula Kamiakin. Of the Yakama Nation."

Susan's stomach dropped to her toes. Standing before her, looking fierce and battle-weary, was the deep-voiced woman they'd heard on the radio weeks before. The two rough-looking mountain men behind her looked ready to blow Susan's head off if she even looked at Paula wrong.

The young woman's eyes flicked over the EKG machine and blood pressure cuff. "We've got injured. Do you know how to use those things?"

It was then that Susan noticed the circle of vehicles in the clinic's parking lot. A delivery van, two pickup trucks, and a minivan waited in the shade of an elm tree. A moan, plaintive and weak, drifted from the back of one of the trucks.

Susan eyed the two mountain men. "If you're asking for my help, put the guns down."

The gesture was subtle, but Susan didn't miss it. Paula made a short, flashing motion with two fingers, and both men lowered their guns.

She's their leader, Susan realized with a little jolt. And by the number of vehicles present, she wasn't leading very many.

Paula was already walking back to the vehicles, forcing Susan to hustle to keep up. "The sons of bitches used gas, probably mustard. We lost three on the way down here. We'll probably lose more."

Susan stifled a gasp when she saw the back of the first pickup. Three badly burnt men lay stretched out on the truck's bed, their torsos wrapped in clumsy bandaging, their faces invisible except for where slits had been cut in the gauze. It reminded Susan of the old black and white photos she'd seen of World War I gas victims, except these men were in color and right before her, the stink of their burnt flesh so strong her stomach pitched.

"These are the worst cases," Paula said tersely, looking down on the men with fury in her eyes. "They and the three dead were holding the main road, when the cult let loose with the gas. It burned the skin right off our guys' bodies and blinded Reb."

Susan gazed at the boy Paula called Reb. By the lankiness of his limbs and the bald smoothness of the small patch of unburnt skin on his chest, Susan guessed he was no older than thirteen or fourteen. He stared sightlessly into space, his bandaged head tilted like he was listening.

Despite his blindness, Susan gave the adolescent the best chance of surviving out of the three. The other men rattled as they breathed, which meant the damage to their lungs was severe.

Paula moved on to the second truck, spitting out information in clipped tones. "These are the walking wounded. Some shot during the first attack. Some injured when we fled for the hills."

Susan surveyed the collection of huddled figures. Half a dozen of them were crammed into the back of the truck, all sharing one disturbing similarity: they wore bandages torn from strips of dirty clothing. One young woman's deformed wrist was crudely splinted with a tree branch.

Seeing Susan's gaze, Paula explained, "We didn't have proper medical care up in the mountains. I'm afraid we lost more than we should have."

"Where's the congressman?"

"Dead," Paula said bluntly. "Killed in the first attack. One of their shells landed on our command center. He died instantly." She glanced over her shoulder at the thin plume of smoke still rising from the tire fire two blocks away. "You better put that fire out. They already know you're here. You don't have to put a welcome mat out for them."

"Who's they?"

"The cult. They're the ones who attacked us. They call themselves the Universal Brotherhood."

Susan felt sick. A thousand questions ricocheted around her brain, but Susan grabbed onto the one that she could do something about. She glanced over at the two other vehicles, wondering how many more wounded were inside them. She figured at least six people needed urgent medical care that she couldn't provide in a plundered, electricity-less family medicine clinic.

She gestured with her head at the EKG machine and blood pressure stand behind her. "You got room for this stuff?"

"We can make room."

"Good. I'm a doctor, and I've got a medical clinic about

eighteen miles from here up the valley. It's nothing fancy, but better than anything you'll find here. Follow me."

Paula put a hand on her sleeve. "Skip the golf cart." She turned to one of her guardsmen and barked out, "Take her cart and go put out the fire. Get rid of the signs while you're at it."

To Susan, she said grimly, "You ride with me."

TWENTY-NINE

In all, there were twenty-four survivors of the Yakima Valley settlement, three of which were so badly injured that Susan was forced to set up a temporary infirmary in the Victorian's living room.

Unfortunately, the new influx of patients also meant that there was no longer a bed for Kayla. Susan sent her and Emmaline to Deb's house so that Susan could focus on what had instantly become a field hospital.

The location was convenient. The Yakima Valley settlement's leader sat at the kitchen table in the room next door, briefing Alan, Etta, Xiangfa, and Carson. When Susan joined them, she noted the warlike atmosphere. Paula's two guards stood behind her like sentries, while Harr and Hondo flanked Alan and Carson on the other side. A bottle of whiskey stood on the center of the table.

"They have assault weapons and SAWs. A couple of mortars," she was saying. "We'd dug trenches around our settlement in the valley and put up roadblocks, but the valley is flat, and they have four-wheel-drive vehicles. They just went off the road and bypassed them. Then they hammered our forward

R.A. SCHEURING

positions with mortar fire. We lost four in the trenches and another four in the command center when a shell hit it. That's when I called a retreat."

"How many attackers were there?" Alan asked.

Paula took a slug of whiskey and answered, "I'd say three hundred."

Susan's mouth dropped open. By Hodis's estimate, there shouldn't have been that many survivors in the entire United States.

"There were more in the second attack," Paula went on. "Maybe four hundred. From what I understand, the cult usually leaves a hundred behind in their compound when they send out a war party. So I'm guessing the cult has maybe five hundred members in total."

Without thinking, Susan's eyes shot to Harr's face, but he wasn't looking at her. He was looking at one of Paula's guards with a sharp furrow between his brows.

"That's a lot of people," Alan said grimly. He poured Paula another finger of whiskey and pushed the glass at her. "What kind of cult?"

"Doomsday. Remember the sarin subway attack in Tokyo back in the 1990s? The group behind it was called Aum Shinrikyo."

"I remember," Etta said. "They built biological and chemical weapons."

"That's right. They wanted to trigger World War III and wipe out mankind because they were convinced humanity had become irretrievably corrupted. They were only because the police linked them to the sarin attack. Well—" She eyed the people at the table grimly. "The Universal Brotherhood wasn't stopped."

To Susan, it felt like an atom bomb exploded in the room. No one spoke. Even Carson looked momentarily taken aback.

"What do you mean?" Alan asked slowly.

"I mean, the Universal Brotherhood cult was behind DRYP. They caused the pandemic." She gazed at the shocked faces around her. "Congressman Cortese told us. He was on the House Subcommittee on Homeland Security when the pandemic struck. They were briefed that the Universal Brotherhood bioengineered DRYP using CRISPR technology."

Susan couldn't breathe. The air seemed stuck in her chest.

"But you said there's hundreds of them," Alan said harshly. "How is that even possible?"

"They have a vaccine." Briefly, Paula's eyes flicked to the cliff-faced guard to her right. He gazed back at her impassively. "It was experimental, but apparently effective."

"My god," Susan whispered. She couldn't fathom it, how anyone could withhold a vaccine that could have saved millions, if not billions of lives. The evilness of it shook her to the very core.

"So they're trying to finish the job then," Alan said grimly. "They want to kill anyone who survived."

Paula nodded. "The Universal Brotherhood is run by a guy named Carlos Massa. You might have seen him on TV. He's a good-looking guy and crazy as a cracker. He claims to be the Messiah. He's probably most famous for leading groups of flagellants during the pandemic. You know, the whole I'll-beat-myself-bloody-to-take-away-the-sins-of-the-world shtick."

Susan reeled inside. "I saw him," she said. "In Los Angeles, on an overpass, before everything really went to hell in a handbasket."

"Yeah, he didn't stay in Los Angeles long after that. He went back to his compound in Nevada and then relocated to a new compound in Oregon, just north of Burns. They call the new compound New Jerusalem."

Xiangfa finally spoke up. "Which makes sense from a

doomsday perspective. New Jerusalem is straight out of the Book of Revelation. According to Revelation, after the battle of Armageddon and the Lord's Final Judgment, all nonbelievers are thrown into a lake of fire and the old Earth is destroyed. A new Earth and City of God are formed. The city is called New Jerusalem."

"That's right," Paula said grimly. "The only problem for Massa is that not every nonbeliever has been purged. Some of us are still alive."

Suddenly Harr moved. He surged around the table and seized the cliff-faced guard in a powerful headlock. Every pair of eyes in the room swiveled in shock.

"What the hell is on your wrist?" Harr snarled.

The guard reacted instantly. He drove an elbow into Harr's abdomen, but Harr twisted and yanked. The man's forehead snapped back so hard Susan gasped. "Did you tell Carlos where they were?" Harr thundered. "Is that how the cult found them up in the fucking mountains?"

For a second, no one in the room moved. Susan stared round-eyed, shocked by Harr's sudden violence. In the space of two swift seconds, the room had rocketed from unpleasant tenseness into flat-out murderous confrontation. Hondo was crouched in front of the other guard, ready to launch.

Susan didn't understand what had enraged Harr. Her eyes shifted from the guard's red face to the tattoo on his inner wrist. It looked like a P superimposed over an X. She couldn't read the words beneath it.

"Stop!" The word rang out sharply. Paula was on her feet.

Harr didn't stop. He pulled the guard's head back further and hissed, "Did you stab those men in Shangri-La? Did you string up their bodies?"

"He didn't do it!" Paula shouted. "Would you listen for a minute?"

Susan realized she herself had come to her feet, that her body was shaking. "John, let him go."

Harr's eyes met hers, a long enough glance that the emotion in his face burned into her heart. In a flash, she understood that she didn't know half of what had happened to him in his journey from Shangri-La, nor half of what had been the cost.

She reached a hand toward him. "John, please."

He was regaining control. She could see it in the tight planes of his face. He pushed the guard from him so hard the man sprawled forward, colliding with the table and knocking the whiskey bottle over.

But no one else made a move. The tension in the room was too fraught, the potential for violence too great.

When no one either supported Harr or admonished him, the eastern Oregon rancher walked out of the Victorian and let the door slam behind him.

———

IN THE SHOCKED silence that followed, Paula said quietly, "Scott, would you give us a moment?"

The guard rubbed his neck where Harr had held him, his breath still ragged from the chokehold. Anger flickered in his eyes.

"You can wait outside on the porch," Paula continued, her voice deliberately soothing. "We'll call you back in a moment."

Alan watched grimly. *Now we're one guard against one guard*, he thought. Without Harr present, there was only Hondo, and Hondo looked ready to brawl.

"Care to explain what that was about?" Alan asked coolly. He had the sense that there was a reason for Harr's outburst and the Yakama woman knew it.

"The tattoo on the inside of Scott's wrist is the cult's tattoo,"

Paula explained. "It's a Chi-Rho Christogram, if you're familiar with that."

Seeing Alan's blank look, Xiangfa explained, "A Christogram is a combination of letters that forms an abbreviation for the name of Jesus Christ. In this case, the Chi and Rho are the first two Greek letters in the name 'Christ.' It's a Christian religious symbol that dates back to the Roman Empire."

Alan gave Paula a hard look. "Why does your guard have that tattoo?"

"Because he was a cult member," Paula answered bluntly. "He and two others defected from the Universal Brotherhood and came to warn us that the cult was coming to attack. They told us to abandon the valley, but the congressman wanted to stay and fight."

Paula took another slug of whiskey, her face grim with memory. "When Roger was killed, we took off for the hills," she went on. "There were only thirty of us left, but we had enough vehicles and gas to make a run for it." She looked at Etta. "That's when you heard me on the radio. During the evacuation, some of our people got separated. I was speaking with one of my tribe trying to regroup."

Alan was silent for a moment. Paula's answer didn't explain Harr's outburst. He turned to Hondo. "How did Harr know the tattoo signified cult membership?"

Hondo kept a wary eye on Paula's remaining guard. "When John arrived in Shangri-La, the town was in ruins. There were dead men and boys hanging from one of the buildings, and half the town was on fire. He only found one survivor, a woman wearing tactical gear and carrying a gas mask. She had the same tattoo." He shot a glance at Paula. "It wasn't hard to put two and two together to figure out the lady dressed like a soldier wasn't part of a peacekeeping mission."

"What happened to her?" Susan asked.

Hondo's face flattened. "She killed herself."

Across the table, Paula nodded. "The cult doesn't have total control over its people. They're not all murderers, but Carlos has them all so brainwashed that they're afraid if they don't do exactly what he says, they'll go to hell. He uses that fear to destroy their ability to distinguish what is true and not true. It causes their psyches to fracture." She looked at Hondo. "For some, it leads to suicide."

"What happened to the two other defectors?" Alan asked.

"The cult recaptured them in the first attack. Scott tells me that they were likely executed, probably in a ritualistic group murder involving cages and spears."

Susan's face went lax with horror. "Why, that's *medieval!*" she cried.

Paula nodded. "Carlos is both a sadist and a masochist. It's a classic brainwashing technique. He uses his own suffering from self-flagellation to justify murdering people in the most heinous ways possible. Scott says he was forced to watch members who had been accused of insufficient belief being burned alive."

Alan met Susan's eyes. She looked pale as a ghost. He turned back to Paula. "You said the cult knows we're here?"

"I'm sure they do. You've been transmitting on open airways, and the cult monitors the radio."

Alan turned to Etta. "Have you been broadcasting our exact location?"

The old woman shook her head. "I said we were north of Vacaville, but I never specifically said we were in Liberty Valley."

"But you said you were in Northern California. I heard you," Paula contradicted. "And you have a signal fire and signs posted on all the surrounding roads directing people to this valley. Unlike us, the cult has plenty of fuel and supplies and

273

can outfit surveillance teams. I guarantee you they know you're here."

"Then why haven't they attacked?" Alan asked.

"Because they wanted to wipe us out first," Paula said grimly. "But now that we're here with you—"

"—they can kill two birds with one stone." Susan finished, her eyes round with horror.

"Exactly," Paula agreed.

"Not necessarily," Alan said.

"How's that?" Susan cried. "They have four hundred people, fuel, and enough weapons to pummel us into the ground."

"We have a weapon they don't have," Alan explained, thinking furiously.

"What weapon?"

"Surprise."

"How in god's name are we going to surprise them?" Etta asked. "They know where we are."

Alan gave her a hard look. "We'll take the battle to them."

THIRTY

It was a crazy plan, cooked up in the middle of the night, over too many cups of coffee. Susan was convinced it was a suicide mission.

But she was apparently the only one who felt that way. Alan, Harr, Hondo, Carson, and Paula labored over maps and inventory lists, counting weapons and calculating fuel needs, as though they really believed they could penetrate New Jerusalem's defenses, as if they really thought they could assassinate Carlos.

But not all was in perfect alignment. At one point, Paula had burst out, "I wish you'd let Scott in here. He can tell you a damn sight better than I can how they guard Carlos."

Harr had been firm. "Scott stays out of this."

Susan understood Harr's reasoning. In private, he'd told her he feared Scott had betrayed the Yakima Valley settlement. He thought the one-time cult member had reported Paula's location in the Yakama Indian Reservation's hills.

But Susan didn't know if it was true. She only knew that Harr and Hondo had volunteered for the mission and that Paula had agreed to send two of her men with them.

Four men against five hundred, Susan thought in anguish. *Our men don't stand a chance.*

She couldn't listen to the planning any longer. Feeling restless and anxious, she went into the living room to tend to the men who'd fought the cult and were now dying, their breath labored, their moans low and agonized.

There was little she could do for them. Without IVs or oxygen, she could only offer small comforts, like giving them sips of water and trying to get them to take the remaining Norcos. She put pillows under their backs to help them breathe.

Sometime in the middle of the night, while she was sitting at the bedside of the sickest man, a voice behind her purred, "What a hero you are, tending to Paula's hopeless wounded while Harr and Hondo plan their hopeless assault."

Carson stood in the dim light, leaning against the wall, smiling down at her. A ray of moonlight fell against his eyes, so that his pale irises looked like silver.

Susan rose from the man's bedside and walked, her back ramrod straight, toward the front door. "For god's sake," she whispered as she passed Carson. "If you want to be an asshole, then do it outside."

When he closed the door behind them, she let him have it. "Have you lost your mind? Those men can *hear* you."

He was very tall, and in the moonlight, his thin face looked bleached and pale. "Oh, come on. Do you really think they'll remember? One will be dead by morning, and the others ..." He seemed to weigh his words, and then shrugged. "I give them two days tops."

She'd had enough. She said in a low voice, "You make me sick."

Her words seemed to genuinely surprise him. "Why?" he asked. "Because I'm honest? Those men will die, and they will not remember what I said or you said or even what their beloved leader, Paula, said. They certainly won't remember how sweetly you plumped their pillows."

She couldn't believe a physician, even an unpalatable one like Carson, could so callously joke about men suffering. "You could help me treat them, you know. You *are* a doctor."

He leaned a shoulder against the porch pillar. "Why? You clearly lack effective tools to care for seriously wounded patients. Why waste two capable people on such a useless endeavor?"

"Because they're suffering, and it's the right thing to do."

"Oh, Susan," he said with great pity. "There are so very few of us, and if you've listened to Paula, so *many* of them. That means we have to ration manpower accordingly. Harr and Hondo will go on their sure-to-fail mission, while the rest of us must prepare for the inevitable assault that will happen once Harr and Hondo are dead."

"How can you be so callous about this?"

"I'm not being callous. I'm being realistic. There is no way four men can overpower five hundred well-armed people in a fortified compound. Maybe Harr and Hondo will assassinate Carlos. Maybe." He shrugged. "But they won't get out once they kill him."

She thought of Harr's austere face, of the airplane flight to Sacramento and the turkey dinner he'd made her. She thought of the herd he'd brought back, guaranteeing the settlement milk and meat, the protein that would carry them through the winter. He was too valuable to risk, too decent to send on a suicide mission. Her heart cried out at the thought.

"They shouldn't go," she whispered.

Carson's eyes glittered in the moonlight. "No, they shouldn't. I argued the point with Alan and Harr but was over-ruled. It seems the cult isn't the only bloodthirsty bunch. We Liberty Valley folk are war-hungry, too. The only problem is that with thirty-something people, being war-hungry is the same as being suicidal. The logic of our leaders is criminally flawed."

She gazed at him for a long, silent moment. "What would you do differently?"

He looked as if he was surprised she'd even asked. "I think we should join the cult. Of course, that may mean enduring some unpleasantries, but remember, cult members are fed and provided for. Paula says they have even labs and factories. I'm sure they aren't wiping their asses with leaves and corncobs."

She flinched. The dwindling supply of toilet paper in the settlement was a silent concern for everyone. But still, what he was proposing was crazy. "Carlos murdered almost the entire planet and tortures his own people. Surely that's a reason not to join his cult."

Carson let out a little laugh. "That may be so, but I guarantee you he doesn't want to murder those who follow him peacefully. After all, it's no fun being a Messiah without a flock."

She stared at him, feeling sick inside.

Her distress must have been evident in her expression, because pity returned to Carson's face. "You always look at everything from a moral standpoint, Susan. If it wasn't so self-destructive, it would be an admirable trait."

"You can maintain your morals and still survive."

"Not when four hundred soldiers of the Lord are coming to annihilate you. Morality is useful when times are good and you want to keep Johnny from stealing Jimmy's lollipop, but it's not particularly useful when you need to consider all options to survive. *Flexibility* becomes key. The occasional unholy alliance must be considered."

He sounded like Alan, only much worse. Alan might accept an alliance with an unsavory person like Carson, but Carson would deal with the devil if it suited his objectives. A terrible possibility occurred to her. "Are you going to betray us?"

He laughed and pushed himself from the porch pillar. As he stood over her, she had the strange feeling that he wanted to caress her face. "No," he said quietly. "I'm going to make an ammonium nitrate bomb, so you can see the man I really am."

Like always, she wasn't sure whether he was mocking her or being serious. She watched uneasily as he descended the porch stairs and crossed the yard to where his motorcycle was parked beneath the olive trees.

"If Carlos conquers us, he won't take you," she called after him. "He'll only take the women."

"Maybe, but somehow I doubt that," Carson said. He waved without looking, his body a shadow in the house's dim light. "Good night, Susan. I'll see you tomorrow."

———

IN THE END, Harr relented. He asked Scott to describe New Jerusalem's layout.

The cliff-faced former cult member leaned over the kitchen table, sketching the compound on a poster-board-sized piece of paper, while Harr, Hondo, Alan, and Paula looked on.

Harr felt bleary-eyed. They'd spent much of the night planning, and though he'd managed to catch two hours of sleep on a cot in the Victorian's basement, his eyes burned as though acid-washed. He sucked down coffee by the cupful.

Scott's diagram of the compound was rough, but it made it clear that breaching the facility would be difficult. Cyclone fencing surrounded the perimeter, and lookout towers rose from the corners like a high-security penitentiary.

"Does Carlos ever leave the property?" Harr asked.

Scott shook his head. "Carlos only leaves the perimeter

when he goes out with a war party. He personally supervises all of the attacks, usually from high ground, where the gas can't get him."

Beside him, Hondo let out a short, frustrated sigh. He shot Harr a grim look. "We'll have to get him in the perimeter, John. We could detonate Carson's ammonium nitrate bomb here." He pointed to the portion of the compound's fence that was nearest to the dormitory, which held Carlos's personal suite. "Maybe we'll get lucky and kill him right then and there."

Harr shook his head. "That dormitory holds a hundred people. This needs to be a clean kill."

There was a knock at the kitchen door, and Susan poked her head in. "Do you mind if I grab some coffee?"

She looked like hell. Unlike him and Hondo, she hadn't gotten any shut-eye, and it showed. Dark circles shadowed her eyes, and her skin was pale with fatigue.

Beside him, Paula nodded toward the living room. "How are they?"

"I'm afraid we'll lose one this morning. The others may last longer, but probably not longer than twenty-four hours."

"Even Reb?" Paula looked stricken. The fourteen-year-old wounded boy had obviously been a favorite.

"He's got the best chance, so long as he doesn't get an infection." She turned dark eyes on Harr. "Deb's coming over to help me in a little while. She'll give you a good rundown on what weapons are left at the bunker."

Harr nodded, wanting to tell her to get some sleep, but knowing from experience that she wouldn't as long as she thought patients needed her.

Alan glanced up from one of the inventory lists. "We have enough fuel to get two trucks to the compound, but you'll have to scavenge for the return trip."

Harr nodded again. No surprise there. He looked around

the room. "For obvious reasons, there won't be any comms on this trip until after we accomplish the mission. Once we do, we'll set up a portable station and transmit on twenty meters from the top of the hour until ten minutes after."

Alan gave a sharp nod. "We'll have someone monitoring."

Just then, Etta pushed her way into the room. She was breathing fast, as if she'd rushed the short distance from the Victorian's radio room to the kitchen. "We've cracked it!" she gasped.

Harr glanced at her sharply. "Cracked what?"

"The code! They started transmitting again this morning ... which gave us enough text ..." She had a hard time getting the words out, she was breathing so hard. "... to run it through Xiangfa's computer program." She turned to Susan in panicked horror. "You were right, Susan. It is the cult, and they're coming for us. They'll be here in less than forty-eight hours!"

———

FOR A MOMENT, no one in the room spoke. Susan's eyes shot to Alan, whose face gave away nothing, and then to Harr, who was staring with murderous intent at Scott.

Anger flickered in Paula's eyes. "They must have followed us."

"Or someone has been reporting on your movements this entire time," Harr said.

Scott glared at him. "It wasn't me."

Susan felt nauseous. The cult had already wiped out Shangri-La and turned the Yakima Valley settlement into a ragtag band of wounded. What chance did Liberty Valley, with its under-armed and under-trained inhabitants, stand against an army of hundreds?

Very carefully, Alan rolled up Scott's diagram. He said

deliberately, "We won't be needing this anymore. What maps do you have of Liberty Valley, Susan?"

Susan felt the insane urge to either laugh maniacally or weep. She tried to marshal herself, to make her voice calm. "There's the plastic relief map on the office wall and a variety of topos."

"Get them," he ordered. "Scott, take the golf cart and go get Carson and Reaper."

Susan hustled past the wounded in the living room, trying not to look at their burnt bodies, trying to blot out their rattling breath. Surely the same couldn't happen here, not after all they'd been through, all the struggle they'd endured to rebuild what little they had.

A voice inside told her it was already happening. Carlos's troops were on the march.

The relief map of Liberty Valley was sturdy and plastic, and showed the valley and the mountain ranges on either side of it. She pulled it down from the office wall and then searched the closet for her parents' map collection. She found a cardboard box labeled *MAPS* and hauled it and the relief map back to the kitchen.

When she arrived, Xiangfa was seated in the chair where Scott had once sat, and Deb was seated next to him.

"A Glock 19, a Smith & Wesson 686, an AR-15, a Ruger Mini-14, and a Springfield M1A. We've got dynamite in the quarry, too, if you need it."

With a little start, Susan realized Deb was listing the weapons at the bunker.

"We'll need it," Harr said. He was leaning forward, his calloused hands gripping the side of the tabletop. "What about ammo?"

"There's lots of it." Deb looked uncharacteristically shaken. "I mean, lots of it if you're trying to fight off a couple of raiders, but not enough for fighting a war against a real army. Good god. How many of these guys did you say there were?"

"Too many," Alan said. He looked up at Harr. "What guns do you have?"

"A Remington thirty-aught-six, a pump action twelve-gauge, and not very much ammo. I've also got this one." He pointed to a 9-mm on his hip. "I found it at the ranch house. There's a box of bullets to go with it."

Alan turned back to Paula. "You said they had a mortar?"

Paula nodded. "At least one, probably a 60-millimeter, but very effective. That's how they got the congressman."

"We can't let them get close enough to use it on us." Just then Alan spotted Susan. She slid the plastic relief map onto the table.

For a moment, all eyes regarded Liberty Valley. The narrow depression of land stood between two mountain ranges, fed at the north by a long, tortuous gorge and emptied in the south by a short, narrow gap. Not far upriver from the gap, a dam held back the Liberty River and diverted its flow into an irrigation canal. The canal traveled through the gap and out into the Central Valley beyond.

There was no way they could defend a valley that size with the number of defenders they had.

Alan was looking at Harr. "How would you attack the valley?"

Harr leaned over the map. "From the south. The gorge at the north end is too steep and long. A few of us could do significant damage to any attack from that route." He pointed to the narrow gap at the valley's southern terminus. "Once they breach our defenses here, it's nothing but flat valley between them and the farm."

"What about over the mountains?" Alan asked.

Susan frowned. "The only road over the mountains is the

Arlington Grade, which has been abandoned for years. It'd be crazy to attack from that route."

Harr peered at the gravel road's laborious track from the River Ranch plateau up over the mountains and down into the neighboring Central Valley. The road was so insignificant that it was barely marked on the map. "But it doesn't mean they won't use it. They could send up a squad to cause trouble."

It's impossible, Susan thought. Looking at the length of the valley, its northern and southern access points, and the Arlington Grade, she didn't know how they could possibly defend it all with so few people and so few weapons.

She looked around her mother's kitchen, and at the painting of her mother and father in the family room. Her eyes drifted to her father's collection of beer steins on the fireplace mantle. She said the unthinkable, "Maybe we should head to the hills."

Paula nodded grimly. "We were better armed than you are and better warned. We didn't stand a chance against Carlos's army."

Susan glanced at Etta and thought of Emmaline. Could the two of them survive life on the run? She thanked god Carson hadn't arrived yet. She knew what he would say, that they should surrender and join Carlos's people, that if they didn't resist they had a better chance of surviving.

But something inside her screamed against the idea of capitulating to the worst mass murderer in the history of mankind. Carlos was worse than Genghis Khan, Hitler, and Stalin combined.

"No," she said.

She felt the collective eyes of the room focus on her, the questioning look on Alan's face.

"If we let Carlos win," she said, "he'll only grow stronger. He'll go after the Colorado settlement next, and then the Georgia settlement. Eventually, he'll go overseas. Nothing will be left of civilization as we knew it. *Nothing*. Carlos will rule the world."

Harr's eyes met hers, and a message passed between them. He nodded once and turned to the others.

"We can beat Carlos," he said and pointed to the dam at the valley's southern end. "And this is how we'll do it."

THIRTY-ONE

Susan heard the first of the dynamite late that afternoon. The explosions sounded muffled and far away, but they still managed to rattle the Victorian's windows, startling Susan as she tried to take a dying patient's pulse. She closed her eyes and willed herself to be calm.

"What was that?" Reb cried. The boy sat up, looking around wildly, his bandaged head swiveling in panic.

Susan went to his side. "Our guys are blasting the gorge to close the road. It's nothing for you to worry about."

Susan's words didn't calm the teenager. Tremors rippled through his thin torso. "What are you talking about?" he cried. "Roadblocks won't stop them. Nothing stops them! They'll use gas again. They'll kill us all!"

Susan reached for a patch of unburnt arm and squeezed gently. "Shhhh, Reb. We've got a plan. It's a good one."

But the words were a lie, and the boy knew it. He turned blind, searching eyes toward her face. "You won't leave me, will you? Tell me you won't let them get me."

"I won't leave you," she assured him, but inside, his fear worked on her composure like steel wool. She felt raw and shaken, haunted by the words Harr had spoken earlier in the day.

We'll make the gorge impassable, he'd said. *We'll force them to attack from the south.*

She hoped Harr was right. It wasn't that she doubted that he could trigger rockslides in the gorge. The crumbly sedimentary rock that lined the canyon walls was notoriously unstable. But it was the unpredictable nature of the slides that worried her. The rock could very easily slide both across the road and into the river, and if they accidentally dammed the river, they would have a whole new set of problems. When the water broke through, the entire valley would be wiped out by a flash flood.

Catastrophe seemed to lie in every direction: from the cult army who was at that very moment bearing down on them, to the desperate dynamiting that might protect them but lead to disaster in other ways.

Once again, she checked the dying man's pulse. It was slow, no more than thirty beats a minute, the last agonal rhythm accompanying his last agonal breaths.

In the kitchen, a door swung open. Susan heard the mumble of Etta's voice and someone else's. A minute later, a dark, closely shorn head poked through the doorway to the living room.

It was Adrienne. "I'm leaving. If you need help—" she eyed the dying patient meaningfully "—you'll need to ask Deb."

Susan understood. Aside from Adrienne and Deb, all able-bodied people had been assigned to shore up the valley's defenses. If she needed to move a corpse, Deb would be the only one available to help.

"Where are you going?" Susan asked.

"Up to the ridge. Etta wants a mobile radio and antenna up there to act as a repeater for valley-wide communications."

"Where are you going to place it?"

"At the top of the Arlington Grade. I also plan to drop a few trees while I'm up there. John wants to make sure if some of them come that way, we make it hard for them." Adrienne sounded remarkably calm, as though assembling a mobile radio and antenna and chainsawing trees were perfectly normal tasks for a former university administrator.

Susan gave her a worried smile. "Be careful up there. The county hasn't maintained that road for years."

Adrienne nodded, as though she had already considered the possibility. "I'm taking the ATV. It should get me around any potholes."

Susan hoped the former administrator was right. Although the hills looked deceptively gradual in places, Susan knew that the reality was far different. The grade was a strictly four-wheel-drive route. Adrienne would have her hands full if she was forced off-road.

The former administrator disappeared into the den and reemerged a moment later, carrying a collapsed antenna, a flat black radio, and what looked like twelve cylindrical batteries wrapped together. A coil of black coaxial cable hung over one shoulder.

"I'll see you tonight," she said as she slipped out the front door.

Reb must have overheard the conversation, because as soon as Adrienne left the room, he said in a small, haunted voice, "We had radios, too. It didn't make a difference."

Susan understood his fear. He was blinded and burnt, a child whose life had nearly been taken from him. It was her job to be strong and comfort him, and she was failing miserably. The odors of burnt flesh and dying men were too powerful. She wanted to run, to join the others as they tried to set up the valley's desperate defenses. At least then she'd be active. She wouldn't be stuck in this room, powerless to help these mortally wounded men as they moaned and rattled, delirious with pain.

Another *whumpf* sounded, louder than the others. Harr and Hondo were getting closer to the farm.

Susan took a deep breath, steadied herself. This was her job: to maintain a field hospital for the wounded, to tend to those already injured. With a quiet murmur, she told the boy not to worry, that he needed to rest.

And then she sat at the dining room table alone, listening to the quiet moans and rattling breath of her patients, while she rolled bandages cut from the last of the Victorian's bedsheets.

———

ALAN HAD to raise his voice to be heard over the din of the chain saws.

"Drop those into the canal," he shouted, pointing at the collection of midsize oaks that lined the irrigation canal as it traversed the gap at the valley's southern end. Reaper nodded and set to work, his saw grinding against the hard wood, a shower of white chips spitting from the blade.

A hundred yards down the road, two of Paula's men worked on a cluster of gray pines beside the dry riverbed. Several of the trees were down already, their twisted trunks turning the rock-strewn channel into an uneven obstacle course.

They were making progress.

Alan had never particularly paid attention to this stretch of land, but now he noted its every detail: the two-lane highway, at least forty feet wide if you included the shoulder; the dry, rock-strewn riverbed that ran parallel to the road's other side; and closer to him, on his side of the asphalt, the straight concrete irrigation canal, pushed up against the rising hillside. Altogether, the gap was no wider than a football field. If they blocked it well enough, they could draw the cult's army into a killing zone. Up the hillside, several of the valley's defenders were already digging in sniper positions.

Alan gazed upstream to the low earthen dam behind which Liberty River collected in a reservoir. He knew that, prior to the pandemic, the river's water had been diverted into the canal behind him to be carried through the gap and out into the Central Valley, but now the water just collected behind the dam, and the reservoir had elongated so that it stretched back nearly half a mile.

For a moment, he allowed himself to lament the infrastructure they would soon destroy. The bridge under which the canal crossed the highway would go tomorrow. Shortly after, they'd destroy the road.

But not today. Xiangfa and Carson were still out in the Central Valley scavenging, and their trucks needed unimpeded access to the valley.

As Alan watched his people hammering nails into home-made spike strips, clearing cover the cult army might use in the gap, and hauling in barbed wire, he thought, *This won't hold the cult back longer than half an hour.*

But if Carson and Xiangfa found what they were looking for, Alan realized, half an hour would be long enough.

———

THE SCAVENGING TEAMS returned within fifteen minutes of one another, passing over the open road at Liberty Valley's southern terminus, as the sun began its downward descent over the western ridge. It was the prettiest time of the day, the grass-covered hills a rich gold, the scattered oaks a deeper green, but Alan didn't notice. His mind was focused on the trucks' cargo areas. To his relief, they appeared full.

As he expected, the trucks didn't stop. The drivers waved without slowing. A few minutes later, they were out of sight.

For a moment, Alan listened to the fading rumble of the trucks' engines, and then he glanced around trying to figure out why the saws had gone silent. His eyes swept the distant riverbed, tangled now with downed trees and piled boulders. Paula's men were pointing to the last tall tree still standing along the riverbank. Alan tried to imagine what they were thinking. Were they remembering their own rout? Did they think the decision to stay and fight was suicidal?

It was impossible to tell. They were stoic farmers, rough-hewn and hardworking. It wasn't in their DNA to complain.

But Alan had to wonder. He knew, looking at the ground before him, that this was where the battle would take place. Carlos's army would do their damnedest to punch through the valley's hastily constructed barriers, and valley men and women would die trying to stop them. He himself would likely die.

For one short minute, he let his brain imagine the rapid fire of machine guns and semiautomatic weapons, the pounding of the mortars, the black plumes of smoke.

He imagined the acrid stink of mustard gas, drifting over anyone unable to run away, burning their skin and scorching their lungs ...

Maybe Susan's first suggestion had been right. Maybe it was smarter to run.

He stared blindly at the riverbed, thinking of how difficult running would be. Since the cult would continue to hunt them down, they wouldn't be able to stop. They'd lose Etta and possibly Xiangfa. He himself probably wouldn't survive.

No, there was no point to running. They would either die on the road or die here.

Once more, the farmers fired up their saws. The last

standing cottonwood shuddered, its leaves winking in the dimming light as the chain tore through its trunk.

God, it's beautiful here, he thought suddenly. The rugged grass and cragged hills, the proud, scattered oaks, even the dried riverbed before him were all gorgeous. He breathed in the scenery, tried to burn Liberty Valley in its present state into his memory before war tore up its beauty and blood ran along its floor.

When the thousand-pound tree shuddered against the ground, Alan called the men in. He wanted them to go back to the farm. He wanted them to eat and rest.

Above all, he wanted them to be ready for battle.

————

"ONLY TWO?" Harr asked. He stood in the Victorian's kitchen, frowning at the lone pair of gas masks on the cherry-wood table. Outside, the night was a thick, impenetrable black.

He was surrounded by Susan, Alan, and Xiangfa. The remnants of a late dinner still stood on the kitchen counters.

"We were lucky to find those," Xiangfa said. "Most of the gas masks were hoarded during the pandemic, but I found these two at the Davis police station. The officers must have taken the rest home when everything broke down."

It wasn't the news Harr wanted. He'd hoped for at least twenty protective masks. He figured a police department in a university town would have at least that many in case of student protests.

"What about Deb?" Harr asked.

"She has three masks from her bunker," Susan reported. "She said she'll bring them over tomorrow."

Harr digested that silently. Five masks weren't enough to

hold off a gas attack. Five masks weren't enough to do anything at all.

He turned back to Xiangfa. "What's the status with the bomb?"

"Carson says he procured three hundred pounds of ammonium nitrate at the Port of Stockton. I'm working on the detonator."

Harr grunted. It wasn't Oklahoma City bombing quantities, but three hundred pounds was enough to put a nice crater in anything they wanted to blow. That was, if the bomb worked. Harr was well aware that a failure in any step in the process—the ignition, the detonation, the chemical makeup of the ammonium nitrate—would ruin their one chance at repelling an attack.

He wished to god he had some C-4. He could blow the whole damn gap with less than ten pounds.

But he didn't have C-4. He had dynamite and ammonium nitrate pilfered from a fertilizer plant. He had two men cobbling together a bomb based on remembered reading and theoretical thinking. And he had a plan that even he thought was too preposterous to succeed.

But it was a plan. He slid one of the masks at Alan. "Don't detonate the bomb until they're all in the gap and you can see the full length of their column."

Alan nodded.

Harr slid the other mask at Xiangfa. "You stay with Alan in case there's a problem with detonation." He picked up the relief map and set it on the table. He pointed to the twin ridges that bracketed the gap. "We'll put twelve of Paula's people up here and here and here. Reaper and Deb will go lower down to give you cover."

Alan said, "What about the north end of the valley?"

"Hondo, Sam, Paula, and one of her guards will take up

positions above the gorge. They'll pick off anyone stupid enough to approach that way." He felt Susan's eyes on him, felt her worry and fear. He looked straight at her. "Susan, you, Etta, and Kayla stay here and take care of the children and any wounded. Adrienne and Scott will go to the top of Arlington Grade and manage comms."

"Where will you be?" she asked.

"Behind their lines," he said tersely. "Outside the valley."

"Alone?"

"Yes. I'll be moving fast."

He could see the bafflement in her face. So he explained the awful reality. "Even if we manage to beat back the cult tomorrow, it won't end it for us. As long as Carlos lives, the cult won't stop until they kill us."

Understanding dawned in her face. "You're going to try to kill Carlos."

"That's right," Harr said.

THIRTY-TWO

They lost two of the wounded the next morning. The men gave their last gasping breaths within twenty minutes of each other, just as the sun was rising above the eastern ridge.

"Do you want me to get Xiangfa?" Etta asked. She stood in the kitchen doorway, the smell of hot coffee a jarring juxtaposition to the foul smell of death in the living room.

Susan rubbed a weary arm against her forehead and shook her head. "He already gave them last rites. They don't need him now."

And we can't spare him from his work anyway, she thought but didn't say. The elderly researcher was working on the detonator for Carson's fertilizer bomb. He and Alan had left the Victorian before dawn.

Which left Susan with two corpses and no way, short of dragging them herself, to get them out of the house. For half an hour, she dithered, hoping that Deb or someone else would drop by the Victorian to help, but as the grandfather clock struck seven thirty, she realized it was better not to procrastinate. Within hours, rigor mortis would set in, and then it'd be hell moving them.

She was just wrapping the first body with twine and an old tarp, when Carson walked through the front door carrying a small shoebox.

"What are you doing here?" Susan asked, frowning. "I thought you were working on a bomb."

"Well, hello to you, too," he replied cheerfully, pale eyes flicking over the twin corpses and then Reb's sleeping form on the couch. "I see the hospital census is declining."

Oh, how she hated him sometimes, with his curled lip and mocking eyes, as if no life had meaning, as if suffering and death were fertile material for irony. She tied off the twine and came to her feet. "Seriously, why are you here?"

He took a step toward her and presented her with the shoebox. "Because, as much as you despise me, you still need me. I'm here to give you a present."

She eyed the cardboard box warily. It was small, the kind of box that contained toddler shoes. Reluctantly, she took it from him.

"Don't be shy. Open it," he urged.

As soon as she lifted the lid, she drew in a sharp breath. Inside were fifteen ampules of fentanyl and three disposable syringes. By post-pandemic standards, it was a treasure trove of narcotics.

"Where did you find these?"

He let out a little laugh. "You sound as if I've committed a crime! Come on, Susan. Accept the medication gracefully. You're going to need it tomorrow when the cult trounces us."

She stared at him. "That's not funny."

"I wasn't trying to be funny. The cult *will* pulverize us tomorrow. It's going to be a rout."

He was trying to provoke her again. She could see it in the slight curve of his lips and the way his nostrils flared. She set the box down on the coffee table next to her stethoscope and folded her arms across her chest. "I thought you were making a bomb."

He shrugged. "I am. It'll blow up a few of those poor bastards, but it's not going to stop an army. But don't worry, Susan, if you and Kayla don't put up a fight, you'll be fine. Carlos likes young women." Carson looked upward as though he were contemplating something. "I guess he'd probably take Deb, too, although she's probably a little older than he'd prefer."

That was too much. She glared at him. "How would you know what Carlos prefers?"

He laughed. "I don't. But you don't have to be Einstein to figure out Carlos needs young, fertile women if he hopes to repopulate the world, and that given the choice, he'd prefer docile ones." His eyes drifted over her face appraisingly. "Not that you're exactly docile, but you are a doctor, and you're good-looking enough. You'd be treated well. Heck, Carlos might even take a fancy to you."

Bile rose in her throat. "You should be worried for yourself, not me. So far as I can tell, you're not a woman, nor do you have superpowers that protect you from bullets and gas."

He ran a finger over the grand piano's surface, held it up, and rubbed it against his thumb. "Which is why I'll be in my lab tomorrow, while the rest of you battle it out in the gap."

Of course, she thought. He wasn't going to fight. He'd never planned to fight. "Hiding out is not going to save you. The cult will find you and string you up just like they strung up all the men in Shangri-La."

For the first time, something like anger flickered in his eyes. "*That* is where you're wrong, Susan. Carlos kills people who oppose him. I'm not going to oppose him. I'm going to join him."

"He won't take you."

"Yes, he will. I'm a doctor, and I know how to make weapons." He smiled down at her, but his curved lips had a sharp edge now. "I know how to make products that a man like Carlos wants."

She didn't know what Carson was talking about and didn't want to know. All of a sudden, she was exhausted by him. She didn't care if he joined the cult. In fact, she hoped he would, as long as he didn't betray them in the process.

The thought caught her up, filling her with sudden fear. "The bomb's going to work, isn't it?" she asked. "You're not going to sabotage it, are you?"

He sighed as though she were a moron. "Yes, the bomb will work. It will make a nice big bang that rattles the hillside."

"I don't get you. If Carlos finds out you built the bomb that killed his people, he'll murder you just as surely as he murders the rest of us."

"But if the valley survives, I'll be a hero. Don't you see I'm hedging my bets?"

She had to admit there was an undeniable logic to his plan. If the bomb did what it was supposed to do and Liberty Valley prevailed, Carson's power in the settlement would increase. If the bomb failed to repel the attack and the valley fell, Carson's offer of his weapon-making services would likely be accepted by the cult. Either way, he'd be okay.

"You're disgusting," she said.

He shook his head, chuckling as he slipped out the door. "Enjoy the fentanyl, Susan. I'll see you after this whole thing settles itself out."

――――――

DEB KNEW how to fire a gun. Actually, she knew how to fire a lot of different guns. Alan watched the hairstylist pick up one weapon after another and go through where the safety was, how to load it, how to fire ("bursts, don't waste ammo"), while Alan's motley platoon of irregulars watched silently.

He turned away. Better her than him. Since half the weapons were hers, she knew how to use them more expertly than he ever would. He wasn't a gun man. He'd never needed to be.

But now was different. Every man needed to handle a gun, as did every woman. The future depended on it in ways that transcended battle.

He slung his Winchester .30-30 hung over his uninjured shoulder. In good hands, the gun was accurate up to two hundred yards, but in his, with his hobbled right arm, he'd be lucky to hit something at fifty. He pushed the thought from his mind. Harr had put him in charge of defending the valley's southern approach not for his gun skills, but for his brain, and his brain was telling him they needed more rock and metal across the road and in the canal. Forcing the cult to attack via the riverbed was the only chance they had.

He pointed at the crag overlooking the gap, called to the demolition team, "Now!", and then watched as two men scrambled up the scree pile on the far side of the canal. The two men buried two sticks of dynamite at the crag's base and then, twenty minutes later, blew the cliff into smithereens.

When the dust settled, Alan realized he'd won a partial victory. The falling rock had buried the canal, effectively making it impassable, but the slide over the road was only four feet deep. True, it was twenty feet wide and would stop a vehicle, but troops could easily scramble over it. He'd only effectively taken out the canal.

He looked at the men and women, now finished with Deb's instruction and awaiting further orders. "Barbed wire," he said tersely, and then watched as they built a crossed post fence, crude in appearance, but effective in practice, across the entire gap.

By three p.m., sharp, steel wire ran in thorny tangles between the posts, and the gap itself resembled the aftermath of a battle scene. No trees stood, and the earth looked pockmarked and denuded. Barricades blocked every route.

It was beautiful once, Alan thought.

Now it reminded him of the Somme.

———

LATER, as he rested in the cab of his truck, exhausted but knowing that he would soon need to check in by radio, he thought of Susan as he'd last seen her, earlier in the day, when he'd violated the agreement he'd made with Harr.

All fuel for the fight, they'd agreed. Every last drop for maximum defensive and offensive capabilities.

But that agreement hadn't stopped him from pressing the Tacoma's keys into Susan's hands in the kitchen that morning. It was the first time he'd been alone with her in days.

"There are two jerricans in the back of the Tacoma," he'd said with quiet urgency. "If the gap falls, the only way out of the valley is over the grade. Take Etta, Kayla, and Emmaline, and get out."

He saw the alarm in her face. "What about the plan?"

"No plan survives contact with the enemy." The quote was from a famous Prussian military strategist, von Moltke the Elder. For Alan, who, as an executive, had studied strategy extensively, von Moltke's meaning had been clear: what happened tomorrow when the cult first attacked would dictate all decisions thereafter. There was no knowing how circumstances would unfold.

By the way her eyes darted back and forth, he could tell she was thinking rapidly. "Then we need to set up a rendezvous point in case the gap falls. Meet us in Davis at the bench where we found Xiangfa. We'll wait there for you."

She didn't seem to realize that if the gap fell, he would, too. "It's more important that you go where the cult won't follow," he said gently. "You'll have to be smart to evade them, which means if you have to go in the opposite direction of Davis, you need to do that."

He could tell he'd upset her. Though she tried to hide it, he could see her hands begin to shake. "Then where are we going to meet? We need a backup plan and a backup plan for the backup plan."

He felt a strange tightening in his throat. He reached a hand to her face, tried to reassure her with his touch. "Just make sure you get out in time. We've dropped trees and rock across the road and blown the bridge over the canal, but Paula says the cult can get around obstacles easily."

She looked stricken. "Don't trust Carson," she said desperately. "The bomb—"

A little kernel of alarm planted itself in his gut. "What about the bomb?"

"Carson says the bomb will work, but I don't trust him."

He looked at her sharply, remembering the barrels of ammonium nitrate and diesel Xiangfa had described. "Why do you think Carson would sabotage the bomb?"

"Because Carson thinks you're all going to die tomorrow, and he's already thinking of how he'll pair up with the cult."

Alan stared at her, dumbfounded. Xiangfa had vouched for the bomb. The elderly researcher had said he'd witnessed Carson working on it. There was no way the infectious disease doctor would sabotage the central piece of the valley's defensive plan.

But he didn't want to fight with her about it now. He pulled her tightly to him, pressed his lips against her hair. "I'll see you when it's over," he'd said. "Don't rush to Davis. Come when it's safe. If I'm able, I'll find you."

But now, as he sat alone in his truck, he realized he might never talk with her again, and the words he hadn't said filled him with an unshakeable sorrow. He should have told her he loved her. That was what men said when they went off to war.

————

THE VALLEY'S defenders checked in one by one at eight p.m. that night, as the last vestige of light faded from the sky, and the heat of the day cooled to an unseasonably mild summer night.

"In position," Hondo reported, his tinny voice cutting in and out on the radio. He was in the most difficult terrain, up in the gorge, where radio signals bounced off rock walls and distorted his transmission.

Adrienne was easier to hear. Her voice came loud and clear from her high position on the Arlington Grade. "In position."

And then Alan's voice, also clear, down at the valley's southern entrance. "In position."

Finally, Harr's voice, scratchy and distant like Hondo's, reporting, "In position."

Susan wondered where Harr was. It had been a group decision to transmit as little information as possible, in an effort to avoid revealing their locations, but the decision left her feeling out of touch and helpless. Harr was on the move, and she had no idea what he was doing.

She gazed at Etta anxiously. "Any more code?"

The older woman leaned back in her chair. Behind her, the radio's electric blue display blinked in its black metal case. "Nope, but they're here. John reported he'd seen them massing outside the southern end of the valley."

A chill ran through Susan. The cult's army was very close to where Alan and his team were dug in.

"They're not even hiding," Susan breathed. She stood up abruptly, anxiety rippling through her body.

"Why would they?" Etta said, watching as Susan paced across the den. "Carlos knows that Paula is here and that she's undoubtedly informed us of the cult's intentions. There's no need for surprise."

In the lamplight, Etta's face looked like it belonged in a Renaissance painting, the shadows of the night giving her wrinkled visage a gravity and nobility that worked like a dagger on Susan's heart. Etta was not afraid.

But Susan was. There was no use denying it. She was terrified for Alan, Xiangfa, Deb, and Paula's people, who were dug in in the deepening darkness, under-armed and outmanned. She couldn't bear that their bravery might cost them their lives. She couldn't bear the suffering that was sure to follow.

She wanted the past back with a ferocity that shocked her. Not the pre-pandemic times, because that seemed impossible, but rather the brief interlude of peace in the valley, when worries about food and medicine and Alan's health had seemed the apex of her troubles. How easily disaster fell upon them again and again, all because of one man.

Carlos.

A chill ran through her, so cold that she felt as if someone had drawn ice across her back. Carlos's spirit was everywhere, slithering through the night like a dark serpent, wrapping itself around the valley and the hills and the people dug in ready to fight.

"Etta, we have to stop him!" Susan cried.

Etta gave her a strange look, as though she thought Susan's equilibrium had finally shattered. "That's what we're trying to do. John's out there right now."

Susan couldn't look at her anymore. She crossed the room and stood at the window, searching the darkness for a man she couldn't see, a man she might not see again. Harr was out there, riding alone, one man against a monster and his army.

She closed her eyes, tried to control her panicked breath.

He hadn't told her his plans. He hadn't told anyone anything other than that he was going to kill Carlos. And now she was staring into the darkness, wondering where he was and what he was thinking. She could almost feel his stillness, as he watched and waited for the right time to strike.

Get him, John, she prayed.

THIRTY-THREE

THE WHIP, BRAIDED AND SLIGHTLY TACKY WITH TAR, FELT like rough velvet in Carlos's palm. He held it loosely, its nine tails brushing against his thigh. Before him, thirty feet from the platform, a bonfire crackled, the heat so strong sweat beaded on his face.

The time is near, he thought.

The robed crowd below him, four hundred strong, was restless. He could feel their tensed energy tingling in his fingers and toes.

He called to them quietly, "*Sum via et veritas et vita nemo venit ad Patrem nisi per me.*"

Their mouths moved. An agitated murmuring, increasingly militant, began to rise.

Good.

His eyes flicked to the armada of pickup trucks and RVs, standing in the outer circle of firelight. Leaning against the vehicles, a line of assault rifles stood upright on their stocks. Something metallic and almost sexual bloomed on his tongue.

The end is at last here. Ours will be the kingdom of purity and exultation.

He lifted his arms, held the whip above his head.

"*Sum via et veritas et vita nemo venit ad Patrem nisi per me,*" he said, louder now.

Chanting began, an electric buzz snapping in the air.

He cracked the whip down, tearing the cloth at his back. The sharp sting of ecstasy burst like a firework in his brain.

"*Sum via et veritas et vita nemo venit ad Patrem nisi per me!*" he shouted.

Somewhere in the back of his mind, he was aware of voices crying, that the chanting had broken into frenzied rage and euphoric adulation. But he was beyond looking, beyond thinking. He only felt the dark glory of the lash, an orgy of agony and pleasure burning like fire across his skin.

I am the way, the truth, and the life. No man cometh unto the Father, but by me.

The words repeated in his head over and over again, melding with the tear of flesh and the warm ooze of blood. When at last he could strike no more, he felt his body slip onto the platform, into a heap of bloodied cloth and exhausted exultation.

We are one now, he thought as his disciples charged the platform.

He felt their fingers upon him, frantic with need, wild with adulation.

Pleasure pulsed in his head like a drumbeat.

Victory was at last at hand.

THIRTY-FOUR

Dawn broke breezy and mild, a faint gray radiating upward from the eastern horizon. Alan Wheeler was already awake. He stood on high ground, just north of the gap, on a stretch of hillside above the low earthen dam.

He regarded the shadowed gravel channel below the dam through his binoculars, checking for the hundredth time the sniper positions overlooking it and the tangled bed of obstacles laid across it. Behind him, another set of sniper positions had been set up to catch any enemy soldiers who might get through.

Liberty Valley had exactly one chance. If any single thing went wrong, the valley's defenses would topple like dominos.

Exhausted and yet amped up, he swung the binoculars downward toward Xiangfa's position. He could just make out the elderly researcher fiddling with the radio-controlled detonator again. Anxiety clawed at Alan. Xiangfa had been struggling with it all night.

Which was why Alan risked a transmission, on the side channel he and Xiangfa had agreed to transmit on. "Everything all right?" he asked.

Alan's handheld radio emitted a burst of static and then Xiangfa's voice, terse: "Yes."

Alan watched as the elderly researcher set the handheld radio down on the rock behind which he'd take cover once he detonated the bomb. Xiangfa would need the protection, Alan thought grimly. The rock was only four hundred feet from the blast site.

Just then, another burst of static sounded on Alan's radio, this one on the all-valley frequency. Harr's voice, scratchy and clipped, announced, "Marching. I estimate two hundred."

"Copy," Alan replied, his voice calm, but his heart instantly racing.

Two hundred! Holy Mother of God!

Alan gazed briefly at the blazing sliver of sun now peeking over the horizon. The cult didn't dillydally. When they set out to kill, they got right to it.

Alan stepped out from his cover position and blew his whistle, two sharp blasts that echoed across the gap, the signal to his people that attack was imminent.

———

SIXTEEN MILES UP THE VALLEY, Susan's heart slammed in her chest when she heard Harr's clipped transmission. She gripped her elbows close to her sides and paced the den, while Etta counted the reports.

All four handheld radios had checked in. Adrienne, up on the ridge, reported a brief wind-distorted "All clear up here."

A gust of wind buffeted the ash trees outside the den's window. Susan peered out at the open field beyond the yard and watched as a dust cloud lifted and skittered across the dried soil.

"It's windy out there," she said with a frown.

Etta came to stand by her at the window. "That's probably a

good thing. It will blow any gas attack right back on their troops."

It was true. The cult was attacking from the south, and thus would be vulnerable to a north wind, but Susan also knew the cult had more than enough firepower and personnel to attack without gas, and wind could work both ways in battle.

"I hope it doesn't affect visibility." She hated to think of dust obscuring the attacking force. The defenders needed to pick off every attacker. Otherwise, the valley's defensive line would be broken.

Etta turned and shuffled back to her seat in front of the radio. "I know you're worried, but there's nothing you can do for them now except be ready to treat wounded and make sure Kayla is taking care of the kids. Worrying about what might happen won't change anything."

She was right, of course. But still Susan couldn't help herself. She gazed out the window, up toward the high ridge on the opposite side of the river, where Adrienne and Scott guarded their critical antenna atop the Arlington Grade. Susan could only imagine the wind gusts buffeting the mobile radio station. It would be hell just keeping the vertical antenna upright.

They've got to keep it working, she thought uneasily. The antenna was the linchpin of the valley's communications. Without it, the handheld radios would be worthless, their range reduced to a matter of miles.

A burst of static filled the room, and then Alan's voice, breathless: "We are under heavy fire," and then the godawful sound of automatic weapons and Alan's breath, heavier now, as though he were moving.

Susan's eyes met Etta's. "Oh my god," Susan whispered. "It's begun."

———

IT WAS A NIGHTMARE. One moment, Alan was lying atop a boulder, scanning the gap with his binoculars, looking for the cult's first troops; the next moment, he was on the ground with his back against the boulder, hunched over and holding his ears as the earth exploded around him.

Jesus! How many mortars did they have?

The barrage was deafening. Explosion after explosion tore up the riverbed and road, blowing gigantic holes in the barbed wire barriers and pulverizing the downed trees. Dust and smoke were everywhere.

Alan reeled inside. He'd expected automatic weapons and the occasional mortar, but not this! All hell was raining down on them. Alan peeked from behind his rock, trying to get an eye on where the firepower was originating. From his position, tucked inside the valley above the dam, it was impossible to tell.

Quickly, he swung his binoculars to Xiangfa's position. The elderly researcher was hunkered down, the detonator control in hand, looking up the hillside at Alan. Alan gave him the *not yet* signal, and then checked each of the gap's six defensive positions. Smoke rose from a forward one, its plume snaking southward toward the Central Valley.

Alan's stomach pitched. He'd expected to lose people, but not this soon, not before the Universal Brotherhood infantry had even reached the gap.

For a second, Alan had the wild impulse to detonate the bomb, to just blow the whole fucking place to kingdom come, but he stopped himself. *Not yet,* he told himself.

But waiting felt near impossible. He and Harr had not counted on such extensive mortar fire. Paula said one, maybe two mortars, but this felt like far more. He watched in horror as a second defensive position went up in smoke.

Then mercifully, the mortar fire ceased. For a moment, Alan could only hear the surge of his breath and the wind whipping by his head. Somewhere far away, he thought he heard someone moaning.

When the smoke and dust cleared, he could see the riverbed was in tatters. Huge holes pockmarked the gravel channel; blasted trees lay in smoking piles. Only the rockslide and barbed wire on the road remained intact.

Somewhere, the plaintive sound of a woman sobbing rose above the wind. Was it Deb?

He pushed the sound from his mind and glanced at the two remaining defensive positions above the road, silently willing the people inside to stick to their positions, to not give up and run. But in his heart he knew it was a damnable expectation. These godforsaken people had survived DRYP. To die like this seemed a mockery of justice, an obscene violation of all that was right and fair.

Goddamn Carlos Massa! Killer of his son and wife! Killer of all man!

A new sound arose: the growl of multiple engines. At the far end of the gap, a line of trucks with massive, angulated grille guards advanced along the road, ramming the smaller downed trees without even stopping.

Behind them, more than a hundred infantry soldiers fanned out across the road and riverbed, silently advancing until the gap suddenly exploded with sound once again. The fury of automatic weapons fire blotted out the wind and the crying, the trucks and even Alan's breath.

The dug-in positions tried to return fire. Alan saw one and then several cult soldiers fall in the gap below. But the valley's defenders were outnumbered, and the Universal Brotherhood troops swarmed through the riverbed mostly unmolested, taking cover behind downed trees, and then rushing through the mortar-blasted holes, cutting the distance between the gap and the dam.

"Now!" Alan shouted into his radio. Even while he yelled the word, an alarm bell rang in his mind. The numbers in the gap didn't add up. Harr had said two hundred were on the march, but Paula had reported an army of four hundred had attacked the Yakima Valley settlement. Where were the other soldiers?

But there was no time to hesitate. The first of the soldiers were only a hundred yards from the dam now.

"Now, Xiangfa! Now!" he shouted into the radio.

Below, tucked behind his rock cover, Xiangfa's hands closed over the radio controller. Every muscle in Alan's body tensed.

But the expected explosion didn't come. Frantic, Alan keyed his radio. "What's wrong?"

The elderly researcher didn't respond. Through his binoculars, Alan saw Xiangfa playing with the radio controller. He had it open and was fiddling with the wires inside. A mortar shell, only forty yards away, knocked the device from his hands and sent the biochemist sprawling.

For a second, time slowed for Alan. He heard screaming, saw the slow-motion scramble of soldiers over the barricades, watched the valley's desperate defenses fall as if they were nothing more than picket fences.

It's a rout, he thought. *The bomb doesn't work.*

And then an even more devastating thought occurred to him. *Carson sabotaged the bomb.*

Below, Xiangfa scrambled to his feet and sent a brief stare up the hillside at Alan. He was too far away for Alan to read his expression, but his hand gesture was unmistakable. The elderly researcher pointed downhill and then ran awkwardly downslope toward the earthen dam, his right hand wrapped around something that looked like a flare.

A second later, Alan's world came apart. A mortar shell landed nearby, blowing him backward onto the ground. He looked around dazedly, realizing that he was on his back, that his ears were ringing like crazy, that something warm was trickling down the side of his head. The thundering roar of rifle fire suddenly retreated. He felt like he was listening underwater.

He pushed himself to all fours, scrambled painfully for the binoculars and found them wedged under the rock. The right lens was cracked and useless, so he closed his right eye, and tried not to throw up when he looked through the left lens. His stomach rose in his throat, threatening to spew out his mouth.

He spotted Xiangfa, wobbly and fuzzy through the binoculars, unscrewing the white cap of one of the blue plastic explosive barrels. On either side of him, Liberty River's gravel-and-dirt dam stretched to either bank.

Alan wanted to shout at him, "Get out of there! You're wide out in the open!" but his brain was slow like sludge, and the words wouldn't form on his tongue.

Xiangfa stuck the flare inside the top of one of the barrels, took one look downstream from the dam, and then pulled a small object from his pocket. The biochemist crossed himself, his eyes looking straight up into the sky.

A second later, Alan realized what the object was. Xiangfa touched the lighter to the fuse and stood there. A minute later the dam exploded in a ball of fire and earth.

THIRTY-FIVE

Freed from its bondage, the Liberty River roared down her dry riverbed, sweeping the cult's soldiers into downed trees and barbed wire, and sending trucks skidding sideways. Though he could not see them, Alan knew the mortars would be destroyed, too. The hydraulic force of water was too great; it rushed through the gap and out into the Central Valley beyond.

Alan could not hear any of it. He only heard his breath, loud like a scuba diver's, deafening in his head. But he knew what he would have heard had the mortar fire not done a job on his ears. The soldiers had been screaming. He had seen their panicked faces as they tried to swim against an unswimmable current, before the racing muddy water sucked their heads down beneath the turbulent surface.

There won't be any survivors, he thought. The bomb had worked after all.

But the exultation he expected did not come. He could only see the destruction: the destroyed dam that would never be rebuilt in his lifetime, the wash of water that had no doubt wiped out the road and the downstream bridges and probably half of Esperanta. And of course, the bodies, just now visible, as the water levels slowly began to drift downward.

Xiangfa, or what was left of Xiangfa, was somewhere in that water.

He picked up his radio, unsure of anything but the words that came from his mouth: "Enemy repelled," he reported on the all-valley frequency. "Standby for further."

But he didn't broadcast more. He was looking at the raging river and the wind rippling through the pockmarked hillside grasses, and he was thinking that one man had caused all this chaos and death.

Carlos.

Alan hoped the cult leader had suffered, that the raging river had smashed his body into nothingness.

But somehow, in the devastating aftermath of battle, Alan doubted it.

———

SUSAN THREW her arms around Etta. "Oh my god, Etta," she cried. "They've done it!"

The wave of relief that washed through her dizzied her. Alan and the others had held the gap, which meant Carson hadn't lied after all. The bomb had worked.

The two women were listening to the radio in the Victorian's den, with Kayla, Emmaline, and two of the Yakima Valley children. It had been Susan's idea to let Kayla and the children in. She didn't think it fair to keep the teenager in the dark, and the children were too young to be left on their own. So all six of them had crowded in the room, waiting for word from the valley's defenders.

Etta threw a quick smile at Susan, but her voice was all business when she responded to Alan's call. "Copy that. Awaiting further." To Susan, she said quietly, "There are probably casualties."

Etta's eyes met Susan's meaningfully. She didn't want to alarm the children. They were watching with anxious eyes.

"How come John's not radioing in?" Kayla asked, her green eyes intense with worry.

"If he's outside the valley, he's out of radio range." Susan tried to sound reassuring, but inside it bothered her that they hadn't heard from Harr since the first terse broadcast of the morning, when he'd announced the cult was on the march.

"When is he coming back into the valley?" Kayla demanded. She seemed to be working herself into a state.

"I don't know," Susan said.

Fearing another unpleasant interaction with the teenager and wanting to avoid it, Susan stepped out to check on the last surviving gas victim. Reb slept on the couch with his mouth open, his breath coming softly and without strain.

He'll survive, she thought. His lung injuries were minor.

While she was counting his respirations, a gust of wind buffeted the house and sent a plastic chair clattering and scraping across the porch. Surprised, she rose from the boy's bedside and went outside to investigate.

The heat in the yard stunned her. It blew like a blast furnace against her face.

For a minute, she just stood there, staring at the swishing, silver-green olive trees in the driveway, amazed by the ferocity of the wind.

A little shiver ran through her, like the fingers of a ghost.

A voice behind her said, "You'd better come."

Susan turned to find Kayla in the front doorway, her face pale with fright.

When Susan reached the den, static poured out of the radio. Susan could understand only bits and pieces of the transmission but understood immediately that it was Adrienne radioing in from the Arlington Grade.

... this way ... Scott ... call back the ...

The transmission abruptly terminated, static blaring from the radio. A moment later, the frequency went dead.

"What was that?" Susan asked, astonished.

"I don't know." Etta was spinning the radio's knobs, trying to pick up other frequencies. There was nothing. She went back to the all-valley frequency. "We did not copy your transmission. Please repeat."

Silence.

Etta tried again. "Adrienne, this is base, do you copy?"

Again silence.

"Maybe the wind took out the antenna and knocked out the repeater," Susan ventured. "Maybe that's what Adrienne was trying to say."

Etta didn't even look at her. "Liberty Team Two, this is Liberty Base, do you copy?"

Liberty Team Two was Hondo's team. Etta and Susan waited for a reply, but the only sound they heard was the low static of an open channel.

"Liberty Team Three, do you copy?" Etta tried again, this time calling for Alan.

When there was no reply, Etta swiveled in her chair, her forehead creased with tension. "The antenna has to be down. We've lost comms."

"Are you sure?" Susan asked.

"At least one of them should have responded. There are four handheld radios out there. You can't tell me that none of them heard me." She rubbed her mouth in agitation. "Something's happening on the grade. Adrienne was trying to warn us."

An icy chill ran down Susan's spine. She realized every eye

in the room was glued on her and that the children looked terrified. She forced calm into her voice. "The wind gusts are at least forty miles per hour up on that ridge. She's probably having a hard time keeping the antenna up. I'll go over to River Ranch and see if I can get an eyeball on her position to make sure."

Susan turned to Etta so that her face was not visible to the others. "Reb is fine. He won't need any additional care while I'm gone," she said. "I'll be back in half an hour."

But her face said something else entirely. She agreed with Etta. Something was wrong on the ridge, and Adrienne was smack-dab in the middle of it.

———

AS SOON AS Harr saw the abandoned RVs, he knew he'd made a critical error. The cluster of vehicles was nowhere near Esperanta or Liberty Valley's southern terminus. Rather, the dozen or so RVs were parked twenty miles north, on a dusty piece of farmland beside a small creek.

Harr's stomach dropped. This was the real staging area. He could see it in the tire tracks and footprints and in the portable platform erected next to a burnt-down bonfire.

How had he been so stupid? All the clues he hadn't recognized suddenly assailed him: the fact that only two hundred soldiers of a four-hundred-soldier army had marched on the gap, the fact that Carlos was nowhere to be seen either before or during the attack.

Scott had warned him. *Carlos likes to supervise his troops*, he'd said. *Usually from high ground.*

Harr slammed on the brakes and grabbed the binoculars from the pickup's passenger seat. He was on a straight stretch of country road just outside the small Central Valley town of

Arlington. Directly in front of him, the Arlington Grade began its arduous westward climb uphill toward Liberty Valley.

He could not see the cult's army, but he knew they were somewhere on the grade. The gate to the gravel road had been opened, and the Road Closed sign kicked into the dirt. Everywhere, there were signs of recent movement.

He snatched the radio from the center console. "Liberty Base, this is Liberty Team Four. Do you copy?"

The radio didn't even emit a burst of static.

He tried again. "Liberty Team One, this is Liberty Team Four. Attack via the Arlington Grade imminent. Repeat. Attack via the Arlington Grade imminent."

The urgency in his voice was met by silence.

Helpless rage filled him. Adrienne's radio hadn't picked up his transmission, which meant either the cult had reached her position or Scott had killed her.

He looked uphill, saw the zigzag of the grade, and threw his truck in gear.

———

THE DOG WAS BARKING like hell and tearing from one end of River Ranch's gravel yard to the other. It occurred to Susan that an animal so upset might bite her, but Seawolf didn't seem to want to attack. Rather, the black-and-gray dog seemed half out of her mind and frantic. She was scaring the cattle to death.

"Shhhhh," Susan said, stepping out of the Tacoma's cab. She threw a glance at the cows, who were sticking their noses through the paddock fencing and mooing plaintively. A rim of panicked white showed around their brown eyes.

She walked past the barn, into the open grazing land beyond. The radio site was too far away to be seen from River

Ranch, but the ridge was clear enough. Pine and oak trees clustered along its sharp edge, interrupted by short sections of rocky crag.

The hillside looked exactly like it did on any other summer day: bone-dry, inhospitable, and deathly quiet. Except for the wind. It rushed through the cottonwoods along the river below her, a sound that in any other time would have worked like velvet on her nerves. But not today. Today the wind seemed ominous, a powder keg ready to blow.

Susan scanned the meandering path of the Arlington Grade with her binoculars. Some of it was visible, but some of it was hidden by trees and folds in the earth. When she reached the midway point, between valley and ridge, she gasped.

In a visible section of road, perhaps a mile distant from River Ranch, a vehicle raced down the grade, dust rising from its back end like a comet's tail. It took Susan all of one second to recognize the knobby wheels of her dad's ATV.

Someone was driving it like a bat out of hell.

Dread pooled like a pit in Susan's stomach. She ran for the truck, took it in a tight turn in the gravel yard, and sped past Seawolf. She was just about to turn up the grade when the ATV barreled around the last sharp corner onto the tree-lined straightaway that marked the end of the road.

The driver didn't slow at all, and for a crazed second, Susan thought the ATV would plow right into her, but twenty feet from the truck, the four-wheeler abruptly skidded and swerved across the road. A second later, the all-terrain vehicle slammed into a pine tree.

"Adrienne!" Susan screamed, recognizing the driver.

She wasn't aware that she was running. She only knew that Adrienne had landed beside the upended four-wheeler and her leg was bent in a horrible angle.

Susan slid to her knees beside the injured woman, her heart

hammering in her chest, horror vibrating in every single nerve cell. Dark red blood soaked Adrienne's shirt, spreading outward from a sharp hole in the fabric.

Adrienne was having a hard time breathing. "They're coming ... Tw-twenty minutes behind me."

Susan grabbed her hand. "Who's coming?"

"The cult. They're massing ... on the other side of the ridge ... there's hundreds of them."

Oh god! Susan's eyes shot beyond the trees, across the small plateau, and up toward the grade. Dust rose along the ridge, whipped southward by the wind. Realization shot through her body like a lightning bolt.

She gripped Adrienne's hand hard. "What happened to the radio?"

"Scott disabled it. He ... he destroyed the antenna. Harr was right, Susan. Scott told the cult everything." A sob wracked her body. "And then he shot me."

Susan's eyes swept back to the ridge. She could see the distant shadow of trucks cresting the ridge and the smudge of troops surrounding them. Futility swept through her. There was no way to fight them now and no place for the valley's residents to flee. The gorge was blocked by rockslides, the gap a raging wall of water. The only way out of the valley was over the grade, and now the cult possessed it!

She wanted to warn Etta, to tell the others to run for the dirt trails on the coastal range at the other side of the valley, but she had no radio, and even if she had one, it wouldn't work without Adrienne's antenna.

They've got us, she thought in agony. *Goddamn you, Carlos!*

She stopped herself, forced her breath to slow. The wind whipped against her back, a hot blast that seemed to strike at her just as the troops above would soon strike at her. In minutes, when the cult soldiers got within range, the mortar shells would begin to fall.

She looked across the river, at the patch of green on her parents' farm, only one mile distant as the crow flew. The proud turret of the Victorian stood above all that had been salvaged of the old world and all they had built for the new. How her parents would weep to know that they had let it fall!

She couldn't let it happen. With a look of sorrow and grief, she peered down at Adrienne's suffering face. "I'm sorry. I have to leave you."

Adrienne's blood-soaked fingers clutched at her wounded abdomen.

"Go," she whispered.

Susan touched the other woman's cheek and pressed a kiss to her forehead, and then ran for the pickup truck. She drove back to River Ranch as fast as she could.

THIRTY-SIX

Hᴏɴᴅᴏ ᴡᴀs ᴛʜᴇ ꜰɪʀsᴛ ᴛᴏ sᴇᴇ ᴛʜᴇ sᴍᴏᴋᴇ. Iᴛ ʀᴏsᴇ sᴏᴜᴛʜ of him, a black and billowing plume, somewhere in the valley.

Alarmed, he keyed his radio. "Liberty Base, this is Liberty Team Two. We're seeing a big plume of smoke just south of here. What's your status?"

Silence greeted him, and Hondo's alarm, which had been low grade up to now, suddenly became overpowering. He hadn't heard a thing on the radio since Alan's terse "Enemy repelled," and now the silence and the smoke struck him as ominous.

"You think there's something wrong with the radio?" Sam asked. She stood beside him, her black-and-red hair ratty, her fingers wrapped around her hunting rifle. The detritus of their watch lay on the ground around them: empty cans of chili, two canteens, and a bag that had contained the corn cakes they'd eaten for breakfast. Their sniper position was a mess.

"I don't know." Hondo's eyes swept the narrow gorge below him, only wide enough to admit the river and the two-lane highway beside it. A tumble of rocks blocked the asphalt, but the river remained open. On either side, sharp cliffs rose above the cascading water, and a hot wind howled.

Abruptly, he said, "We've got to get out." He was already packing up their ammo and supplies.

Sam looked confused. "But what if the cult comes this way?"

He slung his gun over his shoulder. "They won't, and if they do, it'd be suicide." He pointed at the thick chaparral that covered the steep hills around them. "That stuff will burn like a motherfucker in this wind, and anybody who tries to take refuge in the river is going to fry. Come on."

He pulled his whistle from his pocket and blew it hard three times as he scrambled down the rocky slope. Across the river, Paula and her guard popped their heads up from their sniper position. Hondo made the hand signal for "move out" and pointed toward the valley.

Sam was breathless behind him, nearly stumbling as she scrambled down the scree pile. "But that's where the fire is, Hondo. We can't go there," and then as the reality of the fire's location hit her, she cried, "Jim's down there. Oh my god!"

Hondo wasn't listening. He was looking at the plume. It blotted out half the sky now and gave the valley an eerie dark orange glow.

Mother of God, he thought. *The fire's everywhere.* He could smell the smoke even from his upwind position.

They had reached the open end of the valley when the mortar fire began.

———

ETTA SIMON STOOD on the porch of the Victorian with her mouth hanging open. In her entire eighty years of living, she'd never seen such an inferno. Across the river, black smoke blotted out the sun.

She could not see the explosions, but she could hear them.

They thundered somewhere in the flame and smoke, a horrific sound punctuated by the shrieking behind her. Inside the house, the children were screaming in terror, their high-pitched wailing piercing the sounds of the wind and the weapons fire and the godawful roar of the fire.

Etta felt paralyzed. In the open dirt surrounding the house, dust had risen up in a huge rotating funnel. She watched in horror as the twisting tornado grew, throwing off dirt clods and sucking up smoke, and sending the burning ash that floated in the sky toward the house.

It was the end of the world. Birds streaked across the darkening sky. A deer and her fawns sprinted across the field at full gallop. Even the squirrels were running, abandoning their holes and racing across the lawn.

Somewhere a door slammed, and then a figure, wind whipped and hunched, ran across the yard. A moment later, the lawn sprinklers erupted from the grass, spraying dark silver water onto one patch of lawn and then another. Soon the entire irrigation system was raging, and the figure began dragging something from the side of the house.

It was Kayla, lifting the garden hose and spraying the porch, the siding, anywhere the jet of water could reach.

It can't possibly work, Etta thought. Burning ash was already in the air above the house, and Kayla's spray barely reached the second floor.

"*Etta!*" Kayla screamed. "*Help me!*"

The word shook Etta from her paralysis. She stumbled down the porch steps into the yard, aware that her breath had become wheezy, that her heart was pounding in her chest.

Kayla held a bucket. She shoved the hose at Etta and shouted, "Keep spraying." And then the teenager was off, carrying the sloshing container up the porch stairs and into the house. A minute later, the redhead appeared on the second-floor balcony and flung the bucket of water on a burning ember.

It will never work, Etta thought again. Fiery ash was landing everywhere, on the trees out in the orchard and the grass outside the house. It was only a matter of time before some landed on an unreachable part of the Victorian's roof.

But that didn't stop them. Etta wheezed and sprayed and filled bucket after bucket, praying that Kayla would reach the embers before they ignited. The dark heat felt oppressive, like it was sucking up all the air. Etta's heart skittered in her chest.

———

ALAN WHEELER COULD NOT HEAR, but he could see the heavy curtain of smoke rolling down the valley. It swallowed the sunlight in a giant black cloud.

His heart pounded against his ribs. Something was happening up valley, and by the looks of it, it wasn't good.

He picked up his binoculars and scanned the gap below. Now that the water level was dropping, bodies poked up from the muddy torrent. Dozens were pinned against downed trees and wrapped around boulders. Half the road had washed away.

But not everyone was dead. In the sodden grass where the hillside began its steep ascent, Alan spotted a lone soldier crawling on his stomach, dragging a leg behind him. With a little shock, Alan saw that the foot was turned the wrong way, the knee pointing in one direction, and the toes another.

Reaper suddenly stepped into Alan's view, and the soldier's body abruptly jerked in the binocular's focal field. The sound of a shot ricocheted across the hillside .

It was the third cult member Alan had seen the former MMA fighter shoot. Reaper was prowling the gap, killing anybody who had survived.

Later, Alan would pinpoint his failure to respond in this moment as a critical lapse in leadership, but his mind was on the growing fire to the north and the fact that half his people were dead. He made a split-second, fateful decision. He didn't discuss whether to take prisoners or who had the right to make such a life-or-death decision. Instead, he let Reaper kill one more, and then blared his whistle in a signal to move out.

———

THE FIRE WAS ROARING like a freight train up the hillside. Frozen by awe and horror, Susan stood with the empty drip torch in hand, watching as great tongues of flame ripped up the grassy ridge.

As a Californian, she knew the power of wildfires, but to see it up close was terrifying. The day had turned to night. Only the orange glow of the blaze gave the sky any light.

She was not a firefighter. She did not know how to start a proper backfire. She'd only done what a desperate person would do: pour gasoline onto wood and grass and then set it ablaze with flares and the drip torch. The wind did the rest.

But now the fire was out of control. A stream of sparks swirled in the superheated air and blew over her head. Flame creeped back towards her on River Ranch's plateau.

With sudden force, she flung the drip torch toward the fire and ran in the other direction.

She didn't know if she would make it. The air was too hot; it singed her lungs. She stumbled once and went sprawling. She righted herself and ran again.

All the while, she could hear the crazed mooing of the cows. The awful sound wrapped itself in with the wind and the roar of the flames and her own gasping breath.

In some far part of her mind, she realized the mortar fire had ceased, but the observation flashed and didn't hold. She was praying she could reach the Tacoma in time. She wasn't sure she could outrun the fire.

Seawolf tackled her before she reached the truck. For a second time, Susan sprawled to the ground, this time with the black-and-gray dog on top of her.

"Oh, Seawolf," she gasped, clutching the frightened animal. "We've got to get out of here."

She could feel the tremor in Seawolf's chest, see the burning hillside reflected in her dark eyes.

She thinks Harr's out there, Susan thought bleakly. *She thinks her master is caught in the fire.*

Susan's breath caught on a sob. The entire ridge was engulfed, which meant the cult's soldiers were dying. That Harr might be up there fighting against them was more than she could bear.

She gripped the dog to her, watching as flame rushed back across the pastureland. It felt as though the earth had erupted in cataclysm, that the landscape of her childhood had become an inferno-like hell.

She put her face into the dog's fur, trying to calm the shaking animal. In the chaos of the flame and the terrified animals, she didn't hear the hooves until they were right beside her. For a crazed, deluded moment, she thought Harr had come back to her, but when she looked up, it was not Harr. It was Hondo atop a wild-eyed stallion.

The young man cried, "My god, Susan. Get back to the Victorian! They need you there to fight the fire."

He was having a difficult time controlling his horse. The stallion danced one way and then another.

"You have to come with me," she cried.

He shook his head and reined the horse around. "I'm going to save the cattle. Now, go before fire cuts off the bridge!"

She took one look at him and the terrified animals penned up in the corral. An ember landed on the roof, and then another. "Be safe, Hondo," she cried out to him.

But he wasn't looking at her. He was swinging the corral gate open. He hadn't even bothered to dismount from his terrified horse.

———

AT 8:25 A.M., the first slender wisp of gray smoke rose above the ridge line. Twenty minutes later, a full half mile of the rocky summit was in flames.

John Harr stared in shock. In his entire life, he'd never seen a fire chew up ground so quickly. It spread north and south, uphill and down.

He was halfway up the grade on a short section of widened roadway, parked beneath the tilting branches of two scraggly pines. It was a precarious spot, not because the gravel road was in bad shape, but rather because the hillside pinched into two scrub-choked draws on either side of him. Once the draws caught fire, he'd be trapped.

But he didn't flee. Instead, he moved the pickup fifty feet downhill from the pine trees and then pulled a chain saw from the truck's cargo area. Ten minutes later, he returned the saw.

He was not in a hurry as he shouldered his rifle and scrambled up the hillside. Nor was he in a hurry as he steadied his sights. He was not worried about infantrymen, because he knew that they would not survive the fire on the other side of the ridge. He was more concerned about how many soldiers Carlos would bring with him when he fled. That was the real question.

He scanned the gray pines, now lying on their sides across the road, and then let his eyes drift to the orange sky and the fiery ridge above. A trio of trucks was racing down the grade, just as he expected.

He breathed in and out, waiting for their approach.

———

SEAWOLF WHINED as Susan barreled toward the bridge.

"It's all right, girl," Susan whispered to the frightened animal. "It's going to be all right."

But Susan wasn't sure it was true. The fire was out of control in a way that terrified her. It was an inferno that transcended the ten gallons of gasoline Alan had given her, the few flares, and the drip torch.

She bit back a sob, not because her body hurt or she was afraid for herself, but because every jostle of the speeding truck elicited a moan from the woman in back. Adrienne's suffering crept in through the cab's open rear window, a half-conscious sound that tore Susan's heart apart.

"Hang in there, Adrienne," she cried.

Before her, she could see the flickering orange-and-red arches of the Romulus bridge and the scarlet glow of the river below.

No fire burned on the other side of the river yet, but she knew as she raced across the bridge's cement span that this moment of reprieve wouldn't last. Flying embers sailed like fireflies overhead, winking and glowing in the dark sky.

When she reached the turnoff for the farm, she realized she'd been wrong about the fire not touching the valley floor. Half a mile away, a brilliant spire of flame rose above the Morgan property. With a gasp of horror, Susan realized that Adrienne and Deb's home was fully engulfed.

THIRTY-SEVEN

THE BATTLE TO SAVE THE VICTORIAN LASTED ALL DAY. Each time an ember landed on the Victorian's pitched roof, one of Paula's men beat it back with a blanket. For Susan, watching from below, it was an exercise in terror. She kept expecting him to slip and plunge to his death, but the Yakima Valley man moved carefully and deliberately, in one of the bravest displays of courage she'd ever seen.

They were all brave. Deb, who had witnessed the carnage in the gap and the destruction of her belongings at the Morgan house, still ferociously doused spot fires in the yard and garden. Hondo, Paula, and Sam cut fire lines around the solar panels and the barn.

But perhaps the greatest miracle, Susan would think later, was that her father had left the fields around the Victorian fallow. The four acres of open dirt acted as a buffer, stopping the fire from making a direct, fatal run.

Throughout it all, Susan alternated between monitoring the fire outside the house and caring for the wounded inside. Every time she heard someone call out a spot fire, she was sure that the house would burn. Some of the wounded begged to be let outside, but there was no place outside that was safe for them to be, and inside, at least, she had running water and light.

This was the reality of post-pandemic war, she thought dismally. No Life Flight or trauma surgeons. No ORs or oxygen. Just an overtaxed internal medicine doctor racing from one dying person to the next in a house that threatened to go up in flames at any moment.

But it never did. After twelve hours, the howling wind died down, and the smoke cleared enough so that a thin sliver of moon showed through the pall. Across the river and up the ridge, the remnants of the firestorm glowed in scattered red and orange. Everywhere there was smoke and silence.

Those who could sleep, did.

———

SUSAN LOST Adrienne that night and two of Paula's people as well. She saved a third man by amputating his leg in a surgery that would haunt her nightmares, sawing through bone and ligament without anesthetic except a dose of fentanyl that still wasn't enough to stop his screams.

By the time dawn broke on the eastern horizon, her head felt like it weighed a thousand pounds. She rose from the new amputee's bedside and staggered to the kitchen, knowing that there would be no coffee to revive her. The solar-powered batteries were depleted, and the house no longer had electricity.

There was no one in the kitchen, so she went outside. Half a dozen people slept curled up on the trampled lawn. Her heart squeezed painfully when she spotted Alan. He lay in his dirty clothes as though he'd dropped in place. The ends of his hip bone poked up against his jeans.

How much is lost! she thought.

Beyond the open field, her father's beloved walnut trees lay in smoking ruins. Further out, where the river separated the farm from the ridge on the other side, a long section of charred cottonwood and pine gave evidence of the fire's foray across the river and onto the valley floor. But the barn still stood, as did the solar panels and the house. Only the Morgan property two fields over was a complete loss.

She let that mournful thought sink in. It was all her fault—the hundreds dead on the hillside, the destruction of the Morgan buildings and her father's orchard, the fire that was now burning unimpeded south beyond the valley. She, who'd sworn her life to the care of others, had become an agent of annihilation and ruin.

She leaned her elbows against the porch railing and dropped her head in her hands.

The porch creaked behind her. When she looked up, she saw that Alan had risen from the grass and had mounted the steps to join her. His face was haggard, but his expression was certain and firm as he looked down into her face. "We beat the cult, Susan," he said, his voice too loud in the quiet morning. "They won't be coming back for us."

She didn't tell him what she thought, which was that their problems were far from over. There were still a hundred people back at New Jerusalem, and even if they had smashed the cult's military capabilities, there were still enough cult members left to remain a potent threat.

But there didn't seem a point to arguing with him when he couldn't hear her. She pointed at the dried blood on the side of his head and mouthed, "Let me take a look at your ears." She jerked a thumb at the kitchen because she didn't want to examine him in the living room. She knew if he saw the wounded patients inside, his fleeting sense of victory would end.

HONDO AND PAULA returned from scouting the valley's southern expanse as the sun neared the western horizon. They briefed Susan, Alan, and Etta in the kitchen, their exhaustion clearly evident.

"There are no survivors in the gap." Hondo leaned forward blearily on the table, his hand wrapped around a cup of coffee. "We also checked out the area around Esperanta where the cult staged their attack. There's nothing left there except a few trucks."

Susan scribbled *No Survivors at the Gap* on a sheet of paper and slipped it to Alan, who nodded and then slid it back.

"The damage is significant below the dam," Hondo continued. "The road is washed out in two places, and the bridge over the irrigation canal is gone. There's also flooding damage in Esperanta. Half the downtown area is buried under three feet of muck."

Again, Susan scrawled a translation on the sheet of paper and slid it to Alan. He nodded, his face serious and contemplative. She could tell he was assessing the situation, figuring out what could be rebuilt, how soon they could manage it. That was the kind of person he was.

But what kind of person was she? Clinging to the past, trying to preserve as much of the old world as possible, without recognizing that that old world was gone forever?

Alan was asking a question. "Did you check out the back side of the Arlington Grade?" His voice came out too loud, almost as though he were shouting.

But everyone understood. His eardrums were punctured. He couldn't hear himself speak.

Hondo nodded gravely. "It's all burnt. Most of that side of the grade is grass and shrubs, so the fire moved through quickly, but there are still areas that are on fire. We didn't get very far."

Again, Susan translated.

"What about Carlos's army?" Alan asked.

Hondo shot an unreadable glance at Paula. "They were probably killed on the Liberty Valley side of the ridge during the initial firestorm. We spotted four burnt-over pickups on the Central Valley side, but no bodies and no tracks that suggested anyone successfully escaped the fire. In fact, we found what looked like a second staging area on a farm near the grade's entrance. There were eleven RVs there. If anyone did manage to get out, they didn't take their rigs with them."

Silence fell on the room. No one wanted to ask the question, so Susan finally asked it. "What about John?"

A muscle twitched along Hondo's jaw. Susan got the impression of strong emotion, repressed at great cost.

The young man swallowed hard, and his voice was not quite even when he spoke. "One of the burnt-over pickups on the hillside was John's Ford Ranger. We saw it with binoculars. We weren't able to get close enough to look for his body."

THIRTY-EIGHT

THEY HELD THE FUNERALS LATE THE FOLLOWING afternoon when the sun glowed sullen red on the smoke-choked horizon. The twenty-five surviving valley members clustered beneath a large oak on a patch of unburnt land that had become, by virtue of the battle with the cult, the valley's de facto cemetery. The eleven fresh graves broke Susan's heart.

She hoped Harr had killed Carlos, that the cult leader had been in one of the burnt-over trucks that Hondo and Paula had seen on the Arlington Grade the day before. But Susan realized she might never know for sure because Harr had not come back to tell them what had happened, and as the hours stretched into days, she began to accept he never would.

Beside her, Seawolf seemed to sense her grief. Ever since the fire two days earlier, the black-and-gray dog had become her almost constant companion, following her wherever she walked and lying outside the Victorian's front door while she worked with the injured patients inside.

I give you this one thought to keep:
I am with you still—I do not sleep.

I am a thousand winds that blow,
I am the diamond glints on snow,
I am the sunlight on ripened grain,
I am the gentle autumn rain.
When you awaken in the morning's hush,
I am the swift, uplifting rush of
quiet birds in circled flight.
I am the soft stars that shine at night ...

Paula's deep voice carried across the silent crowd. The Yakama woman stood behind the graves, speaking to the group with a face that was both hauntingly young and, to Susan's eyes, also very old. Susan wondered if they all looked like that, if the sorrow of the last few months had become permanently etched in their faces, never to be erased again.

Adrienne, Xiangfa, John ... How her heart wept at their loss!

She let her eyes drift to the grieving people around her: Etta's pale, drawn face; Kayla's raw and swollen eyes; Deb's tear-streaked cheeks.

Only Carson and Reaper looked unaffected. In some bitter place in her heart, Susan understood why. Neither man had fought the fire, nor cared for the dying and injured. Rather, the two men had spent the day of the inferno at their house, miles away from the fire front, because Carson had wanted to protect his solar power system and laboratory in case the blaze made a serious run across the valley floor.

But the fire hadn't, and Carson and Reaper had remained at their house an additional twenty-four hours after the danger had passed. Susan couldn't forgive that.

She looked away from Carson's phony somber face and Reaper's bored one. She didn't want to think of either of them anymore. There was enough to think about with the injured still in the Victorian's living room, tended to, for the moment, by one of Paula's people.

Before her, Alan began quoting Ecclesiastes, reading too loudly from a piece of paper in his hand:

There is a time for everything,
And a season for every activity under the heavens;
A time to be born and a time to die ...

He'll recover his hearing eventually, she thought. Just how long it would take, though, she couldn't quite say. That was the problem with being a doctor just shy of completing her medical residency. She was an expert at nothing. There was so much more she had yet to learn.

Later, after the ceremony ended and the more infirm of the group had loaded themselves into the Tacoma to head back to the Victorian, Deb brought up the matter of housing.

"You can't keep us all at the Victorian," Deb said as she, Susan, Kayla, and Seawolf walked back across the burnt orchard. "I saw there's a house upstream of here that doesn't look too bad. Maybe Kayla, Paula, and I could check it out tomorrow."

Susan knew the house. It was far more modest than the Morgan place and didn't have solar panels, but it was on the river and close to the Victorian. If it hadn't burned, it would be a good choice. "Did it survive the fire?"

"Hondo says so. He wants Paula to have a proper place to live. He's gotten awfully fond of her lately."

Susan smiled tiredly. She, too, had noticed how Hondo and Paula seemed to gravitate to one another. The Yakama woman and the former farmworker had become nearly inseparable.

"What about the rest of Paula's people?" Susan asked. "I can't imagine they like sleeping in the Victorian's basement."

Deb shrugged. "We'll just have to find a place for them. That's how it's going to be from now on. We face one challenge and adapt. And then another one will come along, and we'll have to adapt again." She turned kind eyes to Kayla next to her. "Isn't that right, honey?"

But Kayla didn't answer. The young woman was staring straight ahead, her red-rimmed eyes wide and disbelieving.

"What's wrong, Kayla?" Deb asked, alarmed.

Kayla stuck out a finger and pointed at the Tacoma. It had stopped a quarter mile ahead in the gravel yard near the barn. "Look!"

Susan squinted in the smoke, saw a figure step from the driver's side of the truck. A second later, Seawolf shot across the field at full sprint.

Susan swung around and looked at Deb. "Who is that?"

A smile spread across the hairstylist's face. "Can't you see him? He's coming out of the barn."

Susan looked again and saw the outline of a man limping across the gravel to greet the Tacoma's driver.

Susan's heart slammed in her chest.

"John!" Kayla shrieked and took off after the dog.

———

THEY WELCOMED HIM LIKE A HERO, although Harr hardly felt heroic. He mainly felt exhausted. He'd just walked thirty miles.

"Sit down! Sit down!" Deb cried, ushering him into the Victorian's family room. Alan, Etta, Hondo, and Paula filed in behind him.

"Kayla, honey, go get him a drink," the blonde woman went on. "Make it something strong."

Harr was having a hard time wrapping his head around the

state of the Victorian. Although the curtains were wide open, the light inside was gloomy. Dirt tracks covered the carpet and the kitchen floor. Beyond the living room door, someone was moaning.

"I don't know if I ought to sit on anything," he said. "I'm filthy."

"Honey, the whole house is filthy," Deb said. "Sit down before you fall down."

He wanted to ask what had happened to the Victorian, why there wasn't electricity, and why dirt tracks stained the floor. But he figured they'd want to ask their questions first, and the basic outline of what had happened at the Victorian was pretty much clear anyway: they'd saved the house from the fire, but it had been a hell of a fight.

"Did you kill him?" Etta wheezed. She plopped down on a stuffed chair by the fireplace, her face gray with stress and fury.

He nodded, knowing immediately who she meant, although in truth killing Carlos hadn't been cut and dried at all. There was the small matter that Harr hadn't known what Carlos looked like, and the fact that an onrushing fire made checking identities impossible. He'd barely escaped himself.

No, it was better to let them believe what he himself believed. One of the five men he'd ambushed had been Carlos.

Kayla handed Harr a glass of whiskey and immediately sat beside him. He was too tired to fight her as she clutched his arm. Every bone in his body hurt. He longed to lie down and rest.

Hondo said, "We didn't see you when we found the RVs. Where were you?"

Harr took a slug of whiskey, felt the warmth of the liquor slide down his throat. "I waited at the staging area overnight to make sure none of the cult army survived. When nobody showed up, I took one of the RVs and drove north. I figured since the fire was burning south, my best chance to get back to the valley was to come at it from the opposite direction. Unfortunately, the RV broke down on one of the Bureau of Land Management roads. I wound up walking the last thirty miles on foot."

"Jesus," Hondo breathed. "You're lucky you didn't die of heatstroke."

Harr nodded grimly. The Coastal Range north of Liberty Valley was dry, desolate territory. "I tried to follow the river as much as I could, but there were sections ..." He shook his head. It didn't matter now. He was back.

He realized that Susan had returned from the living room, that she was watching him from the kitchen, and that her eyes had lingered on Kayla's hands before moving to his face. He didn't bother to look away from her.

He wanted her to know, even if he couldn't say it with so many people listening, that he knew she'd started the fire that had killed the cult army and burned River Ranch and the Morgan place, just as he knew that she was having trouble with the fact that she had done so.

He understood. It was the desire not to take lives, but rather to save them, that separated her and himself and all of them from Carlos and his followers The Liberty Valley survivors hadn't wanted to kill but were forced to do so. Carlos wanted to kill and did.

Alan's voice, a little too loud, pierced his musings. The older man was talking about scavenging the fuel and supplies from the RVs, that he wanted to send a group out to do so in the morning.

But Harr wasn't really listening anymore. He was thinking about the praying woman and how she probably hadn't wanted to kill either. But she had and couldn't forgive herself.

Harr hoped he and the rest of the survivors could.

EPILOGUE

EMMALINE RAN LIKE A LITTLE DRUNK. IT GAVE SUSAN A heart attack every time the toddler tripped up and went sprawling.

"She's fine, honey," Deb said reassuringly when Emmaline did another digger in the grass. "It's a soft surface."

It was true. The Victorian's lawn had taken some time to grow back after the fire, but now, in late October, the lawn was once again a lush green, blessed by irrigation and the season's first rain. It was almost possible to forget the muddy, trampled mess the lawn had been in the aftermath of the fire.

Almost. The ridge across the river and the orchard, mostly cleared now except for a few charcoal trunks, remained as blackened reminders of the inferno that still haunted Susan's dreams.

She rose from her garden chair, set Emmaline back on her feet, and watched the towhead take off with a squeal after two of the Yakima Valley children. The kids were an odd misfit of ages—two, seven, and nine—but they played together well, weaving between the adults seated on the lawn and up on the porch.

"It's a nice party," Deb said, as Susan once again took a seat next to her. The hairstylist took a sip of honey-sweetened lemonade and sighed. "I miss having parties. I used to love the dressing up."

Susan let out a rueful laugh. No one was particularly dressed up tonight, although Deb had managed to scramble up a set of scissors to cut many of the men's hair. But Susan understood Deb's meaning. After so much struggle, it felt right to celebrate, even if nothing was perfect, and just surviving was their biggest achievement.

"We should call this the New Hoes Down," Deb went on. "You know, after that harvest celebration you talked about. You know the one that the organic farmers used to put on?"

"That was slightly different," Susan said, remembering the pre-pandemic party. "Thousands used to come to that celebration. They invited everyone near and far."

"But still, it was a party to celebrate harvest and to give thanks. Ours is the same in spirit."

Susan couldn't help smiling at Deb's upbeat attitude. It seemed hard-baked in her, unbroken by the loss of her family and nearly all her belongings. How were some people like that? Susan wondered. So resilient and grateful for everything they had?

Susan knew she herself wasn't really like that. Oh, sure, she was resilient and grateful, but she lacked that magical upbeat enthusiasm that Deb possessed. There was still too much sadness within her. She didn't think it would ever go away.

But still, she was grateful. Grateful that, except for one man, they hadn't lost any further people after the Battle for the Valley. She had to credit Carson's manufactured antibiotics for that. The sulfa drugs were primitive and with limited efficacy, but they still managed to treat infection in all but one of the wounded.

She was grateful that Reb had recovered enough of his

eyesight to walk with a cane unassisted, and Alan's hearing was now near normal. She was grateful that old Jim Waller had recovered enough from the barbaric amputation on the day of the fire to hobble around on his peg leg and play a fine fiddle, which he was doing right now.

Yes, she thought. There was much to be grateful for.

She gazed over to the firepit, where Hondo, Paula, Harr, and Kayla stood beside three roasting turkeys. Kayla's pregnancy was obvious now, and though the prospect of delivery frightened Susan, she was hopeful for more children for the settlement. They would be the much-needed future. She prayed they'd be immune to DRYP, but if they weren't ...

For a moment, her happiness faded. Etta had heard no more from the remaining cult members—she said the radio had been silent except for broadcasts from Colorado and Georgia—but Susan and her fellow survivors knew the cult was still in New Jerusalem. Her best hope was that, without Carlos to lead them, the surviving cult members had renounced their doomsday beliefs, but she couldn't know for sure. As a consequence, she wasn't keen to approach them if they needed vaccine for the newborns.

"Glass of wine?" Alan said behind her. He stood there holding two glasses of white wine with a smile on his face.

"Where'd you get that?" she asked, astonished. She hadn't had wine in months.

"Carson found a case of it on one of his scavenging trips," he said. "You should be prepared to treat a few hangovers tomorrow."

Susan let out a rueful laugh. Now that she was looking, she could see Carson and Sam weaving through the crowd with bottles, pouring glasses for everyone.

He was a manipulative person, Carson was, secretive about what he scavenged and opaque about what he manufactured in

344

his lab. But he served a purpose for the settlement that even she had to recognize. The fact that he could manufacture needed medications forced her to hold her tongue.

But still, she didn't trust him. It was impossible to know what he was thinking or to predict what he would do next. That was the underpinning of what Alan had called an imperfect alliance. As much as she didn't like it, they were stuck with Carson. For now.

Across the lawn, on the patio, Hondo and Paula began to dance to Jim Waller's fiddle. Soon, Harr and Kayla joined in, and then others.

It was a beautiful sight. Out in the open field beyond, the first green shoots of a winter crop of potatoes were beginning to poke above the soil.

Beside her, Alan held out his hand. "It's a hoedown, Susan. Let's dance."

"It's a *Hoes Down*," she corrected, but she was smiling.

She set down her wineglass and took his hand.

ACKNOWLEDGMENTS

I would like to extend my heartfelt gratitude to the many people who made this book possible, either by generously sharing their expertise or reading earlier drafts.

Dr. Jane Davis, veterinarian and educator extraordinaire, thank you once again for patiently answering my seemingly endless questions about animals and for explaining the livestock industry to me. I couldn't have written this book without your help.

Heartfelt thanks also goes out to Jim Thielemann, who introduced me to the wonderful world of amateur radio and answered countless questions about how radios might work in a post-apocalyptic world.

I am also indebted to Tim O'Halloran and Anthony Lopez of the Yolo County Flood Control and Water Conservation District. A big thanks for the hours you spent explaining how dams and irrigation systems work, and for trying to make California's complicated water delivery systems understandable.

I'd also like to extend my gratitude to Robert Falconer, who explained airplanes to me with remarkable clarity and humor.

Having written all of this, I must acknowledge that there

may be places in the book in which I misinterpreted what these generous people have told me or simply chose to ignore it for storytelling purposes. They should not be held responsible for any inaccuracies in the novel!

I would also be remiss not to address the poem recited by Paula at the end of the novel. The authorship of that lovely prose is disputed, but for any reader interested in the poem and the controversy surrounding its origin, please check out https://en.wikipedia.org/
wiki/Do_Not_Stand_at_My_Grave_and_Weep.

And lastly, a big thanks to my beta readers, in particular Eden Manseau, who is not only a great friend but also an insightful reader, and my father, whose input is always intelligent and much appreciated. And of course, Arron, Carly, and Jack, I couldn't have written this book without you. Thank you for your bottomless patience and support.

ABOUT THE AUTHOR

R.A. Scheuring practiced medicine for twelve years before hanging up her white coat to pursue her lifelong dream of writing fiction. DRYP: Revelation is her second novel. It is Book 2 in the DRYP Trilogy.

You can find out more about R.A. and sign up for her email newsletter at www.rascheuring.com.

Printed in Great Britain
by Amazon

42787559R00209